NOVELS BY MERCEDES LACKEY
available from DAW Books

THE BLACK GRYPHON

THE BLACK GRYPHON

Mercedes Lackey & Larry Dixon

DAW BOOKS, INC.
DONALD A. WOLLHEIM, FOUNDER
375 Hudson Street, New York, NY 10014

ELIZABETH R. WOLLHEIM
SHEILA E. GILBERT
PUBLISHERS

For color prints of Jody Lee's paintings, please contact:
The Cerridwen Enterprise
P.O. Box 10161
Kansas City, MO 64111
Phone: 1-800-825-1281

Interior illustrations by Larry Dixon.

All the black & white interior illustrations
in this book are available as 11" × 14" prints;
either in a signed, open edition singly, or in
a signed and numbered portfolio from:

FIREBIRD ARTS & MUSIC, INC.
P.O. Box 14785
Portland, OR 97214-9998
Phone: 1-800-752-0494

Time Line by Pat Tobin.
Maps by Victor Wren.

DAW Book Collectors No. 937.

DAW Books are distributed by Penguin USA.
Book designed by Lenny Telesca.

First Printing, January 1994

1 2 3 4 5 6 7 8 9

DAW TRADEMARK REGISTERED
U.S. PAT. OFF. AND FOREIGN COUNTRIES
MARCA REGISTRADA
HECHO EN U.S.A.

PRINTED IN THE U.S.A.

Dedicated to Mel. White, Coyote Woman
A legend in the hearts
of all who know her

OFFICIAL TIMELINE FOR THE

by *Mercedes Lackey*

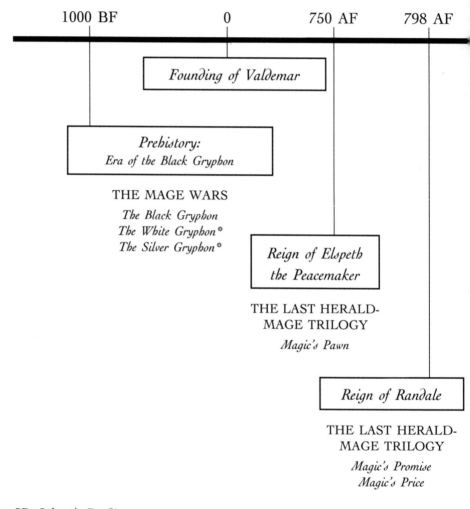

1000 BF   0   750 AF   798 AF

Founding of Valdemar

Prehistory:
Era of the Black Gryphon

THE MAGE WARS
The Black Gryphon
*The White Gryphon**
*The Silver Gryphon**

Reign of Elspeth
the Peacemaker

THE LAST HERALD-
MAGE TRILOGY
Magic's Pawn

Reign of Randale

THE LAST HERALD-
MAGE TRILOGY
Magic's Promise
Magic's Price

BF   *Before the Founding*
AF   *After the Founding*
*   *Upcoming from DAW Books in hardcover*

HERALDS OF VALDEMAR SERIES

Sequence of events by Valdemar reckoning

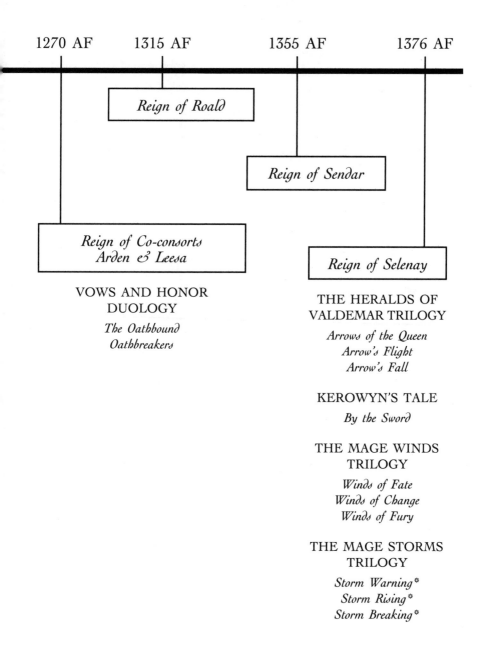

1270 AF   1315 AF   1355 AF   1376 AF

Reign of Roald

Reign of Sendar

*Reign of Co-consorts
Arden & Leesa*

Reign of Selenay

VOWS AND HONOR
DUOLOGY

*The Oathbound
Oathbreakers*

THE HERALDS OF
VALDEMAR TRILOGY

*Arrows of the Queen
Arrow's Flight
Arrow's Fall*

KEROWYN'S TALE

By the Sword

THE MAGE WINDS
TRILOGY

*Winds of Fate
Winds of Change
Winds of Fury*

THE MAGE STORMS
TRILOGY

Storm Warning*
Storm Rising*
Storm Breaking*

Amberdrake

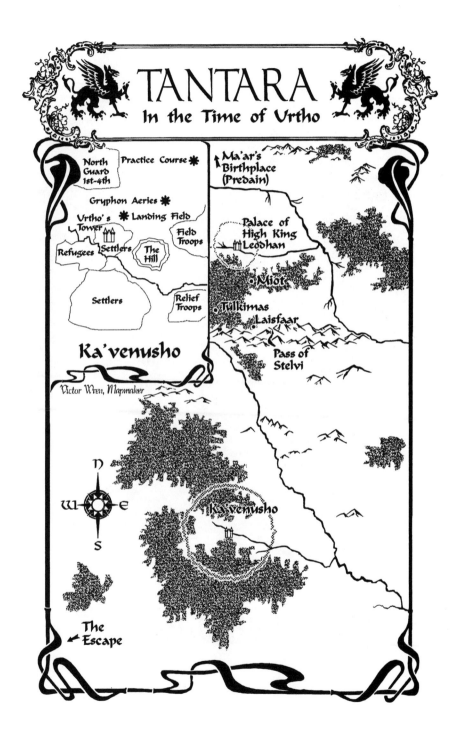

TANTARA
In the Time of Vrtho

North Guard 1st-4th

Practice Course ✳

→ Ma'ar's Birthplace (Predain)

Gryphon Aeries ✳

Vrtho's Tower ✳ Landing Field

Field Troops

Refugees · Settlers · The Hill

Palace of High King Leodhan

• Miot

Settlers

Relief Troops

• Tulkimas

• Laisfaar

Pass of Stelvi

Ka'venusho

Victor Wren, Mapmaker

N
W · E
S

Ka'venusho

← The Escape

Skandranon

One

Silence.

Cold wind played against Skandranon's nares—a wind as frigid as the hearts of the killers below. Their hearts pumped blood unlike any other creature's; thick black blood, warmed when their commanders willed it—only when they flew, only when they hunted, only when they killed.

Their blood was cold, and yet it ran warmer than their masters'. This much Skandranon Rashkae knew; he had fought their masters since he was a fledgling himself. They were cruel and cunning, these *makaar,* and yet the worst aspects of these manufactured horrors paled before the cruelty of their creators.

Silence. Stay still. Quiet.

Skandranon remained motionless, crouched, feathers compressed tight to his body. He was silent to more than hearing; that silence was but one of the powers that had made his master and friend so powerful, although it was the power that had given him his name—Urtho, the Mage of Silence. Urtho's champions had invisibility against magical sight—to mind-scanning, to detection spells, to magical scrying. The enemies of his monarchy had spent much of their resources on foiling that edge—to no avail, it seemed—and now concentrated on more direct methods of destroying Urtho's hold on the verdant central-land's riches.

Skan kept his wings folded, the leading edge of each wing tucked under the soft black feathers at the sides of his chest. It was important to be quiet and keep his head down, even this far from the encampment. The journey here had been one of long soars and kiting, and although he was in his best physical shape ever, flight muscles protested even yet. Better now to rest and watch. The chill wind rippled against his coat of feathers. This day had turned out unseasonably cold, which hadn't helped him any—except that it kept the makaar willing to make only the most necessary flights.

He watched them sleeping restlessly, twitching in their dreaming. Did they know how transient, how fleeting, they were? How their creators built them, bred them, refined them, letting the bad stock die out by assigning them to the border? Did they know their masters designed them with short lives so the generations would cycle quicker, to reveal the defects more conveniently?

They were, despite their horrifying appearances and deadly claws, quite pitiful. They'd never know the caress of a caring lover—they would only know the heat of imposed breeding. They knew their lot was the searing pain of a torture-weapon if they failed. They never lay in the sun with a friend, or dashed in the air with their wingmates. . . .

They'd never risk their lives to do something because they felt it was *right*. Perhaps that was the greatest pity of all; they could not be broken because they had no honor to compromise, no will to subvert.

The makaar and the gryphons were a study in contrasts, despite the darker mages' obvious attempts to mimic the Mage of Silence's handiwork. If gryphons were sinuous, graceful storms, makaar were blustering squalls. The gryphons were bold, intelligent, crafty; the makaar were conditioned to blind obedience. And one need only ask Skandranon which was the more attractive; he'd likely answer, "I am."

Vain bird. You'll make a lovely skin on a Commander's wall.

Skandranon breathed deeply behind the line of trees atop the hill; before him was the Pass of Stelvi. The coming army had stormed it, at the cost of but a few hundred of their soldiers compared to the thousand of Urtho's garrison. Farther down the pass was the split valley which once supported a thriving trade-town. Laisfaar was now the army's quarters, and the surviving townsfolk made into servants no better off than slaves. In the other fork of the valley the commanders had stationed the army's supplies and creatures, including the sleeping makaar.

They might as well sleep; they did not need to fear sorcerous spying. The army's mages had shielded the area from magical scrying, and none of Urtho's many attempts to search the valley by spell had worked. That had left the need for study by stealth—risky at best, suicidal at worst.

Skandranon had, of course, volunteered.

Fly proudly to your doom laughing, vain bird, the best of the best; more suitors than sense, more wealth than wisdom, sharp claws ready to dig your own funeral pit. . . .

His meeting with Urtho had been brief by choice. The offer was made to send guards and mages; Skandranon declined. Urtho offered to bolster his defensive spells, as he had done so many times before; it was declined as well. What Skan asked for was enhancement of his magical senses—his Magesight had been losing sharpness of late due to disuse. Urtho had smiled and granted it, and Skandranon left immediately from the Tower itself, leaping broad-winged onto the wind's shivering back.

That was three dozen leagues and four meals ago; a long time to cover such a distance. It was a tactical disaster for his side that the enemy's army had advanced this close to Urtho's Tower; now it appeared they were prepared to march on the Tower itself. The layout of the encampments showed three separate cadres of troops; the makaar had been assigned equally to two of them. And between those two was the Weaponsmaster's coach, staked firmly and blanketed, flanked by two canvas-covered wagons.

Hold a moment now. With a town nearby—hearths and comfortable bedding—the Weaponsmaster is staying in a tent?

Each side in this war had Seers and Diviners, whose powers could throw secret plans, however perfectly laid, awry. A Seer waking with a premonition of an assassination could thwart the attempt, for instance. The night before Stelvi Pass was taken, a Seer's vision told of a horrible new weapon that would devastate the garrison Urtho had placed there. It was something magical, the woman had said, but was in the hands of common soldiers. That warning alone was enough to make the gryphon wary, and had made him determined to explore this valley.

In a war of mages, the limited number of Adepts and Masters made tactical planning easier; you could study your opponents, guess their resources, even identify them by their strategies without ever seeing the commander himself. What alarmed Skandranon was the idea that the power of a mage could be put in the hands of untrained people—those who did not have the innate powers or learned skills of a mage. The units that could be fielded with such weapons would be an unwelcome variable, difficult to guard against if at all. A Master could ride onto a battlefield and call on his own powers, unleashing firebolts, lightning, hurricanes of killing wind—yet he was still just one man, and he could be eliminated. But soldiers that could do that would be devastating, even if the weapons were employed but once each. And if an Adept had discovered a way for the weapons to draw on power from magical nodes—

That was too horrifying to think of further. Skandranon had faced the Adept commander of all the troops below, the Kiyamvir Ma'ar, twenty months ago. He had volunteered for that mission, too, and had limped home wing-broken, stricken with nightmares. He had seen his wingmates skinned by the Adept's spells, feathered coats peeled back in strips by the Adept's will alone in full daylight, despite Skan's attempts to counterspell. The nightmares had left him now, but the memory made him determined to protect Urtho's people from the Kiyamvir's merciless rule.

Skandranon's eyes focused on the town of Laisfaar. Urtho's garrison had not all been human; there had been hertasi, a few tervardi, and three families of gryphons. His eyes searched the ramparts, noted the wisps of smoke of fires still burning since the attack. There were the aeries of the gryphons; the ramps for visitors, the sunning beds, the fledglings' nests. . . .

. . . the bloodstains, the burned feathers, the glistening rib cage. . . .

All the usual atrocities. Damn them.

She had been alive until very recently; she had escaped

the worst of it by dying of shock and blood loss. The makaar had no love for gryphons, and their masters gave them a still-living one after a battle as a reward. Often it was a terrified fledgling, like this gray-shafted gryphon had been. The rest of the garrison's gryphons had doubtless been wing-cut, caged, and sent to the Kiyamvir for his pleasures by now. Skandranon knew well that, unless Ma'ar was distracted by his business of conquest, there would be nothing left of them to rescue by day's end.

If he could, Skandranon would insure the captives would not last that long. Crippled as they would likely be, he couldn't help them escape; but he might be able to end their ordeal.

Before that, he had a larger duty to attend to.

Now he moved, slinking belly-flat to the ground, catlike; one slow step at a time, eeling his way through the underbrush with such delicate care that not even a leaf rustled. The Weaponsmaster's wagons had plenty of guards, but not even the Weaponsmaster could control terrain. The mountains themselves provided brush-filled ravines for Skandranon to creep through, and escarpments that overlooked the wagons. The encampment was guarded from attack from above by makaar, but only over the immediate vicinity of the camp. It was guarded from penetration from below by the foot-soldiers, but only outside the camp itself. No one had guarded against the possibility of someone flying into the area of the camp, behind the sentry lines, then landing and proceeding on foot to the center of the camp.

No one could have, except a gryphon. No one would have, except Skandranon. The omission of a defense against gryphon spying told him volumes about the military commanders who led this force. The Kiyamvir would reprimand them well for such a mistake—but then, Ma'ar was the only one of their side who understood the gryphons' abilities. Most commanders simply assumed gryphons and makaar were alike, and planned defenses accordingly.

So Skandranon stayed in the shadows, moving stealthily, as unlike a makaar as possible.

Time meant nothing to him; he was quite prepared to spend all night creeping into place. Even in the most strictly ruled of armies, discipline slackens after a victory. Soldiers are weary and need rest; victory makes them careless. Skan had timed his movements to coincide with that period of carelessness.

He noted no sentries within the bounds of the camp itself; his sharp hearing brought him no hint that the commanders prowled about, as they were wont to do before a battle. Doubtless, the commanders were as weary as the soldiers and slept just as deeply.

He spent his moments waiting committing details to memory; even if he died, if his body were somehow recovered, Urtho could still sift his last memories for information. That would only work if he died swiftly, though. Otherwise, the memories would be overcome by sensory input; thus the immediate torture of gryphon captives. Daring rescues had occurred before, and once retrieved, the gryphons' bodies were tremendous sources of information.

That could also be a clue to where the rest of the gryphon families were; it was also not unheard of to use captives as bait for rescue-traps. Captives' minds were often stripped of the will to resist, the prisoners forced to give information to the enemy. This was why Skandranon held a horrible power—a spell of death keyed to gryphons—for mercy.

And he hoped with every drop of blood that he would never be required to use it again.

Halfway to his goal he froze as he heard footsteps approaching the stand of tall grasses where he lay hidden. The cover that had seemed adequate a moment earlier seemed all too thin now—

Clever bird, hiding in grass. Better hope the wind doesn't blow—

But the footsteps stumbled, and Skan held his breath, not wanting to betray his position by breathing steam into the cold air. He froze in mid-step, right foreclaw held a mere thumb length above the ground.

He could not see the human who approached without turning his head, which he would not do. He could only wait and listen.

The footsteps stopped; there was a muffled curse, and the sound of hands fumbling with cloth— Then, clear and unmistakable, the sound of a thin stream of water hitting the matted grasses.

The human grunted, yawned; the sound of trousers being hitched up followed. The footsteps stumbled away again.

Skandranon unfroze and lowered his claw to the ground.

There were no other incidents as he made his way up the escarpment and slid under the shelter of a knot of wild plum bushes, to wait until dawn. He could feel the beetles and spiders of the thicket exploring their newly-arrived piece of landscape as the minutes went by. Despite the impulse to yelp and swat them, though, he stayed still. Their irritation provided a blessing in a way; something to feel, to keep his senses alert after nightfall.

Skandranon's tentative plan was to wait until darkness, then sneak out to explore the camp. Other warriors suspected his stealthiness was a result of Urtho's magicking, although the elder denied it, citing the gryphon's near-obsessive interest in dancing-movements. He had often watched Skandranon mimicking human, tervardi, and hertasi performers in private. Skandranon had trained himself with a dedication he would never admit except as a boast, applying that knowledge to flight, to lovemaking, and to combat. That, in truth, was what made him quieter than a whisper of wind; no spells or tricks, just practiced grace.

Silence alone is not enough. Urtho has learned that the hard way—we've lost border towns for half a generation, and only now begun doing more than simply defending our borders. Eh, well, Urtho had never intended to become Archmage. He's more suited to crafting silver and carving figures than deploying armies.

Such a pity that a man so kindhearted would be pressed into the role of a warlord . . . but better he than a heartless man.

And I'd certainly rather be off making little gryphlets.

That would have to wait until the world became a safer place to raise young, though. For now, Skandranon waited . . . until a shriek rang out from the town, echoing off the walls of the valley. Only practiced self-control kept him from leaping into the air, claws stretched to rend and tear.

One at least still lives. I'm coming, friend, I'm coming

. . . just hold on a little longer. Just a little. Feh, I can't wait any longer.

Skandranon stood and surveyed the layout of the encampment again; he'd heard screams like that too many times in his life. Not again. He spread his wings half-open and leapt, down toward the Weaponsmaster's wagons, depending on speed to be his ally. Knifelike wind whistled against his nares, chilling his sinuses, sharpening his mind. All the sights and sounds of the world intensified when he was in motion, sizes and details of shapes all taken into account for the entire span of his vision.

Snatch and fly, that's your plan, isn't it, damned foolish bird? You're going to die the hero they all call you, for what? Because you couldn't stand another moment of another gryphon's pain? Couldn't wait any longer.

The wagons rushed closer in his sight, and their magical alarms blazed into light, waiting like barbed snares to be triggered. Were they traps, too, besides being alarms? Would they trap him? Were they the bait, not the tortured gryphon?

Would it matter? You're too damned predictable, Skan, too sensitive, couldn't stand to wait. She'd die anyway, you know it, by the time you'd have gone in. Why do it?

Colors and textures rushed past him in three dimensions, as he dove ever closer to the wagons.

It's because you're not bright enough, stupid gryphon. Stupid, stupid gryphon.

Well, death is inevitable anyway, so dying for the right reason is . . .

Just as final.

Stupid gryphon.

Too late for reconsideration, though. The wagon alarm-fields loomed nearer, and Skan had to risk a spell to disarm them—the easiest was one which made them detect another place nearby, instead of the place they were supposed to protect. He focused on them, released the flow into them, diverted their field away to an open part of the camp . . . and they did not sound. Now his troubles stemmed from the soldiers who might still be outside—and the makaar. He might be invisible to the alarms, but he was still pitch black to anyone's vision. A soldier of Ma'ar's army would not wonder at a shadow that moved through the sky—he'd call an alert.

He half-hoped for detection, since he would likely have the quarry before any spells could be leveled against him. Once discovered, he would not have to skulk about any longer . . . he could blaze away with a detection spell to find the gryphon whose scream he'd heard earlier. Otherwise there would be delicate searching around for—who knew how long. Of course, discovery also brought such pesky distractions as arrows and firebolts and snares and spells. . . .

He backwinged and landed, kicking up clods of dirt next to the wagon, and his head darted from side to side, looking for spotters. None yet, but that could change all too quickly. Two steps to the back of the wagon, then under it—*no one ever guards the bottoms of things, only sides and doors*—and he began prying at the wagon's floorboards, next to the struts and axles, where the mud, water, and friction of traveling always rots the wood. He was curled up under the wagon completely, on his back, tail tucked between his legs, wings folded in against his ribs, hind claws holding the wingtips. He didn't dare rip at the canvas of the wagon's bonnet—past experience had shown that apparently flimsy defenses were often imbued with alarm-spells. His claws glowed faintly with the disruption-spell he was using, and the wood shriveled above where his claws slowly raked, silent from the sound-muffling of his cupped wings.

The enemy's wagons traditionally had an aisle down the middle, and that was where Skandranon was working . . . another four cuts, five, six, and he'd be able to pull the boards down under the blanket of a silence-spell. Then he'd get a look inside at their coveted prize.

He began mentally reciting the silence-spell, calling up the energy from inside himself and releasing it around the wagon. He was careful to mold it short of touching the wagon itself, building it up from the ground. The wagon's defenses might yet be sensitive to the touch of just such a spell. It was hard to tell anymore, so many variables, so many new traps. . . .

He hoped that the mages under Ma'ar's command did not sweep the camp for magic at work. Things were going so well, so far. Skan reached up, claws digging firmly into the crossbrace, cracked through it, and the entire aisle section fell to the ground, inches in front of his beak. . . .

. . . and Skandranon found himself face to face with a *very* upset, recently awakened Weaponsmaster, who was drawing *something*—surely a weapon—up from beneath his bedding. The weapon pointed at the gryphon and started changing.

Skan's right claw shot out and struck the human's scalp and squeezed, finding yielding flesh. His thumb pierced the man's eye socket, and inside the envelope of silence, a gurgling scream faded into the wet sounds of Skan withdrawing his talons from the kill.

The man's hands twitched and dropped the weapon, which was still pointing at Skandranon. It was a polished rod, wrapped in leather, with a glowing, spiked tip revealed where the leather ended. It rolled from the dead man's fingers and fell to the ground, and the tip withdrew into the rod.

On your back, underneath a wagon, in an enemy camp, you kill a Weaponsmaster one-handed? No one will ever believe it. Ever. That was too close, too close, stupid gryphon.

Someone will come by soon, Skan. Move. Get the whatever-it-is and get away. That's all you need to do. Get away.

Skan released his wingtips and pulled himself across the body of the slain human, keelbone scraping against the ragged edge of sundered wood. His wing-edges caught, pinning him in the opening, and he wheezed with the effort of pulling himself through. It was dim inside. Only the waning light from outside leaking through the canvas-openings provided any illumination. Around him, stacked in open cases, waited glistening objects, the same as the Weaponsmaster had held, each the size of his foreclaws.

Each far more deadly than his claws, he was sure.

They must be some entirely new kind of weapon, and he needed no spell-casting to know their magical origin. They exuded magic, their collective power making his feathers crawl like being in the heart of a lightning storm abrewing. Now to grab one and leave! Skan reached toward the cases, almost touching one of them, when his inner voice screamed *"No!"*

The Weaponsmaster had one, he was guarding these, these may all be trapped. . . .

A hair-thin crackle of reddish energy arced between the weapons and his extended foreclaw, confirming his fears.

Then there may be only one that isn't trapped. . . .

He moved slowly, wings folded so tight it hurt. Up onto his haunches, then back down to all fours, until he faced the rear of the wagon. Then he reached down through the shattered floorboards, groping for the slain Master's weapon. It didn't make sense to Skan that the man would trap his own weapon, even if he was a mage; Weaponsmasters as a rule tended to be terribly impressed with themselves, and thought they could handle anything. . . . *Too bad, so sad, first mistake and last. What's that, stupid bird, you're getting cocky because you've lasted this long? More to do, and every second is borrowed time.*

At last came the feel of the rod, warm to his touch despite the thickness of his scaled skin. He reared back, eyes closed to the thinnest of slits, concentrating on not touching the racks of trapped arms. He transferred his prize to his mouth, clenching it tightly above his tongue, and fell forward across the gaping entrance he'd made, stretching across it toward the untied flap of the wagon bonnet.

All right. What's the worst that could happen? I touch the canvas, and the entire wagon goes up with all the energy in these things. That'd be just like Ma'ar, if he can't have them, no one else can. . . . I'd better count on it.

Skandranon bunched up his leg muscles, preparing for a massive leap through the exit, when he heard bootsteps outside, and a moment later, a shadowy figure opened the flap, cursing in the enemy's tongue.

Now. Now!

In the same instant, the figure opened the canvas, and the gryphon leapt. Skan used the man's shoulders as a vault, crushing the man's face against the back of the wagon from his momentum. He snapped his wings open, catching the edges, as the human crumpled underneath him. Then a deafening sound exploded around them as the wagon's massive final trap was set off—a crimson circle of fire spread across the ground, incinerating the human, catching the other wagon. A thrashing body was engulfed in the flame arcing from it as Skandranon gained altitude.

The makaar roused.

End of your charmed life, gryphon. At least now you can cast freely before you die . . . find her, wherever she is, accomplish that at least—

Skan's wings rowed at the air, clutching for distance from the camp. There was one thing yet to do before his conscience would let him leave. Somewhere—his mind searched through the camp and town for where—there was one of his own kind being killed, slowly. . . .

He searched, and found her tortured mind as he crested the ridge. It felt as if her body had been lanced deep by thousands of needles, cut on by a hundred mad surgeons, broken by mallets, yet still she lived. There was a wrenching moment as Skan's mind reeled from the backlash of what had been done to her, and he felt his wings fold involuntarily.

:*Kill me,*: she screamed, :*Stop them, something—anything:!*

:*Open up to me,*: Skan sent to her, :*Open up to me and trust—there will be pain at first, then all will be dark. You'll fly again, as Urtho wills. . . .*:

She halted her scream as she recognized the code sign for the death-spell. No one had made a move to block it yet—

He pulled back from her for a bare second, trying to steady himself in his flight. He reached out again, riding the wind, then unleashed the spell, caught her mind, pulled it free of her body for one gut-wrenching second. The spell struck home and stopped her heart.

I am sorry, so sorry . . . you will fly again after the dark. . . . Then he released her spirit to the winds.

Somewhere in the captured inn, a bound and wing-cut body convulsed, then lay still. Above the valley, Skandranon raced away desperately, unable to cry out for her, as seven makaar surged skyward to destroy him.

At last, the General slept.

Amberdrake started to rise, then sank back down to his

seat on the side of the General's bed as Corani woke convulsively, with a tiny gasp. The anguish was still there, filling the room, palpable even to the weakest Empath. For an Empath as strong as Amberdrake, the impact of Corani's pain was a blow to the heart.

Amberdrake waited for the General to speak, while radiating warmth and reassurance, concentrating on the soothing scents still flavoring the air as a vehicle for that reassurance; the gentle hint of amber incense, the chamomile in the oils he had used in his massage, the jessamine covering the taste of sleep-herbs in the tea he'd given Corani. He ignored the throbbing pain in his own temples, his tension-knotted stomach, and the terrible sense of foreboding that had come upon him at the General's summons. His feelings did not matter; he was a kestra'chern, and his client—more patient than client, as was often the case—needed him. He must be the strong one, the rock to rest against. He did not know Corani well; that was all to the good. Often men of power found it easier to unburden themselves to a stranger than to a friend.

The General's suite was in Urtho's keep and not in a tent in the camp; easy enough here to pull heavy curtains to shut out the light and the world with it, to burn dim, scented lamps that invoked a feeling of disassociation from the armed camp beyond the keep. The General himself had not summoned Amberdrake; the few times he had called to the camp for a kestra'chern, it had been Riannon SilKedre he had wanted—slightly inferior to Amberdrake in skill, an accomplished and well-respected female. No, one of Urtho's aides had come to the tent—quietly, with his livery hidden beneath a cloak, which said more about the aide's visit than the boy himself did.

Urtho was still closeted with his General when Amberdrake arrived, but when he finally returned to his quarters, he did not seem surprised to see Amberdrake there. He was clearly distraught, and yet it had taken Amberdrake hours and every bit of his skill to persuade him to unburden himself.

And he knew why Urtho had chosen him and not Riannon. There were times when it was easier for a man to reveal his pain to a man—and Amberdrake was utterly trustworthy. Whatever was revealed to him remained with him forever. He was many things to many people; tonight he had been something of a Healer, something of a priest, something of a simple, noncommittal ear.

"You must be disappointed," the General said into the lamp-lit dimness, his voice resigned. "You must think I'm a weakling now."

That was what Corani *said;* Amberdrake, being what he was, heard what Corani *meant.*

He was really saying, "I must disgust you for falling apart like this, for looking so poorly composed," and, "You must despise me and think me unworthy of my position."

"No," Amberdrake replied simply, to both the spoken and unspoken assertions. He did not want to think what the General's collapse meant to him, personally; he *must not* think of it. Must not remember the messengers that roused the camp last night; the premonitions that had awakened the more sensitive and marginally Gifted among the Healers and kestra'chern from nightmares of blood and fire against the outline of the mountains. Must not think of the fact that Corani's family came from Laisfaar at Stelvi Pass, and that while his sons had posts with the army here, his wife and all his relatives were back *there.* There, where Skandranon had gone. He and Gesten did not know why, or for what reason; Amberdrake only knew that he had gone off without a farewell.

"No," Amberdrake repeated, taking the General's outflung hand before Corani could reclaim it, and massaging the palm and fingers carefully. The muscles felt cramped and tight; Corani's hand was cold. "How could I be that stupid? You are human and mortal; we are the sum of our weak moments and our strong. Everyone has a moment at which he must break; this one was yours. It is no shame to need help and know it."

Somewhere, deep inside, he wondered if it was also *his.* There was pressure building inside him that threatened to break free at any moment. He was not so self-confident that he thought he could do without help. The question was, would there be any there for him? Too many battered spirits

to mend—too many bruised bodies to comfort—the resources of Healers and kestra'chern alike were stretched and
overstretched. That he was near the end of his reserves made
little difference.

Far too many of his clients had gone out to battle and had
not returned. And Skan had been due back this morning; it
had been near sunset when the aide left him in Corani's
quarters. Skan was never overdue.

But for now, this moment, he must put his own strain
aside. None of that must show—he shouldn't let it break his
concentration or his focus. Corani came first; Corani must
be comforted enough, given enough reinforcing, as if he were
a crumbling wall, that he could function and come to heal.
Something had gone wrong, terribly wrong, at Stelvi Pass.
Corani had not told him what, but Amberdrake knew with
dreadful certainty. Stelvi Pass had been overrun; Laisfaar,
and Corani's family with it, was no more. It would be better
for them to be dead than in Ma'ar's hands unless they'd
hidden their identities and vanished into the general population. And that was unlikely.

Corani accepted this, as wise generals accepted all facts.
Corani had accepted Amberdrake's comforting as well. For
the moment, anyway. That was another of Amberdrake's
abilities; it bought time. Time to bring distance, time to
heal. "My sons—"

"I think that Urtho has seen to them as well," Amberdrake replied quickly. Urtho would have seen to everything;
it was his way.

Skan—

Quickly, he suppressed the thought and the anguish it
caused.

The drugs in the General's tea took effect; in the dim light,
Corani struggled to keep his eyes open, eyes still red and
swollen from weeping. The General had fought those tears,
fought to keep them properly held inside with the determination that had made him the leader he was. Amberdrake
had fought his determination with a will of his own that
was no less stubborn. "It's time to sleep," Amberdrake said
quietly.

Corani blinked, but held him with an assessing gaze. "I'm

not certain what I expected when I saw you here," he said, finally. "Based on Riannon—"

"What Riannon gave you was what you needed then," Amberdrake replied, gently touching the general's shoulder. "What I do is what you need now. Sometimes neither is what the recipient expects." He laid a soothing hand on Corani's forehead. "That is what a kestra'chern does, after all; gives you what you need."

"And not necessarily what I want," Corani said quickly.

Amberdrake shook his head. "No, General. Not necessarily what you *think* you want. Your heart knows what you want, but often your head has some other idea. It is the task of the kestra'chern to ask your heart, and not your head, what you need and answer that need."

Corani nodded, his eyelids drooping.

"You are a strong man and a good leader, General Corani," Amberdrake continued. "But no man can be in two places at the same time. You could not be here and there as well. You cannot anticipate everything the enemy will do, nor where he will strike. The War thinks its own way. You are not answerable for the entire army. You did what you could, and you did it well."

The muscles of Corani's throat tightened visibly as he fought for control. Amberdrake sensed tears being forced down. Corani was on the verge of more than tears; he was on the verge of a breakdown. This would accomplish nothing, worse than nothing. The man needed rest, and with Amberdrake's hand resting on his forehead, he was open to Amberdrake's will.

"You must sleep," Kestra'chern Amberdrake said, imposing a mental command on top of the drugs. Corani closed his eyes, and this time he did not reawaken when Amberdrake rose to go.

Gesten would be where he had been since dawn; at the landing field, waiting for Skandranon to return. Amberdrake left the keep, slipping unobtrusively out into the scarlet of a spectacular sunset. The landing field was not far away, and Amberdrake decided to head there, rather than going straight back to his tent.

Depression weighed heavily on his heart, a depression that was not relieved at the sight of Gesten alone on the field, patiently making preparations to wait out the night-watch.

Amberdrake held his peace for a moment, then spoke.

"He's not coming back this time," Amberdrake said quietly.

His hertasi companion, Gesten, looked up at him with his expressive eyes and exhaled through his nostrils. He held his pebble-scaled snout shut for a long minute. "He'll come. He always does," Gesten finally said. "Somehow."

Amberdrake wished with all his heart that the little hertasi would be right this time. Skandranon had flown from the Tower two days before, and Stelvi Pass was less than a day away, flying; he had never been delayed by so much before. Gesten was going about the task of building a watch-fire for their friend, laying out colored smoke-pots amidst the kindling. It might be a useless gesture, but it was all he could really do right now, with dawn so far away. Light up a pattern of blue and white to welcome the flyer home, let him know from afar that safety was close . . . Amberdrake tried to help, but he was awkward, and his heart wasn't in it. How odd, that one so graceful in his calling could be so clumsy outside it.

"Urtho has called a council." That much was common knowledge; no harm in telling the hertasi now. "Two gryphons came streaking in from Laisfaar straight to the Tower, and two hours after that, Urtho sent a message ordering me to tend General Corani."

Gesten nodded, apparently taking Amberdrake's meaning—that Corani needed the peculiar skills of a kestra'chern. The general had been permanently assigned to the Pass, until Urtho needed him more than his home district did. For the last week he'd been at the Tower, pleading with Urtho for some special protection for Stelvi Pass and the town. That much was common knowledge, too.

"What can you tell me?" Gesten knew very well that there was only so much Amberdrake could reveal to him. "What did Corani need?"

Amberdrake paused, searching for the right word.

"He needed sympathy, Gesten," he said as he laid down

a stack of oily fire fuel logs. "Something happened in the Tower that he didn't want to talk about; and I can only assume that from the way he acted, the news was the worst. Kept talking about blind spots—he was near to a breakdown. That's not like him. And now . . . Skandranon is late." Amberdrake smoothed his silk caftan, brushing the wood chips away. He felt worry lines creasing a face even his enemies called handsome, but he was too depressed to care.

Absently, he pulled his long hair back from where it had fallen astray. "I don't think he's coming back this time. I can feel it in my gut. . . ."

Gesten picked up a small log and pointed it up at Amberdrake. "He *will* be back, I feel it in *my* gut, Drake, and I won't put up with your whining about 'poor Skan.' He always comes back. *Always.* Understand? And I'll be here, with this watch-fire, until either he comes back or this army runs out of firelogs."

Amberdrake stepped back, thoroughly chastised, and more than a little surprised at the vehemence of the normally quiet lizard's speech. Gesten stood pointing the stick at him for a moment more, then spit at the air and threw it on the growing stack of kindling.

"I'm sorry, Gesten." Though he meant he was sorry about angering the hertasi, Gesten would probably take it some other way. "It's just that . . . you know how I feel about him."

"Feh. I know. Everyone knows. You seem to be the only one who doesn't know." The hertasi opened the latch on the firebox and withdrew a coal with blackened tongs. His tail lashed as he spoke. "You worry about everything, Drake, and you don't listen to yourself talking. There is no one in Urtho's service who is better than him. No one else more likely to come back." Gesten dropped the coal into the folds of cotton batting and woodchips between the two smoke-pots. "Even if he doesn't come back, he'll have died the way he wanted to."

Amberdrake bit his lip. Gesten thought he was right, as usual; nothing would dissuade him. Nothing Amberdrake *could* tell him would persuade him that the situation was hopeless; only the things Amberdrake could not tell him would do that. And he was right; Skan had died the way he wanted to. "I'll—keep quiet, until we know."

"Damned right you will. Now go back to your tent. You can manage your clients without me tonight." Gesten turned his attention to lighting the center fire, then the blue and white smoke-pots blazed into light. Amberdrake walked in the cooling night air toward the Tower and the semi-mobile city that clustered around it, stopping once to look back at the lonely figure who'd wait for all eternity if need be for the Black Gryphon's return. His heart, already heavy, was a burden almost too great to bear with the added weight of tears he dared not shed.

Oh, not now. I don't need this. . . .
Skandranon struggled against gravity and rough air, jaws clenched tightly on his prize. His heart was beating hard enough to burst from his chest, and the chase had barely begun—the makaar behind him were gaining, and he was only now past the ridge. As if it weren't enough that makaar were quicker than gryphons, they possessed better endurance. All they had to do was cut him off and fly him in circles. That was clearly what they intended to do. His advantage was his ability to gain and lose altitude more quickly than they. With cleverness, he could make them *react,* not act. At least they weren't terribly well organized— it wasn't as though Kili was leading them—

Skandranon twisted his head to assess his pursuers, and spotted an all-too-familiar black and white crest—Kili, the old makaar leader Skan had taunted numerous times. Kili, who had almost trapped him once before, with a much smaller force aflight, was streaking to a pitch a thousand feet above the other six, screaming commands.

Three gray-patched makaar canted wings back and swept into a shallow dive, gaining on him all the faster by trading height for speed. Their trajectory took them below and past him a few seconds later—and they were followed by another three. He tried to watch them all, eyes darting from one to the other, as they split off and rejoined. Why head below him, when altitude was so important against a gryphon?

Altitude—damn!

Instinct took over even as he realized Kili's gambit. He folded his right wing completely, rolling sideways in midair as the elder makaar streaked past him by a featherlength. A shrill scream of rage rang in his ears as Kili missed, and Skan threw himself out of the roll by snapping his wing open again and spiraling nose-first toward the earth—and the six makaar there.

That bastard! *He had the audacity to* learn *from me!*

Skan clamped his wings tightly and plummeted through the massed makaar below him, seeing the claws and razor-edged beaks of the surprised makaar as a blur as he shot past. He followed dead on the tail of Kili. The chances of surviving that move were slim—he'd gambled on his swift-ness, and the makaar did no more damage than removing a few covert feathers.

Distance for speed—let's see if they can follow this.

Kili was so very close ahead that Skan was tempted to strike at him, but he couldn't afford to be distracted from his primary objective—to survive and escape. Already, the two flights of makaar behind him stroked rapidly to pur-sue, crying out in rage. He passed the makaar leader, who predictably took a swipe at him and lost precious speed, and Kili's recovery was further fouled by the wind turbu-lence of his passing underlings. The six rowed past Kili, gaining on Skandranon as he coursed back toward Laisfaar.

Stupid gryphon, the point is to get away *from this place!*

The barrier range swept inexorably closer. Skandranon nar-rowed his concentration to the rockface before him, and studied the erosion channels cut into the stone by ages past. His breath turned ragged through his nares as he struggled against fatigue. From the edge of his vision, he saw the other makaar winging through the Pass, cutting an arc toward the pursuit.

They'll see my wings flare, and assume I'm braking to turn or climb—

Skan cupped his wings as he streaked in a straight line for the sheer cliff-face, feeling but not seeing the bloodthirsty makaar gaining on him from behind. The barrier stone filled his vision as he executed his desperate move: he folded his wings until their leading edges curled under him with a clap and his straining body rolled into a tumbler's somersault. He plummeted in a descending arc as lift abandoned him and momentum hurled him toward unforgiving stone.

Gravity reversed itself; his head snapped into his chest as he fell. Numbly, detachedly, he realized the new, tiny pain in his chest was where the sharp tip of his beak had pierced it. Disorientation took him. All he could do was keep his jaws closed as his world went black, and wonder how many bones this last trick of his would break.

Follow through—do it, bird, do it—

He stretched his hindlegs out, and fanned his tail. Wind rushed against the lay of his feathers as he hurtled backward.

In the next instant, he was surrounded by shocked makaar, three above, three below, whose attention was locked on him instead of the rock rushing to strike them from the sky.

It's going to work—lucky, stupid gryphon—

The dizzying sensations of gravity's pull, momentum's throw, and the rushing of blood mixed with the sound of six makaars' screams and the crunch of their bodies against stone. Skandranon's feet touched the unforgiving rock behind him—and he pushed off.

The strange maneuver stabilized his tumble; gave him the chance to spread his wings in a snap and break his fall, turn it from a fall into a dive.

Only the ground was *awfully* close. . . .

Pull up, stupid bird, pull up!

Wings straining, heart racing, he skimmed the rock at the bottom of the cliff, so close that his wingtips brushed it, using his momentum to send himself shooting skyward again, past the spreading stain on the rock that was all that was left of his first pursuers.

Now get out of here, idiot!

He reversed his course, away from the pass, back toward home and safety—and looked down.

At several hundred crossbows.

Of course, they couldn't see him, except, perhaps, as a fleeting shadow. But they knew he was up there, and they only had to fill the sky with arrow bolts and rocks, and one or more of them would probably hit him. A quick glance to either side showed that he'd been flanked by the two new flights of makaar; they hemmed him in, and had several gryphon-lengths' worth of altitude on him. Kili was not in sight; he was probably up above, somewhere, waiting.

His only chance lay in speed. If he could just get past the archers before they let fly—

Too late.

From below came a whirring sound; the air around him filled with a deadly reverse-rain of crossbow-bolts and slung shot. He pulled in his wings in a vain attempt to narrow the target area.

At first, he didn't feel pain, only impact. Out of the corner of his eye, he saw a mist of his own blood as his right wing came forward on the downstroke.

Then it crumpled.

Then it hurt.

He tumbled again, only nominally under control, shrieking incoherently around his beakful of stolen weapon.

He shuddered under the impact of two more hits; the pain came quickly this time, but he forced himself to ignore it. Once again, he tumbled out of control, and this time there was no handy cliff to push off of.

He pulled in his left wing and rolled over completely; righted himself, still falling. He dared not try and brake completely; the injured wing wouldn't take it. Instead, he extended just enough of both to turn the fall into another steep dive, angled away from the battle and toward friendly territory.

Just after his wings flared, he saw Kili whistle past where he had been.

A little farther—a little farther—

The ground was coming up awfully fast.

He was over Urtho's territory now, on the other side of the enemy lines, but he could not, dared not, flare his wings completely. His dive was a steep, fast one, but it was still a dive. The ground had never looked so inviting. Or so hard.

Ah sketi, *this is going to hurt—*

Tamsin and Cinnabar

Two

Amberdrake could not sleep; weary as he was, there was no point in lying awake and watching the inside of his eyelids. He wrapped a blanket around his shoulders, and made his way down the dark aisles between the orderly tent rows to the landing field.

As he came out into the open, away from the lights of the camp, he saw that the sky to the west was a haze of silvery light from the setting moon; it could not be long now, a few hours at most, until dawn. Gesten waited patiently beside his fire, as he had waited all night. Amberdrake had left the last of his clients to join the little lizard, but Gesten was clearly not in any mood to talk.

The hertasi tended to be silent when something affected his emotions. Amberdrake shared that tendency. In his case, it was due to long self-training; for both of them, it was to preserve the illusion of immutable and eternal stability.

It was Amberdrake's duty to convey an impression of serene concern—for Amberdrake's clients were always damaged in some way these days. Sympathy worked better than empathy, more often than not.

Clients didn't *want* to know their kestra'chern had problems of his own.

Since he couldn't be rid of them, he mustn't let them show, not even for a moment. It was part of the burden of his avocation, and though he'd come to accept it, it still caused a dull ache like a sympathy pain.

Sympathy pain. Yes, that was exactly what it was like.

The depression had worsened with every rumor, every

bit of camp gossip. Skan had never been this late in returning from a mission; even Gesten must know by now that he wasn't coming back. He had often joked about how Skan always rushed back at top speed from a mission; that he couldn't be back to his rewards and admiration fast enough.

By now the news had leaked out of a terrible disaster at Stelvi Pass, worse than any defeat Urtho's forces had faced before. The reaction was not panic, but Amberdrake wondered if there was anyone in the ranks who guessed at what he already knew; that the garrison had been overrun and wiped out completely. As the night grew colder, so did Amberdrake's heart, and wrapping his body in a spiral-knit blanket over his silks didn't help at all.

Gesten still hadn't spoken. Finally, he could bear it no longer. Without a word, he left his place beside the watch-fire and walked away into the darkness, looking back over his shoulder at the little spot of light and the patient figure hunched beside it. His heart ached, and his throat threatened to close with tears he feared to shed—feared, because once they began, he was not certain he would be able to stop them. Tears for Gesten—and for Skan. Wherever *he* was.

Waiting out in the darkness for someone who wasn't going to come home wasn't going to accomplish anything. The war went on no matter who grieved. Amberdrake, like so many Kaled'a'in, had long been thinking of the war as a being of its own, with its own needs, plans, and hungers. Those who chose to obey its will, and those who found themselves swept along in its path, had to go on living and pursuing their dreams, even if it did feel as if they were constantly trying to bail a leaky boat with their bare hands. The skills Amberdrake possessed would be needed regardless of whether the war raged on or ebbed; people would always feel pain, loneliness, instability, doubt, strain. He had long ago resigned himself to the responsibility of caring for those who needed him. No—caring for those who needed his *skills*. They didn't necessarily need him, they needed his skills. It was *that* realization, too, that chilled his heart and had caused him to leave the smoky-white pyre.

Gesten had only his duties to Amberdrake and to the Black Gryphon, and Amberdrake could do without him for a while. Gesten clearly intended to keep his watch no matter what Amberdrake required of him. Amberdrake, on the other hand, always had his duties. And right now, he felt terribly, horribly *lonely*. After all, once you've given up a large slice of yourself to someone and they're suddenly *gone*—how else *could* you feel? He'd never had a magical bond to the Black Gryphon, nothing that would let him know with absolute certainty if Skandranon were alive or dead. So he only had his reasoning and the known facts, and they pointed to the loss of a friend. A trusted one.

He neared the camp.

He entered the lighted areas of the camp, fixed a frozen, slight smile on his face, and checked his walk to ensure it conveyed the proper confidence and the other more subtle cues of his profession. There were few folk awake at this time of the night—or rather, morning—but those few needed to be reassured if they saw him. A frowning Healer was a bad omen; an unhappy kestra'chern often meant that one of his clients had confided something so grave that it threatened the kestra'chern's proverbial stability—and since Amberdrake was both those things, anything other than serenity would add fuel to the rumors already flooding the camp. And for *Amberdrake* to be upset would further inflame the rumors. As long as he was in a public place, he could never forget who and what he was. Even though his face ached and felt stiff from the pleasant expression he had forced upon it.

Urtho kept an orderly camp; with tents laid out in rows, every fifth row lighted by a lantern on a perching-pole, anyone who happened to see Amberdrake would be able to read his expression clearly. It must look as if nothing had changed in the past few hours.

And yet, before he could do anyone else any good, he was going to have to deal with his own sorrows, his own fears and pain. He knew that as well as he knew the rest of it.

He strode into the Healers' bivouac, his steps faltering only once. There was a distant part of him that felt ashamed at that little faltering step. He attributed that feeling to his tumultuous state of mind—hadn't he soothingly spoken to others that there was no shame in such things? Still. . . .

Help was not far off—if he asked for it. It was his right, of course. He was entitled to counsel and Healing, and all of the skills of his own profession he wished. He had taken comfort in such ways before and had given it many times. And though a small internal voice might echo words of weakness from the walls of his mind—tell him to just hold it in, not to succumb to the strain, he was not too proud to ask for that help. Not at this point, not when he was a mass of raw nerves and trembling on the edge of a breakdown. He had seen the signs of such things too often not to recognize them in himself.

In tents and shacks he passed, small lanterns or lightstones illuminated solitary figures. They carved surgical instruments or sewed torn clothing and bandages. The surreal acoustics of the still night made an old Healer's work-time whistling seem louder than it should be, as he cut and assembled arm slings by lantern light, apparently oblivious to the world outside his opened tent. On perches by the surgery tent, messenger-birds slept with their heads tucked under soft-feathered wings, with *kyree* sleeping soundly in front of them. The soft jingling of hanging harness and tackle sounded like windchimes from a tranquil garden. How odd that such poignant moments could still occur even in the middle of upheavals.

Healer Tamsin and his lover and coworker, Lady Cinnabar, were on night duty for the next ten days or so. He should be able to find them inside the surgery tent. There, past the Healers' and surgeons' tents, on the little rise ahead of him called "Healer's Hill," stood the common tents being used for infirmaries and treatment centers. Several of the tents had been used, in happier days, to hold Kaled'a'in celebrations, and had the capacity of housing a hundred or more. Their colors had been allowed to discreetly fade over the years since their current uses were anything but festive.

Lights in the central tent, and shadows moving inside it, told him that *someone,* at least, was there. He pushed aside the flap and moved quietly inside, and found Tamsin and Cinnabar bandaging a middle-aged land-scout, surrounded by tables bearing the debris of a thorough patching job. A mercenary; Amberdrake caught sight of the badge on his shoulder and recognized the wolf-head of Pedron's Wolves. Urtho was very careful about the mercenaries he hired, and the Wolves had a particularly good reputation. Even the gryphons spoke well of them.

Even Skan had spoken well of—

Sketi, *Drake, you're fixated. It's a downward spiral, and it's got to be broken—before you are.*

He sagged against a tent brace and hid his face in the shadows as he lost control over his expression. He wanted to be within sensing distance, but he also didn't want to be obtrusive. He shielded as much of his grief as he could, but these were fellow Healers, Empaths—and the closest friends he had.

Next to Gesten and Skan. . . .

Tamsin didn't look his way, but Amberdrake sensed his attention, and in the next moment he said to the mercenary, "You'll do well enough, fire-eater. What you need now is some rest. Limit your activity to complaining for a few days. Here's your green chit for days off." He signed the wooden square with a silver-rod and handed it off. "Three days, and six more at light duty."

Now Tamsin looked up, as if noticing Amberdrake for the first time, and added quietly, "I think I have a friend in need of a little help himself at the moment."

The merc looked up, caught sight of Amberdrake standing in the shadows, and grunted. "Thankee, Master Tamsin. I 'spect you'll send me the charge, eh?"

Tamsin laughed at the tired old joke, and the mercenary shuffled off, passing Amberdrake with a nod, and pushed through the tent flap into the warm dark beyond. Amberdrake laid himself down on the cot the scout had just vacated, disregarding the binding of the silk caftan against his body as he rolled over. He threw his arms over his eyes, hand bunched into a fist. A fist was a sign superstitiously avoided among Healers as being bad luck, but his mind was not on wards and omens. He heard the sounds of hands being washed and toweled dry, and instruments being laid back in trays. Minutes passed without a word, and the after-Healing cleanup was concluded. He heard a curtain being drawn around them for privacy.

"The rumors about Stelvi are true—the truth's probably worse than you've heard," he said to the waiting silence. "And Skandranon didn't make it back."

He felt one hand lightly touch his cheek; felt someone else take his hand. Both touches released the flood of grief he had pent up within him and, lost in the dark waters of mourning, he couldn't tell which of the two was touching him. Focus wavered in his mind. It didn't matter which of the two touched him where; what mattered was that they did. He welcomed them both.

Tears threaded their way down his face, soaking the hair at his temples. The knot in his throat choked further speech.

"Don't mourn for one who might still be alive," Tamsin chided gently. "Wait until you know—"

But they both knew that if Skandranon were able, he'd have made it back by now or somehow have sent a message. Tamsin made a swallowing sound, as if he had stopped himself before he said anything stupid.

"I think it's the fact that we don't know," Lady Cinnabar said as Amberdrake fought for control. "Drake, we love him too, you know—but we've seen too many times when people we've given up as lost made it back. Skandranon—"

"Has never failed a mission in his *life*," Amberdrake cried, half in anger, half in grief. "If he didn't—if he couldn't—"

The rest was lost in tears, as he finally stopped trying to control himself and simply let himself weep. The cot creaked as two weights settled beside him; one of them kissed his forehead, the other embraced him, and he buried his face in the proffered shoulder as a wave of compassion and reassurance spread from both of them.

"This is too much!" he sobbed bitterly, as whoever was holding him rocked him a little, like a child. "Waiting here, waiting to see who comes back in pieces—who doesn't come back at all. Not being *there* when they're hurt and dying."

"We know," Tamsin murmured, a world of sorrow in his own voice. "We know."

"But you don't know the rest of it—rewarding the ones who survive, when inside I cry for the ones who didn't."

There was nothing they *could* say to that.

"I'm *sick* of detaching myself!" he burst out, in another flood of tears. "They come to me to forget *their* pain, but when am I allowed to mourn?"

There was no spoken answer for that, since they *were* the answer. They simply held him while he wept, held him and tried to give him the little comfort they had. Finally, after he had cried himself out in their arms, he was able to talk a little more calmly.

"Drake, you've heard it all before," Cinnabar said as Tamsin got up to retrieve a damp cloth for Amberdrake. "But I'll tell you again; we are here to help you, just as you help others. You've been bearing up through all this better than anyone else. No one has ever seen you lose control, but you don't have to be superhuman."

"I know that," he said, exhausted by his bout of emotion. "Gods, that's exactly what I just got through saying to someone else tonight. But I've never felt like this before. It's *Skandranon* this time—he was my constant. I always knew he'd be all right, that it was safe to love him because I never thought I'd lose him. He never comes back with anything worse than a lost tailfeather."

Cinnabar smoothed Amberdrake's damp hair back from his forehead with the cool cloth, cool as winter skies, as the ache in his heart struck him once again. "Now—just losing *him*—I can't bear it. It hurts too much!"

Early morning sounds, muffled by the cloth and canvas of the tent, punctuated the talk. Wasn't it too early, yet, for all of that? Maybe time had simply gotten away from them. Maybe that was the next lesson in all of this—that no matter how Amberdrake felt, all would still go on without him. Still. . . .

Tamsin settled on the other side of him as Cinnabar captured his hands in hers.

"There's nothing I can say that you don't already know," Tamsin said quietly. "You have a harder task than we—a double burden. We have flesh to make whole again; you have hearts and minds to heal as well. The only comfort I can offer is to say you aren't alone. We hurt, too. Skan is our friend, and he—"

The noise outside didn't settle to the dull murmurs of daybreak. Instead, it kept rising.

It sounded, in fact, as if a small riot was approaching the surgery tent. A pang of *what have I done now?* struck Amberdrake in his self-pitying state, but left when reason returned a heartbeat later.

Amberdrake pushed the cloth away from his eyes and sat up—just as a pain-filled shriek ripped through the pre-dawn air, shattering his eardrums, and ensuring that all three Healers had their full attention taken by the noise outside.

"What in—" Tamsin leapt to his feet, Cinnabar beside him, just as the tent flap flew open and the mob shoved its way inside.

In the center of the mob was an unholy mating of gryphon and brush pile, all liberally mired in mud. Amberdrake would not have recognized it as Skandranon, except for the black feathers and the incredible vocabulary of half-delirious curse words.

He rolled off the cot and to his feet, as Gesten directed the litter team—for there was a litter under all that mess—to get what was left of the gryphon up onto one of the surgery tables. The hertasi looked around for a Healer; spotted Tamsin and Cinnabar, and Amberdrake behind them.

"You'll do. Here!" Gesten snapped.

Gods, if he *ran the army. . . .*

But the three Healers had begun their work before he spoke; Tamsin getting the clattering trays of surgical instruments, Cinnabar calling for their assistants, and Amberdrake pushing aside the litter bearers to get at the injured gryphon, heedless of anything else.

Amberdrake touched the Black Gryphon and felt Skandranon's pain as if it screamed through his own nerves, striking him like a hammer blow to the forehead. This was the draw-back of working on so close a friend. He shielded somewhat, automatically, but that pain also told him what was wrong, so he dared not block it all out.

As Cinnabar's assistants scraped and washed the mud from the tangled flesh and cut branches away from broken limbs, Amberdrake took Skandranon's pain deeper into himself, warning the others when they were going to cause more damage by moving something. He could feel his mouth agape as he sucked in halting breaths; felt his eyes widen in double-Sight, his mind split between seeing the physical and Seeing inside. It seemed an eternity before they got Skandranon's body free of the remains of the tree he'd crashed into, another eternity before they got him washed down so that they could see the external injuries clearly.

Wordlessly, the other two left the wings to Amberdrake and concentrated on Skan's legs and body. Amberdrake was one of the few in camp who knew the gryphons' anat-omy well enough to Heal wings to be flightworthy again. Muscle, tendon, bone, vein, all were dependent on each other in living bodies—yet in an avian's body this seemed doubly true. Alter *this* and balance and weight distribution and control surface and a hundred other things would change.

The right wing had a crossbow wound, still bleeding slug-gishly. The left was broken in several places. Amberdrake directed Gesten to put pressure on the bleeding bolt wound. Gryphon wingbones tended to knit almost as soon as they broke, like a bird's, and the sooner he got to the breaks, the less likely that he would have to rebreak anything to set it properly.

Skandranon whimpered a little and coughed, until a fourth Healer, still sleepy-eyed and robed from bed, came to stand at his head, and with one hand on either side of the huge beak, willed the gryphon into slumber. Skandranon's throat gurgled as his beak parted.

The wing muscles relaxed, and Amberdrake went to work.

He eased the shattered fragments of each broken bone to-gether, then held them in place with his bare hands while his mind forced the bits and pieces into the right order and prodded them into the process of knitting, all the while drawing away the fluids that built up around the damage. When the bone started healing, he called for splints and bandages, wrapped the section of wing tightly, and went on to the next, pausing only to wipe the drying blood from his hands before it caked so thickly it interfered.

"Drake?" Gesten said, barely making a stir in his concentration.

"What?" he asked shortly, all of his attention focused on getting the final bone to draw together.

"I think you'd better hurry." That was all the hertasi said, but it was enough. He left the splinting of the final bone and the binding of the wing as a whole to one of the assistants, and came around to Gesten's side of the table.

He knew with a glance why Gesten had called him; the sheer dead weight of the injured wing was so great that the bolt wound was tearing open, and the great wing vein was perilously close to the site of the wound. A fracture under that pressure could simply break wide open and sever the vein as it went.

Quickly, he directed Gesten under the gryphon's wing, to take some of the strain off, and reached out to hold the wound closed, being careful not to pinch. He closed his eyes and concentrated, Seeing the injury, examining it with his inner sight, bringing together the torn muscle fibers, rejoining bleeding veins, goading it all into the process of Healing at a rate a thousand times faster than it would naturally, and providing the energy the body required to do so from within himself. Infection threatened; he burned it away ruthlessly. He strengthened the rest of the muscles, taking some of the strain off the injured ones. When they threatened to cramp, a finger's touch soothed them. He found smaller broken bones, wounds and cuts he had not noticed in Healing the larger ones. He dealt with them all, searching out dangerous blood clots and filtering them from the bloodstream, until the wings had been wrapped in a binding of energies that would, in time, allow Skandranon to fly again.

Skandranon moaned and coughed weakly, as if something

were caught in his throat. His breathing steadied as the fourth Healer pushed him back into slumber, but he was taken by a fit of coughing again that caused everyone near to hold onto him tightly. Amberdrake was peripherally aware of Tamsin putting his arm down Skandranon's gullet while an assistant held the beak open with a metal bar, and then the badly wounded gryphon wheezed, shook, and fell into deep sleep again.

The assistants administered fortifying herbal and mineral infusions of all kinds into the gryphon while Amberdrake set Skandranon's fractured forearms and splinted his foreclaws.

Finally, it was over, and he swayed away from the table, letting the assistants do their mechanical labor of bandaging and bracing. He saw then that Tamsin and Cinnabar had already finished; Cinnabar was telling the litter bearers where to take Skan, and Tamsin had disappeared. The early morning sun shone brightly through the walls of the tent, making them glow with a warm amber light.

The tables and floors were a disaster. Blood—*how could a flyer hold so much blood?* he thought—and cut-away feathers pasted bits of bark and leaves to the floor. On the table, a length of a crossbow bolt lay amid the other debris, next to something that was relatively clean—a leather-wrapped handle of some kind, perhaps a broken sword. *That must have been what was blocking his throat,* Amberdrake thought numbly. *How would it get there...?*

Amberdrake blinked once and staggered back.

"No, you don't!" Gesten left Skandranon's side to go to Amberdrake's, getting under the kestra'chern's arm and bracing him upright. "It's bed for you, Drake. Skan's going to be fine—but you'd better lie down before you pass out!"

"I think you're right," Amberdrake murmured, actually finding a chuckle somewhere. *Skan's going to be all right. He made it back.* That was all that really mattered, after all. The cold place inside him had warmed; the emptiness erased. *Skan made it back.*

With Gesten's help, he tottered off down the slight slope to the kestra'chern's portion of the camp, just beyond the Healers'. He was so tired, he hardly noticed when he was guided into his own tent, except that the bright light of the morning sun dimmed, and the cool, fresh air took on a tinge of incense and body-scent. That was when he pulled away from Gesten, staggered to his bed, and collapsed across it. He managed to position himself the right way, but after that, he knew nothing more.

Amberdrake felt Skandranon's pain and frustration as he awoke. Even after—how many?—hours of needed oblivion, there was a dull ache in Amberdrake's body in all the places he'd helped Heal in Skandranon's body the night before. In all the places that Amberdrake *didn't* have a direct analog to—the wings and tail, especially the wings—there was an ache. It was an aftershock effect that Healers knew well and had to live with; in the case of the wing pain, it bunched in Amberdrake's shoulder blades and upper arms, like a bruised muscle cramping to the bone.

Amberdrake had awakened feeling as if he had run for days carrying a full pack; as if he had worked for two days without a rest—

—in short, as if he had served his full roster of clients, then Healed a gravely injured gryphon.

Gesten—loyal, competent Gesten—had drawn the sleeping-curtains to block as much light as possible from reaching the exhausted kestra'chern and was, no doubt, away from the tent clearing Amberdrake's schedule of responsibilities.

Amberdrake pulled the blankets from himself and stood up, steadying himself on a ring set into the oversized bed frame. He washed quickly and gulped down a meal of meat strips and flatbread, then pulled on the caftan and belt Gesten had laid out for him. By his clothes was a roster-sheet of appointments for the day; all but one had been crossed out, and that one was not due for another two hours.

Amberdrake stepped out from the spell-quieted canvas of his multiroomed tent into the afternoon daylight of the camp. Messenger-birds shot past, brightly colored, calling their descending chittering cry, while smoke from cook-fires scented the air they flew through. Three laughing children ran by, wearing the green and yellow ribbons of their parents' cadre, chased by a playful kyree with a bright red ball in its mouth. This was the way life should be. Amberdrake stretched, then ran a hand across his chin and cheeks as he squinted in the light; time to shave again before serving that client. A thorough general grooming was in order after he insured that Skandranon was healing properly. Being immaculately groomed always made him feel better.

He threaded his way through the shacks, forges, and service huts to the great tent where he'd left the Black Gryphon languishing that morning. In the daytime, the camp was far more inviting, despite the tension that was apparent everywhere you looked.

Assistant Healers and surgery aides surged past Amberdrake as he stepped inside, all intent on taking care of small administrative tasks and stocking supply shelves while the luxury of time was theirs. Casualties could course in like an overwhelming wave at any moment, so any spare minutes had to be spent in preparation. The war hadn't left the Healers much time to rest; they (and the grave diggers, body burners, and clergy) had few hours of leisure time. That was the nature of a war, after all. It ate spirits and bodies. It fed like any other creature.

War forced individuals and species together in ways no peacetime situation would duplicate, and some of the oddest friendships—even loves—came out of that. Amberdrake's affection for Gesten was natural, given the long association that hertasi had with the Kaled'a'in. Only the war and the needs of the fighters for support personnel had prevented Amberdrake from acquiring an entire troop of the little lizard-folk. As it was, he had to share Gesten's services with Skandranon.

But the bond between himself and the Black Gryphon—that was something that would never have occurred in peaceful times. The gryphons were literally unnatural—creations of Urtho, the Mage of Silence—and they would never have been found near the rolling plains that the nomadic Kaled'a'in called home. At least, not in Amberdrake's lifetime. He had heard Urtho mention some kind of vague plans he'd had, of planting them in little aeries in some of the wilder parts of the mountains, creating yet another population of nonhuman intelligences, as Urtho's predecessors had done with the hertasi and kyree. But that plan, of course, had come to nothing with the onset of war among the Great Mages.

Urtho had tried to stay out of the conflict, with the result that the conflict had come to him. Amberdrake wondered if he sometimes berated himself for waiting. There had probably been a point early in Ma'ar's career when Urtho could have defeated him easily, had he not stayed his hand. But who could have known that war would have come to roost in Ma'ar's willful head? Urtho couldn't be blamed for not bottling up the Kiyamvir long ago.

There were little joys amid all the pain, and some of those joys could come from the bindings of affection that just sprang up, like wildflowers in a battlefield.

Amberdrake sighed a little. He loved Skan as much as if he and the gryphon had been raised in the same nest, in the same home, but he wondered now if Skan felt anything more than simple friendship. It was hard to read the gryphon; the raptorial features reflected emotion in far more subtle ways than, say, a kyree's mobile face. And Skan was—well, Skan. He often kept his deepest feelings to himself, covering them with jokes and pranks—or complaints and feigned irritation. If he felt affection for someone, he was just as likely to mock him as praise him.

Caring for the gryphon certainly had its drawbacks.

Amberdrake made his way quietly and unobtrusively through the rows of smaller tents housing the recovering wounded. There was a special section for gryphons; an array of tents with reinforced frames, built to be used for traction, to keep any of the gryphons' four limbs or two wings immobile.

He spotted Gesten leaving one of the tents just as the hertasi saw him. Gesten looked uncommonly cheerful, all things considered; his eyes twinkled with good humor and he carried his tail high.

"His Royal Highness has one demon of a headache, and he says he's too nauseous to eat," Gesten reported. "Cinnabar says that's because he's got a concussion, and His Highness irritated his throat with the thingummy he stuffed into his crop, and since I couldn't get him to eat anything, she wants you to try."

Amberdrake nodded. "What was that thing he tried to swallow?" he asked. "It kept intruding on my dreams last night."

Gesten ducked his head in a shrug. "Some magical weapon Urtho sent him after," the hertasi said indifferently. "There was a big fuss over it after I got you to bed—half the mages in the Tower came looking for it when Himself found out Skan had been carried in. One of 'em woke Tamsin and tried to dress him down for not reporting it right away."

Amberdrake noticed the careful use of the word "tried." "I take it that Tamsin gave him an earful?"

Gesten chuckled happily and bobbed his head. "It was a pleasure and a privilege to hear," he said with satisfaction. "It was *almost* as good as you do when someone gets to you."

"Hmm." Amberdrake shook his head. "So, it was some kind of mage-weapon. Well, I suppose we'll never know the whole truth of the matter." It occurred to him that this "weapon," whatever it was, may have been the reason that Laisfaar had been taken. Or it might have been the single factor that made its loss possible, which made it imperative for Skan to have found one and gotten it back so that Urtho's mages could create a counteragent.

If Skan knew that, he wouldn't reveal it. The less anyone knew, the better, really. It was terribly easy for a spy to move through Urtho's camp—precisely because Urtho's people as a whole were far less ruthless than their counterparts on Ma'ar's side of the conflict. And camp gossip, as he had seen last night, spread as quickly as flame in oil-soaked tinder.

Amberdrake had long since resigned himself to the fact that he was going to overhear and accidentally see a million tantalizing details that would never make sense. That, too, was in the nature of his profession.

"Anyway, if you can get His Grumpiness—"

"*I heard that,*" came a low growl from the patient behind the tent flap.

"—His Contrariness to eat something, I can get the place ready for your next client," Gesten concluded smoothly.

Amberdrake chuckled. "I think I can manage. For one thing, now that I know his throat is irritated, I can do something about that."

"Don't strain yourself," Gesten warned, as he pulled back the tent flap to go inside. "He isn't your only charge. And *he* isn't even *paying*."

That last had to have been added for Skandranon's benefit. The gryphon only raised his chin off his bandaged forearms a moment, and said with immense dignity and a touch of ill temper, "I sshould think thisss sssort of thing came underrr the heading of 'jussst rewarrrd for a missssion sssatisssfactorilly completed.' "

"I would agree with you," Amberdrake said absently, noting that Skandranon was pointedly rolling his sibilants for "emphasssisss." Skandranon's diction was as crisp as any human's, when he wanted it to be. Amberdrake extended his finely-honed senses and found nothing more amiss than healing bones, healing wounds, and—yes, a healing concussion.

"How's the head?" he asked conversationally, letting his awareness sink into the area of Skan's throat and crop, soothing the irritation caused by the foreign object Skan had (inadvertently?) swallowed. It was something of a truism that a gryphon could not store anything in the crop that was bigger than he could successfully swallow, but that did not mean that the object in question would be a *comfortable* thing to store. Particularly if it was angular and unyielding as Amberdrake thought he remembered.

"The head isss missserable, thank you," the gryphon replied with irritation. "I sshould think you could do ssssomething about it."

"Sorry, Skan," Amberdrake replied apologetically. "I wish I could—but I'm not a specialist in that kind of injury. I could do more harm than good by messing about with your head."

He exerted a touch of Healing energy—being careful not to overextend himself; he hadn't needed Gesten's warning on that score. He'd run himself into the ground once already;

if he did it again, he was asking for trouble, and it generally took two or more Healers to fix what a stupid Healer did to himself. In a moment, the heat that meant "soreness and irritation" to Amberdrake faded and died from Skan's throat, and the gryphon swallowed experimentally.

"Well, I suppose you aren't going to go away unless I eat something," Skan said, without a sign of any kind of gratitude. "So I'd better do it and get you out of here so I can sleep."

Amberdrake didn't make any comments; he simply held out hand-sized pieces of fresh, red meat for Skan to swallow whole. Like all gryphons, Skan preferred his food to be fresh killed, as fresh as possible, although he could and would eat dried or prepared food, and actually enjoyed breads and pastries. Gesten had left a large bowl of the meat chunks; Amberdrake didn't stop handing them to the gryphon until the bowl was empty, even though Skan looked as if he would have liked to take a piece of Amberdrake's hand with his meal.

Amberdrake tried not to let his feelings get hurt. He'd seen this kind of thing often enough in other cases of those who had been extremely active and had been forced by injuries to depend even a little on others. Skan had been completely immobilized by his injuries, and couldn't even use his forelegs. Add to that the pounding of his concussion-headache, and he really wasn't behaving too badly, all things considered.

But on the other hand, Amberdrake was a friend, and Skan was treating him in ways that he wouldn't have inflicted on an indentured servant.

Some of this must have shown in Amberdrake's expression, for just as the last strip of raw meat went down Skan's throat, Gesten returned, took one look at the two of them, and proceeded to give Skan a lecture on gratitude.

"You'd *think* that the smartest gryphon in Urtho's army would have a mudcake's sense, wouldn't you?" he railed. "You'd think that same gryphon might recall Amberdrake putting his wings together for him until Drake fell over with exhaustion! You'd think that same gryphon might possibly remember that Drake would be feeling phantom pain this afternoon from all that Healing. But *no*—" Gesten snorted. "That takes common sense, and common courtesy. So when Drake isn't sitting here right by the tent, waiting for a certain gryphon to wake up, that gryphon pouts and thinks nobody loves him and then acts like a spoiled brat when Drake does show up *even before he's had a shave.*"

Skan couldn't possibly have looked worse, but his eartufts, which had been lying fairly close to his head, now flattened against his skull. And the gryphon looked distinctly chagrined.

And penitent.

Silence followed Gesten's lecture, as the hertasi gave Skan his "you messed up" glare, and Skan sighed.

"Drake," the gryphon said softly. "I am sssorry. I have been verrry rrrude. I—"

Amberdrake knew this mood. Skan was likely to keep apologizing for the next candlemark—and perversely, getting more irritating and irritable with every word of apology.

"Skan, it's all right," Amberdrake said hastily. "You haven't been any ruder than some of my clients, after all. I'm used to it." He managed a weak chuckle. "I'm a pretty rotten patient myself when I'm sick. Just ask Gesten."

The hertasi rolled his eyes, but said nothing.

"So don't worry. We're just glad you're back, however many pieces you came back in." Amberdrake slid his hand in among the neck-feathers and scratched places where he knew Skan had not been able to reach—and would not for some time.

The gryphon sighed, and put his head back down on his bandaged and splinted forelegs. "You arrre too patient, Drrrake."

"Actually, if I don't get him moving, he's going to be too *late*," Gesten interjected, apparently mollified by the apology. "You've got a client, Kestra'chern. And you're going to have to make up for the fact that you had to cancel out all your morning appointments."

"Right." Amberdrake gave Skan's neck a final scratch, and stood up, brushing out the folds of his robe. "And I'd better shave and clean up first. How much time have I got?"

"Not much, for the grooming you need," Gesten replied. "You'd better put some speed on it."

A little later, Amberdrake wondered why he'd bothered. This was not one of his usual clients, and he had not known what to expect, but he could have been a wooden simulacrum for all the man looked at him.

He was a mercenary mage, one of the hire-ons that Urtho had taken as his own allies and apprentices proved inadequate to take on all the mages that Ma'ar controlled. While he was probably a handsome man, it was difficult to tell that at the moment. His expression was as rigid and unreadable as a mask, and his needs were, to be blunt, basic.

In fact, if he wanted what he *said* he wanted, he need not have come to Amberdrake for it. He could have gone to any of the first- or second-rank kestra'chern in the cadre and spent a great deal less money. The illusion of grace and luxury, relaxation, pampering—and the inevitable: a kestra'chern was not a bedmate-for-hire, although plenty of people had that impression, this mage included. If that was all he wanted, there were plenty of sources for that, including, if the man were up to it, actually winning the respect of someone.

Amberdrake was tempted to send him away for just that reason; this was, in its way, as insulting as ordering a master cook to make oatmeal.

But as he had told the General, as every kestra'chern must, he had learned over the years that what a client asked for might not be what he wanted—and what he wanted might not even be something he understood. That was what made him the expert he was.

When a few quiet questions elicited nothing more than a growled order to "just do your job," Amberdrake stood up and surveyed the man from a position of superior height.

"I can't do my job to your satisfaction if you're a mass of tension," he countered sternly. "And what's more, I can't do it to *my* satisfaction. Now, why don't we just start with a simple massage?"

He nodded at the padded table on the brighter side of the

chamber, and the mage reluctantly rose, and even more reluctantly took his place on it.

Gesten appeared as if Amberdrake had called him, and deftly stripped the man down and put out the oils. Amberdrake chose one scented with chamomile and infused with herbs that induced relaxation, then began with the mage's shoulders. With a Healer's hands, he sought out and released knots of tension—and, as always, the release of tension released information about the source of the tension.

"It's Winterhart," the man said with irritation. "She's started pulling away from me, and damned if I know why! I just don't understand her anymore, but I told her that if _she_ wasn't willing to give me satisfaction, I could and damned well would go elsewhere for it."

Amberdrake surmised from the feelings associated with the woman's name that "Winterhart" was this fellow's lover—or at least, he thought she was. Odd, for that kind of name was usually worn by one of the Kaled'a'in, and yet he seldom saw Kaled'a'in associating intimately with those of other races.

"So why did you come here?" Amberdrake asked, prodding a little at the knot of tangled emotions as he prodded at the knotted muscles. "Why not someone—less expensive?"

The man grunted. "Because the whole army knows your name," he replied. "Everyone in our section will know I came here this afternoon and there won't be any question why."

Very tangled emotions, he mused. Because although the top layer was a desire to hurt by going publicly to a notorious—or famed, depending on your views—kestra'chern, underneath was a peculiar and twisted desire to flatter. As if by going only to the best and most expensive, he was trying to say to Winterhart that nothing but the best would remotely be a substitute for her.

And another layer—in doing so he equated her to a paid companion, thereby once again insulting her by counting her outside his personal, deeper emotional life. Still, there was that backhanded flattery. Amberdrake was not a bedmate for hire, he was a kestra'chern, a profession which was held in high regard by Urtho and most of the command-circle.

Among the Kaled'a'in, he was the next thing to a Goddess-touched priest. The word itself had connotations of divine insight and soul healing, and of friendship. So, then, there was wishful thinking—or again, the desire to impress this "Winterhart," whoever she was.

There were more mysteries than answers no matter where he turned these days.

"You do know that what happens in this tent depends upon what I decide is best for you, don't you?" he asked, just to set the record straight. If all the man wanted was exhausting exercise, let him go elsewhere for it.

Amberdrake was massaging the man's feet, using pressure and heat to ease twinges all through the body, without resorting to any actual Healing powers. Amberdrake had detractors who thought he worked *less* because of his power to Heal flesh and soothe nerves. His predecessors had used purely physical, learned skills—like this massage—for generations, driven by sharp senses and a clear mind. In his role as kestra'chern, he used his Healing gifts only when more "conventional" skills were ineffective. Still, one *did* complement the other, and he would use the whole of his abilities if a client warranted it. So far, though, this merc hadn't warranted it; he hadn't even warranted the kind of services he would get from a *perchi*. This was still at the level of banter-and-pose.

"Well . . . urrgh . . . I'd heard that—" He said it as if he hadn't quite believed it.

"If you aren't satisfied with that, I can suggest the name of a *perchi* or two, accustomed to those of rank," Amberdrake ventured. There was no point in having the man angry; he was paying for expensive treatment, and if he felt he hadn't gotten his money's worth, he might attempt to make trouble.

"What you do . . . ah . . . isn't important now, is it?" the mage replied shrewdly. "It's what Winterhart thought you did. You *are* required to keep this confidential, that much I know, so I'll let her use her imagination. It'll probably be more colorful anyway."

Amberdrake was tempted at that point to send the man

away. He was right; what he was planning was also very cruel to his lover.

Assuming she didn't deserve it; she might. He could have no way of knowing.

Amberdrake sighed. There was still his professional pride. He decided to give the man his money's worth—and to make certain that, as it progressed, as little of it as possible was what the client had anticipated.

Urtho

Three

"I hope that's all for tonight, Gesten," Amberdrake said, as the curtain dropped behind him. He rubbed the side of his nose with his knuckle and sighed. "I'm exhausted. That last client wanted a soft-hammer-massage and an argument. Roster indicated a gentle counseling session."

"That's all you've got for the night," Gesten replied, a bit smugly. "The last two made up for all the clients you canceled this morning, since they were straight-pay and not reward-chits. I'd have warned you if I'd known about the last. He didn't say anything about the hammers; I'd have had them warmed and ready for you if I'd known. He was pretty closemouthed."

"I'm not complaining. You'd probably have sent him elsewhere if he *had* said anything; I'm certain he would have made it into an insult somehow." Amberdrake didn't elaborate. The last two clients had been, to be charitable, annoying. And since Gesten always discreetly monitored the workroom, he was probably well aware of that. The hertasi simply laid out a clean sleeping robe, simple and unadorned (unlike the robes Amberdrake wore for his clients), and uncovered a plate of army-bread and cheese. Few delicacies appeared in the hands of Urtho's folk these days, even for those who could afford them; the ones Amberdrake got his hands on he reserved for his clients who often responded well to gustatory pampering. Rumor had it that Urtho himself had given up his favorite treats. One thing there was no shortage of, at least, was water. There was a hot bath waiting in the corner, steam rising invitingly from the frame-and-skin tub.

"Thank you, Gesten," he said with genuine appreciation.

Amberdrake stripped off his sweat-dampened silks and slipped into the bath, wincing a little at the heat. He was going to look as if he'd been boiled in a few minutes, but it would be worth it to relax his muscles. He recalled, as from a distant past, that before they had packed up their families and herds and moved here, the Kaled'a'in had created hot springs where they settled, if there were none there already. But much had changed; mage-created hot springs required an enormous expenditure of magical energy, and that was now a luxury no one could afford.

The war tried to eat up everything in its path. For Amberdrake and those who supported the warriors, it was the war they fought, not the army, spells, and makaar. This was the way many of the warriors saw it, too—saw war as a natural enemy, to be dealt with firmly and then put behind you. But war's devouring power was why Urtho had tried to avoid it for so long—why he had successfully avoided it until it came to his very doorstep. Folk from northern climes referred to the people of the South as "civilized"; it had little to do with their technologies and powers, but far more with their philosophy—and they were as pragmatic as they might be idealistic. When Ma'ar's army threatened at the border, opposition was there to meet it.

That was why Amberdrake's services, which in peacetime would have been divided between the wealthiest of outsiders and the needs of his own people, had been volunteered to be the reward for heroes. . . .

And as the very expensive indulgence for those whose egos demanded the best.

That thought brought him uncomfortably right back to that merc mage, a man whose cold soul he had been unable to warm. Most of the mages in Urtho's forces were there because they felt Urtho's cause was right, or because they honored Urtho as one of the greatest Adepts ever born and hoped to be able to learn from him as they helped to defend his land. Or simply because they hated Ma'ar, or their own lands or overlords had been destroyed by the rapacious conqueror. Few fought in this army simply for the money.

This man, Conn Levas, was one who seemed to care only

about the money. He had few friends and few interests outside his own skill and power. He was, in fact, one of the
most monofocused people Amberdrake had ever seen: a nar-
cissist to a high degree. Everything for him was centered
around how he could increase his personal wealth and prestige. To him, the war was a convenient way to do that.
Urtho was the master to serve because Urtho gave his mages
much more autonomy and better rewards than Ma'ar.

Still, it was that kind of focus that made the hunting
beasts of the world so successful, so perhaps he shouldn't be
faulted for it. But how a Kaled'a'in woman had ever become
his lover, Amberdrake could not guess.

Levas had at least admitted that his own coldness was
a part of why this Winterhart was disenchanted with him.
Amberdrake had the feeling that such an admission that *anything* was due to personal fault was a major concession.

Disenchanted . . . now there was a thought. Could this
mage have worked a beglamorment on the woman? He couldn't
have used a stronger spell, since other mages would have
noticed, but a beglamorment, at the right time, would have
made him what she most wanted to see. She could have
found her way into his bed long before she realized he wasn't
what she had thought. To have a Kaled'a'in lover was considered a coup by some mercs in Urtho's forces; to have a
Healer as a lover even more so. She might represent just
another symbol of success to be acquired. And—

Why was he worrying about *her*? He didn't even know
her, only that her name sounded Kaled'a'in. She might not
be Kaled'a'in at all; there were others who took on colorful
names or were given them at birth. For that matter, why
was he worrying about Conn Levas? The man had gotten
good and ample service for his money. He was unlikely to
return, given his uneasiness with Amberdrake's probing
questions; Amberdrake knew the merc had been disturbed
by how much he had revealed. Well. The service he'd ren-
dered was easy enough, even by kestra'chern standards.
Still. . . .

*If you worry about every man and woman in the army,
you'll tie yourself up in knots for no good reason,* he told
himself. *You're making things up out of nothing, then wor-*

*rying about them. You've never even seen this Healer Win-
terhart. Why work yourself into a headache?*

Oh, he knew why he was worrying about them; it was to
keep from worrying about Skan.

As if he didn't have enough to worry about already.

Skandranon was grateful to be alive, even more grateful to
have gotten his mission completed successfully, and *entirely*
grateful to have been put back together. He'd been assured—
repeatedly—that he would be able to fly again. But he was
in constant pain, his head pounded horribly, and on top of
all of it, having to be *that* grateful made him want to bite.

This was very bad of him, and he knew it, which made
him want to bite even more. He only liked to be bad on his
own terms. If only he could have someone show up to see
him who deserved a good, scathing dressing-down—the fool
who had assured Urtho that Stelvi Pass had been in no danger, for instance, or the idiot who had issued the orders that
grounded the gryphons between specific missions. Even the
imbecile cook who had first sent him raw fish for breakfast
instead of good, red meat, then had made it worse by sending
yesterday's stew instead of fresh, still bleeding meat. But the
only people who came near him were those he was supposed
to be *grateful* to—how *annoying!*—Gesten and Drake, Tamsin and Cinnabar, the members of his wing, and the scouts
and mercs who had risked their lives to get him home. After
Gesten's lecture, he made doubly sure to convey his proper
gratitude to them.

But he still wanted to bite—so he did. The camp could
find another pillow somewhere.

Now if only his beak didn't hurt; there was a persistent
sting from small scratches around his nares, and an itch
across his cere, and his sinuses felt like—

*Like you hit something hard after a prolonged plummet,
bird.*

It didn't help that he was forced to lie in a completely
unnatural position, forelegs stretched in front of him, hindlegs stretched straight under him and bound by splints, unable to get comfortable. He knew Healers could fuse the
bones of a mage-bred creature like himself in a single session

of concentrated Healing. He also knew that there was plenty of pain on the front lines, and people in real danger of dying if they didn't get to a Healer, and that such a session was fairly low on the list of priorities.

That didn't help.

But much to his surprise, late in the afternoon, Tamsin and Cinnabar made an appearance at his tent—and from the implements their hertasi was carrying, this was no social call. Tamsin was in his usual simple green breeches and shirt, his short-cropped blond hair and beard in stark contrast to many of the other Healers, who usually let their hair grow long and went clean shaven. And he could not have made a better foil for the graceful and tall Lady Cinnabar; he was as stocky and muscled as a wrestler. Cinnabar, of course, was as elegant as if she had just come from holding court, her scarlet gown cut to mid-calf, showing scarlet leather boots and slender ankles, her sleeves cut tight, displaying her graceful arms without an unseemly show of flesh. Skandranon had heard that by human standards she was not beautiful, not even handsome, but her strong-nosed face, so like a proud falcon, seemed attractive enough to him. She even had a crest; her hair was cut short on the sides and top so that it stood up, and flowed in a braided tail down her back. Lovely.

Both of them looked relatively rested and full of energy. Skan's hopes rose. Were they—?

"All right, old bird," Tamsin said cheerfully as he held the tent flap open for the laden hertasi. "We need to do something about those legs so you can get a proper rest. Think you're up to it?"

"Do you think I would sssay otherwisse?" Skan countered. "I would do anything!"

"Anything?" Cinnabar replied archly. Then, at Tamsin's eloquently raised eyebrow, she added hastily, "No, don't answer. You are the most insatiable creature I have ever met!"

Skan wanted to leer but couldn't manage it. "Pleasssse," he near-whimpered instead.

By near sunset, after much effort on their part and pain and cooperative effort on his, the fractured bones of his forelegs fused, and the hindlegs healed enough that the splints could come off and he could carefully walk a few steps. He could attend to his personal needs—which was just as well, since so far as he knew, no one had come up with the equivalent of a chamber pot for a gryphon. He would be able to feed himself, and since Cinnabar had blessedly done something about the headache, he was ravenous. Now he could lie back down in a much more comfortable position to listen to his bowels rumble.

Cinnabar looked as serene and composed now as when they had started; Tamsin was clearly tired, but just as cheerful. "That should do you, old bird," he said, slapping Skan on the flank. "Dinner first, or visitor?"

"Both," Skan replied. "If it isss sssomeone who cannot bearrr to watch a gryphon eat, let him come back laterrr. And if it iss sssomeone I do not want to sssee, *he* will be the dinner."

He would not be eating little chunks of meat tonight; no, Cinnabar and Tamsin knew gryphons, and unless that idiot cook mistakenly countermanded their orders, there would be a nice fat haunch of something fresh-killed and bloody, something Skan could tear into and take out some of his frustrations on. Maybe even half a deer or ox—he was quite hungry enough to eat either.

A silver-brocaded hertasi signaled from beside the canvas doorway, and the other hertasi disappeared as if they had evaporated. A moment later, the tent flap was pushed aside, to reveal a beloved and unique personage.

"I should think I can bear to watch a gryphon eat," said Urtho, the Mage of Silence.

He swept into the room with a single step; he said nothing more, but projected a soothing *presence* into the damp, warm room. It was impossible to tell Urtho's real age; he could be sixty or six hundred. For as long as Skan had known him, Urtho had looked the same, an eternal image of genius. Tall and thin, storklike, with a waist-length fall of curly silver-gray hair, huge gray eyes, a nose as prominent as Lady Cinnabar's and a lantern jaw kept scrupulously clean-shaven, he did not look like the finest of Adept-class mages. He did not look like any kind of mage. He looked more like a scribe, or perhaps a silversmith or retired acrobat.

Skan thought there might be Kaled'a'in blood in Urtho's veins. That might well be true, given his nose and the long-standing association he had with them. But if that were true, no one had ever confirmed it in Skan's hearing.

Urtho held the flap open for two hertasi bringing in the forequarters of a deer; both front legs, shoulders, and the chest, hide and all. No head, though, but perhaps that was a bit much to ask. Humans were so queasy when it came to delivering a gryphon's dinner with head intact, never mind that the head was delicious. Well, humans were queasy about a great many silly things. Skan seized the prize in his foreclaws as soon as the hertasi had laid it in front of him, and tore off a mouthful of meat and hide before acknowledging the commander of one of the two largest armies that Velgarth had ever seen.

He tossed his head and swallowed the bite whole. Like the raptors the Kaled'a'in bred, he needed the hair and stringy hide to clean his crop. "Join me for dinner?" he offered.

Urtho laughed. "Is that like a falcon offering to meet a mouse for lunch?" Tamsin and Cinnabar both bowed respectfully and made a somewhat hasty exit. Urtho's power tended to overawe people who didn't know him well. He nodded to them both, took one of the two seats the Healers had left, and settled himself down onto it.

Skandranon tore off another mouthful of meat; it tasted wonderful, rich and salt-sweet. He swallowed, feeling the striations of the blood-slick muscles slither against his throat, down into his crop. He flicked an ear and cocked his head at his leader. Their gazes met, and tales sped between them in the flicker of their eyes.

"Well, old man, I sssurvived afterrr all. I hope you have *it.*"

Urtho nodded casually. "So you did. And you were right, when you insisted you were the one to go. You did very well, Skan, and yes, I have it. Even though you tried to swallow it whole."

"I wasss the only one ssstupid enough to trrry, you mean,"

Skan replied, trying not to preen with pride. He scissored another bite out of his meal.

"I seem to recall that you not only volunteered, you insisted." Urtho made it a statement and a bit of a challenge. Skan simply grunted.

"Perhapsss," he suggested teasingly after a moment, "your memorrry isss faulty."

Somewhat to his surprise, Urtho sighed. "It is," he said wearily. "I've been forgetting a great deal lately. Kelethen has been most impatient with me."

"You have much to rrrememberrr," Skan pointed out quickly. "Kelethen isss as fusssy as any other herrrtasssi. You ssshould tell him that if he isss upsssset, he can jussst keep an appointment calendar, asss if you werrre a kessstra'cherrrn."

"Sometimes I feel like a kestra'chern," Urtho told him ruefully. "Expected to please everyone and generally pleasing—"

"Almossst everrryone." Skan interrupted. "Besssidesss, sssomeone hasss to lead, and I am too busy. What arrre you doing down herrre anyway? Isssn't there a weapon to invessstigate, a Passss to retake? I am only one sssstupid grrryphon, afterrr all."

"True." Urtho sighed again. "But you are a very special stupid gryphon; I was concerned and I wanted to see that you were doing as well as the Healers claimed. The weapon has been dealt with, and a counterattack on the Pass is in the hands of the commanders; there is little I can do from here now that it has been launched."

Urtho's face was a little thinner, and Skan guessed he had not been sleeping or eating much in the past few days. He could sympathize with the mage for wishing to escape from his Tower for a little. Still . . . "I hope that sssomeone knowsss where you are."

"Kelethen does. I wish that this were over or, better still, had never begun."

Skandranon wiped his beak against the fur and cast his eyes supportively to Urtho. "Urtho. It isss begun and continuesss. We fly thessse windsss together. You did not cause the windsss to become a sssstorm."

"I would say that I had done nothing to cause this, but the simple fact of our existence was enough to trigger this assault from Ma'ar. I've studied him. Even as a young man, he wanted power far more than he wanted anything else, and he enjoyed having power *over* people." Urtho shook his head, as if he simply could not understand anyone with that kind of mind. "Whatever he had, it was never enough. It was a kind of hunger with him, but one that could not be sated. There could only be one master of the world, and that one must be Ma'ar."

"Insssane," Skan replied.

"Not exactly," Urtho said, surprising the gryphon. "Not insane as we know the meaning of the word. But his sanity holds nothing but himself, if that makes any sense."

"No," Skan said shortly. What he had seen of Ma'ar and Ma'ar's creations did not convince him that the Mage of Black Fire was anything but evil *and* insane.

"I would help him if I could," Urtho said softly.

"What?" Skan squawked, every feather on end with surprise. He felt very nearly the same as he had when he'd hit the ground; breath knocked out of him and too stunned to even think.

"I would," Urtho insisted. "If he would even stop to think about all the harm he has caused and come to me, I would help him. But he will not. He cannot. Not and still be Ma'ar." He shook his head. "His obsessions are like mine, Skandranon. I understand him far better than he understands me. He thinks I am soft enough that at some point I will surrender because so many have died and more will die. He thinks I don't realize that the killing would not end just because we had surrendered. I don't think he has the barest idea what we will do to stop him." There was no mistaking the grim determination in Urtho's voice.

Skan relaxed; for a moment he had thought that the latest turn of the conflict might have unhinged the mage.

"He isss a mad dog," Skan said brusquely. "You do not try to help a mad dog, you ssslay it."

"Harsh words, my child." Urtho frowned a little, although by now he should have been well aware of the gryphons' raptorial and somewhat bloodthirsty nature.

Skan thought of the tortured gryphons at Stelvi Pass, and hissed. "Not harsssh enough. I did not tell you what they did to the Ssstelvi Wing. Everrrything you have everrr hearrrd of. All of them, down to the nessstlingsss, and worsse than you could imagine."

Urtho turned pale, and Skan instantly regretted what he had blurted out. Urtho had never wedded and had no children. He considered all of his intelligent creations to be his children, but that was especially true of the gryphons.

An awkward silence loomed between them for a moment, and Skan cursed his habit of blurting out the first thing he thought. *Stupid bird; you might think before you say something once in a while. It would be a distinct improvement.*

During the silence, the camp sounds seemed particularly loud and intrusive; people shouting to one another, and somewhere nearby, the hammering of metal on metal. Skan continued eating, his hunger overcoming his manners, as he thought of a way to apologize.

"I am sorry, Urtho," he said finally. "I am hungry, hurt, and a very irritable and stupid bird. Think of me as being in molt."

"You're right, Skan," Urtho said finally. "You're right. Despite what I just said, I sometimes don't think of what Ma'ar is capable of. It stretches my imagination and willpower to think like Ma'ar, and it isn't something I—enjoy."

Skandranon had no reply for that; perhaps there was no possible reply. He simply swallowed another beakful of meat.

"Well, thanks to you, those new weapons of his will no longer threaten us," the mage continued, changing the subject. "And what I really came here for, my friend, was to discover what you want as your reward. You more than deserve one. Offspring, perhaps? You certainly have a high potential, and any female in the wings would be happy to oblige you. I would like to see the Rashkae line continued."

The offer of the reward did not surprise Skan, but what Urtho had called him—"my friend"—certainly did. And yet, the simple words should not have been such a revelation. Urtho had spent many hours talking to him, not as commander to subordinate, nor as master to servant, nor even as creator to creation—but as equal to equal. Skandranon alone of the gryphons was privileged to come and go at will from Urtho's Tower, and to interrupt the mage at any time of the day or night.

"I will think about it," Skan replied. "At the moment, I ssshould be verrry glad merrrely to be healed and flying again."

Urtho nodded. "As you will. I'm sure you'll think of something. Just please be mindful of our limited resources! And the impossibility of transporting massive libraries wherever you go!"

Skan gryphon-grinned; Urtho had not forgotten his love of books. "I am sssure I ssshall think of something."

Urtho showed no disposition to rise and go his way, however, so Skan simply continued eating while the greatest single power in their entire army spoke of camp gossip. And it was in the midst of this that Commander Loren found them.

No doors to knock on existed in a tent, of course, but the ostentatious clearing of a throat outside the closed flap told Skan that there was a visitor, and one whose voice he did not recognize. Skan instinctively bristled, all his reactions trying to force his body into readiness to protect Urtho, even though he was in no shape to do so.

Urtho did recognize the voice, of course; it was one of those traits of his that Skan could only marvel at, that he knew every leader in his huge army well enough to recognize their voices. Urtho's memory was remarkable and reputedly utterly reliable, so much so that forgetting even minor things upset him.

"You might as well come in, Loren," Urtho said immediately. "If it's all that important that you tracked me down."

When Commander Loren pushed aside the tent flap, Skandranon recognized the bricklike face and body, although he could not have put the proper name to the man. Loren was neither outstandingly good in deploying the gryphons assigned to him, nor outstandingly poor at it. Only one or the other would have made a gryphon take notice of him.

So Loren's first words made Skan raise his head from the remains of his meal in surprise.

"I need you to reward a gryphon, Lord Urtho," Loren said,

apologetically. "And I would never have troubled you when you had so obviously gone to the effort of losing your aides, except that I didn't want this one to slip through the cracks."

"Obviously, this gryphon has done something exceptional—" Urtho paused significantly.

"Very." Loren's beefy face reddened with pride. "She was on patrol in what was supposed to have been a safe sector, and discovered and eliminated three makaar."

Three makaar? Skan was impressed. "Who isss flying with herrr?" he asked. "I ssshould like to know who ssset them up for herrr." Setting someone up for a triple kill took almost as much skill and more courage than actually making the kills.

"That's just it, Black Gryphon," Loren said, face practically glowing. "She did it by herself. Alone. It was supposed to be a safe area; as thin as my patrols are spread, we thought it was reasonable to fly safe areas in singles instead of pairs, to give the younger or smaller gryphons experience without risking them too much. Her name is Zhaneel."

To destroy three makaar was remarkable; to destroy three at once was uncommon even among experienced frontliners. *Who is this "Zhaneel?"* he thought, beak agape with surprise. *And why have I never heard of her before this?*

From the dumbfounded look on his face, Urtho's surprise was just as great as Skan's, and that was astonishing in itself. The gryphons were his favorite creations, and he knew and kept track of every promising youngster. Yet he did not appear to know of this one.

"You mussst bring herrr herrre," Skan said imperiously before Urtho could speak.

Loren looked to Urtho for permission first. When the mage nodded, he pushed back the tent flap and stalked out into the sunset-reddened dust and activity of the camp.

He returned much more quickly than Skan would have expected, though not too soon for the gryphon's impatient nature. He had bolted the last of his meal and called the hertasi to come take the remains away and light the lamps before they arrived, partially to be able to devote all of his attention to the visitors, and partially out of a wish to be seen at his best, limited though that "best" might be at the moment. He hardly presented a gallant sight—swathed in bandages, propped up by pillows, and without having had a proper bath in days. Still, Gesten had groomed him as best he could manage, and it did not do to be presented to a brave lady with the leavings of a greedy meal in front of him.

You just want to look good for the lady, vain bird. As if you want to be sure that you could add her to your harem if you wanted, like a collector of figurines lusting after yet another little statue.

Still, he didn't want her to think that he was some kind of ragged-tailed hooligan. The gods only knew what she'd heard about him; Drake and Gesten wouldn't repeat half of the stories they *said* they'd heard about him. But then again, he had only their word for the fact that they'd heard these stories at all. . . .

It was a good thing that this was a relatively large tent, made for two gryphons as patients, and only holding Skan at the moment; once Commander Loren brought his young gryphon in, things became just a little crowded.

"This is Zhaneel, my lords," Loren said formally. "Lord Urtho, Skandranon, this is young Zhaneel, who today disposed of three makaar single-handedly."

While Urtho made the usual congratulatory speech, Skandranon kept very quiet and examined Zhaneel. She was small and lightly built, with a deep keelbone but narrow chest. Her ear-tufts were compact and dainty, her feathers very smooth, and she had no neck-ruff at all. In color she was a light brown with a dusty-gold edge to her primaries; like most gryphons except the unassigned, her primary feathers had been bleached, then dipped in the colors of her wing—in this case, red and gold. On her head and face, she had malar-stripes of a slightly darker brown, and eye-markings flowing down her cheeks, like soft-edged tear tracks.

While Loren and Urtho spoke, she kept her head down and turned to the side, as if shy or embarrassed—the gryphon equivalent of blushing. Was she simply shy, or was she truly uncomfortable in their presence? Most of the gryphons that Skan knew might have been subdued in the presence of their overlord and creator, but they wouldn't have acted like this.

When Loren finally coaxed her to speak, her voice was low and soft, and she spoke in simple sentences with a great deal of hissing and trilling—and yet it was not because she was stupid. A stupid gryphon would not have been able to do what she had done. It was as if she simply could not get the words past her shyness.

"It wasss nothing," she insisted. "I only fly high, verrry high. Sssaferrr it isss. Makaarrr cannot fly ssso high. I ssssee them, thrrree, below me."

Skan could readily picture it in his mind's eye; especially if she had been flying as high as he thought she was. Those tapering wings—surely with wings like those the aspect ratio would be remarkable, and the narrow leading edge would complement the long primaries. The makaar would have been halfway between her and the earth; she would have been invisible to them.

"Too farrr to rrreturrrn to rrreport, it wasss," she continued. "They would be gone when warrrriorrrsss came. They mussst have been looking for sssomething. Ssssent. They would have found it and gone."

Now Skan nodded. "True," he rumbled, and Zhaneel started at the sound of his voice. "Quite true. Your duty was to try to stop them."

Her hissing had made him conscious of his own speech; normally he only hissed and trilled when he was under stress or very, very relaxed, among friends. When he chose, he could speak as well as any human, and he chose to do so now. Perhaps it would comfort her.

"But how did you kill them?" Urtho persisted.

She ducked her head. "I wasss high. They could not sssee me. I sssstooped on them; hit the leader. Like thissss—"

She held up one foreclaw, fisted.

"I ssstruck hissss head; he fell from the sssky and died."

No doubt; coming from the height Zhaneel had been at, she must have broken the leader's neck on impact, and the ground finished him.

"I followed him down; the othersss pursued, but I climbed again, too fasssssst for them to follow." She pantomimed with her foreclaw, and Skan saw then what he had not noticed before—a reason she may not have struck to slash, or bind to her quarry as he would have. Her talons were actually very short; her "toes" long and flexible, very like stubby human fingers. A slash would only have angered the makaar unless she had managed against all odds to slash the major artery in the neck.

"I go high again, verrry high; the two follow, but cannot go sssso high. I turrrrrn, dive, hit the first asss he fliesss to meet me." She sat back on her hindquarters and mimed that meeting with both of her odd foreclaws; how the makaar struggled to gain height, how she had come at him head-on, angling her dive at the last possible moment to strike the top of his head with her closed fists.

"He wasss ssstunned; he fell, brrroke hisss neck when he hit. I follow him down, to be sssure, then turrrn dive into climb again." She would not look at any of the three of them, keeping her eyes fixed on some invisible point on the ground. "The thirrrd one, he isss afrraid now, he trrries to rrrrun. I go high again, asss high asss I can, and dive. He isss fassst, but my dive isss fassster. I hit him. He fallssss." She ducked her head. "It isss overrr. It isss nothing ssspecial."

Nothing special—except that these were tactics few, if any, gryphons had tried before. Spectacularly successful tactics, too, if Zhaneel's experience was anything to go by. Most gryphons, when they fought makaar, closed for the kill, binding to the prey's back and bringing it down, or slashing with talons in passing strikes. Hawk and eagle tactics, not falcon. Zhaneel had fought as would a very hungry—or very brave—falcon, when taking a goose or very large duck, prey that would outweigh her twofold or more—knocking the prey out of the sky, and *not* using her talons.

"Zhaneel, your act of courage has probably saved any number of our people, and no few of your own kind," Urtho said, as these thoughts passed through Skan's mind. "I am quite impressed and quite pleased that Commander Loren thought to bring you to my attention personally. At the very least, my dear child, I am going to present you with the reward you richly deserve."

With that, he reached into a pocket and pulled out one of the reward-tokens he used instead of medals or decorations. Urtho felt medals were fairly useless; he rewarded bravery directly. This particular token was the highest possible; a square of gold with a sword stamped on one side and a many-rayed sun-in-glory on the other. He slipped this into the tiny pouch Zhaneel wore around her neck, an accessory that most gryphons not on duty wore. She could trade that particular token for virtually anything in the camp, from a fine tent to the exclusive services for a month of her very own hertasi. Or she could save it and add it to others to obtain other luxuries. Skan simply kept a running account with Gesten, whose services he shared with Amberdrake. Before he had left on this last mission, he had been quite a few months ahead, and Gesten would be a very wealthy hertasi when the war was over.

"But child, I am curious," Urtho continued, his eyes fixed on her, as Loren beamed his approval and the young gryphon stammered her thanks. "Who are your parents? Who trained you besides them?"

"My parentsss arrre no morrre," she replied. "They died when I wasss jussst fledged and I have no ssssiblingsss."

Urtho's disappointment was clear even to Skan; there would be no more like Zhaneel unless she mated. But before he could persist in finding out how she had been trained, since her parents had obviously been unable to give her that training, one of his aides burst into the tent without so much as an "excuse me."

"Lord Urtho! The counterattack at Stelvi Pass—"

That was all the boy needed to say; Urtho was off, following him at an undignified run that belied his silver hair, out into the lamplight, and from there into the darkness.

This was not the first time Urtho had left Skan holding the line, and it probably would not be the last. Skandranon knew what to do; summoning as much dignity and aplomb as his injuries permitted, he proceeded to deal with the situation.

"Lord Commander, thank you for bringing Zhaneel here," he said, raising his head and then bowing it slightly to Loren. "Once again, you have gone beyond mere duty, and if Urtho had not been forced to leave, he would have told you so himself."

He hoped that Loren would take that as a hint, and so he

did. "Thank you, Black Gryphon," he replied, then continued, with an honesty that was not necessarily common among the commanders, "it has taken me a while to learn the best way to employ fighters other than human, but I hope that Zhaneel's success is a harbinger of more such victories to come. Now, if you will excuse me, news from Stelvi Pass is going to affect all of us, and I must go at once."

He turned to Zhaneel. "Scout Zhaneel, you are officially on reward-leave for the next two days. I will inform your wingleader, and I hope you can enjoy your well-earned rest."

Loren turned and pushed aside the tent flap, following Urtho into the night, though at a more dignified fast walk.

Skan had hoped that the departure of the humans would relax the youngster, but she was clearly still terrified. It was a bit disconcerting. No one had ever been terrified of him before, not among those on Urtho's side, least of all one of his own kind, and an attractive lady at that. He would have expected flirtatiousness, not fear.

He fluffed his feathers and let his eyelids droop a little, hoping his posture of relaxation would make her relax in turn. A good theory, but unfortunately, it didn't work.

"Since Urtho has been called away, I must ask the rest of the questions he wanted to ask you," Skan told her, in a very low, coaxing voice. "Believe me, it is not that we wish to make you uncomfortable, but we need to know these things to improve the training of the next batch of fledglings."

She bobbed her head stiffly but gave no indication of relaxing. "It wasss no grrreat deed," she insisted. "I did not clossse and fight prrroperly. No one can learrrn prrroperrr fighting frrrom thisss."

Skan had heard any number of "modest" protestations in his time and had made a few of them himself, but this didn't seem to be the kind of modesty that covered the very opposite. On the contrary, Zhaneel apparently believed what she was saying; that she had done nothing of note.

"Not all gryphons are large and powerful enough to close with makaar," he reminded her gently. "And for even those, it is not always wise to try, particularly when there are more than one of them. Who trained you to strike like a falcon?"

"N–n–no one," she stammered. "I did thisss becaussse I *cannot* fight like a prrroperrr grrryphon, becausssse I am too sssmall and weak to be a prrroperrr grrryphon."

Small, perhaps, but she was certainly not weak, and Skan would far rather have brains on his side than brawn. He'd seen too many muscle-bound specimens close with makaar believing themselves invincible and had to go to their rescue when they found out otherwise. Whoever, whatever her trainer was, Skan was just about ready to put the being on report. This little female had emerged with a load of self-doubt from training that should have given her confidence in her own abilities. She would have been useless except for her own courage, determination, and sense of responsibility. It was also fairly obvious that this self-doubt carried right on down to how she felt about her physical appearance. She held herself as if she was certain there was nothing attractive about her—in fact, as if she thought she was a horrid freak.

Didn't he recall some of the fledglings in training baiting a smaller one a while ago, about a year or two? It could have been—

Yes, he remembered now, as Zhaneel continued to protest that what she had done was less than nothing, unworthy of reward. Three or four, all nest-brothers by the look of them, surrounded the smaller one and had been name-calling and insulting the little one. The object of their taunting could have been Zhaneel; he only remembered that he had broken it up when the trainer did not appear to intervene, and that the youngster was a small, awkward adolescent. Considering the way she was trying to disappear into the tent canvas now, it would not be surprising that—if it had been her—he did not remember her.

But that had been some time ago, and the only reason he remembered it was because the appropriate authority had not stepped in to handle the problem, and the noise had gotten on his nerves. There was a certain amount of competition among the youngsters; gryphons were still not a "finished" race, and Urtho took those who could not succeed in training for the less demanding jobs of messenger and camp-helper. These were, of course, never permitted to breed.

But if that youngster had been Zhaneel, she had proved

herself by completing her training. Now, Zhaneel was a working member of a wing, and entitled to the same care and protection Skan himself got. There should be no reason why she should continue to suffer these feelings of inferiority. There would be a *Trondi'irn* assigned to her wing, whose job was to see to everything but serious injuries, whose duty was to know every gryphon in the wings assigned to him by name and peculiarity. So why hadn't the Trondi'irn noticed Zhaneel's problems?

Well, there was someone who *would* take notice of her mental state, do something about it himself, and then see to it that the Trondi'irn in question would get an earful afterward.

"If you have no plans for your token, you might take it to Amberdrake," he suggested casually. "He's the best there is."

Drake will have her feeling better in no time—and by the time he and Gesten get done massaging, grooming, and adorning her, she'll be so elegant that she'll have half her wing at her feet. That should make her feel better about herself. That was one of the many things a truly talented kestra'chern and his or her assistants did; spending hours, sometimes more, taking an ordinary creature and transforming her (or him) into the most stunning example of her race possible within her physical limitations. Most gryphons went to a kestra'chern before a mating-flight, though few could afford the services of one like Amberdrake.

"That is simply a suggestion, of course," he added. "You may already have something in mind."

"N–no," she said. She seemed a bit stunned, though whether it was the suggestion itself or that Skan had made it, he couldn't tell. "If you think it isss a good thing to do. I have neverrr had a token beforrre. . . ."

"Well, this is likely to be only the first of many tokens for you. You might as well spend this one on something you are going to enjoy," Skan told her. "You won't regret going to Drake, I promise you."

She seemed to take that as a dismissal, although it had not been meant as one, and stammered her thanks, backing out of the tent before Skan could ask her to stay. He thought about calling her back, but it was already dark, and she probably had things she wanted to do.

He wondered about Urtho's interest in her; it had been something more than the usual interest in a successful fighter. It was as if something about either the gryphon herself or the way she had fought had brought back a memory that Urtho had forgotten for more pressing concerns.

But now that the visitors had left, and darkness had crept over the camp, not even the lamps could keep Skan awake. His pain was bearable; he could lie down in relative comfort, and he had a full crop. Urtho had that mysterious weapon, and in any case, there was nothing for Skan to do until he healed. Sleep seemed in order, and there were no mysteries so pressing that they could not wait until tomorrow.

He shifted himself around on his cushions until he found the best possible position. He put his head down on his forelegs and yawned once—and that was the last thing he remembered doing or thinking until the Healers woke him at dawn.

Zhaneel's Feather

Four

Gesten had rearranged Amberdrake's schedule to include Skan as a regular "patient" for the next several days. Amberdrake discovered the change when he checked the roster the next morning. He didn't bother to comment on it; he knew that Gesten's reply would be sardonic. Dear Gesten, whom he'd hired on so long ago, liked to think he fostered a heartless image, constantly spitting barbed comments and double-entendres. Even though the little hertasi failed utterly at posing as a bossy ogre, Amberdrake was not going to tell him so, directly or by implication. So often the gruffness people showed the world was a defense, meant to protect the ones they loved. That was how it was with Gesten. It was also how it was with Skandranon, and when Amberdrake wasn't indulging himself in self-pity, he was well aware of that.

And Skan was first on the day's roster, with a generous amount of time allotted to him. Amberdrake could visit him, add his own touch to the Healing meld, and spend some time simply enjoying Skan's company before returning to work at the tent.

This was interesting; his schedule was bracketed by gryphons today. The first patient was Skan, and the last a gryphon named "Zhaneel." A female, according to the log, with a gold-square token. He'd have to make certain Gesten had the bleaches and dyes ready; she might want a feather-tip job in addition to whatever other pampering and primping she desired. Amberdrake's other talents often obscured this one, and few knew he had ended his apprenticeship at the ancient trade of kestra'chern as a feather-painter, and still enjoyed doing it. Skan, of course, wouldn't let him practice on *his* feathers, no matter how Amberdrake tried to assure him that it would be a subtle pattern, sophisticated and elegant. No, the Black Gryphon was the *Black* Gryphon, and black he would remain. Skan had made it clear time and time again that the only dye to touch *his* feathers was the stark black he himself had chosen.

But female gryphons, to whom nature and Urtho had given fairly drab coloration, tended to be very fond of painted feathers. In peacetime they had sometimes sported patterned feathers as gaudy as a Kaled'a'in weaving or a messenger-bird's bright plumes—now they had to confine themselves to something that made them less of a target. *If she's got goshawk coloring, perhaps I can persuade her into something in blue and gray,* he mused. *That way she'd have the advantage of sky-camouflage when she was flying, but up close she would be dappled in fishbone patterns and ribbons.*

That would be a pleasant way to end the day.

He washed and shaved, tied his hair back, then donned a plain linen tunic and breeches to stroll over to the mess tent for breakfast. He could eat in his quarters, and often did when he was pressed for time or tired, but he preferred to share at least one meal with the other kestra'chern. Experience and observation had taught him that if the top-ranked kestra'chern acted no differently than the rest, there would be less acrimony and jealousy, both of which could lead to unpleasantness and outright sabotage. He was careful to dress plainly when off duty, shared his knowledge and experience freely, and when forced to cancel appointments, did his best to see that the canceled clients had been distributed fairly among the others. Thanks to this, the rest of the kestra'chern tended to regard him as their unofficial leader and spokesperson. He had mixed feelings about *that,* but it was probably better that he was in that position, rather than someone else. He was the only Kaled'a'in among them; the other Kaled'a'in kestra'chern chose to work among the Healers and save their other skills for their own people. No other working kestra'chern in the camp had as much training as Amberdrake, and when the Kaled'a'in had moved to Urtho's

Tower and the question of what his job should be had come up, he had felt no hesitation. He made, at best, an ordinary Healer, and to operate under the constraints of a Healer would have made him feel as if he worked with half his fingers gone. It was best to do what he was truly good at.

Breakfast was unusually quiet; Amberdrake's companions were tired and subdued. Like the rest of the army; after all, the kestra'chern were by no means immune to what had happened at Stelvi Pass. Even if none of them had friends or acquaintances there, the fighters themselves would, inevitably, bring their troubles to the anonymous comfort of those whose business was pleasure and support.

No one seemed in any mood for conversation on a personal level; no one looked at Amberdrake with the desperate eyes of someone who had taken on more pain than he or she could handle, nor asked Amberdrake for advice in affairs of their own hearts. At first, he simply ate his breakfast, keeping the conversation light, intending to leave with a quiet greeting for everyone.

One of the junior kestra'chern inquired about Corani, and was met with a brief, sharp glance from Amberdrake. This served as an impetus for several other kestra'chern at the table to start talking about the news from Stelvi Pass, Laisfaar, and the Tower, each adding their own slices of information. They had likely as not gleaned it from their clients as much as from camp gossip. As long as no one revealed the identities of the clients, many of them thought, putting the pieces of the puzzle together in the confidence of other kestra'chern was something of a challenge to all concerned. It was done all the time, and Amberdrake knew it, and although it was a source of some of the kestra'cherns' hidden power, he didn't entirely approve of this free sharing of basically private knowledge. Still, the war made its own rules, and they fought the war itself, and not the army of the enemy. Perhaps this *technical* transgression of kestra'chern protocol could yield valuable insights. So he told himself.

Regardless of Amberdrake's private mullings about the talk, it went on unabated, and he found himself offering up the occasional "It may well be" and "From what I know, unlikely" comments, which helped lay in more pieces of the puzzle. When he felt it was time to go, he directed the discussion back toward client care and techniques, then slipped out unobtrusively.

When he reached the Black Gryphon's tent, Skan was awake, and evidently in a much better mood this morning, as he looked Amberdrake up and down in mock amazement. "Tchah, the kestra'chern has lost his commission? All your fine plumage is gone, strutting-bird!"

"Heh, dressing to match the job."

"It seems likely you turned in here mistakenly on the way to the horse-stalls, then," Skandranon replied smoothly. Yes, he was definitely feeling better. Yesterday he would have growled.

"Has anyone looked at your wings?" Amberdrake asked.

"Not since you did," Skan told him. His pronunciation was much improved from yesterday, too. He hissed his sibilants only a little, hardly enough to notice. "All who have come have said it was best left to the expert."

"They're probably right, but lacking an expert, I'll have to do," Amberdrake said absently, running his hand just above the surface of the splinted and bandaged right wing. He extended his awareness down into the wing itself, into the muscle, tendon, and bone. "You're doing all right, though. Bear with me for a minute, here, I need to probe some more."

He shifted from simple awareness into true Healing with a deft twist of his mind. Carefully, for if he sped the Healing of the bones too much, they would not Heal properly but would remain weak, as the bones of a very old person might be after setting. He sent energy to the torn muscle, to the tiny arteries and veins that had been savaged, and then, delicately, to the bones.

Finally he pulled his awareness away and came back to himself, shaking his head a little to clear it of the shared pain. "I'd leave the bandages on for now," he continued. "It's going to take another couple of days of work to mend those wings, and a couple of weeks to strengthen them enough that you can use them. Having them bandaged like that keeps them from being strained. I hope you have feathers saved from your last molts; we're going to have to imp a lot of broken secondaries and primaries. That's one thing we can't do for you—grow new feathers."

"You're the Healer," Skan replied philosophically. Then he looked sheepishly at Amberdrake out of the corner of his eye. "I have to apologize to you, Drake. Again, I mean. The apology I gave you yesterday wasn't exactly sincere." He took a deep breath and let it out slowly. "I treated you badly yesterday. It wasn't fair, and it wasn't right. My only defense is that I was in pain, and I'm not at my best when I hurt."

Amberdrake snorted. "Not at your best? Skan, you could give a makaar lessons in surliness!" But he smiled and scratched Skan's ear-tufts, while the gryphon feigned indignation. "That's all right; I'm not a good patient either, you know. It's just a good thing I'm not hurt or sick very often, or I'd probably lose Gesten."

"Not Gesten, he enjoys suffering. He enjoys letting you know he's suffering even more," Skan replied wickedly—and accurately. "What's happening out there? Nobody tells me anything; they're afraid I might not want to heal up."

"Ma'ar's forces threw back our counterattack," Amberdrake told him, knowing that if he didn't, Skan would find some other way of getting the information. "We've lost the Pass, for now at least, unless Urtho can come up with some way of dislodging them."

Skan shook his massive head and sighed. "I can't see how, Drake. Stelvi was built well, as impregnable as possible, with water supplies in every part of the fortress. That was part of the reason why no one took an attack there seriously." He stared at the canvas wall of his tent, as if by sheer force of will he could see beyond it to the Pass. "So it's to be another retreat, then. Eventually abandoning the Tower, if this goes on."

Amberdrake nodded. "I'm afraid so."

"Damn them." Skan glared at the tent wall until Amberdrake was afraid he might burn a hole in it. Then he shook his head, and when he turned back to Amberdrake, his eyes were clear, although wrinkles betrayed a deep and abiding anger burning at the bottom of them. "Has Ma'ar given us any new and unpleasant surprises?"

It was Amberdrake's turn to shake his head, but this time

it was with relief. "Like that mage-shot he pelted us with last month? Not that I've heard, and I heard most of the rumors three times over between my tent and yours."

"Good." Skan had been tense; now he relaxed a bit. Amberdrake would have given a month's pay to know what had prompted that question—and knew very well that Skan would never tell him. He could surmise that there had been some kind of new weapon in use by Ma'ar's army—and that Skan had neutralized it somehow. He could surmise it, but Skan would never reveal the truth of the matter.

"So, wicked one, what have you been up to while I have been wallowing at my ease in a nest of pillows?" Skan asked, quickly changing the subject before Amberdrake had a chance to ask him anyway. "Any new and interesting clients?"

"One new one yesterday, who I *hope* is never going to come back," Amberdrake told him. "A more unpleasant man I have never met, and a mercenary mage on top of that."

He told Skan all there was to tell about Conn Levas, without revealing the man's name or divulging anything that might identify him—not even the fact that the man's lover might be Kaled'a'in. He didn't often break client confidentiality, and even then it would only be to a superior, like Artis Camlodon, the Chief Healer, or to Urtho himself, should he ever find himself in that exalted being's presence. Few people overawed Amberdrake; he had seen too many of the great and powerful unclothed both physically and spiritually, but Urtho always left him feeling as if his mouth were hanging wide open. The blazing intellect, the aura of controlled and absolute power, and the overwhelming competence of the man added up to the kind of charisma that left Amberdrake weak in the knees. What he looked like didn't matter; Amberdrake invariably saw the Mage of Silence with a kestra'- chern's eyes—the eyes of one who saw past the surface, always.

Still, Amberdrake found himself telling Skan more than he would have told anyone else, and Skan listened with every indication of interest. It was marvelous, simply having a friend to talk to this way, and they both exulted in it behind their calm and rehearsed exteriors.

"I feel sorry for that one's lover," Skan said finally. "Very sorry, actually. She seems more important as a possession than as a person to him."

"That was the conclusion I came to," Amberdrake admitted. "What was worse, though, was that I was supposed to be dealing with my client's problems, and I found myself wishing there was a way I could have a good long talk with his lover instead. That wasn't very professional of me, I suppose, but then again, he wouldn't *let* me help him."

"The more fool he," Skan said scornfully, "to pay good money and then refuse to take what it purchased."

Trust Skan to put the situation into the simplest possible terms! Amberdrake had to smile. "Thank you, Skandranon Rashkae, you'll make me a *perchi* yet. Should I simply become a baker, and save myself some worry?"

"You would find another way to take on the army's burdens as a baker. Each little slice of bread would have a soldier's very life and spirits slathered upon it," Skan snorted.

Amberdrake laughed in response. It was, after all, a good return volley. "I suppose that in the grand context of an entire army, one mage's emotional problems aren't too high on the list of things I need to worry about."

Skan chuckled. "That is a reasonable statement. More reasonable than the fretting. You've spent more time with me than you should have. Your other clients will be unhappy if they find out."

"Then they won't find out." Amberdrake got up to leave. "This is going to be a very interesting day; I'm going to begin and end with a gryphon. It's the first time something like that has ever happened."

"I thought I was your only gryphon client," Skan mock-chided. "I may become jealous!"

"Don't bother, old bird," Amberdrake told him. "This is just a once-only, a reward. I'm not sure why this gryphon chose me when she could have had the same treatment from an apprentice at a fraction of the fee, but it will be a nice change from emotionally-damaged fighters and deservedly-traumatized mages."

Skan snorted approval at the small insult to Conn Levas. He had long maintained that Amberdrake was too gracious. "I may still be jealous."

Amberdrake smoothed his unwrinkled tunic as a mocking gesture. "She's a young female, I believe, and if you're *very* good, I might introduce you to her after Gesten and I finish prettying her. Not that you'll be in any shape to seduce her, but you might be able to persuade her you'll be worth keeping in mind when you heal!"

Skan's face wore a very peculiar expression, as if he tried to hold back something. He seethed with amusement. Amberdrake couldn't for a moment imagine why, though; the female gryphon hadn't been listed as being from any wing Skan had ever flown with, and was several years his junior besides. Whatever his secret was, however, he managed to keep it behind his beak. Amberdrake waited for him to betray himself, but he said only, "I should like very much to meet this young lady once you've been with her."

"I'll see what I can do," Amberdrake said. And since Skan didn't seem disposed to reveal anything, he finally waved good-bye and went back to his scheduled work.

Very much like to see her, indeed . . . vain bird, he's probably planning his post-mating dinner with her already.

Amberdrake was wiping thick oil from his hands with a rag when Gesten reminded him of his last client for the day. It had been a day marked by trauma and pain, from the emotional trauma of a young Healer who had seen one too many die, to the pain of a horseback skirmisher who'd had three beasts shot out from under her at the attempt to retake Stelvi Pass. She had had so many wrenched and displaced vertebrae from falls that Amberdrake almost sent her to the Healers instead, regardless of what she said she wanted. But she swore to him that she would rather have "the best kestra'chern in the world" put her spine back in place than any Healer and seemed thrilled to be with him, as if she spoke to a great dancer or singer. She'd sworn that she could bear the pain he would have to put her through to do so.

The reason? An admirable one; she'd felt that the Healers were overburdened, and that they would feel obliged to pain-block her, which would add to their burden. Yes, she'd known that the Healers would treat her for nothing, and that his services cost a high-ranking reward-chit. No, she hadn't cared. "I've got a pile of these things already, so I'm saving them up for a better commission once the war's dead," she'd said gruffly. "Urtho's aides brought me a new horse—Kaled'a'in-bred at that. I've got a new tent. I don't crave pretties. I look like a horse myself, so fancy clothing on me would look like barding on a mule. So what else am I going to spend a chit on? Besides, this way I get an attractive man to put his hands all over me. That, I can use."

So he manipulated her vertebrae as she stifled her gasps of pain, until her gasps turned to ones of sheer relief. He was so impressed by her courage and sense that he'd had Gesten prepare a hot soaking tub for her, with aromatic oils in it. He had her soak until her muscles completely relaxed, then he gave her the massage she had paid for, rubbing her down gently until she was just dozing. Then he did for her what he would not do for Conn Levas. They were good hours.

She left his tent smiling and exhausted. He sat back while Gesten cleaned up and prepared for the last client of the day, smiling just as widely as she had. Once in a while, he got a client who was worthy of his skills in every way—that skirmisher was just such a one, and it had been a privilege to help her. Odd; both she and Conn Levas were mercenaries, and yet they were so unlike each other. Ah, well, experience had shown that the only thing similar about most soldiers was the uniform they wore.

"That was a fine lady," Gesten observed as he expertly put away the oils and stowed the massage table. "I think I ought to go over and suggest she spend one of those 'useless' chits of hers on a makeover with us. I don't see any reason why she has to keep on looking like a wild mare. She's lean enough to be elegant, and if she'd just let me do something with her hair . . ."

"That's a good idea, if you want to," Amberdrake agreed. "I'd take the exotic approach with her. You know, she could carry off some of the Kaled'a'in costumes quite impressively. Maybe with a cat-stripe paint pattern across her shoulders—"

"That's what I like about you, Drake," Gesten interrupted cheerfully. "You always see the potential. Think you can exercise that one more time today? That gryphon Zhaneel will be here shortly."

"Gryphon?" Amberdrake replied, momentarily confused. Then he hit his head with the heel of his hand. "Right! I nearly forgot! My mind is still muddled from this day. I'm just tired. Did you—"

"I've got the oils and the satin cords and the beads and feather-paint," Gesten said, snorting a little. "As if I'd forget! Listen, I'd like to go over and put Skan to bed if you don't mind. Do you think you can handle this youngster alone?"

It was Amberdrake's turn to snort. "As if I hadn't been taking care of gryphons all by myself long before *you* came looking for some *fool* to hire you! Of course, I can."

"All right, then, fool-who-hired-me," Gesten replied, giving him back as good an insult as he'd gotten. "I'll go make sure that featherhead up on the hill gets his sleep, then I'll see to it you don't drown yourself in the tub when I get back."

Gesten indicated a bright but battered wheeled storage chest with a nod of his snout. "Everything you need is in there, and I replaced whatever had dried out or was too old to use. If I do say so myself, I don't think there's a kestra'-chern in the army with a better stock of 'gryphon pretties.' By the time you get done, she should be stunning. Provided you can do *your* job."

He whisked through the curtain before Amberdrake could make a rejoinder. Amberdrake just laughed and took his time getting out of his chair. He changed into a utilitarian pair of loose linen breeches and baggy shirt, tying a sash about the latter. He would not need any fancy robes with this client; instead, he needed clothing he could work in, clothing that could be splashed with dye and not take harm. Over that he wore his receiving robe, with its intricate designs.

Amberdrake stepped outside the tent to take in some of the camp's relatively fresh air before the client arrived. "Small" feathers—the size of a hand—drifted by in the breeze, discards from some gryphon's vigorous preening, no doubt. Activity in the camp had stepped up a bit from earlier that day; it seemed that the rumors had fed a packing frenzy. The children that he'd seen before were engaged in tying blankets and packs, with the help of two kyree tugging with their teeth. He saw adults mending wagon covers and double-checking the wheels of carts. Farther beyond that, a set of soldiers and an Apprentice mage—who looked to be Vikteren, one of Amberdrake's social acquaintances—leveled and tested a hovering-sled. The large sleds floated half a man-height above the ground—although they could be raised higher—and were mainly used for troops' supplies. A few of the kestra'chern, Amberdrake included, had bought one for use in moving their own gear, rather than relying on the army to do so for them.

Next to them, the horse-skirmisher he'd cared for earlier—who was moving much more freely than before he'd begun—was keeping a number of her fellow warriors enthralled with some great tale. Or if not great, certainly one that called for a substantial amount of gesturing.

Maybe she's talking about me. . . ? That would be good if she was. Let them know I treat the lower ranks as well as I do their commanders.

Hidden back behind the cluster of humans, though, was a mere wisp of a gryphon—a fledgling, judging by her size, or a subadult. She—yes, definitely a female—was eavesdropping on whatever it was the horse-skirmisher was saying. How strange. Normally, gryphons simply walked into conversations they wanted to be a part of, invited or not.

Then Amberdrake's attention was taken by a flight of messenger-birds winging past, darts of living paint flittering across the sky. Their bounding flight carried them and their messages toward the Tower; with luck, they carried news that the war's hunger was sated for a while.

Amberdrake turned back inside, and set about finger weaving feather-shaft-adornments for his next client. It would be so relaxing, for a change.

Zhaneel, when she arrived, turned out to be the little gryphon he'd seen lurking behind the warriors earlier. She was a very pretty thing, in a quiet way; lean and fit, with long wings and feathers set very close to her body. He'd walked out from the back room of the tent with a handful of finger-woven satin cords, and found her in the receiving area, hesitantly nosing around the cushions and boxes.

She's never been to a kestra'chern before, I can tell that right now. Nervous, expectant, unsure of herself.

He cleared his throat gently, and she started. "Welcome, Zhaneel," he said in a soft but commanding voice. "My name is Amberdrake. I am honored to serve you." He executed the sweeping, graceful bow that customarily accompanied the greeting and ended it down on one knee, so that he would not be looming over her. His receiving robe gathered around him in glossy folds as he knelt, a shimmering contrast to the work clothes underneath it.

Her eyes darted across his entire body as he bent forward to touch one of her forelegs, as was also customary. It was in this first touch that an experienced kestra'chern could tell the way the session was going to go. Involuntary reactions mixed with postures and poses, hopeful or desperate projections, all would be caught by a sensitive kestra'chern in good form. One did not have to be an Empath to read body language; that was a skill taught to every kestra'chern during his or her apprenticeship.

In this case, the signals were decidedly odd. Zhaneel slicked her feathers down and turned her head until her delicate beak touched the wrist joint of her folded wing. A soft, sibilant voice came from that beak, in as near to a whisper as gryphons could manage.

"The Black Grrryphon sssent me to you. You are my k—kessssstrrra'cherrrn." Then her head dipped and her wings fluttered near her body, spread ever so slightly.

"Yes. I am the kestra'chern that will serve you, Zhaneel, as you requested, and as your reward for bravery. I will adorn, comfort, and help you and give you the attentions you may deserve and the insight you may need." Amberdrake raised his other hand and touched the remaining foreleg, reading her physical reactions clearly while another part of his mind reasoned out what to do about it.

She's practically seething with sexual tension . . . definitely worked herself up into a frenzy somehow over the past candlemark. Well, I know what that usually means. Some feather-work and oils should increase this unique beauty of hers, so her lover will be especially pleased by her after our session. Still . . .

Still, this sleek little creature wasn't coming across like the usual gryphon client to be prepared for a special tryst. There was anticipation, and an electric desire, but there didn't seem to be any *confidence* in the outcome of the night, nor the sense of certainty that gryphons were so well known for. And no gryphon went for an expensive tryst-grooming unless she was *positive* she had a partner waiting for her!

Suddenly, Zhaneel looked directly at him and stepped forward, causing Amberdrake to rebalance himself—and then she kept moving forward. Amberdrake fell backward as Zhaneel straddled him. Her long wings spread to either side of them, with her tail up and neck feathers roused. Her beaked face was nearly touching his nose when she asked, "You will give me pleasssurrre, Amberrrdrrrake?"

Oh, gods . . . that explains what . . .

He stared at her beak, remembered the size of gryphon talons, and felt himself blanch. "Zhaneel, no—wait—you'll hurt me," he begged. "Please let me up!"

Skandranon marked his page with a discarded feather and stretched, looking back to where Gesten meticulously brushed and treated his back just above his tail. Urtho had sent down a book by an explorer who had been in his employ from before the war had started, and the heavy tome was filled with small notes written in the margins, observations and anecdotes by others that the book had been loaned to. Urtho had sent it by messenger-kyree to make up for his hasty departure earlier; yet another small gesture that told the Black Gryphon of his status in Urtho's eyes. Gesten had been there for at least two candlemarks, quietly putting all of the details right for Skandranon; cutting, sanding, and rounding partially snapped feathers, rubbing in soothing gels around strained feather-shafts. Without saying a dozen words, he'd moved Skandranon—who was twice the weight of most human men—into easier positions for tending tiny cuts the Healers hadn't gotten. He had sanded down the chips in Skan's beak, filling in near-invisible cracks with cement, and coping his overgrowing talons. He then moved on to a deep and thorough combing, removing all the tiny snags and remaining bits of burr and twig from Skan's black coat.

Skan was in good shape—much better than even this morning, he mused—and in little pain, thanks to one of Lady Cinnabar's clever abilities, a trick with shunting pain away. She was a delight to know, even peripherally, and seemed to have the sort of personality he'd like to find in a gryphon mate one day.

Skan counted himself fortunate that he'd lived this long. Ah, but taking a mate? Seriously considering the possibility of fathering young had been reduced to a worn pastime over his years of service, one that at some times felt like his only reason for persevering, and at others like an impossible fantasy from a laugh-singer's tale. The concern was not one of merely finding sex. He had no lack of lovers; there were few gryphons who wouldn't be ecstatic to raise their tails to him, but, still, they were at best casual friends, and none of them fertile. Mmm, but there were those that had been so sweet, so warm. . . .

He shifted the way he was lying; thinking about lovers was causing his belly to tighten with longing. He'd never been embarrassed about his virility before and felt no pangs about such now, but his healing state kept poking reminders at him about how limited his movement really *was*.

Gesten didn't miss a stroke while grooming Skan's flank and tail, although he surely noticed the outward signs of Skan's line of thought. There seemed to be very little the little hertasi missed; but, as with other topics that came up around him daily, Gesten's best comment was not to comment at all.

Tchah, by now little Zhaneel is settled in warm and comfortable with Amberdrake. Amberdrake knows how to make everything right. He's such a good kestra'chern; so clever, so graceful, so intelligent. I'm proud to know him; I'm glad I sent her to him.

I'm going to kill Skandranon for this, Amberdrake fumed as he faced away from Zhaneel. Surely that mindless, oversexed, bug-bitten, arrogant mass of black feathers had given Zhaneel the impression that Amberdrake was going to make love to her somehow. This was an unforgivably cruel joke on Skan's part! After this situation was handled, Amberdrake resolved to go over and give Skan a verbal flaying—asleep, injured, or in whatever condition he happened to be.

Zhaneel had disentangled herself from him only a moment before and was now watching his every move for some cue to resume, her head bobbing up and down and hind-claws clenching.

Amberdrake wiped a palm across his face and turned back to speak to her pointedly. "Zhaneel, I can't be the kind of lover you want. You and I aren't physically compatible. I just can't—"

A moment passed.

An unmistakable, inexplicable look of horror transformed Zhaneel's entire demeanor from one of desperate desire to one of emotional devastation. She let out a gurgling cry and suddenly bolted through the opened tent flap and into the darker and more private inner room.

Skandranon finished the annotated chapter on social organization among the southeastern tribes, and luxuriated in the attention Gesten was giving his recently-battered crest.

By now she must feel like the most beautiful and capable gryphon in the entire world! Amberdrake always knows how to say exactly the right thing to make someone feel good. He's given me so many compliments, and he's hardly ever wrong. Maybe once I'm recovered, he can give me a tryst-grooming, and we can talk about how much good my suggestion did Zhaneel.

The Black Gryphon sighed and settled down for a nap, smug in the knowledge that all was right with the world as far as Zhaneel and Amberdrake were concerned.

Amberdrake found Zhaneel curled into a ball in the farthest corner of the tent, shivering, her head tucked under her wings. It was a saddening, unnerving thing for Drake to see; this was the gryphon equivalent of racking sobs, as bad as any he'd seen in mourning or after nightmares. Surging, palpable waves of shame pounded at him; feelings of self-blame hissed in his mental "ears" the closer he got to her. He braced himself to receive a backlash and reached out to touch her quivering body.

Instead of the expected strike, she didn't acknowledge his presence at all. Nothing. Yet, with the touch, a staggering rush of sickening emotions blinded Amberdrake for the span of a heartbeat.

She hates *herself. She genuinely hates herself. Self-doubt, self-pity, an overwhelming sense of worthlessness, of loss. From a gryphon! This I could expect from a human, but from a gryphon? They're all convinced that Urtho created them as an improvement on all other races! Who or whatever made her this way was long in building. If it* can *be stopped, it has to stop now. If I can change her—it has to start* now.

He spoke quietly, soothingly. "Zhaneel?"

She whimpered, the barest whisper of sound.

"Shh, little one, I am here for you. Please listen. Please listen. I'll make you feel better, I promise it. I am here for you." He moved in closer and folded his robed body across hers, to comfort her as he had other distressed gryphons with the sensation of protective, caring wings wrapped over them. He could feel her underneath him, body temperature high, breathing fast, and there, yes, her eyes tightly shut. Her delicate ear-tufts folded back tight to her head. Drake stroked her neck feathers and spoke more reassuring words, keeping his voice steady and deep, speaking "into" her, and held her as her shuddering subsided.

The sexual anticipation earlier can help some, at least. . . . Amberdrake swam through Zhaneel's nerves with his Healing powers, found her pleasure-centers, and gently stimulated them while he soothed her with his words. Gryphons' bodies held stores of specialized fluids, elements, in various glands and repositories, and the delicate touch of an experienced Healer could release them at the right time. A careful nudge *there* and a feather-light stimulation *so,* and the "rewarding" sensation following a mating coursed through her veins; in a small amount, by no means as great as the euphoria following a real mating, but definitely there. It had the desired effect; she slowly went from quivering to a state of relaxation—physically, at least—and uncurled from her ball after what felt like a harrowing eternity. All the while, Amberdrake reassured her and spoke encouragements. It didn't cure any of her problems, no, that could come later, but her gradual relaxation at least opened a doorway toward a cure.

A candlemark must have passed since her arrival before she spoke again. It was a time in which her kestra'chern held her and scratched her ear-tufts, all the while carefully touching her mind and soaking in the feelings she unknowingly projected into him. He could not help thinking that it was a good thing she had chosen him, rather than a kestra'-chern with no Empathic or Healing abilities. Anyone else would have had to send for her Trondi'irn—and an apprentice would have been as terrified and traumatized as she.

"Zhaneel," he said urgently, "you must tell me *why* I distressed you so. I had no intention of hurting you."

She shivered all over. "You . . . kessstra'cherrrn. Think I am mmmisssborrrn, too. No desssirrre, neverrr. . . ." She hunched her shoulders and hung her head, deep in purest misery. "Should have died," she cried softly. "Not worth raisssing, ssshould have died. Trried."

Amberdrake didn't hesitate a moment; strange how, after waiting in silence for so long, a moment's delay in a reply could cause damage. "No, lovely child, you misunderstood me entirely! You're far from misborn, Zhaneel. You were made by Urtho as his proudest creation. And you are lovely to me."

She uncoiled some more, and nervously looked at him with one eye. "But you sssaid—no lover. Physssically. Not even you want me—"

He rubbed his cheek against hers, as a gryphon-sib would do, and replied quickly. "Zhaneel, no, little one! I said I *can* not, not that I *would* not if I could. I am only a human. Thin skin, and smaller than you. We wouldn't fit, you and I, our sizes and bodies are too different. And you'd tear me up trying." He allowed a small chuckle. "Dearheart, believe me, if I were a gryphon, you and I would be in the sky together the moment after I saw you."

She opened both eyes and blinked, twice, as if the dry observation that humans were perhaps a third the size of a gryphon—in every salient way—hadn't even occurred to her.

Some people think a kestra'chern can do anything!

"Never learned how mating goes. Parents died. Left me, left me alone." Zhaneel slumped down, her beak touching the floor. "Misborn, wings too long and pointy, too long for body, head too big, too round, no ear-tufts at *all!*" she cried out, shivering. "That's why they left me, why they flew and died. I was misborn, and they were ashamed."

Amberdrake scratched her head, fingers disappearing into the deep, soft down-feathers, and projected more calm into her, soothing her, lest she ball herself up again and never uncurl. "I just can't believe that, Zhaneel. You are lovely and strong. Your parents must surely have treasured you and looked forward to seeing you fly."

Apparently, a floodgate had been released when she had first started speaking. She continued to pour out her feelings. "Not enough talon to hurt even mites—"

Amberdrake surveyed the outstretched forefoot dubiously. The talons looked plenty long to him.

"—freakish, misborn, should have *died*," she whispered hoarsely. "No one wants Zhaneel in wing. No one. No one wants Zhaneel as mate. Worthless."

Amberdrake lifted her head up, a more difficult task than he tried to make it appear, and caressed her briefly around the nares, then held up the forgotten reward-square.

"If you're so worthless, then how did you earn this? They don't give these away for digging latrines, sky-lady. Only the bravest receive this kind of reward."

His left arm was complaining bitterly about supporting the weight of her head when she finally lifted it herself and blinked. Then she looked down.

"Not brave," she insisted faintly.

Amberdrake smiled gently. "Why don't you tell me how you earned it, and let me be the judge of that? I would sincerely like to hear, Zhaneel. Join me. I'll make you a fine strong tea." He stood up creakily and gestured for her to come with him; she rose, took three hesitant steps toward his bed, and then sat beside it.

"No one would accept me into their wing. But I wanted to fly for Urtho. So I—I just moved into a wing. Kelreesha Trondaar's wing."

Ah. Interesting, the same wing that merc mage Conn Levas is attached to. Amberdrake prodded the coals in the ever-burning brazier, then set a copper kettle of water on it. "And then. . . ?"

"I flew patrols. The back patrols—the ones fledglings fly in relays." Her voice broke at that. The duty she described was humiliating for an adult gryphon, usually reserved for punishment because of its length and uneventfulness, and for training fledglings in procedure. "It gave me—time away from the camp. Time to fly. Can fly the circuit faster than anyone else."

Amberdrake dropped herb-packed cloth pouches into the kettle, and spoke gently. "Faster than any other gryphon; that is wonderful in itself. How much faster, Zhaneel?"

"A third faster. I fly the circuit alone." Amberdrake raised an eyebrow in surprise and appreciation. "I was at fifth-cloud height," she continued. *Half again higher than other gryphons fly on patrol—even more interesting.* "And I found makaar. There were three, leaving our territory. They had to be stopped somehow, they must have been spying. But I can't Mindspeak well—I couldn't call for help. So I dove on them and fought them. It didn't matter if I died stopping them."

Amberdrake's thoughts ran quickly, despite the practiced, impassive expression on his face. *She means that. She means that if she died trying, that was better than living. It's plain why she said she wasn't brave. She was suicidal. And she wanted her death to* mean *something.* He took a deep breath and smoothed back his hair.

"Zhaneel, I've known many warriors, many shaman and priests and High Mages. So many of them have felt inadequate, and I've spoken to them as I am doing to you, dear sky-lady. When warriors feel afraid they lack something, it is only because they are forgetful. They have forgotten how capable they truly are." He settled down on the bed beside her and caressed her brow as she listened. "If you were anyone besides Zhaneel—lovely, powerful, sleek Zhaneel—you would have gone for help, or flown away frightened, or attacked the makaar and failed. You succeeded wholly because of who and what you are, and by the power of your mind as well as your body. That is no small thing, given that *some* gryphons I know have no more brains than an ox."

Again, he held up the token and gently touched it to her beak. "And now you have this, given by Urtho's own hand. Do you know how rare that is?" She shook her head, humanlike, indicating she didn't. "It's very rare, Zhaneel, very unusual. It shows that you are exceptionally *good*, dear one, and not a freak. Not misborn. And *far* from worthless."

"Doesn't matter," she croaked. "Everyone thinks I am."

"Everyone didn't stop three makaar, and everyone didn't get this token." He shook his head, certain that he had her attention now. "Sometimes 'everyone' can be wrong, too. Didn't 'everyone' say that Stelvi Pass was impregnable?"

Her ear-tufts rose just a little, and she bobbed her beak once in cautious agreement.

He considered her; her build, her very look. "You are different, Zhaneel, just as I am different from my own people. And when I came here, I felt a little like you do—no, a lot like you do. I was scorned simply because of who I was, and what I do. The Healers wouldn't accept me because I was kestra'chern. The kestra'chern were wary of me because I could Heal. Yet as I saw them dance away from me, I studied the moves of their dance." Amberdrake smiled again as Zhaneel relaxed some more and gazed at him, an enraptured raptor listening to a storyteller. "They would look at me and I was a mirror. They could see parts of themselves in me, layers and shards of their own lives they'd tucked away in their sleeves. When I spoke, the Healers knew I had that kestra'chern insight and they felt threatened. And the other kestra'chern distrusted my station and Healing abilities. Yet through it all, there I was. Still myself, Zhaneel, just as you are still you. Those who push you down fear you. They are jealous of you. And you are stronger than you know."

Zhaneel fidgeted, uneasy under his care-filled eyes. "Not strong, sir."

He shook his head, and chuckled again. "Nah, sky-lady. Please don't call me 'sir,' I am only Amberdrake—a friend. Ah." He moved gracefully to the tea kettle and poured two cups, one large, one small, as he spoke. "If you were not strong, I would never have met you, Zhaneel. You would have been dead and forgotten, not honored by the Mage of Silence himself. And *not* noticed by the Black Gryphon."

Zhaneel turned her head aside, and her nares flushed in embarrassment. *Ah, so she's as impressed with Skandranon as he is by himself. I'm still going to skin him later, but I'll certainly use his image to Zhaneel's advantage.*

"Let me tell you of Skandranon, Zhaneel," he began. "*They* make fun of Skandranon, too. He is called a glory-hound, reckless, arrogant, petulant, and some say he has the manners of a hungry fledgling. Still, he is there, doing what he is best at. *They* are jealous of him, too—mainly because he actually *does* what *they* only talk about doing. Actions define strength. And you, sky-lady, fly faster and farther than *they* do, and can strike down three makaar alone."

She blushed again, and once more he wondered what went wrong in her childhood. Where were her teachers, her parents? The simple things he told her should have been the most basic concepts that a young gryphlet was raised on. *Normally*, though, was the key word. Amberdrake had seen a thousand souls laid bare, and knew well that what most called "normal" was anything but reality. He also felt the warmth in his chest and belly, and the simmering heat in his mind, that told him that the hunt was good this time—that this young Zhaneel was going to survive.

"Always, I hear how *they* have said this or that, and yet, I have never come face-to-face with one of *them*. Who are *they* anyway?" he asked—rhetorically, since he did not truly expect her to answer. "What gives them a monopoly on truth? Why are they any more expert than you or I?"

Another few steps, and he presented her with the larger cup. He marveled at the deftness with which she grasped the cup, with a single foreclaw—no—with a single *hand*. And she followed his gaze.

"No claws to speak of. Have to wear war-claws like silly kyree," she murmured, and looked down again.

"Tchah, no. That's no defect, sky-lady. See my arms and legs, my muscles? They match my body well, as the parts

of your body match well. Now see my hands, and their proportion to my arms." Her sight fixed on his hands.

And her eyes widened as she realized what she was seeing.
"Your hands—are like mine."

"Yes! Very similar. All the Powers made me this way."
He nodded his approval. "And Urtho created you, with exactly *this* shape to your foreclaws, your body, your wings.
Do you believe that Urtho would be so incompetent as to
create an ugly, mismatched creature?"

That went against the most basic of gryphonic tenets; even
Zhaneel would not believe that. "No!"

He smiled; now he had her. "Of course, we all know that
Urtho would not. He has always been thorough and detailed,
with a vision unmatched by any Adept in history. No, I
believe, Zhaneel, that you are something new. Sleek and
small, fast—like a falcon. The others, they all have the
shapes of broad-winged birds, of hawks and eagles—but you
are something very different. Not a gryphon at all, but something new—gryphon and falcon. *Gryfalcon.*"

Her eyes sparkled with wonder, and she caught her breath,
still holding the cup of steaming tea. She spoke the word
that Amberdrake had just made up, testing it on her tongue
as she would try a sweet apple or cold winter wine.
"Gryfalcon."

This was going so much better than a candlemark ago.
Amberdrake took a sip of his cup of tea and luxuriated in
the play of flavors—rich and bitter, sweet and acidic, each
in turn. Complex blends that suited the mood of a complex
problem.

Outside the tent, dusk had darkened to night as they
talked further, and Zhaneel had told him, in words that faltered, of her parents' fate. They had both been killed on what
should have been a low-risk mission; once again, the war
had hungered, and had fed as all things must feed. Zhaneel
had been left alone, a fledgling cared for thereafter by a suc-
cession of foster parents and Trondi'irn who felt no particular
affection for her. One by one, they changed or disappeared, and
the memories of her parents became a soft-edged memory of

nurturing acceptance, a memory so distant it came to seem like a dream or a tale, having nothing to do with her reality.

It was the *contrast* between the fledgling's memories of loving care and the subadult's reality of indifference that had suffocated her in the cold box of self-hate.

Conversely, however, the same thing had kept her from killing herself.

The knowledge, only half-aware, that when she was still in the downy coat of a fledgling she was *loved* had given her soul the broad feathers it needed. There were no specific images now, and no remembered words; there was only the sensation that, yes, with certainty, they had trilled their affection as she drowsed and taught her when she awoke. Brief as that time had been, it had given her an underlying strength, and a reason to endure.

By the time their cups were empty, most of the night had passed by, and they had wandered into mutual observations. Zhaneel asked about the life of a kestra'chern. He'd wondered aloud, once he knew the subject would not alarm her, where she had gotten her idea that Amberdrake would be her lover.

Her nares flushed. "The horse-rider was telling the others about you, and I listened. I didn't understand some of it, but I thought it was because she was a human." She ducked her head a little as her nares flushed deeper. "I thought, this must be what you do with all who come to you. I thought, this was why Great Skandranon had told me to come to you when I was given the reward."

He clenched his jaw for a moment. *I might have known Skan was at the bottom of this! No wonder he was acting so—so smug!* But a confrontation with Skan would have to wait. Now, all unknowing, she had given him another opening to bolster her self-esteem.

"Skan sent you here?" He blinked as if he were surprised, but he continued quickly before she could burst into frantic protest that he really *had,* as if he might doubt her truthfulness. "Do you realize just how impressed he must have been with you, Zhaneel? Why, it was only two days ago he was brought in, injured—he is still not Healed, and he has made it very clear to me, his friend, that he does not wish to be troubled with inconsequential things. And yet he thought enough of your proper reward to send you to me! How much time did he spend with you?"

"I—do not know—half a candlemark, perhaps?" she said, doubtfully.

"Half a candlemark?" Amberdrake chuckled. "I cannot think of any other he has spent so much time with, other than his Healers. Truly, he must have found you fascinating!"

"Oh," she replied faintly, and her nares flushed again. "Perhaps he was bored?" she suggested, just as faintly.

Amberdrake laughed at that. "If he was bored, he would have sent you elsewhere. Skan's cures for boredom are reading, sleeping, and teasing his friends, in that order. No, I think he must have found you very interesting."

By now, from her body-language and her voice, it was fairly obvious to him that Zhaneel had—at the very least—a substantial infatuation with the Black Gryphon.

"He doesn't pay that kind of attention to just anyone," he continued smoothly. "If he noticed you, it is because you are noteworthy."

She perked up for a moment, then her ear-tufts flattened again. "If he noticed me, it wassss sssurely to sssee how freakish I am."

"How different you are—not freakish," he admonished. "Skandranon is not one to be afraid of what is different."

"Am I—" She hesitated, and he sensed that she was about to say something very daring, for her. "Am I—different enough that he might recall me? Notice me again?"

Amberdrake pretended to think. "I take it that you want him to do more than simply take notice of you?"

She ducked her head, very shyly. "Yessss—" she breathed. "Oh, yessss—"

"Well, Zhaneel, Skan is not easily impressed. You would have to be something very special to hold his interest. You would have to do more than simply take out a couple of makaar once." That was a daring thing to say to her, but fortunately she did not take it badly; she only looked at him eagerly, as if hoping he could give her the answers she needed. "I know him very well; if you want Skan, Zhaneel, you will have to impress him enough that he wants you—enough to make him ask you to join his wing." Before she could lose courage, he leaned forward and said, with every bit of skill and Empathy that he possessed, "You can do this, Zhaneel. I know you can. I believe in you."

Her eyes grew bright, and her ear-tufts perked completely up. "I could—I could entrrrap the makaar." She paused as he shook his head slightly. "Perhaps if I made of myself a target, outflew them to ambush?" Again he shook his head. Both her ideas were far too impulsive—and suicidal.

"It will have to be something that only you can do, Zhaneel," he suggested. "You don't have to make a hero of yourself every day. You don't have to have an immediate result, either. But whatever you do must be something only *you* can do—just as the way you killed those three makaar was done in a way only you could have performed. Perhaps something that Urtho or Skan said to you could help you think of something. . . ."

She sat, deep in thought, while Amberdrake got himself a second cup of tea. Finally she spoke.

"Urrtho asked me what training I had, and he was disappointed that no one had given me any special attentions." She looked up at him intently, and he gave her an encouraging nod. "Skandranon also seemed surprised that I had no special training. And if I cannot fly and fight as the others do—perhaps—perhaps I should train myself?" Again she looked to him, and he nodded enthusiastically. "Perhaps I should ask for—for courses, such as they put the young humans across, only for flying."

"That is a *good* plan, sky-lady," he told her firmly. "It is one that will benefit not only you, but others who are also small and light. And as you become skilled, you will definitely attract Skan's attention."

But now she had turned her attention to his hands, and then to her own foreclaws.

"Amberdrrrake, I have hands, like humans—I can do human things, can I not?" She flexed her hands, first one, then the other, as if testing their mobility. "Perhaps I can use a weapon—or—perhaps I can *fly* to help wounded!" Her beak parted in excitement, and Amberdrake had to work to suppress his own excitement. The idea of a gryphon-Healer, even the kind of field-Healer who could only splint bones and bandage wounds—*that* was enough to make him want to jump up and put the plan into motion immediately. How many fighters had bled their lives out simply because no one could reach them? The mobility of a gryphon would save so many of those otherwise lost lives.

"This is going to take time, Zhaneel," he cautioned, repeating the words to himself as well as her. "All of it is going to take time to learn, more time to practice. But it is a *wonderful* idea. I will help you all I can, I swear it!"

Zhaneel listened to his cautions, then bobbed her head gravely. "One weapon," she declared. "I ssshall learn one weapon. Crosssbow; it ssseems easy enough to massster. And I shall learn the simple healing that the green-bands know."

By "green-bands," she meant the squires and sergeants who wore a green armband and acted as rough field-Healers, who knew the basics. Enough to patch someone up long enough for them to get to a real Healer.

Enough to save lives.

"And I would be honored to teach you that Healing, my sky-lady," Amberdrake said softly.

"And—" she dropped her voice to a shy whisper. "And Skandranon will notice me?"

Amberdrake chuckled. "Oh, yes, my lady. He won't be able to help himself. You will be one of the few things that he does notice, I think."

She cocked her head to one side. "Few things?" she asked curiously.

He shook his head, and shrugged. "Oh, sometimes I think he is so obsessed with topping his last escapade that he does not notice much of anything, including his friends."

She continued to stare at him quizzically and finally said, "He notices. He loves you. The whole camp knows this."

That was not what he had expected to hear, and for once, he was taken by surprise. "He—what?" Amberdrake replied. He thought for a moment that he had misheard her, but she repeated her statement.

"He loves you as if you were a nestmate," she insisted.

"Perhaps he does not say so, but all the camp knows that Amberdrake and Skandranon might as well have come from a single mother."

As his mouth dropped open a little, she gurgled—a gryphon-giggle, and the first sound of happiness he had heard from her yet. "I heard this—I heard him tell some of the captains that you were a being of great integrrrity!"

"You what?" he said, trying to picture Skan doing anything of the sort.

"I heard him," she said firmly, and with coaxing, the story emerged. She had, once again, been eavesdropping when she shouldn't have. Some of the mercenary captains had been bandying about the names and reputations of several of the *perchi* and kestra'chern, and Amberdrake's name had come up just as Skan passed by. That would have been enough to attract his attention, but one of the captains had called out to him, tauntingly, asking him to verify what they had heard "since you know him so well."

And Skan had, indeed, defended Amberdrake's problematical honor, at the cost of some ridicule, which Skan hated worse than cold water.

"So," Zhaneel concluded. "You see."

Amberdrake did see—and he was rather overwhelmed at this evidence of affection, affection that he had hoped for but had not really believed in. A kestra'chern had so few friends—so few of those more than the merest of superficial acquaintances. . . .

He blinked, finding his eyes stinging a little.

"Amberdrake," she said into the silence. "You are a Healer."

He blinked his eyes clear and returned her grave stare, expecting a return to the earlier topic of discussion. "Of course, sky-lady."

But she turned the tables on him. "And when you are hurt, who heals the Healer?"

Has she suddenly turned into Gesten, or Tamsin, to sense my feelings before I know them? he thought, startled again. But he chuckled, to cover his confusion, and replied, "My lady, I am not likely to be needing the services of a Healer, after all. I do not ply my various trades on the battlefield."

She snorted, in a way that sounded very like Skan, but she said nothing more. And just at that moment, the sentries called midnight, and they both blinked in surprise.

Half the night has gone—but why am I surprised? It almost feels like half a year.

"You should take some rest, lady," he said, taking the half-forgotten token and putting it back in her pouch. She started to protest; he placed a hand on her beak to stop her. "It is at my discretion to determine my fee. You keep this. If you have some difficulty convincing your wingleader that you need special training and equipment, you could use that to deal with him. And when you find someone worthy of you, then come to me with it, and I shall turn you from simply lovely into the most breathtaking creature ever to fly."

Her nares flushed again, this time with pleasure. She started to leave, then paused on the threshold.

Tugging a hand-sized covert-feather loose, she gravely handed it to him. "And when you need—anything—you bring *me* this. Healer."

Then she was gone, leaving him with a slate-gray feather in his hand, and a great deal to think about. He let down the entrance flap, closing his tent against the night and any observers, and ran the feather between the fingers of his right hand.

Who heals the Healer. . . ?

Aubri

Five

"Well, great hero," Tamsin said dryly, pushing his way through the tent flap, "I see you have a tent-mate now. Did they discover you weren't a general, and you weren't supposed to have private quarters?"

Skan chuckled; it was amazing how much better a tiny improvement in his condition made him feel. Not great, but less like snapping someone's head off anyway. "No, they decided that I must be lonely, but instead of giving me a lithe young female, they sent this disgusting heap of tattered feathers. Meet Aubri. Be careful not to step in him."

The other gryphon in the tent, swathed in bandages covering burns, raised one lazy eyebrow and snorted. "I thought *I* was being punished. I was put in here with you, feather-head." He raised his head from his foreclaws and regarded Tamsin and Cinnabar with a long-suffering gaze. "I'll have you know," he continued, in mock aggravation, "he whistles in his sleep."

"So do you," Skan countered. "I dreamed I was being attacked by a giant, tone-deaf songbird, and woke up to discover it was you. Maybe it was yourself you heard, loud enough to wake yourself up!"

"I *don't* think so," Aubri countered, then put his head back down on his foreclaws and pretended to sleep.

Skan chuckled again. "I like him," he confided to Tamsin in an easily-overheard feigned whisper, "But don't let him know. He'll get arrogant enough to be mistaken for me."

A single snort of derision was all that came from the "sleeping" Aubri.

"Well, you know why we are here," Cinnabar told him, coming up behind her lover and giving him a greeting that was more than half a caress.

"Yesss," Skan said. "You are here to pretend to tend to my hurts, while you put your hands all over each other. Tchah! You lifebonded types! Always all over each other! Bad enough that as humans you are always in season—"

"And you are not?" Aubri rumbled from the background.

"What?" Skan asked. "Did I hear something?"

"No," Aubri replied. "I am asleep. You heard nothing."

"Ah, good." Skan returned his attention to the two humans who were doing their best not to break into laughter. "As I said, bad enough that you are always in season—but you lifebonded types are always preening each other. It's enough to give an honest gryphon sugar-sickness."

"Then Skandranon is in no danger, for he is hardly honest," came the rumble.

Skan shook his head, sadly. "What did I tell you? The lout not only whistles in his sleep, he mumbles nonsense as well. Perhaps most of his injuries were to his rump, since that is surely where his brain resides."

"He's upset I'm not succumbing to his imagined 'charisma,' " Aubri grumbled, raising his head. "And upset I beat him in his fledgling-baiting 'logic puzzles.' "

"You have no logic to use. Lucky guesses, all of them. I beat Urtho with them." Skandranon looked back to the Healers, chagrined.

Cinnabar moved to the gryphon's left, hands moving expertly over his wing and flank. "Gesten did a fine job with you, I see—you look very fit. You'll soon be in good enough shape to dazzle all the potential mates you like, Skan. Are you finally going to take a mate?"

Skandranon flicked his wings suddenly and stabbed a glare at her which was much harsher than he'd really intended. He felt his nares darkening. How *maddening* to be constantly asked that! As if they had placed bets on who and when and how!

Cinnabar bit her lip and backed off, pretending—pretense that was just a little too obvious—to search for something in her belt packs. Tamsin broke the tension by clearing his throat and pulling Skan's head toward him.

"Here now, Skan, let me look at your eyes."

"He'll just think you're in love with him," Aubri snickered.

Before Skan could make any retort, Tamsin clamped Skandranon's beak closed with one hand and stabbed a Look at him. This was serious business. Gryphons could judge relative distance and speed from each eye independently, and could clearly compare minute details of objects directly ahead. The paper texture of the book Skandranon had been studying, for instance, had been in sharp relief to him, even the furrows left by the pen. Like many other parts of a gryphon's body, though, the eyes were used to judge the health of the rest of the body. Tamsin leaned in until his face was barely inches away from the lens of Skandranon's right eye, becoming an encompassing blur which filled most of his wide field of vision. "You're dilating well. Not as scratchy as I'd expect. No problems with focus? Good depth perception from each eye?"

"With Aubri, therrre's little depth to ssstudy," Skandranon said dryly. "But yes, all seems to be well enough. I want to be back in action immediately."

"There'll be plenty of action for you, warrior, and that surely means we'll see you back in surgery soon enough," Cinnabar joked. "By now, Ma'ar's troops have stopped wagering on you. They know that sooner or later every one of them will get a chance to shoot at you."

Skandranon stood, feeling more lively than before, and mantled in indignation. In walked an opportunity for mischief. "They haven't killed me yet! Have they, Jewel?"

A laden and bewildered hertasi looked at Skan wide-eyed, having just come in bearing rolls of blankets for Aubri. "N . . . no?" she said, with a nervous glance at the Healers.

This, of course, was a favorite trick of the Black Gryphon's—getting people involved in his arguments, whether they liked it or not or whether they had any knowledge of the subject at hand. Always fun! Especially when the topic of discussion was *him*, and it had turned unflattering. "There, you see? Jewel knows. This was just a temporary setback, and I'll be back to save Urtho's army in no time at all." He puffed up his chest feathers and struck an heroic pose.

"Oh, *save* me from him!" came Aubri's plaintive cry. Tamsin and Cinnabar broke up in laughter, while Jewel scurried about positioning the rolls of blankets for Aubri's comfort, still bewildered by the whole scene. Skan, of course, continued to play to his audience.

"He's unaccustomed to being near greatness." Skan gave Aubri a lofty and condescending sidelong glance.

"I'm unaccustomed to drowning in such *sketi*! I can't stand him asleep or awake!" Aubri moaned. "Healers, could you *please* either still his tongue or eliminate my hearing? Something? Anything?"

"Tchah! Blind fledgling," Skandranon retorted. "I am forced to take up company with the unappreciative. It's worse than physical wounds, I tell you honestly."

Jewel paused for a heartbeat, took in the tableau of laughing and posturing, and evidently decided that folding fresh bandages for Aubri was the right thing to do. She fell into doing so with religious fervor on the far side of the tent. Lady Cinnabar recovered from her laughter and flashed her wide grin at Skandranon as Tamsin tweaked Skan's tail. Tamsin then wiped his hands as if he'd just finished a day's work and shot a satisfied look at his lover.

"I'd say our labor is done here, Lady. He's as good as he'll ever be."

"What a sad thought," Aubri muttered.

"Oh, please," Skan countered. "I have capacities I've . . ."

"Boasted about for years," Aubri inserted quickly. "And never fulfilled."

Skan decided that a quick change of subject was in order. "Are you two keeping an eye on our Lord and Master?" he asked. "When Urtho visited me, I thought he looked underfed."

"It hasn't been easy, but I've been making certain he gets at least a bite or two out of every meal brought him," Cinnabar replied with a sigh. "And his hertasi have been bringing him meals every two candlemarks or so. Still—no sooner does he settle down to eat than more bad news comes from the front lines, and off he goes again, food forgotten."

"He's giving more than he can afford to," Skan told her, sitting down and becoming serious for a moment. "He never wanted to be a warlord. He isn't suited to it."

"He's doing well enough. We're all still alive," Cinnabar offered. "The only reason he's in charge is because the King folded up. And all the King's men, the gutless lot."

Aubri's eyes twinkled. "She only says that because it's true."

But Skan stuck his tongue out in distaste. "She's being charitable, Aubri. When Ma'ar first swept down, the border lands burned up like kindling. All the Barons were terrified, and the King's best efforts couldn't hold them together. It all fell apart, and we had only Urtho to turn to. No one else had any knowledge of what we faced. Cinnabar's family and a few others stood against the Kingdom's dissolution; the rest fled like frightened hens, and were just about as witless."

"We remembered that we serve our subjects. The ones who ran served themselves and left their people crying in their wake," Cinnabar added. "We don't know what happened to most of them. Some had their faces changed. Some went mad or died. Most are still in hiding. Urtho doesn't blame them even now. He told the King that Ma'ar sent a spell of fear into them. However," she said while rebraiding a lock of hair, "it seems not all of us were affected."

A shadow fell across the threshold and was followed a second later by a severe-looking, impeccably uniformed woman. Her brown hair was short-cut but for three thin braids trailing down her back, each as long as a human's forearm, all placed in mathematical precision along her smooth neck. As she stepped in, her hazel eyes flicked from human to gryphon to hertasi in that order; she then flowed like icy water toward Aubri. Or rather, she would have flowed, had she not been trying to cover a limp. Skan stared at her; to intrude uninvited into a tent was not only rude, it was dangerous when the tent contained injured gryphons. Yet Aubri did not look surprised or even affronted, only resigned.

"May we help you?" Tamsin asked, openly astonished that the woman had not offered so much as a common greeting.

The woman did not even look at him. "No, thank you, Healer. I am here to tend to this gryphon."

"And you arrre. . . ?" Skandranon rumbled, his tone dangerous. Either she did not catch the nuance, or she ignored it.

"His Trondi'irn, Winterhart, of Sixth Wing East," she replied crisply—not to Skan, but to Tamsin as if Skan did not matter. "His name is Aubri, and he has suffered burns from an enemy attack," she supplied.

Oh, how nice of her. She's provided us with details of the obvious, as if we had no minds of our own or eyes to see with. How she honors us! Except that she was paying no attention to the nonhumans, only the humans, Tamsin and Cinnabar. *What does this arrogant wench think she is? Urtho's chosen bride?*

But the woman was not finished. "I've also come to reassign you, hertasi Jewel. Your services are required in food preparation with Sixth Wing East. Report there immediately." Jewel gulped and blinked, then nodded.

Winterhart drew a short but obviously sharp silver blade from her glossy belt and cut one of Aubri's bandages free, looking over the blistered skin underneath.

"I don't think—" Tamsin began. The woman cut him off as Jewel scurried out of the tent.

"Aubri doesn't require her any longer," she said curtly, "and the Sixth is shorthanded."

Skan ignored the rudeness this time, for Winterhart had caught his attention. "Sssixth Wing—that of Zhaneel?" he asked.

The woman looked at him as if affronted that he had spoken to her, but she answered anyway. "Yes. That is an extraordinary case, though. She surprised us all by somehow distinguishing herself." Winterhart's shrug dismissed Zhaneel and her accomplishments as trivial. "Rather odd. We've never had a cull in our ranks before."

Skandranon's eyes blazed and he found himself lunging toward the woman. *"Cull?"*

Tamsin and Cinnabar held onto both of Skandranon's wings. He repeated his incredulous question. *"Cull?"*

Winterhart ignored both his obvious anger and his question. Instead, she rebandaged Aubri and held her hands over his burns.

Even Skan knew better than to interrupt a Healing trance, but it took him several long moments to get his anger back under control. "Cull, indeed!" he snorted to Tamsin, indignantly. "Young Zhaneel is no more a cull than I am! These idiots in Sixth Wing don't know how to train anyone who isn't a musclebound broadwing, that's their problem! Cull!"

Tamsin made soothing noises, which Skan ignored. Instead, he watched Winterhart closely. The fact that this cold-hearted *thing* was Zhaneel's Trondi'irn explained a great deal about why no one had tended to the youngster's obvious emotional trauma and low level of self-esteem. Winterhart simply did not *care* about emotional trauma or self-esteem. She treated her gryphon-charges like so many catapults; seeing that they were war-ready and properly repaired, and ignoring anything that was not purely physical. Zhaneel needed someone like Cinnabar, or like Amberdrake, not like this—walking icicle.

But she was giving Aubri the full measure of her Healing powers; at least she was not stingy in that respect. And she was good, very good, provided that the patient didn't give a hung-claw about bedside manner or empathy. Aubri was clearly used to treatment like this; he simply absorbed the Healing quietly and made neither comment nor complaint when she had finished.

But for the rest of her duties—those, she scanted on. She did not see that Aubri was comfortable. She did not inquire as to any other injuries he might have, other than the obvious. She did not ask him if there was anything he needed. She simply gave Tamsin and Cinnabar another curt nod, ignored Skan altogether, and left.

No one said a word.

"Well!" Cinnabar said into the silence. "If that is the quality of Healers these days, I should have Urtho look into where that—woman—got her training!" Tamsin nodded gravely, but Cinnabar's expression suddenly turned thoughtful.

"Odd," she muttered. "I could have sworn I'd seen her before, but where?"

But a moment later, she shook her head, and turned to Aubri and said, "I'll have one of my personal hertasi come see to your needs until we can get Jewel back for you. Is there anything I can do for you now?"

Aubri's ear-tufts pricked up in surprise. "Ah—no, thank you, my lady," he replied, struggling to hide his amazement. "I'm really quite comfortable, actually."

"Well, if there is, make sure someone sends me word." Having disposed of the problem, Cinnabar turned back to Skan. "Do you think you can keep your temper in check when *that one* comes back?" she asked. "If you can't, I'll have Aubri moved so you won't have to encounter her again."

"I won't promisssssse," Skan rumbled, "but I will trrrry." It was a measure of his anger that he was hissing his sibilants and rolling his r's again.

"I won't ask more of you than that," Cinnabar replied, her eyes bright with anger as she glanced at the still-waving tent flap. "It is all I could expect from myself."

Tamsin mumbled something; perhaps he had forgotten that a gryphon's hearing was as acute as his eyesight. It would have been inaudible to a human, but Skan heard him quite distinctly.

"I *must* speak with Amberdrake about that one. . . ."

Tamsin chewed his lower lip for a moment, his brow wrinkled a little with worry, and then sighed. "Well, greatest of the sky-warriors," he said lightly, with a teasing glance to the side, "I think *you* won't have any real need for us in the next few hours, so we'll go tend to those with greater hurts and smaller egos."

Skan pretended to be offended, and Aubri snorted his amusement; Cinnabar lost some of her anger as her lover took her hand and led her out.

Aubri settled back down, wincing a little as burns rubbed against bandages. Skan arranged himself in his own nest of cushions with a care to his healing bones and watched his tent-mate with anticipation, hoping for another battle of wits. But the Healing had tired Aubri considerably, and the easing of some of his pain had only left an opening for his exhaustion to move in, assassinlike, to strike him down. Before either of them had a chance to think of anything to say, Aubri's eyes had closed, and he was whistling.

Skan snorted. "Told you," he whispered to the sleeping gryphon.

At least the poor thing was finally *getting* some sleep. Skan was only too well aware that Aubri's sleep had been scant last night and punctuated by long intervals of wakeful, pain-filled restlessness. Skan had wondered then why his tent-mate's Trondi'irn hadn't come to ensure that the gryphon at least got some sleep. Well, now he knew why.

Because this "Winterhart" doesn't care for us. We're just weapons to her; weapons that have the convenient feature of being able to find their own targets. All she cares for is how quickly she can get us repaired and back on the front line again. She might as well be fletching arrows.

Winterhart wasn't the only person in Urtho's forces to think that way; unfortunately, two of Urtho's commanders, General Shaiknam of the Sixth and his next-in-command, Commander Garber, had the same attitude. Urtho's most marvelous creations meant the same as a horse or a hawk or a hound to them. If a gryphon didn't do *precisely* as ordered, no matter if the orders flew in the face of good sense, there was hell to pay. Obviously, Shaiknam picked underlings who had that same humanocentric attitude.

Skan put his chin down on his foreclaws and brooded. It wasn't often he had his beak so thoroughly rubbed in the fact that he was *incredibly* lucky to have Amberdrake as his Trondi'irn and Tamsin and Cinnabar as his assigned Healers-of-choice.

And if anything ever happened to Amberdrake?

I could end up with another cold, unfeeling rock like Winterhart. And I would have no say in the matter . . . just as I have no say in when I may sire young, which commander I must serve, nor any way to change battle-plans if the commander does not wish a gryphon's viewpoint.

The gryphons found themselves treated, as often as not,

as exactly what Shaiknam and his ilk thought them to be; stupid animals, deployable decoys, with no will, intelligence, or souls of their own.

The more he brooded, the more bitter his thoughts became. Thanks to Amberdrake, he had led a relatively indulged life, insofar as it was possible for any of Urtho's combatants to be sheltered. But Zhaneel was an example of how a perfectly good gryphon could be turned into a self-deprecating mess, simply by neglect.

Because too many of Urtho's folk—and sometimes even Urtho!—treat us as if we aren't intelligent beings, we're things. We have no autonomy.

From where he lay, he had no trouble reading the titles on the spines of the books Urtho had loaned to him. Biographies and diaries, mostly—all humans, of course—and all great leaders, or leaders Skan considered to be great. Did Urtho have any notion how Skan studied those books, those men and women, and what they did to inspire those who followed them? How he searched for the spark, the secret, the words that turned mere followers into devotees? Or did he think that Skan read them as pure entertainment?

Make your motivations secret to the enemy, fool them into false planning, use their force against them, lead them onto harsh ground, hold true to the beliefs of your followers, and show them the ways they may become like you. Lead by example. Those weren't fictions on a page, they were a way of life for those who had become legends in the past. *Urtho knew half of these writers. A quarter of them worked for him when he created us. One he served.*

Urtho had learned from all of them, and now so did Skandranon. So *why* must things remain the same?

Amberdrake came awake to the smell of simmering bitteralm-and-cream. Gesten bustled about with fluid efficiency as the kestra'chern awoke, whistling jaunty hertasi tunes while he folded towels and polished brass, pausing only to check the bitteralm pot on the brazier between tasks. Amberdrake couldn't help thinking of morning-wrens greeting the dawn, like the hertasi tale of how the sun had to be coaxed from slumber each day with music.

Amberdrake rolled over and slid sideways, stretching his legs underneath the glossy red and silver satin cover that Urtho had sent to him when he had joined Urtho's forces as a kestra'chern. He curled up around a body-pillow and hoped that Gesten wouldn't realize he was awake, but it was too late. The hertasi pulled back a corner of the blanket and offered a cup.

"Morning and daylight, kestra'chern. Much to be done, as always."

Amberdrake blinked and mumbled something that could have been interpreted as rude, if it had been intelligible. Gesten was as unimpressed by it as he'd been the last hundred times and proceeded to prop up pillows behind the Healer's head. "There's hot bread and sliced kilsie waiting outside. We have three clients today. Losita has pulled muscles and can't take her usual clients, so I accepted one of hers for us. Should not take long. And before you ask, nothing has gone wrong with Skandranon. He is fine and sends his best regards."

Amberdrake took a sip of the hot, frothy bitteralm-and-cream and smiled at Gesten. What would any kestra'chern do without hertasi, and what would he do without Gesten? "So things are back to normal."

"As normal as ever in a war. Tchah," the hertasi spat, and flicked his tail. "New orders are down from Shaiknam and his second, Garber. 'All hertasi of convalescing personnel are to be reassigned to more important tasks, according to the judgment of the ranking human officer.'" He thumped his tail against the bedframe. "I don't think Urtho knows. It's the most stupid thing I've heard in years—we aren't tools to be traded around! Hertasi know their charges. It takes time to learn someone! And to send off a hertasi when their charge is in pain—it's unthinkable. Worse—it's rude."

Amberdrake finished his cupful and thought for a moment. Gesten apparently expected him to do something about this—an assumption that was confirmed when Gesten produced Amberdrake's full wardrobe for the day, laid out his sandals, and stood with his arms crossed, impatiently tapping his foot.

★   ★   ★

"So, just how *did* you manage to get yourself bunged up?" Skandranon asked his erstwhile companion when they had both finished the hearty breakfast that Gesten brought them at dawn. Somehow—possibly from Cinnabar, or one of Cinnabar's hertasi—the little fellow had learned that Aubri was without an attendant and had simply added one more gryphon to his roster of duties. Hence, the double breakfast; a lovely fat sheep shared out between them. *With* the head, which Skan had courteously offered to Aubri, and which Aubri had accepted and had Gesten deftly split, so that each of them could share the dainty.

Aubri had been profuse with his thanks, and Skan had thoughtfully kept his requests to an absolute minimum so that Gesten could concentrate on Aubri. By the time Gesten left, Aubri was cradled in a soft nest of featherbeds that put no pressure on his burns, and the telltale signs of a gryphon in pain were all but gone.

"How was I hurt?" Aubri asked. "Huh. Partly stupidity. We were flying scout for Shaiknam's grunts; we had one report of fire-throwers coming up from behind the enemy lines, but only one. And you know Shaiknam."

Skan snorted derision. "Indeed. One report is not enough for him."

"Especially when it comes from a nonhuman." Aubri growled. "Needless to say, one report was certainly enough for *us*, but he ignored it. He didn't even bother to send out a second scout for a follow-up on the report."

The broadwing grunted a little and flexed his talons, as if he'd like to set them into the hide of a certain commander. Skan didn't blame him.

"Anyway," Aubri continued after a moment, "I was just in from my last flight and officially off-duty, so he couldn't order me on one of his fool's errands, and I figured I was fresh enough to go have a look-see for myself. And I found the fire-throwers, all right."

"With your tail, I see," Skan said dryly.

Aubri snorted laughter as Tamsin arrived with Cinnabar and two of the Lady's personal hertasi. "At least Shaiknam believed the evidence of his eyes and nose, when I came in smoking and practically crushed him!" Aubri chuckled.

"You should have seen his face! I set fire to his tent when I landed, and I only wish I could have seen how much of it burned."

"Not as much as you or I would like, Aubri," Tamsin said. "By the way, flaming hero, we've had you reassigned for the duration of *this* injury, anyway. You're our patient now, and if Her Royalness Winterhart comes giving you orders, you tell her to report to *me* first."

Skan blinked in surprise; it wasn't often that Tamsin made room in his overcrowded schedule for a patient from another wing and another commander. Winterhart must have truly angered him yesterday!

"Tchah, Shaiknam should be set down to scrub pots a while," Cinnabar added, wrinkling her elegant nose in distaste. "My family has known his since our grandfathers were children, and it is a pity that anyone ever gave the cream-faced goose any vestige of authority. The only thing he truly has a talent for is losing interest in one project after another."

"And spending someone else's money," Tamsin reminded her.

She shook her head and brushed her hair back over her shoulders. "That was for peacetime," she corrected him. "Now he simply trades upon his father's reputation, rather than spending his father's gold on one incomplete project after another." She began telling off some of them on graceful fingers, as Skan and Aubri listened with pricked-up ears. "There was the theater company he abandoned, with the play into rehearsals, the scenery half-built, and the costumes half-made. They struggled on to produce the play, no thanks to him, but since it was written by one of his friends with more hair than wit, it did not fare well and the company disbanded quickly. Then he set himself up as a publisher, but once again, when the tasks proved to entail more than an hour or so of work at a time, he lost interest and left half a dozen writers wondering what would ever become of their works. Then there was the pleasure garden he planned—oh, Amberdrake knows the tale of *that* better than I—but it was the same old story. The garden languishes weed-filled and half-finished, and a number of talented folk who had turned down other offers of employment to take up with him ended up scrabbling after work and taking second and third place to those with less talent but more perception when it came to dealing with Shaiknam and his enthusiasms."

"His father was Urtho's first and greatest general," Tamsin told the two fascinated gryphons, "and with my own ears I have heard the man say that he is certain he is heir to all of his father's genius. As if wisdom and experience could be inherited!"

Skan laughed aloud at that. "I would say that Shaiknam is living proof that intelligence can skip entire generations."

Cinnabar's lips twitched, and her eyes gleamed with amusement. "Well, as proof that the so-observant Skandranon is right, this is the latest of Shaiknam's orders—that 'hertasi of convalescing personnel are to be immediately reassigned to tasks of more immediate importance.' That is why I brought Calla and Rio; right, little friends?"

She looked down fondly on the two hertasi, who gave her toothy grins. "Let some fool from Sixth Wing East come in here and try ordering *us* about," said Rio who, like his fellow, was clearly clad in the personal colors of Lady Cinnabar's retinue. "We'll send him out of here with boxed ears."

"You'll have to share us, though," added Calla. "The Lady is seeing how many injured there are from Shaiknam's command, and we're to tend them all if we can. You don't mind?"

"Mind?" Aubri replied, clearly surprised, pleased, and a little embarrassed. "How could I mind? I didn't expect *any* help! I can only thank you, and know that thanks are inadequate—"

But both Lady Cinnabar and Rio waved away any thanks. "My friends have been itching to do *something* besides tend to my nonexistent needs," she replied. "If my family had not insisted that I take a retinue due my rank, they would not be here at all."

"For which we are grateful," Rio butted in. "And grateful to be able to do something useful. So we will return when we know how many patients there are and see what it is you will be needing from us. Eh?"

Aubri nodded, speechless for once.

"It isn't surprising that Shaiknam would have someone like that Winterhart woman as a Trondi'irn," Tamsin observed, checking Skan's healing bones, as Cinnabar and her two helpers rebandaged Aubri's burns with soothing creams and paddings.

Aubri let out his breath in a hiss of pain but replied, "It's typical of him. She won't stand up to him at all; that's why he picked her. Honestly, I don't think there's a Trondi'irn in the army that would put up with his *sketi*, other than her. But she's just like him; thinks we're nothing more than self-reproducing field-pieces. We're like fire-throwers, only better, because we repair ourselves if you leave us alone long enough. *Very* efficient, is Winterhart."

"Efficient enough to requisition Jewel as soon as she knew you were down," Skan observed.

Aubri snorted. "Surprised she left Jewel with me as long as she did. Maybe she just didn't notice I was gone. She's been *quite* efficient about that new order."

"Who actually issued that particular chunk of offal?" Tamsin demanded in disgust.

"Garber. Shaiknam's second. In case you don't know him, he's by-the-book, and every inch an *officer*." Aubri's tone made it very clear what he thought of *officers* like Garber.

"So in the meantime, those who have been injured in the front line—where presumably, Shaiknam and Garber never go—are supposed to do without those who might serve as their hands and make their recovery more comfortable," Lady Cinnabar's cold voice told Skan that there was a great deal of heat within. The angrier she became, the chillier her voice. "We'll just see about that."

Skan quickly bent his head to keep from betraying his glee. Lady Cinnabar rarely *used* that rank of hers—she was one of Urtho's most trusted advisors when she chose to give that advice—but when she did, mountains moved, oceans parted, and strong men trembled until she was safely satisfied. If it had only been a case of one-on-one combat, Urtho could have sent the Lady in against Ma'ar and been secure in the knowledge that Cinnabar would return from the combat with not a single hair disarranged and Ma'ar would be on all fours, following at her heels, begging for her mercy.

But she never, ever, forgot courtesy, even when most angry. She bade Aubri and Skan a polite farewell, instructed Calla and Rio to stay with Tamsin to review the rest of the patients from Shaiknam's command, and only then stalked off.

Tamsin chuckled; Skan joined him. Aubri stared at the two of them in wonder.

"What has gotten into *you* two?" he asked, finally, eaten up with curiosity.

Skan exchanged a knowing look with Tamsin, a look which sent him into further convulsions of laughter. Skan answered for the both of them.

"Lady Cinnabar has Urtho's ear in a way that no one else does," he explained. "I think she's a combination of younger sister and respected teacher. And when she's angry—aiee, she can melt glass! She won't be satisfied with simply talking with Urtho and getting a change in those orders, she'll insist on seeing Garber *and* Shaiknam and delivering a choice lecture in person. By the time she is done, you won't be the only one nursing a scorched tail!"

Urtho's Tower

Six

Since Gesten was obviously not going to be satisfied until after he *had* done something about the situation with Shaiknam, Amberdrake put off his own breakfast until after he had a chance to schedule a conference with Urtho. He had hoped to simply slip in and have a quiet chat with the Wizard, but that was not in the stars; Urtho was chin-deep in advisors long before Amberdrake arrived at his Tower, and it was evident that there were other matters far more pressing—or disastrous—than the assignment of a handful of hertasi.

The situation would probably be taken care of, at least in the short-term, as soon as senior Healers Lady Cinnabar and Tamsin got wind of it. It could easily be dealt with permanently later, when Urtho had a moment of leisure to spare and Amberdrake could have that quiet word with him. Provided, of course, that Lady Cinnabar *herself* did not save Amberdrake the effort and broach the subject to her kinsman. That was only reasonable. But Gesten was not noted for taking a reasonable view when it came to things *he* considered important, so Amberdrake avoided a confrontation by avoiding *him*. Instead of returning to his tent for a solitary breakfast, he went to the mess tent shared by all the kestra'chern. The food would be exactly the same there as he always had when he was alone; Gesten generally fetched it directly from the mess cooks. And even though he enjoyed the peace of a meal by himself, it was part of his duty as the highest-ranking kestra'chern to spend as much time in casual company with the others as possible. While the kestra'chern had nothing like a regular organization, it fell upon Amberdrake to see that no one was overburdened, that those who needed help got it, and to keep this corps of "support troops" functioning as smoothly as the rest of the army. They were all Healers, after all, and not just "of a sort." They had a real impact on the combat troops.

A delicate undertaking, being "leader" of a group with no leaders—and not a position he would have chosen if it had not been forced upon him.

Whatever was going on that had Urtho up to his eyebrows in work hadn't yet worked its way down to the underlings, it seemed. The tent hadn't more than half a dozen kestra'chern seated at their makeshift tables of scrap wood, sipping bitteralm and conversing over bread and porridge. That wasn't unusual; kestra'chern were not early risers, given that they generally worked late into the night. No one seemed overly tense or upset. They all greeted Amberdrake with varying degrees of respect and warmth, then went back to their conversations. Amberdrake got himself another cup of bitteralm and a slice of bread and a hard boiled egg, and took a seat near enough to all of them that he could listen in without being obtrusive.

Two of the women had been having a particularly intense conversation; soon after Amberdrake seated himself, it grew increasingly heated. He knew both of them, and neither was Kaled'a'in; one was a robust redhead called, incongruously enough, Lily. The other, named Jaseen, was a thin, ethereal, fragile-looking blonde who could probably have taken any man in the infantry and broken him in half without working up a sweat.

It was Jaseen who was the angrier, it seemed, and all over a client who had been reassigned to Lily. Amberdrake bent his head over his cup and listened, as her voice rose from a whisper to something a great deal more public.

"I don't care where he's been assigned or who did it!" she hissed. "You don't have the background to handle him, and I do."

"You don't have the skill!" Lily interrupted rudely. "And I do! That was why he was reassigned to me."

"Oh, really?" Jaseen replied, her voice dripping with sweet

acidity. "I suppose the ability to drive a man into exhausted collapse is called a *skill* and counts more than experience!"

Lily sprang to her feet, both hands clenched into fists, and her face flushed. "Superior skill in anything is nothing to be ashamed of!" she cried.

"Tell her, Lily," urged one of the bystanders, as another rose from his seat and moved to Jaseen's side.

They're taking sides. It's time for me to stop this! Amberdrake got up quickly.

And just in time; Lily pulled her arm back to deliver a slap to Jaseen's cheek. Amberdrake moved as quickly as a striking snake and grabbed her wrist before she could complete the blow.

"What are the two of you doing?" he not-quite-shouted, bringing the argument to a sudden halt. All parties involved stared at him in shock; they had clearly forgotten that he was there.

He let go of Lily's wrist; her cheeks were scarlet with shame, and she hid both hands behind her back. He looked from her to Jaseen and back again, making no secret of his disapproval.

"I know that the tension has gotten to everyone, but this is no way to handle it! You two are acting precisely as our critics *expect* us to act!" he accused. "Don't you think that you're both being utterly childish? Bad enough that the two of you started this—but in *public*, in a common mess tent! The Healers use this tent, and what would one of them have thought if he had come in here to find you two brawling over a client like a pair of—of—" He shook his head, unable to force himself to say the word.

Now it wasn't only Lily who was flushing; Jaseen and the two who had taken sides in the argument had turned scarlet with humiliation as well.

Now that he had their attention, he would need to engage in a verbal dance as intricate as anything woven by a priest or a seasoned diplomat. Somehow he must chide both of them without touching on the tragedies that had made them kestra'chern in the first place.

"No one knows hurt and heartache like a kestra'chern," his teachers had said, *"because no one feels more pain than*

their own. Not so with us." There were tragic stories behind every pair of doe-soft eyes and tears behind all the comely smiles in this camp, and no one knew that better than Amberdrake.

"Neither of you has ever lacked for clients," he scolded. "It is not as if you are not well-sought-after! And if you hear anyone rating you like athletes, I want to hear about it! You both have the same rank; you differ only in your strongest characteristics. This client you argued about—he has specific needs. Jaseen, *what* comes first—your own pride, or the client's well-being?"

At all costs he must never say the word "poison" around Jaseen—she had spent three years imprisoned for poisoning her lover, only to be freed when his brother confessed that *he* had done it. By then, the "tender" ministrations of the guards had left her a changed woman.

She hid behind the curtain of her hair, but her blushes were still clearly visible. "The client," she replied, her voice choked with shame.

"Exactly," he said sternly. "That is what we are all here for. And what is the second rule, Lily?"

Lily had trained as a fighter and had served in Urtho's army. Injured and left for dead, the experience had shattered her nerves and the injuries themselves left her unfit to face combat again. Lily had been treated as a hopeless cripple, destroyed in both nerve and body, until she fought her way back to what she was now. She looked him in the eyes, but her face was so scarlet that it matched her hair. "The client receives what he *needs*, not what he wants."

"And you may—if, in your sacred judgment, and not merely your *opinion*—deliver what he wants *after* he gets what he needs," Amberdrake told them both.

Jaseen sniffed a little and looked up at him to see if she'd had any effect on him with that sniffle of self-pity. Amberdrake's expression must have told her that she wasn't winning any points, for she slowly raised her head and brushed her hair back although her red face was a match for Lily's.

"Jaseen. Just now it was *my* judgment, as it was the judgment of your old client's Healer that he needed a little less cosseting and a little more spine." He leveled his gaze right into her eyes so that she could not look away. "You are quite good at sympathy, but your chief failing is that you don't know when to stop giving it. Sympathy can be addictive and can kill strong men as surely as a diet of nothing but sugar."

She whispered something inaudible, but he was good enough at lip-reading to know she had said only, "Yes, Amberdrake." He turned to Lily.

"It was *your* job to challenge him. I hope that you did—I will only know after his Healer talks to me. And by 'challenging' him, I don't necessarily mean physically. You could even have challenged him by making him *earn* what he got from you." The fact that she avoided his gaze told him she hadn't exactly done that. "We aren't even primarily bedmates," he reminded both of them sternly. "That's what makes us something more than—what our critics claim we are."

Both these women had mended from their past shatterings; he knew that, every kestra'chern in this encampment knew that. If they hadn't, they simply wouldn't be here. They'd been given guidance in reassembling themselves from the splintered pasts fate had left them, and were obligated by that training to help others as much as they had helped themselves. Amberdrake would not permit incompetence— and although he was not officially a "leader," he had that much power among the kestra'chern without needing the title. In his experience, true leaders seldom had or needed flamboyant titles.

Jaseen and Lily bowed their heads, their blushes fading. "Yes, Amberdrake," Lily murmured. "You are right, of course. But it's easy to forget, sometimes, with the way we're treated."

"People treat you as what they wish you were, and that is not always what you are," he said gently, reminding them both of their pasts. "You must always remember what you *are*. Always. And always believe in each other."

Jaseen nodded wordlessly.

He raised his voice slightly so the rest of the observers could hear better. "Whatever the kestra'chern have been in the past, we are now something very important to these warriors. The war may turn upon what we do. We are the rest after the battle, and the blanket to warm them when they shiver. We are comfort in the darkness when death has become far *too* personal; we are the listeners who hear without judgment. We are priest and lover, companion and stranger. We are all the family many of them have, and something so foreign they can say *anything* to us. They need us, as they need their rations, their weapons, their Healers. Keep that always in mind, no matter how you are treated."

Both of them stood taller and straighter, and looked him right in the eyes. Several of the others nodded in agreement with his words, he noted with satisfaction.

"Now, let's get back to the business of living," he told them. "You are both too sensible to quarrel over this." He summoned an infectious grin for the two recent quarrelers and the others, and it caught all around. "We could be spending our time complaining about the seasons. Or the weather. Something productive, something useful."

With that he turned back to his own neglected breakfast, to leave the two of them to patch things up on their own. Or not—but they were both responsible adults, and he was fairly certain they would behave sensibly.

They whispered tensely for a few moments, then took themselves elsewhere. Well, that was fine, and even if they were foolish enough to continue the quarrel, so long as they did so privately, Amberdrake didn't care. . . .

I'm slipping, he thought as he held out his cup for a hertasi to refill, rewarding the little lizard with a weak smile. *I would have cared, a while ago. I would have stayed with those two until I was certain they had reconciled their argument. Now I'm too tired to make all the world happy.*

Too tired, or perhaps, just too practical. He used to think that everyone could be friends with everyone else, if only people took the time to talk about their differences. Now it was enough for him if they kept their differences out of the working relationships, and got the job done.

I'm settling for less these days, I suppose. I just pray there isn't less out there to settle for. Right now he couldn't have said if this lack of energy was a good thing, or a bad one. It just *was,* and he harbored his resources for those times when they were really needed. For his clients, for Urtho, for Skan—if he spent every last bit of energy he had, he'd wind up clumsy at the wrong time, or weak when the next emergency arose. That—

"Are you Amberdrake?"

The harsh query snapped him out of his reverie, and he looked up, a little startled. A young man stood over him, a Healer by his green robes, and a new one, by the pristine condition of the fabric. The scowl he wore did nothing to improve his face—a most unlikely Healer, who stood awkwardly, held himself in clumsy tension, whose big, blunt-fingered hands would have been more at home wrapped around the handle of an ax or guiding a plow. His carrot-colored hair was cut to a short fuzz, and his blocky face, well-sprinkled with freckles, was clean-shaven, but sunburned. Not the sort one thought of as a Healer.

Well, then, but neither was I. . . .

"Are you Amberdrake?" the youngster demanded again, those heavy hands clenched into fists. "They said you were."

Amberdrake didn't bother to ask who "they" were; he saw no reason to deny his own identity. "I am, sir," he said instead, with careful courtesy. "What may I do for you? I must warn you my client list is fairly long, and if you had hoped to make an appointment—"

"*Make* an appointment?" the boy exploded. "Not a chance! I want you to take my patient *off* that so-called 'client list' of yours! What in the name of all that's holy did you think you were doing, taking a man that's just out of his bed and—"

The young Healer continued on in the same vein for some time; Amberdrake simply waited for him to run out of breath as his own anger smoldered dangerously. The fool was obviously harboring the usual misconceptions of what a kestra'chern was, and compounding that error by thinking it was *Amberdrake* who had solicited his patient for some exotic amorous activity.

All without ever *asking* anyone about Amberdrake, his clients, or how he got them. *One word in the Healers' compound would have gotten him all the right answers,* Amberdrake thought, clenching his jaw so hard his teeth hurt. *One word, and he'd have known clients come to me, not the other way around . . . and that "his" patient has been sent to me for therapeutic massage by a senior Healer. But no— no, he'd much rather nurse his own home-grown prejudices than go looking for the truth!*

When the boy finally stopped shouting, Amberdrake stood. His eyes were on a level with the Healer's, but the outrage in them made the boy take an involuntary step backward.

Amberdrake only smiled—a smile that Gesten and Tamsin would have recognized. Then they would have gleefully begun taking bets on how few words it would take Amberdrake to verbally flay the poor fool.

"You're new to Urtho's camp, aren't you?" he asked softly, a sentence that had come to represent a subtle insult among Urtho's troops. It implied every pejorative ever invented to describe someone who was hopelessly ignorant, impossibly inexperienced—*dry-seed, greenie, wet-behind-the-ears, clod-hopper, milk-fed, dunce, country-cousin*—and was generally used to begin a dressing-down of one kind or another.

The boy had been with the troops long enough to recognize the phrase when he heard it. He flushed and opened his mouth, but Amberdrake cut him off before he could begin.

"I'll make allowances for a new recruit," he said acidly. "But I suggest that you never address another kestra'chern in the tones you just used with me—not if you want to avoid getting yourself a lecture from your senior Healer and possibly find yourself beaten well enough your own skills wouldn't help you. Did you even bother to *ask* why 'your' patient was sent to me? For your information, 'your' patient was assigned to me by Senior Healer M'laud for therapeutic massage, and I had to *seriously* juggle my overcrowded schedule to fit him in. I am doing *you* a favor; the man needs treatments that you have not been trained to give. If you had tried, you probably would have injured him. *If* you had bothered to *ask* your Senior Healer why he had scheduled this patient for other treatments, instead of barging in here to insult and embarrass me, you would have been told exactly that."

The boy's mouth hung open, and his ears reddened. His

eyes were flat and expressionless, he had been taken so much by surprise.

"Furthermore," Amberdrake continued, warming to his subject, "If you had taken the time to ask your Senior Healer why anyone would send a patient down the hill here to the kestra'chern for treatment, you would have learned that we are considered by all the *Senior* Healers to *be* Healers with skills on a par with their own—and that there are some things that you, with all your training, will never be able to supply that a kestra'chern can. Our preliminary training is identical to yours—with the exception that most kestra'chern don't have the luxury of Healing Gifts to rely on. We have to do our job with patience, words, and physical effort. Healing means more than mending the *body*, young man—it means mending the heart, the mind, and the spirit as well, or the body is useless. That doesn't make us better or worse than you. Just different. Just as there are times when you heal what we cannot, so there are times when *we* can mend what *you* cannot. You would do well to learn that, and quickly. Inexperience can be overcome, ignorance be enlightened, but prejudice will destroy you." He allowed his anger to show now, a little. "This war is not forgiving of fools."

The Healer took another involuntary step back, his eyes wide and blind with confusion.

Amberdrake nodded, stiffly. "I will see your former patient at the arranged time, and if you wish to overrule it, I will speak with Urtho personally about the matter. The word of Healer M'laud should take precedence over your objections."

And with that, he turned and left the tent, too angry to wait and see if the boy managed to stammer out an apology, and in no mood to accept it if he did.

He returned to his tent, knowing that it would be empty while Gesten made his own rounds up on Healer's Hill. That was good; he didn't really want anyone around at the moment. He needed to cool down; to temper his own reaction with reason.

He shoved the tent flap aside and tied it closed; clear warning to anyone looking for him that he did not want to be disturbed. Once inside, he took several deep breaths, and considered his next action for a moment, letting the faintly-perfumed "twilight" within the tent walls soothe him.

There were things he could do while he thought; plenty of things he normally left to Gesten. Mending, for one. Gesten would be only too pleased to discover that chore no longer waiting his attention.

Fine. He passed into the inner chamber of the tent where no client ever came, to his own bed and the minor chaos that Gesten had not been able to clean up yet. *Clothing needing mending is in the sage hamper.* He gathered up a number of articles with popped seams and trim that had parted company with the main body of the garment; fetched the supply of needles and thread out from its hiding place. He settled himself in a pile of cushions where the light was good, and began replacing a sleeve with fine, precise stitches.

The chirurgeons that had been his teachers had admired those stitches, once upon a time.

No one knows hurt and heartache like a kestra'chern, because no one has felt it like a kestra'chern. If he had told the boy that, would the young idiot have believed it?

What if I had told him a story—"Once on a time, there was a Kaled'a'in family, living far from the camps of their kin—"

His family, who, with several others, had accepted the burden of living far from the Clans, in the land once named Tantara and a city called Therium. They had accepted the burden of living so far away, so that the Kaled'a'in would have agents there. His family had become accustomed to the ways of cities after living there for several generations, and had adopted many of the habits and thoughts of those dwelling within them. They became a Kaled'a'in family who had taken on so many of those characteristics that it would have been difficult to tell them from the natives except for their coloring—unmistakably Kaled'a'in, with black hair, deep amber skin, and blue, blue eyes.

Once upon a time, this was a family who had seen the potential for great Empathic and Healing power in one of their youngest sons. And rather than sending him back to the Clans to learn the "old-fashioned" ways of the Kaled'a'in Healers, had instead sent him farther away, to the capital of the neighboring country of Predain, to learn "modern medicine."

He took a sudden sharp breath at the renewed pain of that long-ago separation. It never went away; it simply became duller, a bit easier to endure with passing time.

They thought they were doing the right thing. Everyone told me how important it was to learn the most modern methods.

Everyone told me how important it was to use the Gifts that I had been born with. I was only thirteen, I had to believe them. The only problem was that the College of Chirurgeons was so "modern" it didn't believe in Empathy, Healing, or any other Gift. The chirurgeons only believed in what they could see, weigh, and measure; in what anyone with training could do, and "not just those with some so-called mystical Gifts."

The Predain College of Chirurgeons *did* provide a good, solid grounding in the kinds of Healing that were performed without any arcane Gifts at all. Amberdrake was taught surgical techniques, the compounding of medicines from herbs and minerals, bone-setting, diagnoses, and more. And if he had been living at home, he *might* even have come to enjoy it.

But he was not at home. Surrounded by the sick and injured, sent far away from anyone who understood him—in his first year he was the butt of unkind jokes and tricks from his fellow classmates, who called him "barbarian," and he was constantly falling ill. The Gift of Empathy was no Gift at all when there were too many sick and dying people to shut out. And the chirurgeons that were his teachers only made him sicker, misdiagnosing him and dosing him for illnesses he didn't even have.

And on top of it all, he was lonely, with no more than a handful of people his own age willing even to be decent to him. Sick at heart and sick in spirit, little wonder he was sick in body as well.

He had been so sick that he didn't even realize how things had changed outside the College—had no inkling of how a mage named Ma'ar had raised an army of followers and supporters in his quest for mundane, rather than arcane, power.

He heard of Ma'ar only in the context of "Ma'ar says" when one of his less-friendly classmates found some way to persecute him and felt the need to justify that persecution.

From those chance-fallen quotes, he knew only that Ma'ar was a would-be warrior and philosopher who had united dozens of warring tribes under his fist, making them part of his "Superior Breed." Proponents of superior-breed theories had come and gone before, attracted a few fanatics, then faded away after breaking a few windows. All the teachers said so when he asked them.

I saw no reason to disbelieve them. Amberdrake took his tiny, careful stitches, concentrating his will on them, as if by mending up his sleeve he could mend up his past.

He had paid no real attention to things happening outside the College. He didn't realize that Ma'ar had been made Prime Minister to the King of Predain. He was too sunk in depression to pay much attention when the King died without an heir, leaving Ma'ar the titular ruler of Predain. *King* Ma'ar, the warrior-king.

But he certainly noticed the changes that followed.

Kaled'a'in and other "foreigners" throughout Predain were suddenly subject to more and more restrictions: where they could go, what they could do, even what they were permitted to wear. Inside the College or out of it, wherever he went he was the subject of taunts, and once or twice, even physical attacks.

By then, the teachers at the College were apologetic, even fearful of what was going on in the greater world; they protected him in their own way, but the best they could do was to confine him to the College and its grounds. And they were bewildered; they had paid no attention to "Ma'ar and his ruffians" and now it was too late to do anything about them. Intellectual problems they understood, but a problem requiring direct action left them baffled and helpless.

And in that, how unlike Urtho they were!

The restrictions from outside continued, turning him into a prisoner within the walls of the College. He stopped getting letters from his family. He was no longer allowed to send letters to them.

I was only fifteen! How could I know what to do?

Then he heard the rumors from the town, overheard from other students frightened for themselves. Ma'ar's men were "deporting" the "foreigners" and taking them away, and no one knew where. Ill, terrified, and in a panic, he had done the only thing he could think of when the rumors said Ma'ar's men were coming to the College to sift through the ranks of students and teachers alike for more "decadent foreigners."

He ran away that very night with only the clothes on his back, the little money he had with him, and the food he could steal from the College kitchen. In the dead of winter, he fled across country, hiding by day, traveling by night, stealing to eat, all the way back to Therium. He spent almost a week in a fevered delirium, acting more like a crazed animal than the moody but bright young Healer-student he was. He was captured by town police twice, and escaped from them the first time by violence, the second time by trickery.

Before he was halfway home, his shoes, made for town streets, had split apart, leaving his feet frozen and numb while he slogged across the barren countryside. He had stolen new shoes from farmhouse steps, hearing more of the rumors himself as he eavesdropped on conversations in taverns and kitchens. Then, from many of his hiding places, he saw the reality. Ma'ar was eliminating anyone who opposed his rule—and anyone who might oppose war with the neighboring lands. He had mastered the army, and augmented it with officers chosen from the ranks of his followers. Ma'ar intended to strike before his neighbors had any warning of his intentions.

Ma'ar was making himself an emperor.

And at home, indeed, as the students had said—all the "foreigners" were being rounded up and taken away. Sick with fear and guilt, Amberdrake hid in the daylight hours in an abandoned house with a broken-down door. Ma'ar's troopers had been there first, and when night came, he took whatever food he found there and continued his flight.

Looting the bones of the lost. May they forgive me.

It would have been a difficult journey for an adult with money and some resources, with experience. It was a nightmare for Amberdrake. The bulk of his journey lay across farmlands, forests, grazing lands. Most of the time, he went hungry and slept in ditches and under piles of brush. Small wonder that when he stumbled at last into Therium, he burned with fever again and was weak and nauseous with starvation.

I came home. And I found an empty house, in a city that was in a panic. Ma'ar's troops were a day behind me.

No one knew what had become of his family. No one cared what became of him.

He found the neighbors preparing to evacuate, piling their wagon high with their possessions. They had no time for him, these folk who had called themselves "friends," and who had known him all his life.

I begged them to tell me where my family was. I went to my knees and begged with tears pouring down my face. I knelt there in the mud and horse dung and falling snow and pleaded with them. They called me vile names—and when I got to my feet—

Old sorrow, bitter sorrow, choked him again, blinded his eyes until he had to stop taking his tiny stitches and wait for the tears to clear.

I never knew till then what "alone" truly meant. Father, Mother, Firemare, Starsinger, little Zephyr—gone, all gone— Uncle Silverhorn, Stargem, Windsteed, Brightbird—

He had flung himself at the false neighbors, and they had shoved him away, and then raised the horse whip to him. One blow was all it took, and the world and sky disappeared for Amberdrake. He awoke bleeding, at least a candlemark later, with a welt across his chest as thick as his hand. Half-mad with terror and grief, he staggered on into the snow.

He fell against the side of another wagon full of escapees.

The wagon belonging to the kestra'chern Silver Veil, and her household and apprentices.

He forced his hands to remain steady. *This is the past. I cannot change it. I did what I could, I tried my best, and how was I to know what Ma'ar would do when older and wiser folk than I did not?*

Silver Veil did not send her servants to drive him away; although by now he hardly knew what was happening to him. In pain, freezing and burning by turns, he barely recalled being taken up into the moving wagon, falling into soft darkness.

In that darkness he had remained for a very long time. . . .

His hands shook, and he put the mending down, closed his eyes, and performed a breathing exercise to calm himself—one that Silver Veil herself had taught him, in fact.

He had heard of her, in rude whispers, before he had been sent away. As little boys on the verge of puberty always did, his gang of friends spoke about her and boasted how they would seek her out when they were older and had money. She was as beautiful as a statue carved by a master sculptor, slim as a boy, graceful as a gazelle. She took her name from her hair, a platinum fall of silk that she had never cut, that trailed on the ground behind her when she let it fall loose. He had always thought she was simply a courtesan, more exotic and expensive than most, but only that.

It took living within her household to learn differently.

She tended him through his illness, she and her household. He posed as one of her apprentices as they made their way to some place safer—and then, after a time, it was no longer a pose.

Silver Veil did her best to shelter her own from the horrors of that flight, but there was no way to shelter them from all of it. She had no Gifts, but she had an uncanny sense for finding safe routes. Unfortunately, many of those lay through places Ma'ar's troops had lately passed.

Ma'ar's forces were not kind to the defeated; they were even less kind to those who had resisted them. Amberdrake still woke in the night, sometimes, shaking and drenched with sweat, from terrible dreams of seeing whole families impaled on stakes to die. Nearly as terrible was the one time they had been forced to hide while Ma'ar's picked men—and his makaar—force-marched a seemingly endless column of captives past them. Amberdrake had watched in shock from fear and dread, searching each haggard face for signs of his own kin.

Was it a blessing he had not seen anyone he knew, or a curse?

Silver Veil plied her trade as they fled—sometimes for a

fee but just as often for nothing, for the sake of those who needed her. And sometimes, as a bribe, to get her household through one of Ma'ar's checkpoints. The apprentices, Amberdrake among them, tried to spare her that as much as possible, offering themselves in her place. Often as not, the offer was accepted, for there was something about Silver Veil that intimidated many of Ma'ar's officers. She was too serene, too intelligent, too sophisticated for them. It was by no means unusual to find that the man they needed to bribe preferred something less—refined—than anything Silver Veil offered.

And finally, as spring crept cautiously out of hiding, they came out into lands that were in friendly hands. But when Silver Veil reviewed her options, she learned that they were fewer than she had hoped. Soon she knew that she must seek a road that would take her away from the likeliest direction his family had taken—back to Ka'venusho, the land of the Kaled'a'in.

And once again, she provided for young Amberdrake, she found another kestra'chern to take him as an apprentice and be his protector, one who would be willing to go with him to Ka'venusho. This time, the kestra'chern was old, mostly retired—and unlike Silver Veil, Lorshallen shared with Amberdrake the Gifts of Healing and Empathy. Silver Veil took a tear-filled leave of him and his new mentor, and she and her household fled on into the south. One of the apprentices claimed that she had a place waiting for her in the train of one of the Shaman-Kings there, in a land where winter never came. Amberdrake hoped so; he had never heard anything more of her.

The war encroached, as Silver Veil had known it would, and Amberdrake and his new mentor Lorshallen fled before it.

Lorshallen taught him everything he knew about his ancient art; Amberdrake learned it all with a fierce desire to master each and every discipline. All the things that the chirurgeons had not believed in, he mastered under Lorshallen's hands. And he, in his turn, taught Lorshallen the things that they *had* known. Silver Veil had completed his erotic education and had done her best to heal his body; Lorshallen completed his education as a Healer and had done his best to heal Amberdrake's mind and heart.

Eventually, they came to the Clans, and Amberdrake briefly took his place among his own people, an honored place, for the Kaled'a'in knew the value of a kestra'chern, particularly one as highly trained as Amberdrake, and they respected the pain he had gone through. The Kaled'a'in had a deep belief that no pain was meaningless; something always came of it. He knew that tales of what he had gone through were whispered around cook-fires, although such a thing was never even hinted at to him. Those in pain could look for strength to someone who had suffered more than they.

Always, he searched for word of his family. His people understood, for to a Kaled'a'in, the Clan is all. The Clan he settled among, k'Leshya, did their best, sending out messages to all the rest, looking into every rumor of refugees, searching always for word of Kestra'chern Amberdrake's lost family.

And they never found it. In a nation of close-knit families, I remain alone, always alone. . . . There will be no brother to share man-talk with, no sister to comfort for her first broken heart. No father to nod with pride at my accomplishment, no mother to come to for advice. No cousins to ask me to stand as kin-next at a naming ceremony for a child. And when I die, it will be to go alone into that last great darkness—

I have lost so much that sometimes I think I am nothing inside but one hollow husk, an emptiness that nothing will ever fill. Still, I try to bail in more and more hope, in hope that the sorrow will seep out.

When the call came for volunteers from the Mage of Silence, Amberdrake answered at once. At least he would no longer be surrounded by Clans and families to which he would never belong, but by others torn from their homes and roots. And he would fight Ma'ar, in his own way, with his own skills.

Eventually, all of the Clans came to settle at the base of Urtho's Tower, but by then, he had already carved his place among the kestra'chern.

He shook his head and bit his lip. Gesten might think he was blind to the workings of his own mind, but *he* knew why he felt the way he did about Skan. The Black Gryphon and Gesten had become the closest thing he had to a family, now.

And the closest thing I am ever likely to have.

When—best say, *if*—a kestra'chern ever found a mate, it was nearly always someone from within the ranks of the kestra'chern. No one else would understand; no one else would ever be able to tolerate sharing a mate with others. But for such a pairing to work, it had to be between equals. The altercation between Jaseen and Lily had only shown how easily quarrels could spring up over a client. And if one kestra'chern in a pairing was of a higher rank than another, such quarrels and, even deadlier, jealousy were more than likely, they were inevitable. Beneath the surface of every kestra'chern Amberdrake had ever met was a lurking fear of inadequacy. So unless both in a pairing were equal—

The lesser would eventually come to envy and fear the greater. And fear that his or her own skills would not be enough to hold the partner.

Amberdrake was the equal of no kestra'chern here; that was an established fact. And it meant even temporary liaisons must be approached with great caution.

Which left him even more alone.

Even more alone—no. This is ridiculous. If I were a client, I'd be told to stop feeling sorry for myself and concentrate on something that would make me feel good. Or at least stop me from being engulfed by the past.

The sleeve was done; he picked up a second garment and began sewing a fringe of tiny beads back in place. Thousands of tiny beads had been strung into a heavy, glittering fall of color, in luxurious imitation of a Kaled'a'in dancing costume where the fringe would be made of dyed leather. It was a task exacting enough to require quite a bit of concentration, and with gratitude, he lost himself in it.

Until someone scratched at the tied flap of the tent door, and he looked up in startlement. The silhouetted shadow on the beige of the canvas was human, not that of a hertasi.

Now what? he wondered, but put his mending down and rose to answer it.

He was a little disconcerted to find yet *another* young Healer—another stranger, and another newcomer—waiting uneasily for him to answer the summons. "Are you—ah—Amberdrake?" the youngster asked, blushing furiously. "The—ah—kes-kes-kes—"

"Yes, I am Kestra'chern Amberdrake," he replied, with a sigh. "How may I help you?"

The youngster—barely out of a scrawny, gawky adolescence, and not yet grown into the slender and graceful adult Amberdrake saw signs he would become—stared down at his shoes. "I—ah—have a patient, and my Senior Healer said my patient needs to see you and if I wanted to know why—I, ah, should ask you myself."

"And who is your Senior Healer?" Amberdrake asked, a little more sharply than he had intended.

"M'laud," came the barely audible reply.

At that, Amberdrake came very near to destroying the poor lad with a bray of laughter. After having sent *one* of M'laud's juniors up the hill with his tail on fire, the Senior Healer had evidently decided to teach his juniors about kestra'chern directly.

But he kept control of himself, and when the lad looked up, it was to see a very serene countenance, a mask that would have done Silver Veil herself proud.

"Come in, please," Amberdrake said, calmly. "I think you are probably laboring under a great many misconceptions, and I would be most happy to dispel those for you."

When he held the tent flap wide and gestured, the boy had no choice but to come inside. Amberdrake noted with amusement how the youngster stared around him, while trying not to look as if he was doing so.

What does he expect to see? Never mind, I think I can guess.

"Take a seat, please," he said, gesturing to a hassock at a comfortable distance from the cushion he took for himself. "I take it that you are afraid that I am going to hurt your patient, is that true?" At the boy's stiff nod, he smiled. "I take it also that you have never had the services of a kes-tra'chern yourself?"

"Of *course* not!" the young Healer blurted with indignation, then realized how rude that was and winced. But Amberdrake only chuckled.

"Young man—what is your name, anyway?"

"Lanz," came the gurgled reply.

"Well, Lanz—by now, I should think that M'laud has made you aware that the preliminary training for Healers and kestra'chern is practically identical. And I *know*. I began my training as a Healer." Amberdrake raised his eyebrow at the boy, who gaped at him.

"But why didn't you—I mean—why a *kestra'chern?*" Lanz blurted again.

"You sound as if you were saying, 'why a chunk of dung?' Do you realize that?" Amberdrake countered. "When you consider that the Kaled'a'in rank the kestra'chern with shaman, that's not only rude, that's likely to get you attacked, at least by anyone in the Clans!"

Lanz hung his head and said something too smothered to hear, but his ears and neck turned as scarlet as Amberdrake's favorite robe.

I seem to be making a great many people blush today. Another Gift? "Lanz, most of the reasons I became a kestra'chern are too complicated to go into for the most part, but I can tell you the only simple one. I am also Empathic, too strong an Empath to be of any use as a conventional Healer." Amberdrake nodded as Lanz looked up cautiously from beneath a fringe of dark hair. "That doesn't mean I became this because I am afflicted by some horrible mental curse—but as a kestra'chern—well, I never see those who are so badly injured that their physical pain overwhelms everything else. But I *can* use my Gifts and my training to Heal the deeper, and more subtle pains, injuries of mind, body, and heart they may not even be aware they have."

"But not all kestra'chern are Healers," Lanz said doubtfully. "Or Empaths."

Amberdrake smiled. "That is true. Most of them are not. And those who have no Gifts must work the harder to learn how to read the languages of body and tone; to see the subtle signals of things that the Gifted can read directly." As Lanz's blushes faded, he allowed himself a chuckle. "My friend, there is one thing that the kestra'chern have learned over the centuries; people who believe they are coming to someone only for an hour or two of pleasure are *far* more likely to unburden themselves than people who are confronted with a Healer or other figure of authority. If we honey-coat the Healing with a bit of enjoyment, of physical pleasure, where's the harm? Now—is your patient the last one on my roster tonight?"

"I think so." Lanz sat up a little straighter now, and he had lost some of the tension in his body that had told Amberdrake that the boy was afraid of him.

"M'laud sent me a briefing on her. The reason she is coming to me is that she is under some kind of great inner tension that M'laud has been unable to release, as well as some severe battlefield trauma, and that is making it impossible for her damaged body to heal." Lanz's face lit up, and Amberdrake decided that *he* must have thought her failure to heal was *his* fault. "M'laud suspects that she suffered some kind of abuse in her childhood, which is the real root of her problems. Essentially, she is unconsciously punishing herself for being such a bad person that she deserved abuse." He sighed and shook his head. "I know that this makes no sense, but this is something that kestra'chern in particular see and hear all the time. And it is not something you have any chance of dealing with, for I greatly doubt you would ever get her to trust you enough. Not because you are not trustworthy, but simply because of her own problems. You have other responsibilities to take your time, and you are less experienced with this kind of problem than I. I am a stranger, and it is often easier to say terrible things to a stranger than it is to someone who has known you, for the stranger will not prejudge. I will not be anywhere near the front lines, *ever*, and thus she will know that I have no chance of being cut down by the enemy. I become safe to think of as a friend because she knows she will not lose me."

Lanz shifted a little in his seat, looking rather doubtful, and Amberdrake decided to overwhelm him, just a little.

"Here—I'll prove it to you," he said, in an authoritative voice.

And he recited the litany of all the formal training he'd had, first with the chirurgeons, then Silver Veil, and finally Lorshallen. It took rather a long time, and before he was finished, Lanz's eyes had glazed over and it looked to Amberdrake as if the poor boy's head was in quite a spin.

"You see?" he finished. "If you've had *half* that training, I'd call you a good Healer."

"I never knew," the youngster said in a daze, "and when Karly came up the Hill from talking to you—"

"Karly? The redhead?" Amberdrake threw back his head and laughed.

Shyly, Lanz joined in the laughter. "I heard that one of the other Senior Healers said, 'I hope he has a regular bedmate, because after talking to Amberdrake the way he did, there isn't a kestra'chern in all of the camp who'll take him for any price!' I suppose he was awfully rude to you."

"Rude?" Amberdrake replied. "That doesn't begin to describe him! Still, Karly needn't worry. We're *obligated* to take those in need, and I can't imagine anyone more in need of—our services—than he is!"

Lanz smiled shyly. "And Karly's rather thick," he offered. "After talking to you—you being so kind and all—well, if you take any of my patients, I think I'm going to be awfully grateful, and kind of flattered."

This time Amberdrake's smile was as much full of surprise as pleasure. "Thank you, Lanz. I will take that as a very high compliment. Can I offer you anything?"

The boy blinked shyly. "I don't suppose a cup of bitteralm would delay me much—and could you tell me a little more about some of the others down here?"

Amberdrake rose, and Lanz rose with him. "Why not come with me to the mess tent and see for yourself?" he asked.

"I think—I will!" Lanz replied, as if he was surprised by his own response.

By such little victories are wars and hearts won, Amberdrake thought with a wry pleasure, as he led the way.

Zhaneel

 Seven

Zhaneel flexed her talons, digging them into the wood of her enormous block-perch. She checked over her harness again—wire-scissors, bolts, spikes, rope-knife, preknotted ties, all sized for her large, stubby "hands"—and stared out over the obstacle course she herself had set up. The course covered several acres by now, built mainly in erosion trenches and brook-cut hollows that were of little value to anyone in Urtho's camp, dotted with fallen trees and sandstone boulders. To get from here to the end of it, she would have to fly, dodge, crawl, and even swim. There were water hazards, fire hazards, missiles lobbed by catapult—

And now, magic.

She had already gotten the help of Amberdrake's hertasi, Gesten, in this endeavor. He'd been there from the very beginning; somehow he had known, perhaps through Amberdrake, what she was going to attempt. He had never asked her *why.* He simply showed up unasked, acted as her hands, then found three others to aid him in setting up the course and in triggering the hazards. At first, no one had paid any attention to what she was doing, but gradually her runs attracted a small audience. At first, this had bothered her, until the day when, after several unsuccessful tries at passing a hazard of simulated crossbow bolts, she made it through untouched and the tiny group applauded wildly.

That was when she realized that they were *not* there to make fun of her, but to cheer her on.

She had honestly not known what to make of that; it bewildered her. Why should anyone take an interest in *her?*

Then again, she had never been able to effectively figure out why hertasi and humans did most things. . . .

But today, she had a larger audience than ever before, and she knew precisely *why* this time. Word had spread that her obstacle course included magic.

She hadn't planned on including magical traps; those took effort and much energy, and she had never for a moment believed that there was any mage in the entire camp willing to devote so much as a candlemark of practice time to helping her. Or so she had thought, until a few days ago.

A young mage, a Journeyman named Vikteren, approached *her* for help. He needed spell-components. *Still-living* spell-components, which were not at all interested in becoming components of anything.

Zhaneel's speed and agility were what caught his attention; speed and agility were precisely what he lacked in going after starlings, rabbits, and other small, swift creatures. So they struck a bargain; she would hunt for him, and he would provide her with magical obstacles.

He had been doing so for several days now, and he had told her yesterday, grinning, that he was very impressed. Actually, what he had said was, "You're *good*, gryphon! Very *damned* good!"

So, much to her shock and amazement, had the gryphons' trainer, Taran Shire. The day after Vikteren began helping her, Taran showed up on the sidelines. Now, along with the young Journeyman, the seasoned trainer joined her every day, working with her on his own time.

She tried to put her audience out of her mind, although that was far from easy: her own kind were out there, other gryphons, those from other wings as well as her own. And what was more, some of those same gryphons had taken to training on the course, and leaving her tokens of appreciation.

Every time she made a pass on the course, people cheered her efforts, from hertasi to humans, from gryphons to a lone kyree who seemed to find her fascinating. Now, they waited for her to start yet again.

A white and red striped flag midway down the course went up and waved twice, and she launched from the block. This

was a rescue mission to free a captured gryphon. The details
had been kept secret, at her request, so she had only a general idea what to expect. One thing she knew for certain—
Vikteren and the hertasi planned to make her work harder
than ever before.

The first danger came only twelve wingstrokes after starting—a sudden gust of wind from her right. It hit her hard
and pushed her toward a downed tree's spidery limbs, an
easy place to lose feathers and find lacerations. She reacted
by rolling in midair and grounding, folding her wings in
tightly while she clutched at stones and brush. The wind
gusts ceased, and Zhaneel leapt over a ravine, to the cheers
of the audience.

She crept into the next erosion channel, popping her head
up every few seconds to look for danger. A quick bolt of fire
shot toward the ravine from behind a boulder and was followed by a huge fireball that roared like a sustained lightning
strike. It burned slowly through the ravine, catching the underbrush afire. She heard the audience gasp even over the
roar, as Zhaneel scrambled out of their line of sight, disappearing from their view. She knew what was in their minds.
Had the game gone too far?

But she couldn't worry about them. They'd see her soon
enough—

She popped up again at the far end of the adjoining erosion
cut. She leapt to the sandstone boulder with a growl, and
drew her rope-knife on the surprised mage hiding behind it.
Hah! Hello Vikteren.

"You die!" she sang out, and Vikteren grinned and fell
backward.

"I'm dead *here*," he reminded her as he stood up and
brushed off his robes. "See you further on, maybe."

"You might not see me at all, dead body!" she laughed,
then sheathed the knife. There was a mission to accomplish,
a gryphon to rescue, and the adventure had barely begun.

Amberdrake felt like a proud and anxious father as he
watched the young gryphon waiting on her block-perch.
Every line and quivering muscle betrayed her tension and
her concentration. He had arrived after she took her position,

but still managed to commandeer a place in the front beside Skan. The Black Gryphon had recovered nicely from his injuries although, on the orders of Lady Cinnabar, he was still officially convalescing. He was keeping an uncharacteristically low profile, however—as if he were afraid his presence would distract the young female at some crucial moment.

Well, it might. The youngster had been patently overawed by the Black Gryphon; if she knew he was watching, she might well lose her concentration.

Skan's tail twitched impatiently, but as Amberdrake put a comradely hand on his shoulder he gave Amberdrake a sideways gryph-grin before riveting his attention on the distant gray and buff figure of Zhaneel.

At the end of the course, a flag dropped. Zhaneel left the block with a leap, followed by an audible *snap* of wings opening.

Amberdrake had never seen a gryphon run an obstacle course before, though he'd heard from Gesten that Skan had been out here to watch for the past three days in a row. He hadn't been able to imagine what kinds of obstacles *could* be put in front of a gryphon, whose aerial nature made ordinary obstacles ridiculous. He was impressed, both with Zhaneel's ability to create the course, and her ability to run it.

More to the point, so was Skan.

He gasped with the others, when it appeared, briefly, that a rolling fireball had accidentally engulfed her; he hadn't realized that there would be some hazards on this course that were *real*, and not just illusions. He sighed with relief when she reappeared, and cheered when she "killed" someone, a Journeyman mage by his clothing.

Skan remained absolutely motionless, except for the very end of his tail, which flopped and twitched like a fish on land. Like a cat, the end of his tail betrayed his mental state.

Well, every other gryphon in the audience was watching her closely, too; gryphons were by nature impressed with any kind of fancy flying. It was part of courtship and mating, after all. But none of the others had quite the same rapt intensity in their gaze as Skan did.

In point of fact, he looked as much stunned as enraptured, rather as if he'd been hit in the back of the head with a club.

Amberdrake smothered a chuckle when he realized that Skan's eyes had glazed over. Poor Black Gryphon! He was used to impressing, not *being* impressed!

Zhaneel neatly dodged a set of ambushes; crossbow bolts, dropping nets, and an illusion of fighters. "She's good, isn't she," he said, feeling incredibly proud of her. She wasn't just good, she was smooth. She integrated her movements, flowing from flight to ground and back again seamlessly.

"She's beautiful," Skan rumbled absently. "Just— beautiful. . . ."

His beak gaped a little, and Amberdrake had to choke back another laugh. So the great Black Gryphon was a little bit *more* than simply impressed, was he? Well, fancy flying *was* the gryphon equivalent of erotic dance.

"Skan," he muttered under his breath, "you're going to embarrass both of us. That tongue looks really stupid sticking out of the corner of your beak."

Skandranon hadn't realized that he was making his interest in Zhaneel *quite* so obvious.

"Pull it in, Skan," Amberdrake muttered insistently. And annoyingly, but that was the privilege of an old friend. Better him than anyone else, though. There were plenty of other folk who enjoyed a chance to get a jab in; why give them more fuel for their fires?

More to the point, such teasing might be turned against Zhaneel, and he already knew that her fragile self-esteem would not survive it. He wasn't even certain she'd recognize teasing if she encountered it.

One of the Second Wing West gryphons, a female named Lyosha, sidled up beside him, and preened his neck-ruff briefly. It was a common enough sort of greeting between gryphons, one which could lead to further intimacies or simply be accepted as a greeting and nothing more. He and Lyosha had flown spirals together before, and she was obviously hoping the greeting would lead to the former, but he was not interested this time. Not with Zhaneel dancing her pattern with danger before his eyes.

"Lyosha," he said simply, acknowledging her presence in

a friendly manner, but offering nothing more. "This is fascinating."

Lyosha gave his feathers one last nibble, then subsided with a sigh. "True enough," she replied with resignation. "I'm tempted to start running this course myself. It's enough to set a gryphon's tail afire!"

He ignored the hint and coughed politely. "Well," he said, his eyes never leaving Zhaneel, "if she's not careful, the tail that's afire may be *hers*."

And let Lyosha make of that what she will. . . .

Zhaneel slunk over a decaying tree trunk toward four up-right sacks of hay. The sacks had been clustered around a burning campfire and wore discarded uniforms. A sign next to them read, "Off duty. Talking. Eating." Next to them was a midsized tent and pickets for four horses, but no horses were there.

Tent is big enough to hold ten. Four here, four horses gone, may mean eight. Four still out or on mission. Ma'ar's squads are eight and one officer, but officers get separate tents. Where is the officer, then, and the others?

Zhaneel drew her hand-crossbow. A tug with her beak, and it was cocked for a bolt to be laid in the track. She pulled one from her harness and laid it in, ready to fire.

Use the cover you have available. Steady with solid object.

She lowered herself behind the trunk, braced the hand-crossbow on the crumbling bark—and fired. The shaft hit the sack on the far left, and she hastily drew a second bolt while recocking the weapon with her beak. The second shot hit the next sack dead center and pitched it forward into the fire. She then snapped the hand-crossbow onto its tension-buckle and leapt over the tree trunk to maul the remaining two sacks of hay.

That was when the barrage began.

The tree-line to her left erupted with slung stones as the hidden miniature siege engines on the right shredded their foliage. Zhaneel power-stroked high into the air and avoided major damage, although some of the stones stung her on the feet and flank. That put her in the open for the fan of firebolts from the hillside, where she saw her objective—a gryphon. A *real* gryphon, under a wire net, staked out in a very unflattering position.

Oh, no! I hadn't asked for that!

So Vikteren's promised surprise was that she wouldn't be rescuing a bundle of cloth called a "gryphon"—she would have to deal with an actual one! But if Vikteren had gotten the cooperation of a gryphon as a prisoner, then what else could he have—

A whistling flash from the sky was her only warning. Two broadwings—from Fourth Wing West, by their wingtip markings—stooped down on her. They trailed white ribbons from their hind legs—sparring markers. *Simulated makaar!*

So be it!

Amberdrake's hand tightened on Skan's shoulder, and he felt Skan's muscles tense up underneath his fingers. The two "makaar" swooped down on Zhaneel from above, and he could not see any way that she could escape them.

He couldn't, but *she* most clearly did!

She ducked—and *rolled,* so that the "makaar" missed her by a scant talon-length; as they shot past her, she leapt up into the air behind them. By luck or incredible timing, she snagged the trailing white streamer of one, and ripped it off.

The "dead makaar" spat out a good-natured curse and a laugh, then obligingly kited out of the way of combat. It was a good thing he did so because Zhaneel had shot skyward, gaining altitude and speed, and was just about to turn to make a second attack run. The second broadwing had tried to pursue her, but his heavy body was just not capable of keeping up with her. If her objective had simply been to survive this course, she would already have won.

But it wasn't, of course. She still had to "free the trapped gryphon," and get both of them off the course "alive." The trapped one was Skan's old tent-mate Aubri, whose injuries still had him on the "recovering" list, and who would not be able to move very quickly. Again, that was a reflection of reality; any gryphon held captive would be injured, perhaps seriously, and his speed and movement would be severely limited.

Aubri had volunteered for the ignominious position he was currently in partly out of boredom, partly out of a wish to help Zhaneel, and partly because it pleased him to irk their commander in every way possible. And Zhaneel's success in these special training bouts must be irking the very devil out of their commander, who could hardly encompass the notion that a gryphon might have a mind of her own, and must be in knots over one who had *ideas* of her own.

Zhaneel wheeled and started her dive. The "makaar," who had been trying vainly to pursue her, suddenly realized that although he would be more than a match for her in a straight-on combat, he was never going to be able to take her on in strike-and-run tactics.

And she was not going to let *him* close.

He turned, heading for a place that Amberdrake suspected held that young mage—would Zhaneel see it, too?

Or would she be so involved in the immediate enemy that she would forget there were others on this course?

Like a falcon stooping on her prey, her wings folded tightly along her back, and she held her talons up against her body— but unlike the broadwings, who held their talons ready to strike and bind, hers were fisted. She had learned how to knock her foes out of the sky once, and now it was second nature to her—was she so caught up in the euphoria of combat that the "kill" was all she saw?

Skan held his breath as Zhaneel dropped down out of the sky. He was certain she had forgotten the Journeyman mage, but he certainly had not forgotten her—and the best place for him was somewhere near the staked-out "prisoner." She might get her immediate foe, but Vikteren would certainly get *her*—

But as the broadwing pumped frantically to evade her, she shot past him completely, ignoring him!

Instead, she stooped on an insignificant-looking mound of shrubbery, leveled out into a shallow curve, and buffeted it with fists and wings until the illusion of brush dissolved and Vikteren tumbled out of the way, laughing.

"All right!" he called, scrubbing dust out of his eyes with

his fists. "Holy Kreeshta, you've got me already! Give me a moment, will you?"

"You die twice, Mage!" she cried, as she leapt skyward again. She looked around for the second "makaar," but the broadwing had followed the example of most makaar left to face a gryphon alone, and had fled the scene, his ribbon and his "life" intact. Of course, unlike a real makaar, he would remain unpunished for such desertion.

Skan rumbled approval deep in his chest, as she landed as close to the staked-out and netted "prisoner" as possible—which in her case, was practically on top of him. There were probably traps all around her, but she avoided setting any of them off, simply by dint of remaining within the narrow margins that humans would have used while restraining the prisoner. A broadwing couldn't have pulled this off; nor could a broadwing have used foreclaws as cleverly as she did, snipping the wire net free with special scissors, then cutting the ropes holding Aubri down with a heavy knife she had already used once to good effect.

Oh, clever, clever, little gryphon! he applauded mentally. *Now, how do you guard the back of the injured one? That will be the real test.*

Zhaneel's gaze darted all over Aubri. "Can you fly?" she asked impatiently.

"No. Can't move any faster than a broken-legged horse, either. And my wounds are real, hey?"

Zhaneel spat a curse away from Aubri and looked around for anything she could use. Within a few winglengths there were tree limbs, and she had the lengths of rope she'd just cut, as well as the remains of the wire net. She grasped the lengths of rope readily available, coiled them up and held them to her keel.

"Two questions," she said. "How far can you jump, and can you hold a pole steady?"

Aubri narrowed his eyes, obviously trying to second-guess what this odd rescuer had in mind. He also, just as obviously, gave up. "Could leap . . . maybe twice my length, if I had to. But I wouldn't enjoy it. And I can hold a pole steady. I still feel strong enough to chew makaar."

"Good. Stay here." She parted her beak in what was meant to be a reassuring smile, then bunched her legs up and concentrated. She leapt high into the air with her burden of cord. At the zenith of her jump, she power-stroked out of Aubri's immediate area toward the tree limbs nearby.

Conventional gryphon-traps were usually built to fire sideways across a broad area, the kind she had been stung by at the fake-soldiers' camp. Magical ones were often designed to detect a low flyer approaching, shoot high up, blossom, and spread while falling. They could kill or maim at any point after they deployed. Since Vikteren—a mage—was involved, she had every reason to assume she would be facing both types.

So, the best way to sweep for traps is . . . to not be near them at all!

Within a few minutes, she had what she needed. A long branch, snapped off with her beak and trimmed of snags, for Aubri to hold. At its narrowest end, it forked for two clawlengths, and she had carved indentations for the two branches that were now tied across it. They were firmly in place.

Now to deliver my little nesting-gift.

A few minutes' more work, and the long pieces of rope were one very long length of rope—inelegant, but effective. Zhaneel used four of her preknotted ties to bind up the foliage and small branches she had trimmed scant minutes earlier to one end of the rope. She bobbed her head, measuring the range to Aubri and the "safe" ceiling she had flown at already without triggering traps, then took wing, the loose end of the rope clutched tightly in her hind claws.

Magical gryphon-traps are triggered by something living flying over their kill range, but not always. Can sometimes be triggered by anything—have to go high!

Zhaneel circled up, straining only for altitude—and it was *work*, hard work because the higher she went, the heavier the burden of the rope became. Finally there was a shudder as the bundles of foliage lifted. She angled away from the still-perplexed Aubri, carrying the rope higher and higher until the bundles below were above what she had determined to be safe. Then, she turned her struggle for altitude into an exhausting dive from the far side of the clearing, toward the tied branches. She judged, hoped—and let go.

The bunches of foliage sailed down, heading directly for the hapless Aubri. Behind them, the rope coiled and twisted wildly, gaining on the clusters of branches that had more wind resistance than the rope. While Zhaneel surged back up into the sky, the green leaves and twigs struck Aubri's wings and back. It was surely uncomfortable, but easily less painful than anything a makaar would have done to a captive gryphon. Amid indignant curses from the "captive," the rope fell in a snaky line across the clearing. As hoped, no traps triggered immediately from the rope's impact.

Next trick.

She landed and collected her thoughts, taking deep breaths. Aubri glared at her indignantly, but voiced no ill thoughts toward his "rescuer" for the moment. She waved a reassurance to him, looped the rope around the fork of the branch-affair she'd made earlier, and tied it off.

Several heartbeats later, she was in the air again, with two stripped branches clipped to the back of her harness. She followed the air path she knew was safe and dropped straight down to land next to Aubri.

"I assume you have a good reason for pelting me with salad?" he rumbled.

"I'm sorry. But I have a plan to get you out safely. Hold this . . ." she muttered while unclipping the branches from her back. "They scratch—! There. Now. Lie sideways and curl up. Hold these sticks up, one in hindclaws, one in fore-claws. So both are that way." She indicated the direction the rope lay. "Be patient."

Aubri sighed. "Where would I go? My life is yours."

Zhaneel pulled the wire mesh until it faced as Aubri did, and used two more ties to anchor it to the two sticks. Then understanding dawned in Aubri's eyes as she fastened the foliage bundles to the net.

"A shield."

"Yes. Not a big one, but could help us." She smiled and nibbled his crest reassuringly. "Now, let me down there in the hollow of your belly, where the rope goes under the net."

Aubri complied, fascinated. After settling herself in, Zhaneel reeled the rope in claw-over-claw until the heavy branches tied to the other end ground their way toward the two gryphons.

"Searching for ground traps," Zhaneel muttered. "If one goes, hold tight to the sticks! Let me protect your belly." *Only makes sense—he can't fly, so I am as good as ground-bound. If I can shield him from a fatal injury by taking an injury myself, we will still both be alive to return home.*

A deep thudding sounded, like a massive crossbow cord releasing, and a hail of stones showered much of the clearing. Both gryphons squinted their eyes while pebbles struck the greenery protecting them, then resumed pulling. Two ground panels lurched open and drove stakes into the ground nearby. A few minutes later, Zhaneel could reach out and grasp the quarry herself.

Last trick.

She patiently explained to Aubri what she was doing as she worked and allowed herself a moment of satisfaction when she was done. The crowd watching had approved of the way she'd triggered the ground traps. They waited, enraptured, wondering what she would do next. Zhaneel knew they saw her raise the canopy she had just finished, made of wire net, foliage and branches, above Aubri.

"You *must* hold this steady, understand? Must!"

Aubri nodded. "Y'got me this far, skydancer."

Zhaneel's nares blushed red and she leapt straight up, gaining altitude madly. When she had reached twice the height she counted as "safe," she rolled over on her back, straightened, and folded her wings in tight, hurtling faster than any crossbow bolt. Her shadow streaked across the ground below as she flattened the dive. She felt the wind cut across her body and saw the landscape become a blur as she shot across the clearing, scant winglengths above the ground, following the same path in the air that her sweep earlier had done on the surface.

Behind her, she could hear fireballs erupting, and saw flashes of yellow light. Moments later, she traded speed for altitude and pulled up, to see sparks raining down on the entire clearing—and Aubri's shield.

The improvised shield held and protected him from harm.

With the first victory cry she had ever uttered, she closed on him to lead him from his captivity.

Winterhart grimaced as the audience began cheering. Someone jostled her, jarring her back and sending a jab of pain down her right leg, further souring her mood.

Garber had ordered her to come here, orders she hadn't much liked and wasn't sure she agreed with. Right now, though, she wasn't very fond of gryphons; it was a gryphon that had injured her back.

Be fair. It wasn't her fault. She'd been having backaches and ignoring them—after all, who *didn't* have a headache or a backache by day's end around here? She had been restraining an hysterical and delirious broadwing with severe lacerations who had lashed out with both hind feet and sent Winterhart twisting and tumbling sideways. She hadn't broken anything, but her back spasmed as soon as she got up, and it had been getting worse, not better, with time.

She was a Healer; she *knew* she should be seeing another Healer, or should at least stay in bed, flat, for a while. She was even fairly certain that she knew what was wrong. But there were no Healers and no time to spare, so she simply hadn't mentioned it to anyone. She moved as little as possible, said she had "sprained" her back, and used that as an excuse not to do things that made it hurt worse. But she was in constant pain; there were only two positions she could take that allowed the pain to stop, and neither of them were appropriate for getting any work done. It was *embarrassing*. A Healer should be able to keep herself in one piece. This was altogether too much like a display of incompetence.

The pain wasn't doing much for her temper, and getting jostled and making it worse didn't help.

Damn Garber. He's right, but for all the wrong reasons.

She'd been watching Zhaneel herself for several days, since she'd gotten wind of this "obstacle course" business, and long before dimwitted Garber had any notion that it was going on. Even before today she'd found herself torn between two violently conflicting opinions.

On the one hand she had to admire the little gryphon; obviously unsuited for combat, she had found ways to *make* herself suited to it. She had been pushing herself, finding her absolute limits, turning handicaps into benefits. The number of things she'd had to work out for herself to overcome her own deficiencies was incredible, and the ingenious ways she had done so were amazing. It was difficult to believe that this was the little runt Garber saw no use at all for.

But on the other hand, Zhaneel was exhausting herself completely with these so-called "training sessions"; no one had ever *authorized* her to do what she was doing, which made them quasi-legal at best. But that could be ignored. What could not be ignored was the fact that she had led other gryphons into trying her unorthodox tactics, with very mixed results.

Zhaneel herself had come out of these sessions with pulled muscles; she hadn't come to Winterhart for any help, but that made no difference. The gryphon had been hurt, and she was the one who had invented the course and the training. Winterhart was afraid that one of the others was very likely to be seriously injured trying some of her nonsense.

Even if the other gryphons didn't manage to hurt themselves on this course, the fact still remained that they burned off energy and resources they *might* need later, where it counted. Out on the front lines. The war escalated, resources diminished. Although it was not common knowledge, Urtho's forces had lost ground, a little more every day. There was a new breed of makaar in the air now, and they took a toll on the gryphons. If the gryphons wasted their energy or strained themselves on this obstacle course of Zhaneel's, they might not have that little extra they needed to survive an encounter with these new makaar.

Garber, of course, only knew that the gryphon cull was doing things he hadn't ordered, not so much flouting his authority as ignoring it. No gryphon in Sixth Wing was allowed to think for itself; the very idea was preposterous. He was already aching with humiliation at the lecture the Lady Cinnabar had delivered—on Urtho's behalf—concerning the reassignment of injured gryphons' hertasi. Winterhart had not been present, but several who had overheard the Lady had indicated she had been less than flattering concerning Garber's intelligence and ability to make a sound decision.

Then came news of Zhaneel creating some unorthodox training program, encouraging others to join her in it, completely bypassing Garber's authority. This could not be permitted, so he had sent the gryphon's Trondi'irn—the lowest ranking officer in the wing, she acidly reminded herself—to dress her down for it. Never mind that it was a *successful* program so far. That was hardly the point.

Winterhart threaded through the crowd, more uneasy with every passing moment. She did not like confrontations. She particularly disliked them when there was a possible audience involved.

But she had direct orders. She also had an exact speech, delivered to her by Garber's aide-de-camp, and duly memorized. Presumably the commander did not trust her to deliver a proper dressing-down . . . or perhaps he was as contemptuous of her intelligence as he was of the gryphons'.

Abruptly, she found herself in a clear space, and practically nose-to-beak with the runt.

Zhaneel blinked in surprise, and backed up a pace or so. "Winterrrharrt," she said blankly. "What do you herrrre?"

That was all the opening that Winterhart required. "It is more to the point to ask you what *you* are doing here, gryphon," she said coldly. "You are here without orders, you have commandeered equipment and personnel that you have no right to, and you have subverted other gryphons inside and outside of your wing into not only aiding you, but following in your ill-conceived plans. Your commander is highly displeased. What have you to say for yourself?"

She expected Zhaneel to behave as she always had; to cower a little, stammer an apology, and creep off to her aerie, forgetting and abandoning her ridiculous "training program." She had readied a magnanimous acceptance of that apology before she was halfway through her speech. Something that would make her look a little less like Garber's mouthpiece. . . .

"I?" the cull replied, and every hair and feather on her body bristled. She drew herself up to her full, if substandard, height, and looked down her beak at the Trondi'irn with eyes full of rage. "*I?*" she repeated, raising her voice. "How isss it that *I* am to blame becaussse the commanderrr of

Sssixth Wing hasss no morrre imagination than a mud-turrr-
tle? How isss it that it isss *my* fault that therrre isss only
one trrraining progrrram for all, no matter the cirrrcum-
ssstancesss, norrr if they change? What isss it that I am doing
wrrrong? What isss it that I am doing that I ssshould be
accusssed of doing wrrrong?" Her voice rose to full volume,
and the audience, which had begun to disperse, regrouped in
anticipation of another sort of spectacle. It was clear in an
instant that they would *not* be siding with Winterhart.

"I do *nothing* wrrrong!" Zhaneel shouted. "I do what
ssshould have been done, that no one carrred to do! And
you, my Trrrondi'irrrn, *you* ssshould have ssseen that it
needed doing!"

By now the audience had surrounded the two of them,
leaving Winterhart no route of escape. She couldn't help herself, she flushed with profound embarrassment.

"You had no orders and no permission—" she began.

"Orrrderrrsss?" the gryphon interrupted with shrill incre-
dulity. "I am on leave time! Thessse who help me arrre off-
duty! What need have we of orrderrrsss, of perrrmisssssionsss?
Arrre we to requesssst leave to *pisssss* now?"

Growls from behind her, a little laughter on all sides, and
nods and angry looks on the faces she could see. Winterhart's
face burned painfully.

"We arrre off-duty," the gryphon repeated. "When hasss
Garrrberrr the rrright to decrrree what we do off-duty?"

"He doesn't," Winterhart admitted reluctantly. "But he
gave me the orders. . . ."

Before she could say anything more, a huge, black-dyed
gryphon with no regimental marks pushed through the
crowd and faced her with challenge in every line of him.
"Then why," rumbled the infamous Skandranon, the Black
Gryphon, "don't you tell that overbearing half-fledged idiot
that his orders are a pile of steaming mutes? You're a
Trondi'irn, you have that right *and* duty for your gryphons."

She stared at him. She had never heard the Black Gryphon
speak before—at least, not more than a word or two. When
he had shared a tent on Healer's Hill with her gryphon
Aubri, he had not spoken more than a word or two in her
presence at most. He was either asleep or ignoring her. She

had no idea he was so articulate, with so little gryphonic accent. Hearing that clear, clipped voice coming from that beak—it was such a shock, she addressed him as she would have another human.

"I couldn't do that!" she exclaimed automatically. "He's my superior!"

But the Black Gryphon only shrugged. "In what way? I don't see why you shouldn't tell him he's being hopelessly thick," he replied. "I tell *my* superiors when they're idiots often enough. I generally tell them they couldn't tell their crest from their tailfeathers on a daily basis. And that includes Urtho."

Urtho? This—this creation, this construct, talked back to *Urtho?* She was aghast, appalled, and tried to put some of that into words, but all that came out was, "B–but that's n–not the way things are *done!*" She'd stammered which made it sound all the stupider.

Skandranon only snorted his contempt as equally contemptuous laughter erupted around the circle. "That's not the way *you* do things, maybe," the Black Gryphon replied. "It seems to me that the main problem we have is that there are too many officers thinking that books and noble birth give you all the answers you need—and too many order-takers who *believe* them without question." He took a step or two closer to her, looming over her, and staring down his beak at her. "Amuse me. Bring me up on charges. You didn't even think for yourself when Garber handed you that scoop of manure to deliver here. Didn't it ever occur to you that the real reason you were told to lecture this young lady was *not* that she was doing anything wrong, but because she was doing something Garber and Shaiknam didn't think of—or steal—first? It must gall them both that what they would call a 'mere beast' has been more clever than they were. Without asking for permission. Without being *told,* Trondi'irn."

Winterhart opened her mouth to say something—and could not think of anything to say. Certainly, she could not refute what the gryphon had just said. Hadn't she been thinking it herself? And she could not bring herself to defend Garber, not when his aide had been condescending to the point of insulting when he had delivered those orders. All she could do was to stand there with her mouth hanging open, looking stupid and shamed.

It was Zhaneel who salvaged what little was left of the situation. "Trrrondi'irrn," she said crisply, "I will have worrrdsss with you. In prrivate. Now."

Winterhart took the escape, narrow as it was, and nodded. After all, there was nothing else she could do but follow. But then, wasn't she used to that by now?

Garber and Shaiknam

Eight

Amberdrake managed to get Skan out of earshot of most of the camp before the Black Gryphon exploded, pulling him deeply into the heart of the obstacle course and into a little sheltered area with a tree or two for shade and a rock to sit on. He counted himself lucky, at that; this obstacle course of Zhaneel's was large enough for privacy even at the level of shouting Skan was capable of. Large gryphons had large lungs.

The course should be safe enough with all the traps sprung, and now that the "show" was over, anyone who might happen to overhear Skan's outburst was likely to be sympathetic anyway. Up until today there hadn't been anyone unfriendly among the spectators.

Zhaneel's first "show" had been utterly eclipsed by her second; standing up for her rights to that officious Trondi'-irn, Winterhart. It was nothing anyone had expected, given Zhaneel's diffident manner up until this moment.

She must just have been pushed too far. Not surprising. That woman would have pushed me over the edge.

Even the Sixth Wing trainer had been disgusted with the woman, and even more disgusted with Garber. If everyone who said they would actually *did* lodge a protest with Urtho—bypassing Shaiknam altogether—Garber would go down on record as the commander most disliked, *ever*. Even the humans had been appalled by the precedent that would be set if this action was not met with immediate protest, a precedent that permitted a commanding officer to decree what could and could not be done during off-duty hours.

Well, the woman had at least enough conscience left that she was embarrassed by those orders she was supposed to deliver. That's about all I can say in her behalf. If first impressions are important, I can't say she's made a very good one on me. A Trondi'irn should have enough fortitude to stand up for her charges, not roll over and show her belly every time the commander issues some stupid order. And wasn't she the one Gesten told me about, that ordered the hertasi to be reassigned? Can't she do anything but parrot whatever Garber wants?

Amberdrake took a seat on the sun-warmed rock, and let Skan wear himself out, venting his anger. He was annoyed with the woman, and *very* put out with her commander. But Skandranon was enraged enough to have chewed up swords and then spit out tacks. It was better for him to show that anger to Amberdrake than sweep into camp and get himself in trouble. It wouldn't have been the first time that his beak had dug him a hole big enough to fall into.

"*This* is what I mean!" Skan fumed, striding back and forth, wings flipping impatiently. His talons tore up the ground with every step he took, leaving long furrows in the crumbling earth. "This is *exactly* what I've been trying to tell you! Now you see it for yourself—this whole sorry business! We gryphons are *constantly* being ordered about by humans who know and care nothing about us! We get chewed up trying to keep them alive, and they won't let us figure out ways to keep *ourselves* alive! Damned idiots can't tell their helms from the privy, and *they're* trying to tell *us* what to do! And now they're ordering us around when we're *off-duty,* and the dungheads think it's their *right* and *privilege!*"

There was more, much more, in the same vein. Amberdrake simply remained where he was on his rock, nodded, looked somber, and made appropriately soothing noises from time to time. He wished there was something else he could do, but right now, all he could provide Skan with was a sympathetic ear. He was, himself, too angry to do Skan any good. If he tried to calm the gryphon through logic games, he'd only let his own anger out. Besides, Skan didn't want to be calmed; he wanted a target.

The trouble was, Skan was right on all counts; Amberdrake had seen it time and time again. And it wasn't as if the gryphons had any choice. They couldn't simply pack up and leave their creator, no matter now onerous conditions got. They were, in a sense, enslaved to their creator, for only Urtho held the secret of their fertility. Without that, they could not reproduce. Without that, if they left, they would be the last of their kind.

Skan knew that, better than anyone else, since every time he returned from a mission, intact or otherwise, someone asked him when he was going to pick a mate and father a brood. It was a constant irritant to him; he never forgot it, no matter how cavalier he might seem about it. And yet, he had never once brought it up to Urtho directly.

Why? I don't know. Maybe he's afraid to, for all his boasting that he speaks to Urtho as an equal. Maybe he keeps thinking that Urtho will realize on his own what an injustice has been done.

Amberdrake wished there was some legitimate way that he could calm his friend down; by now Skan had worked himself up into a full gryphonic rage-display—crest up, hackles up, wings mantling, tearing the thin sod to shreds with his talons. He agreed with the Black Gryphon more with every moment. How could he calm Skan down when he himself wanted to carefully and clinically take Garber and Shaiknam apart on Skan and Zhaneel's behalf?

Not just their behalf, either. How long before they try that sketi *on the other troops? Or before they try to command the exclusive services of one or more Healers, or even kestra'chern? If they're willing to break the rules once, how many more times will they break them? And then, when* they *make* the *rules, who can oppose them?*

He'd thought that Skan's display had cleared the area. No one really wanted to get too near a gryphon in that state, especially not when the gryphon was Skandranon. He'd never actually hurt anyone, but when he was this angry, he got malicious enjoyment out of coming within a feather's width of doing so. But after listening to Skan for a quarter candlemark, Amberdrake spotted someone else storming up over the rough ground toward them, short Journeyman's robes marking him as a mage, and carrot-colored hair identifying him as Vikteren.

He's heading straight for us. Good gods, what now? Another disaster?

"Gods!" the young mage shouted as Skan paused for breath. "I would have the *hide* off that fatuous, fat-brained idiot, if only I knew how to make it hurt enough!"

"Garber?" Amberdrake asked mildly.

"Gods! *And* Shaiknam!" Vikteren said bitterly, dropping his voice below a shout. The young mage snatched up a fallen branch as he reached them, and began methodically breaking it into smaller and smaller pieces. "Anthills and honey spring to mind—and harp-strings, delicate organs, and rocks! I thought this bigoted business with poor Zhaneel was bad enough—but now—!"

He struggled with the press of his emotions; clearly his rage was hot enough to choke him, and even Skan lowered his hackles and cocked his head to one side, distracted from his own state of rage by seeing Vikteren's. The youngster was one of the coolest heads in the mage-corps; he prided himself on his control under all circumstances. Whatever had happened to break that control must have been dreadful indeed.

"What happened?" Amberdrake asked anxiously, projecting calm now, as he had not with Skan. Not much, but enough to keep the young mage from exploding with temper.

Vikteren took several long, calculated breaths, closing his eyes, as his flush faded to something less apoplectic. "I heard Skan just now, and I have to tell you both that it isn't just his nonhuman troops that Shaiknam's been using up. He's been decimating everyone with the same abandon. I just talked to the mages from Sixth Command. We almost lost *all* of Sixth Crimson this morning, the mage included, because Shaiknam led them into an ambush that he'd been *told* was an ambush by his scouts. Ividian covered their retreat; he *died* covering that retreat, and it was all that saved them. Ividian *died!* And Shaiknam reprimanded the entire company for 'unauthorized maneuvers'! And I'm not just livid because Ividian was my friend. Shaiknam killed three more mages today—and he has the brass to claim it was *by accident.*"

Amberdrake let out his breath in a hiss, his gut clenched and his skin suddenly became cold. The loss of any portion of Sixth Crimson was terrible—and the loss of their mage dreadful. And all through prideful stupidity, like all of Shaiknam's losses.

But what Vikteren had just implied was more than stupidity, he had very nearly said that Shaiknam had murdered the other three mages. "How," he asked carefully, "do you kill a mage by accident?"

Vikteren's face flushed crimson again. "He forced them—ordered them—to exhaust themselves to unconsciousness. Then he *left them there,* where they fell. Ignored them. Got them no aid at all, not even a blanket to cover them. They died of power-drain shock where they lay. He said that there was so much going on at the time that he 'just forgot' they were there, but I heard someone say that he ordered them to be left alone, said if they were such powerful and mighty mages they could fix themselves. Called them weaklings. Said they needed to be taught a lesson."

Amberdrake and Skan both growled. That *was* more like murder-by-neglect. A mage worked to unconsciousness needed to be treated immediately, or he would die. Every commander knew that. Even Shaiknam.

There was no excuse. None.

"Shaiknam's a petty man, a *stupid* man—the trouble is he gives petty orders that do a lot of damage," Vikteren finished, his scarlet flush of anger slowly fading. "He has no compassion, no sense of anything outside of his own importance, no perspective at all. He used those three up just so he could recoup the losses he took on the retreat—*just* so that he wouldn't look bad! That was the *only* reason he ordered them to attack; they fought there against ordinary troops, there was no need for mage-weaponry!"

Vikteren took another deep breath and dropped the splinters still clenched in his hands. "I came to tell you two that there's going to be a meeting of all the mages tonight. We're going to tell Urtho that none of us are going to serve under Shaiknam or any other abusive commander, ever again.

We're tired of being treated like arbalests and catapults. I'm going to have a few things to say at that meeting, and before I'm done, you'd better believe they're going to follow my vote!"

"But *you* won't have a vote," Amberdrake protested. "You're just an apprentice—well, a Journeyman, but—"

But Vikteren snorted. "Hah! I'm not a Journeyman, I'm a full Master mage at the least, but my master never passed me up. He saw who was in charge and snarled the status on purpose so I'd work back here, and not get sent out on the lines to get killed by a fool. He saved my life today, that's how I feel. I could be a Master if I wanted to get slaughtered, and every mage in the army knows it."

Amberdrake glanced over at Skan, who nodded slightly. One Master mage could always pick out another. Well, that was certainly interesting, but not particularly relevant to their situation.

But Vikteren wasn't finished. "Dammit, Skandranon! We're not makaar, we're not slaves, and we're not replaced with a snap of the fingers! We're going to demand autonomy, and a say in how we're deployed, and I came to tell you that all the mages I've talked to think you gryphons ought to do the same! Maybe if both parties gang up on Urtho at once, he'll be more inclined to take us seriously!"

Skan's hackles went up again, and his claws contracted in the turf with a tearing noise. "We are *not* going to gang up on Urtho! He is my friend. Still—we might as well be stinking makaar," he rumbled. "While Urtho is the only one who can make our matings fertile, he holds all of us bound to him." Then in a hiss, "Much as I care for him, I could *hate* him for that."

Vikteren started. "What are you talking about?" he asked, obviously taken aback. "I've never heard of anything of the sort."

"Let me—" Amberdrake said hastily, before Skan could rouse back to his full rage. "Vikteren, it's because they're constructs. Urtho alone knows the controls, what triggers fertility, and what doesn't. Gryphons that survive a certain number of missions are the only ones permitted to raise a brood. There're some things only Urtho knows that trigger fertility, and they are different for male and female gryphons; both have to have something secret and specific done to them before their mating results in offspring—plus they have to make an aerial courtship display. Only if all three of those things happen do you have a fertile coupling."

"We can go through the motions of breeding as much as we like," Skan said tonelessly. "But without that knowledge, or that component that Urtho keeps to himself, it's strictly recreational." He shook his massive head. "Not only is it slavery, or worse than slavery, it's *dangerous*. There are never more than a tenth of us fertile at any one time. All it would take is one spell from Ma'ar—or for Urtho to die—and our race would die! You can't have a viable breeding population with only a tenth of the adults fertile! Even the breeders of hounds know that."

"But why?" Vikteren said, bewildered. "Why does he hold that over you?"

Skan sighed gustily. "I have no idea. None. We don't *need* to be controlled. Do you know how much we revere him? We'd continue to serve him the way the kyree do. We'd do it because he is *right*, and because we respect and care for him, not because he controls our destiny. We'd probably serve him better if he *didn't* control us like that. Damn! If he doesn't give it to us, maybe we ought to *steal* it."

"So—steal it? The spell, or whatever it is?" Vikteren said slowly. "That's not a bad idea." Amberdrake stared at him, not believing the mage had said anything so audacious even though the words had come out of his mouth.

"What good would that do?" Amberdrake asked. "If you need a mage to make it work—"

Skan closed his eyes for a moment, as if Vikteren's words had caused a series of thoughts to cascade. "About half of the gryphons are apprentice-level mages or better," he rumbled. "We are magical by nature. We wouldn't need a mage to cooperate with us. I'm a full Master, for instance."

"Even if you lacked for mages among yourselves, you'd find plenty of volunteers with the human mages," Vikteren insisted. "Do it, Skan! You're right! If he won't give it to you, steal the damn spell! And if you're a Master, then make the change permanent! Don't put up with being manipulated like this!"

Much to his own surprise, Amberdrake found himself agreeing.

Think of the families sundered by Ma'ar. They, who did not deserve such horrors, and now these gryphons you know and love cannot have families at all unless their lord wills it.

"Take your freedom, Skan," Amberdrake whispered. "Steal the spell, and teach it to everyone you trust."

Skandranon backwinged in place, then pulled himself up to his full, magnificent height.

The brisk wind from the Black Gryphon's wings sent Vikteren's hair into his face and kicked up a bit of dust that made Amberdrake squint for a moment.

"Stealing a spell from Urtho, though . . ." Vikteren's eyes lit up with a manic glee. "You know, that'd be nearly impossible? Not working the spell itself, that would be pretty simple, fertility spells nearly always are. No, it's the stealing part that would be hard. Getting into Urtho's Tower, getting past all the protections . . ."

From the look on Vikteren's face, he relished that very challenge and impossibility.

"It would not be impossible for *me*," Skan replied, his crest-feathers rising arrogantly.

But Amberdrake shook his head. "Be realistic, Skan. You've always flown directly to Urtho's balcony when you went to see him. You have no idea what safeguards are in that Tower, many of them built only for human hands. It would be impossible for you. But not for *us*."

"Us?" Skan asked, eyeing them both. Vikteren nodded gleefully, seconding Amberdrake.

"Exactly," the kestra'chern said with immense satisfaction, feeling as if the weight of a hundred gryphons was lifted off him. "Us."

In the end, the "us" also included Tamsin and Cinnabar. After a brief discussion, the means of bypassing all those special protections turned out to be absurdly easy.

Cinnabar crafted a message to be sent to Urtho *just* before

Urtho was to meet with the leader of the mages' delegation. She claimed that there were some problems she and Tamsin were encountering with gryphon anatomy—not even a lie!—and that she and he needed to consult the records on the gryphons' development so that they could tell what Urtho used for a "model."

She did not specify who she would have with her, only that she needed some "help."

"Urtho keeps records on everything he's ever done," she said, as they waited in her tent for the reply. She sat as calmly and quietly as if they were all her guests for an evening of quiet social chat and not gathered to perform what could, by some standards, be considered a major theft. Her hands were folded in her lap, and she leaned into Tamsin's shoulder, wearing an enigmatic little smile. Her pale green robes were as smooth and cool as tinted porcelain; beside her lover, she looked like an expensive doll propped next to a peasant-child's rag-toy. "I know he has extensive records on how he put your race together, and what he modeled you on. I specified 'internal problems,' which could be anything in the gut, and that's difficult stuff to muck about with when you don't know what you're doing. It isn't enough to be a Healer familiar with raptors in order to be successful with gryphons, even though that is *how* I became a default Healer to your people, Skan. You aren't all, or even mostly, raptoral. I'm counting on his being preoccupied with this mages' meeting; he should simply give us access to the Tower rather than taking the time to explain things to us in person."

"A pity about the timing on that," Skan observed dispassionately. "Vikteren did want to be here, and he has some—ah—unusual talents for a mage. He could have been very useful. Still, he will surely keep Urtho's attention at the meeting." The Black Gryphon lay along one side of the tent on Cinnabar's expensive carpet of crimson and gold, where the furniture had been cleared away for him. Until he moved or spoke, he looked like an expensive piece of sculpture, brought in to match the carpet. Or, perhaps, like a very expensive and odd couch.

Amberdrake chuckled. "Well, he'll be here in spirit, anyway," he said, patting his pocket where the bespelled lock-breaker Vikteren had loaned him resided. "It's just as well, given that we've been huddled together like conspirators for the whole afternoon. This way, if anyone has seen us all together, they can assume we won't do anything without him, and won't be watching us."

Tamsin laughed and reached across Cinnabar for a cup of hot tea. "You've heard too many adventure tales, kestra'-chern," he mocked. "Who would be watching us? And why? Even if Urtho catches us, the worst he'll do is dress us down. It's not as if we were trying to take over his Power Stone or something. We are not even particularly important Person-ages in this camp."

Skan raised his hackles at that. "Speak for yourself, Tam-sin!" he responded sharply. Tamsin only laughed, and Cinna-bar smiled a little wider.

Before a verbal sparring match could begin, one of Cinna-bar's hertasi scratched at the tent flap, then let herself in, handing the Lady a sealed envelope. Cinnabar opened it, read the contents, and nodded with satisfaction.

"As I thought," she said, to no one in particular. "Urtho is so caught up with the mages that he didn't even ask me what the complaint is. He's leaving orders to pass us into the Tower. We have relatively free access to the gryphon records; he warned me that some things have some magical protections on them, and that if I want to see them, I'll have to ask him."

"Which, of course, we will not," Amberdrake said. "Since we have other means of getting at them."

"So, you see, we didn't need all that skulking and going in through windows that you three wanted to do," Cinnabar replied, with just a hint of reproach in her voice.

"Lady, don't include me in that!" Amberdrake protested. "It was Tamsin, Skan, and Vikteren that wanted to go break-ing into the Tower! I knew better!"

"Of course you did," Tamsin muttered under his breath, as they all rose to go. "And *you* never collected ropes and equipment for securing prisoners. I don't even want to know why you conveniently had all that stuff on hand!"

Amberdrake raised an eyebrow and pretended not to hear

him, and simply rose with all of the dignity that years of practice could grant.

They all walked very calmly into the Tower, a massive and yet curiously graceful structure of smooth, sculpted stone. They gave a friendly nod to the guard on duty, and received one in return; very clearly he was expecting them. They didn't even need to make up some excuse for Amberdrake and Skan being with them. The guard didn't bother to ask why they were there.

There were no fences; the Tower didn't need them. It probably didn't need a human guard, either, but such things made mere mortals feel a little more comfortable around a mage like Urtho. The entrance was recessed into the Tower wall, and the door opened for them at the guard's touch. They passed out of the darkness and into a lighted antechamber, bare of all furnishings, with a mosaic of stone inlaid on the floor. Three doors led out of it; Cinnabar had been here before and she led the way.

Ah, bless the mages, Amberdrake thought yet again. *If it hadn't been for them—*

Then again, perhaps Lady Cinnabar would have found another excuse. She was a woman of remarkable resources, the Lady was.

The area where Urtho kept his records on the gryphons was several floors up, but all of them were fit enough that they didn't much mind the climb. The circular staircase was wide enough for Skan and, other than the fact that it was lit by mage-lights, seemed completely ordinary. It was constructed entirely of the native stone of the area, planed smooth, and fitted together so closely that the joins looked hardly wider than the blade of a knife.

However, as they reached the floor they wanted, a gently-curved door opened itself as they approached. All the other doors they had passed remained securely closed, with no visible means of opening them. They passed through that open door into an area of halls and cubicles, all lined floor-to-ceiling with books.

It certainly looked as if they'd found the right place. Amberdrake wondered how Urtho kept the air moving and fresh in a place like this; there was no more than a hint of dust in the air, no mold, and no moisture. If he stood very still, there *was* a gentle, steady current of air running past him, but where it came from and where it went he simply couldn't tell.

This place, too, glowed with mage-lights; a wise precaution with so many flammable books around.

Interesting that Cinnabar herself said we ought to simply take the secret without confronting Urtho. She knows him better than any of us. I wish I knew why she'd come to that conclusion, but she must have some reason to think he would have refused to give away his hold over the gryphons.

As a kestra'chern, Amberdrake's curiosity had been aroused by that. He could think of many possible motivations, but he would have liked to know which of them was the most likely.

So while Tamsin and Cinnabar perused the index to the record room to find the books on the gryphons' reproductive system, he browsed through the notations written on the spines of the books in search of clues.

Unfortunately, he didn't find any. The notations were all strictly impersonal, mostly dates or specific keywords to the contents. *Eggs, raptor, failure rate,* said one. *Breeding records, Kaled'a'in bondbirds.*

So he had a hand in that as well? Or did he just study what my people did?

Next to it, *Breeding records, Kaled'a'in horses.* Amberdrake had to chuckle at that. Just one book? Then Urtho had no real idea of what the Kaled'a'in were up to with their horse herds. Unless, of course, this was a very limited study of what they did with the warhorse breed.

That might be his only interest, but even so, Amberdrake doubted that the Kaled'a'in horsemasters had parted with their inmost secrets even for the mighty Urtho, Mage of Silence and their titular liege lord. Kaled'a'in Healers and Mages together worked on both the warhorses and the bondbirds—and while the results with the raptors might be more obvious, the ones with the horses were far more spectacular, though never to the naked eye.

The raptors had been given increased intelligence and curiosity, the ability to speak mind-to-mind with humans, and the ability to flock-bond to each other and to the humans who raised them. To compensate for the increased mass of brain tissue, and to make them more effective as fighting partners, they were larger than their wild counterparts.

But the horses had been changed in far more subtle ways. Bone density had been increased, hoof strength increased, in some cases extra muscles had been created that simply didn't exist in a "normal" horse. The digestion had been changed; the warhorses could forage where few other horses could feed, taking nourishment from such unlikely sources as thistle and dead or dried plants, like a goat or a wild sheep. As with the raptors, the intelligence had been increased, but one thing had been utterly changed.

The warhorses were no longer herd beasts. They were pack animals. Their behavior was no longer that of a horse, but like a dog. Properly trained, there was nothing they would not do for their riders—and unlike a horse, the rider could count on his mount to continue a command after the rider was out of sight. "Guard," for instance. Or "Go home."

Very few people knew this, or the amount of work it took to change a *behavior* set rather than a simple physical characteristic. Did Urtho?

He was reaching for the book when Cinnabar called him. Regretfully, he pulled his hand back. Another mystery that would remain unsolved, at least for now.

"We've found the book we want," Tamsin said, as he followed Cinnabar's voice into yet another book-lined cubicle. "Very nicely annotated in the index, with the fact that it contains the fertility formula. He refers to it as that, by the way, rather than an actual 'spell,' so Cinnabar and I are assuming that only a small part of it actually requires magic."

"That's good news for the gryphons, then," Skan said with interest, padding in from the opposite direction to Amberdrake. "If it only requires a little magic, most should be able to do it for themselves."

"As we expected, however, the book is mage-locked," Cinnabar interrupted, gesturing to a large leather-bound volume securely fastened with leather and metal straps. There were no visible locks, but then, there wouldn't be, not with a volume that was mage-locked.

But, thanks to Vikteren, that was not going to be a problem.

The "lock picks" didn't look like anything of the sort; rather, they looked like a set of inscribed beads of various sorts. "Urtho only uses about a dozen different spells to hold his ordinary magic books," Vikteren had said. "There aren't more than a hundred common spells of that sort in existence. Of course, there's always a chance he used something entirely new, but why? Most people don't know more than two or three mage-lock spells, even at the Master level. The chances that he'd use something esoteric for a relatively common book that he's going to *want* to consult easily are pretty remote."

Amberdrake had looked over the string of beads curiously. "So how many counterspells are there here?" he'd asked.

"Seventy-six," Vikteren had replied with a grin. "My Master is a Lock-master among his other talents. I paid attention. You never know when you may need to get into something."

"Or out of it," Amberdrake had remarked sardonically. But he'd taken the "picks."

Now it was just a matter of trying the beads against the place where all the straps met, one at a time. Vikteren had strung them in order—from the most common to the least, and that was how Amberdrake would use them. All it would take would be patience.

He didn't need to try more than a dozen, however; as he took the bead away and fingered up the next, the straps suddenly parted company, unfolding neatly down onto the stand, and leaving the book ready for perusal.

Cinnabar exclaimed with satisfaction, and flipped the cover open. "Ah, Urtho," she said with a chuckle. "Just as methodical as always. Indexed as neatly as a scribe's copy, and here's what we want on page five hundred and two."

She and Tamsin leafed rapidly through the pages and soon located the relevant formula. They planned to make two copies, just in case they were discovered; they would turn over one, but not the second, unless Urtho somehow *knew* that they'd made it.

Suddenly, Skan's head snapped up, alarm in his eyes, his crest-feathers erect and quivering.

"What is it?" Amberdrake whispered, afraid to make a sound. Was there a guard coming?

"There's—another gryphon up here!" Skan muttered, his head weaving back and forth a little, his eyes slightly glazed with concentration. "It's in the next room, but there's something wrong, something odd—"

Before Amberdrake could stop him, the Black Gryphon had snatched the lock-pick beads out of his hand. He turned and trotted down the hall to a doorway barely visible at the end of it.

Tamsin and Cinnabar became so engrossed in their copying that they didn't even notice Skan's abrupt departure. It was left to Amberdrake to chase after him and snatch the beads out of his talons as he shoved them in a bundle against the door lock.

"What are you trying to do?" he hissed, as the gryphon turned to look at him with reproach. "Do you *want* us to be discovered?"

"I—" Skan shook his head. "I just felt as if there was— something I should do about that other gryphon. It felt important. It felt as if I needed to get in there quickly."

Amberdrake did *not* make the scathing retort he wanted to. "And what if that was the point?" he asked, instead. "What if there is some kind of trap in there and this feeling of yours is the bait? We both know how tricky Urtho is! That's exactly the kind of thing he'd do!"

"He wouldn't be mad, at least not for long," Skan replied weakly. "I could talk him down."

"Until he figured out that we had taken his precious fertility formula!" Amberdrake retorted. "Now will you be sensible? Did you actually unlock that door?"

"I thought I heard a click," the Black Gryphon told him, with uncharacteristic meekness. "But I don't know, I could have heard the beads clicking together."

These were meant to unlock books, not doors—maybe nothing happened. "Look, Skan, whatever it is behind that door, it can wait until you have a chance to ask Urtho yourself. If he wants you to know, he'll tell you. You were supposed to be here, after all, and you can say you sensed another gryphon—then you can ask him what was going on. He'll probably tell you."

"Just like he's told me the fertility formula?" the gryphon replied scornfully, sounding *much* more like his usual self. He walked beside Amberdrake with his usual unnerving lack of sound. "Oh, please—"

"We're done!" Tamsin grinned. "We copied legitimate information to cover the notes on the fertility formula, if we meet Urtho on the way out and he asks. Let's get out of here. I'd rather not try and bluff him."

"Right." Amberdrake said. "Come on, Skan. You can solve mysteries later."

He stuffed the "picks" into a deep pocket, one full of other miscellaneous junk of the kind a kestra'chern often collected; bits of trim, loose beads, a heavy neck chain, the odd token or two. He hoped that among all that junk the beads would appear insignificant. And hopefully, Urtho, if they met him, would not check him over for magic.

He hurried down the hall to join the others, assuming Skan followed. The mage-lights extinguished in his wake, leaving darkness and silence behind him.

Kechara

Nine

Skan pushed the unlocked door open the tiniest bit. *Stupid gryphon. Stupid, stupid gryphon. Going to get yourself into trouble again. This time with your own side!* Skan shoved the door open a little more, carefully, listening, watching for moving shadows as he opened the portal, taking a huge breath of air and testing it for scents other than dust. His bump of curiosity was eating him alive. His weaker bump of caution was screaming at him to turn around and join the others on the staircase. As always, his bump of curiosity won.

Metal doors, and I wonder why! Never mind, Urtho's not going to like this, stupid gryphon. He puts locks on things for a reason.

Yes, but what could that reason be? Why would paternal, kindly Urtho hide something that called to him like a gryphon—only not quite? What if it was something important, something out of keeping with Urtho's kindhearted image? What if Urtho was as bad as Ma'ar beneath that absentminded and gentle exterior? After all, hadn't the Mage of Silence been withholding the fertility secret all this time? What if he was hiding something sinister?

Stupid and *paranoid, gryphon. Maybe you addled your brains when you struck the too-hard earth. It's been known to happen.*

Still. Just because you were paranoid, that did not mean your fears had no foundation. What if Urtho had no intention of giving the gryphons their fertility and their autonomy because he already had their replacement waiting in the wings, so to speak?

Some kind of super-gryphon, but one that wouldn't do such an inconvenient thing as begin to think for itself and hold its own opinions. A prettier sort of makaar?

Stupid, stupid gryphon. And if you find out that's really the case, what then? Take the chance that Urtho won't know and stay to tell the others, or fly away before he can catch you? If so, to where?

The door moved, slowly, a talon-width at a time. Then, suddenly, it swung open very quickly indeed, all at once, as if he had triggered something.

For a moment, he looked into darkness, overwhelmed by a wash of gryphon "presence," so strong that surely, surely it must be from *many* gryphons.

Then the lights came up, albeit dim ones that left the far walls in shadow-shrouded obscurity, and he found himself staring at—

Gryphon-ghosts!

That was his first thought; they hung in midair, floated, and he could see right through them. *They* were the source of most of the light in the room. Wasn't that the way ghosts were supposed to look? Surely they must be the source of the "presence" that had hit him so strongly!

But then he saw that they didn't move at all, they didn't even breathe; they stared into nothingness, with a peculiar lack of expression. *Not dead . . . but lifeless,* he thought. *As if they never lived in the first place.*

And as he continued to stare, it occurred to him that it wasn't only their *surface* that he saw, it was their insides, too! Every detail of their anatomy, in fact. If he concentrated on *stomach* when he stared at one, there would be the stomach, eerily see-through, suspended inside the transparent gryphon.

Fascinated now, if a trifle revolted, he stepped inside, and the door closed softly behind him.

They hung at about knee-height to a human above the floor, so that one could, if he chose, crawl under them to view the detail from below. Each one differed from the one next to it, some in trivial ways, some very drastically. Here was a rufous broadwing, like Aubri; there a dark gray gos-type, with the goshawk's mad red eyes, blazingly lifelike even in the lifeless face. There was the compact-bodied sun-tail that was best at flying cover—

They're all types. *I'm looking at* types *of gryphons! All of them, every kind I've ever seen! We aren't just one race, we're* many *races! Why did I never see that before? Is that why Urtho keeps the fertility secret to himself? Is he trying to keep the types pure?*

Dazed with the revelation, he wandered past another three of the transparent models, to find himself beak-to-beak with—

Zhaneel!

Only it wasn't Zhaneel at all, it was a creature with no personality. But there was her general build, her coloration and configuration.

He looked back along the line of gryphons, following them up to where he stood, and the Zhaneel-type. Back and forth he looked, a thought slowly forming in his mind. There was something about this line of gryphons, something that had struck an unconscious chord. What was it? Of course. The types that were closest to the door represented more numerous populations than the ones nearest him, and as far as he knew of the Zhaneel-type there was only Zhaneel—

Because she is the first?

That was it! This was a visual record of Urtho's entire breeding program! Zhaneel *wasn't* a freak, she wasn't mal-formed, she was the very first of an entirely new gryphon type!

Now—all those questions Urtho asked her, about her parents, her siblings, her training, they begin to make sense! Surely her parents knew that she was a new type—and if they had lived, they would have seen to it that she got special training for her special skills! But with them gone, she was left to flounder, and Urtho cannot remember everything—

As Urtho himself had reminded Skan. He could not re-member everything, and evidently he had forgotten that one, solitary gryphon of a new falcon type—

Amberdrake called her a gryfalcon!

—who survived, was alone, and needed an eye kept on her. Skan had been angry with Urtho, and now he was furious.

How could he have *done* that to her? Surely he knew what lay ahead of her when she didn't look anything like the others! Surely he knew how the gryphons felt about runts, sports, the "misborn."

But there was the war. How could he remember? He could only trust to his trainers to be clever and see that she was not some misborn freak, but something entirely new. It is as much their fault as his, if not more. His anger faded, he sighed and rounded the image of the gryfalcon.

And he looked upon his own feet, his own chest, his face. His own beak, eyes, and crest, lifeless, mutely staring through the living Skandranon.

The shock was a little less, this time. He was quicker to see that it was no more him than the other was Zhaneel. Still, the shock was of an entirely different sort; he was perfectly well able to think of the other gryphons as the end result of a breeding program, and even think of Zhaneel that way—but it was profoundly harder to think of himself in those terms.

It was, in fact, uncomfortable enough that he had to remind himself to resume breathing.

But as he studied the model, he took some comfort in noting that his proportions were rather better than its were. Especially in some specific areas.

And I'm definitely handsomer. Better-feathered. Smoother-muscled. Longer—

:FEAR-ALARM-ANGER!:

The emotion hit him like a boulder shot from a catapult, and before he could even get his mental "feet" underneath him, something physical hit him from behind. It hurtled from a place he had subconsciously noted was a doorframe, but had dismissed because there were no lights on the other side.

The strike sent his feet slipping out from under him, causing him to fall sideways through the image of himself. He tumbled into a wall, and his dancer's grace was not helping him in the least at the moment. Whatever wanted his hide was only about half his size, and it smelled like gryphon— only not *quite* like gryphon. It was muskier, earthier—

But this was no time to start contemplating scents! Whatever this was, it jumped him again and kicked his beak sideways into the wall. Only reflexes kept him from being blinded by the next slash—and then the assault began again.

This thing is like a wildcat! Too small to take me, and too crazy to know better. It just might hurt me bad. I don't like being hurt bad!

And if this is something of Urtho's—oh, damn and blast, I have to stop it without hurting it!

A scratch across his cere carried up over his eyes and sent blood down into them. He was momentarily blinded, but he blinked the haze away and rolled. He gathered his hindlegs under him, ignored the pain of the bites and claw-marks for a moment, then tucked both of his feet under its belly and heaved.

It tumbled into the other wall, without any sign of control, as if parts of it got tangled up with the rest of it. But it was game, that much was for certain; as soon as it stopped rolling, it sprang to its feet again and faced him, claws up and hissing.

It *was* a gryphon.

It was what Zhaneel had misnamed herself, something that the gryphons referred to as a "misborn." It was actually about a quarter of Skan's size, not half. Its head was small in proportion to its size, and very narrow, more like a true raptor's head than a gryphon or gryfalcons' broader cranium. The wings were far too long for its body, and they dragged the floor so badly that the ends of the primaries had been rubbed off by the constant friction.

In coloration, it was a dusty gray and buff. It was *that* which made Skan realize why it looked slightly familiar.

It was a misborn—of Zhaneel's type.

It was at that moment that it finally penetrated that the creature wasn't hissing. It was trying, and failing, to produce a true gryphonic scream of challenge.

He blinked again, clearing the blood from his eyes with the flight membranes. The powerful telepathic "presence" of *gryphon*, a presence so strong he had thought that it must come from several of his kind, was all emanating from this single small creature that valiantly tried to howl defiance at him.

The mental hammering of alarm-fear-rage had come and was still coming from it.

Skan had reared instinctively into a fighting stance while his mind was putting all this together. The misborn looked up at him—four times larger than it was—

Its eyes widened for a moment, and it cringed.

But in the next second, it had gone back into a defensive posture. The intensity of its mental radiations increased, and Skan dropped back a little. It wasn't consciously attacking him with those thoughts, but they were strong. Very strong.

The moment he dropped back, it glanced to the side and scrambled away, into the next room. Lights came on in there as it entered, leaping up onto a table with incredible speed considering how clumsy it was. It scattered books and instruments in all directions with its too-long wings, and reared up again from the advantage of this greater height.

"Bad! Bad!" the thing hissed. "Go away!"

Skan forced himself to relax, and got down out of his fighting posture. The bites and claw-marks stung, but his injuries weren't *that* bad, no worse than he got when playing with a rowdy bunch of fledglings. This poor little thing was obviously scared witless.

"What—ah—who are you?" he asked carefully. It *did* have enough language to tell him to go away; surely it would understand him.

"Go away!" it hissed again, feinting with a claw. "Go away! Where is he? Did you hurt him?"

It reared up again into a ridiculous parody of full battle display, and it was clear that its anger was overwhelming its fear. But why was it so frightened and angry? And who was "he?" "I hurt you!" it tried to shriek. "I hurt you! I will!"

Skan was completely bewildered, and he could only hope that there was some kind of sense behind all this. If the creature was completely mad, he would have to render it unconscious or trap it before he could make his own escape, and he really didn't want to hurt it.

Urtho be damned; it would be like hurting a cat defending its litter. This creature doesn't know what I am and that I don't intend any harm—and unless I can get that through to it, I don't think it's going to stop attacking me.

"Hurt who?" he asked. "I haven't hurt anyone; I haven't even *seen* anyone here! Hurt who? Urtho? Who are you?"

He put his ear-tufts and hackles flat, and gryph-grinned, trying to look as friendly as possible. Evidently it worked, for the little creature stared at him for a moment, then suddenly sat down on the shredded desk blotter. It came out of its battle posture, instantly deflating, and wiped its foreclaws free of Skandranon's blood. "Not bad?" it asked plaintively, its anger gone completely. "Not hurt Father? Where *is* Father?"

Father! What on earth can this creature mean! Surely no other gryphons have ever been up here; no one could keep a secret like this for long! No, of course there haven't been any gryphons here, otherwise this little thing would recognize me for one.

He looked around at the room for clues who "Father" was, but there weren't any; just the table with odd bits of equipment and a few books and papers, an old cabinet that looked mostly empty, and a sink. In fact, it looked more like a Healer's examination room than anything.

"No," he said persuasively. "I'm not bad. I haven't hurt anyone. I just opened up a door and came inside." He edged a little closer to the creature as it relaxed. "Who is Father? Who are you?"

"Father is Father," the creature replied, as if stating the obvious for a very slow child. "Father calls me Kechara."

Skan moved right over to the table and sat beside it, which put him just about beak-to-beak with the little one. "Tell me about Father, Kechara," he said softly. "Everything you can. All right? There are a lot of people where I come from, and I need you to tell me what Father looks like so I know which person he is."

Kechara (which meant "beloved" or "darling" in Kaled'-a'in) was a female, as near as he could tell. It might have been more appropriate to say that Kechara was a neuter, for she had none of the outward sexual characteristics of a female gryphon. That peculiar muskiness of hers was not a sexual musk, just an odd and very primitive scent.

"Father comes here, Father goes," Kechara told him. "Father bring me treats. Father brings toys, plays with me. He not here for a while, and I play."

"What does Father look like, Kechara?" Skan asked. The little creature wrinkled up its brow with intense thought. "Two legs, not four," it said hesitantly. "No wings, no feathers. No beak. Has—long stuff, not grown, not feathers, over legs and body. Skin, smooth skin, here—" it pawed its face. "—long crest-hair here—" it ran its paws down where the scalp would be on a human. "And Father makes pretty cries when he comes, so I know he here. Cries like songbirds, and he dances with me."

That clinched it; the only person that would come into this area that whistled was Urtho. Oddly enough, Skan had noticed that most mages couldn't whistle. Vikteren and Urtho were the only exceptions in this camp.

"How long have you been here?" he asked, trying to get some sense of how long Urtho had concealed the creature here.

But it just stared at him blankly, and when he rephrased the question several times, Kechara could only say that there was nothing else *but* here, for her. Only Father went somewhere else.

Which meant that Urtho had confined this poor thing to this section of his Tower for her entire life. There were places Urtho had taken her where she could look out through windows, which was how she had seen and heard songbirds, but that was the closest she had come to the outdoors.

For a scant heartbeat, Skan was outraged. But after attempting a few more questions with Kechara, he understood why Urtho had thought it better to keep her here.

She couldn't possibly function in normal gryphon society without protectors. She couldn't *do* anything productive. Zhaneel had been made fun of as she grew up, and she was marvelous. This poor thing would be tormented if there wasn't always someone watching out for her. Zhaneel was highly intelligent, resilient, and capable of remarkable things; this little one wouldn't even know how to defend herself without risking injuring herself.

She seemed to be very much on the same level of intelligence as some of Urtho's enhanced animals, and the biggest difference between her and one of those animals was that she had a rudimentary ability to speak. She didn't seem to have much of a concept of time, either. She never actually lost track of the conversation, but sometimes there was a long wait between when he asked a question and she answered it, a wait usually punctuated by a short game of chase-her-shadow.

Then again, that might not be a lack of intelligence, that might be because she hasn't had anyone to model her behavior on but Urtho. The winds only know he's done the same thing.

He coaxed her down off the table and into taking a short walk with him since she seemed restless and kept fidgeting when he talked with her. After that, the conversation seemed to flow a little better; she bounded ahead or lagged back with him as he strolled through the gallery of "models." She paid them no attention whatsoever, which didn't much surprise him. She must be as used to them by now as he was to the messenger-birds or Amberdrake's eye-blinding clothing.

But suddenly, as they drew opposite the "Skandranon" type of model, she looked from it to him and back again, as if she could not believe her eyes. She blinked, shook her head, and looked again.

"That *you!*" she said, as if she'd had a major revelation.

"Oh, it does look something like me," he replied casually. "Just a bit." He left it at that, and she promptly seemed to forget about it.

A moment later, she made a dash into another room, and once again, the lights came up as she entered. She headed straight for a bowl sitting beside what must have been her bed, a nicely made nest of bound straw lined with soft, silky material. There was a box with a pile of brightly-colored objects in it; toys, probably. The top ones looked like the normal sorts of balls and blocks that young gryphlets were given to play with as nestlings, before they fledged. She grabbed for a clawful of something brown and moist—then, like a child suddenly remembering its manners, she shyly offered him some of it—her food, presumably. It did not look like much, and Skan declined, although Kechara wolfed it down with every evidence of enjoyment.

I can't tell how old she is, he thought, watching her eat. She did manage that fairly well; gryphons were not the daintiest of eaters at the best of times. *She has no idea of the passage of time, she can't see the rising and setting of the sun from in here. She eats when she's hungry, sleeps when she's tired, and Urtho comes and goes at unpredictable intervals. But if I were to guess—misborns don't tend to live very long, and I'd guess she's near the end of her "normal" lifespan.*

The notion revolted him as much as the food had. All her life had been spent in close confinement, never feeling the free wind, only seldom seeing the sky, the sun, the moon and the stars.

When she was bred *for the skies, and only accident and bad fortune made her the way she is, and not like Zhaneel—*

—or like—me—

He ground his beak a little in frustration. Then there was the other side of the rock. How could she live outside? Maybe that was precisely why she was in here, because she *couldn't* live outside the Tower. Misborn were also notoriously delicate, prone to disease, weaknesses of the lungs and other organs.

Maybe only living here in complete shelter made it possible for her to live at all.

This may be kindness, but it has a bitter taste.

He noticed that all of his earlier bleeding had stopped, and that reminded him of his own internal time sense. He was surprised at how long he had been in here with her. "I must go, Kechara," he said at the first break in conversation. Such as it was.

She blinked at him for a moment. Then she asked him something completely unexpected. "You come back?" she asked hopefully. "You come play again?" And she looked up at him with wide and pleading eyes.

Oh, high winds and rock slides! She may not know the emotion for what it is, but she's lonely. *What can I tell her?*

He ground his beak for a moment, then told her the truth.

"I don't know, Kechara. I have to talk to Father first. He makes the rules, you know."

She nodded, as if she could accept that. "I ask Father, too," she said decisively. "I tell him I need you to play with me."

Then, as he paused at the door, she reared up on her haunches and spread her forelegs wide. It was such a *weird* posture that at first Skan could not even begin to imagine what she was up to. But then he understood. She was waiting for a hug, a human hug. The kind she always got from "Father" when he left her.

That simple gesture told Skan all he needed to know; whatever Urtho's motives were in keeping this little thing here, they were meant to be kindly, and he gave her all the affection he could.

It was awkward, but somehow Skan managed. Then he gave her a real gryphonic gesture of parting, a little preening of her neck hackles.

It would have been much worse if she had put up some kind of a fuss about his leaving, but she didn't; she simply waved a talon in farewell, and turned and trotted back to her nest room, presumably to play by herself.

She's learned that fussing doesn't change anything, he decided, as he walked stunned through the book rooms and touched the door to the staircase to open it. *She's learned that people come and go in her life without her having any control over where and when they do it. Poor thing. Poor little thing.*

The lights dimmed behind him as he made his way down the stairs; slowly, for staircases were difficult for gryphons to descend, although climbing them was no real problem. When he got to the bottom, he was very tempted to try one of the other doors in the antechamber.

Stupid gryphon! Don't tempt your luck. You'll be in enough trouble with Urtho as soon as you bring up Kechara.

Oh, dear. That made another problem. *How do you bring up Kechara without revealing you got into a locked room? And if you got into a locked room, how much else would he guess you got into?*

The guard nodded to him and grinned as he left. "Damned hard for you critters to manage staircases, eh?" he said, as

Skan realized that some of his injuries from the spat with Kechara must *surely* be visible.

And he hadn't come in with fresh scratches on him.

But the guard had just offered him a fabulous excuse for his appearance, and he seized it with gratitude. "More than damned hard," he grumbled. "I must've slipped and fallen once for every dozen steps. And would the others wait? Hell, no! They were in such a hurry to scuttle off with their Healer-stuff that they didn't even notice I was lagging!"

The guard laughed sympathetically and patted Skan on the shoulder. "Know how you feel," he replied. "With this gimpy leg I can't even climb *one* staircase good anymore. Never much thought about how you critters managed until I got that crossbow bolt through the calf."

Some chat might not be a bad cover at the moment, and I don't really have anywhere to go . . . Tamsin and Cinnabar will be deciphering the text they copied and putting it into terms we gryphons can use. They'll be so busy with that they wouldn't know if I was there or not.

"Kyree and hertasi can manage all right," he replied. "But us, the dyheli, the tervardi—staircases are hell, and other things are worse! You'd think with all the veterans hurt that can't walk that they'd put in some ramps. But *no*—"

The guard sighed. "Well, that's the way of the world, everybody sees it according to what *he* needs. If a man don't need a special way up the stairs, why, he don't think nobody else needs it, neither."

Skan snorted. "You figured that right, brother! And my bloody aching head agrees with you, too!"

"Best run along and catch up with those Healer friends of yours, an' make 'em patch you up," the guard advised. "Maybe then they'll think twice before they rush off an' leave you alone!"

Skan laughed and promised he would do that; the guard limped on his rounds with a friendly wave as Skan headed back toward camp, and Healer's Hill.

All right, I'd better get this all in order. We'll get the fertility spell straight; I'll pass it on to the rest. Then, once I know everyone has it—I'll come to Urtho and tell him what I did. That's when I bring up Kechara. That would take a few days at the best, and his conscience bothered him about leaving her alone in there for so long—

But she's been alone in there for all of her life. A few days, more or less, will make no difference.

There was an additional complication, however. What if Urtho made a visit to his—well—pet? If Kechara happened to mention Skan—

I'll have to hope that she doesn't. Or if she does, Urtho just thinks she's talking about the models.

Complications, complications.

Stupid gryphon. You're trying to do too much too fast. But doesn't it need to be done? If not you, then who?

The walk down to the camp was a long one. There weren't many people out at this time of night. Most of the ones still awake were entertaining themselves; the rest had duties, or were preparing their gear for combat tomorrow. It was a peculiar thing, this war between wizards; the front lines were immensely far away, and yet the combat troops bivouacked here, below Urtho's stronghold, in the heart of his lands.

It was the Gates that made such things possible, the Gates and the gryphons.

The first meant that Urtho could move large numbers of troops anywhere at a moment's notice. There were even permanent Gates with set destinations that did not require anything more than a simple activation spell, something even an apprentice could manage. Because of this, Urtho's troops were highly mobile, and the problem of supply lines was virtually negated.

Of course, that was true for Ma'ar's men as well. The defender had the advantage in a situation like this. A mage setting up a Gate had to *know* the place where he intended it to go, and Urtho or his mages knew every inch of the territory he was defending. Ma'ar's mage could only set up Gates where they had been, places that they *knew*, so Ma'ar's Gates would always be behind his lines.

There had even been one or two successful forays early on in the campaign where Urtho had infiltrated troops *behind* Ma'ar's. That, however, would only work once or twice before your enemy started setting watches for Gate-energies, in order to blast the Gate as it was forming. This tended to cost your mage his life as the energies lashed him at a time when he was wide open and vulnerable. That was why Urtho's forces didn't do that any more, and there wasn't a mage in the entire army who would obey an order to do so.

Not that Shaiknam hasn't tried. But only once.

The gryphons were the other factor that made this war-at-a-distance possible. Aloft, they could cover immense stretches of territory, and their incredibly keen vision allowed them to scout from distances so high that not even the makaar would challenge them unless they were in the very rare situation where they were at a greater altitude than the incoming gryphon. Makaar were not built for the winds and the chill of high altitude; there were gryphons who were, though they were not the best fighters.

And there were gryphons built for long-distance scouting who had ways of overcoming their physical shortcomings that made them poor choices for combat. The one who could do it best was Zhaneel.

One gryphon, anyway. Maybe . . . one day, more.

As Skan took to the air for the brief flight to Healer's Hill, his sharp eyes picked out the glow of the tent shared by Tamsin and Cinnabar. *Hard at work already. They may even have it by the time I get there. Good.*

The Black Gryphon used a thermal to kite in that direction, appreciative that the night was so clear and calm. He noted that Amberdrake's tent was also aglow.

Hard at work, too! He chuckled. *Well, the night usually is when most of his work is done. He bears the hearts of many, mine included. He is there when he is needed, even this late at night. I shall not tease him about it.*

This *time!*

Winterhart

Ten

Amberdrake did not notice that Skan wasn't behind them on the stairs until they reached the outside of the tower, beyond the antechamber. That was when he turned to say something to the Black Gryphon—

And the Black Gryphon wasn't there.

They were already beyond the immediate perimeter of the Tower. Amberdrake swore under his breath. It was too late to go back and get him; the doors probably wouldn't admit them a second time, and the guard would wonder what was going on when they returned, looking for Skan.

A light breeze blew at Amberdrake's back, and camp sounds carried up from the tents below. It would be better to go back to his tent and go on with the plan as if nothing was out of the ordinary. Gryphons had a hard time with staircases. With luck, the guard knew that. Maybe he would figure that Skan was still inching his way down, step by painful step.

Not that Skan had any trouble with staircases, spiral or otherwise. He was as graceful as a cat under any circumstances. It was the dancing that did it; Amberdrake had seen him climbing trees, eeling through brush and scaling the outside of tower walls with equal ease and panache. But Amberdrake was one of the few people who knew that.

Amberdrake lingered in the shadows as Tamsin and Cinnabar hurried on ahead. He waited on the off chance that his friend might simply be sauntering along as if time had no meaning. *He's been known to do that . . . "It's image," he says.*

Skan still did not appear. Whatever he was doing, it was not just a case of lagging behind. *Where the hell is that idiot featherhead?* he thought with irritation. *Caught up in his own reflection somewhere?*

Far more likely that he had found some book that had caught his eye and was leafing through it, oblivious to the time. Amberdrake could only hope that it was something as innocent as a book that had detained him.

But time was running out, for Amberdrake at least. Wherever he was, whatever he was doing, the Black Gryphon would have to make his own excuses, and bail himself out of any trouble he got into. Amberdrake could not wait any longer. He had an appointment; a last-minute appointment set up by Urtho himself. This was not a client to keep waiting.

Especially not tonight. If he broke that appointment, or was even a tiny bit late for it, *someone* might put that together with Tamsin and Cinnabar's request, ask the guard who had been with them, and put two and two together and figure they had all been up to something. And that *someone* would probably be Urtho.

Skandranon was a big gryphon; he could take care of himself. If he had been asked, that is exactly what he would have said.

The way back to camp was as clear as the night sky; with no one in sight anywhere close. That meant there was no one to take note if he broke into a sprint and wonder why he was running—or at least not close enough to recognize a distant runner as Kestra'chern Amberdrake. He took off at a lope, and didn't pause until he was just within sight of his own tent.

I'm in better shape than I thought, he thought, with pardonable pride, as he composed himself before making his "entrance," right on time. *I'm not even out of breath.*

Fortunately, his hertasi assistant, Gesten, would have everything he needed for this client prepared for him ahead of time. It had been a very long time since Amberdrake had performed the simple chores that surrounded his profession—getting out the massage table, warming the oils, putting towels in the steamer, preparing incense. Simple chores, but time-consuming. Things it would be impossible to take care of before a client came, if the kestra'chern in question happened to be doing something he didn't want anyone to know about. For instance, in case a kestra'chern absolutely had to snoop around in the Great Mage's Tower.

Thank goodness for hertasi.

The client was not waiting, which could mean a number of things. She could simply be late; she might be a little reluctant to go to a kestra'chern; new clients often were, until they realized how little of a kestra'chern's work had to do with amorous dealings. That was fine; it meant he had time to change into his work clothes in peace. He *could* have done a massage in his current outfit, but he didn't want to. He had a reputation to uphold, and much of that reputation involved his appearance. Clients should see him at his very best, for that was what he always gave them.

So he pushed the draperies aside and slipped into his private quarters; quickly shed the clothing he had on and donned one of the three appropriate massage-costumes that Gesten had laid ready for him. Tunic and breeches again, but of very soft, thick, absorbent material in a deep crimson with vivid blue trim. The cut was more than loose enough to permit him to take whatever contortion was required to give his client relief from stressed or sore muscles. And in the soft lighting of the tent, it looked opulent, rich, *special.* That would make the client feel special as well.

He braided his long hair up out of the way, but fastened the ends of the braids with small chiming bells which would whisper musically when he moved. He had found that the rhythmic chiming that followed the motions of the massage soothed his clients.

The new client still had not appeared when he moved back to the "business" side of the tent, so he double-checked on Gesten's preparations. Not that he had any doubt of Gesten's thoroughness, but it never hurt to check. The laws of the universe dictated that the one time he did *not* check, something would be missing.

The bottles of scented oil, already nicely up to temperature, waited in their pan of warm water. The hot stones had been set in the bottom of the towel-warming chest, and the steam that rose from the cracks in the upper portion, carrying with it the scent of warm, clean cloth, told him that all was in readiness there as well. The massage table had been unfolded and covered with a soft pad, of course, and a crimson chair was beside it in case the client was too stiff or sore to be able to get on it without assistance.

The wooden rollers were ready; so were the warming ointments for after the massage, in case the muscles needed herbal therapy. There was a pot of vero-grass tea steeping in case he needed to get her to relax beforehand.

And, most importantly for a new and possibly shy client, all the other tools of his many trades had been packed away out of sight. Most of them, in fact, currently cluttered up his private quarters. The only hint that he might not be a simple Healer was the incense in the air, the opulent hangings, and the scattering of pillows around the floor.

He prowled the room anyway, rearranging the pillows, making *certain* that nothing had been left out by accident, checking the oils to be certain they hadn't gone the least tiny bit rancid. It was all energy-wasting, and he knew it, but the energy he was wasting was all from nerves, and it was his to waste if he chose.

He wouldn't have been here, now, if he'd had any other choice. He'd be waiting outside the Tower for Skan or lurking outside the mages' meeting.

I wish I knew what was going on at the meeting, he thought fretfully. *I wonder if the hertasi have anyone there? If they do, Gesten will know the results as soon as they let out. Maybe before. I hope so—but of course Vikteren will tell me whatever happened.*

Gods, I hope Skan got out of the Tower without tripping some alarm or other. I hope the guard doesn't figure he was up to something. I hope he wasn't up to something. He simply spotted a book he could not resist, I'm sure. I hope Tamsin and Cinnabar really can find a way to give the gryphons their fertility....

Mental nattering, really. Fretting over things he could not control and could not change was a habit of his. If he could change something, he did so; if he couldn't, he fretted it to pieces in hopes of finding a way he *could* affect the situation.

Fortunately he didn't have time to work himself up over either the mages' meeting or Skan; Gesten finally poked his nose through the door flap and motioned someone inside.

A female, but Amberdrake knew that already. But now he knew why Urtho had not specified *who* was coming, in making this appointment.

Stiff, severe posture, mathematically precise hair, with three thin braids down the back of her neck, pinched expression, perfectly pressed and creased utilitarian clothing— *Winterhart!* Oh, gods.

His shoulder muscles tensed, and his head started aching. He stopped his lip from curling with distaste just in time and dropped his mask of impassiveness into place.

I am a professional. Urtho sent her to me, and the fee he included should quite cover the fact that she is a pain in the tail. I can take care of her without becoming the least involved. She is only here for physical therapy. I don't have to know her inmost secrets, I don't even have to speak more than a dozen words to her.

All that flashed through his mind, as he altered his expression into a carefully indifferent and businesslike smile. She was moving very stiffly, more so than he remembered, and it wasn't all because she was not happy to be here. What had the note Urtho sent said? *Back injury.* Interesting; she was far stiffer than even a back injury would account for.

I don't have to open up to her to know that she is as tense as a cocked catapult. It's written in every muscle. I can't work on her like that, and she is not going to relax. . . .

Interesting; I don't think she recognizes me as having been with Skan. Maybe the dim light is working for me.

There was certainly no sign of recognition in her eyes— and then, there was recognition, but no sudden pulling back that would indicate she realized he had watched while Skan and Zhaneel made her look the fool.

Well, that tenseness was the reason there was vero-grass tea steeping. She wouldn't be the first client who had come to a kestra'chern too tense to get any benefit from the visit.

"You look thirsty," he said quickly as she looked around suspiciously. "Please, do drink this tea before we begin. It will help you."

And as a Trondi'irn should know, vero-grass was thick with minerals; someone with a back injury was in need of minerals.

She accepted the cup of tea dubiously, waved aside his offer of honey to sweeten it, and took a sip. Her eyes widened as she recognized what it was, but she said nothing; she simply gulped it down.

Grimly, he thought. As if she dared him to do his worst.

Well, he wouldn't do his worst, he would do his *best*, and to hell with her and her opinions.

"I'd like you to disrobe, please," he said, taking the cup away from her and placing it out of the way. "And lie on the table."

Winterhart had not known until she stepped into this tent that Urtho had ordered her to the hands of a kestra'chern. But she knew Amberdrake by sight—it seemed that he was always messing about with the Healers and the gryphons in one way or another—and she knew what his profession was.

She had *thought* she was being sent to a minor, unGifted Healer for her back problems—on Urtho's direct orders of course, and after that rather painful interview following the altercation with Zhaneel. How the Mage had wormed the fact of her injury out of her, she had no idea.

Then again, she had told him any number of things that she hadn't intended to, and that was only one of them. At least the fact of the injury and the pain she was in had apparently saved her from a reprimand; Urtho evidently counted it as a reason for her irritation with the world in general and gryphons specifically.

When he had told her that—and that he was ordering her to get treatment that he himself would schedule, she had been resentful, but just a little relieved.

Now she was resentful, not at all relieved, angry—and truth to tell, more than a little frightened. Angry that Urtho had set her up like this without telling her. Resentful that he had interfered in her private life, arbitrarily assuming that there was something wrong with her sexual relations and setting her up with a kestra'chern.

And frightened of what could happen at the hands of this particular kestra'chern.

She had heard very embarrassing things about kestra'chern in general and this Amberdrake in particular, stories that would curl the hair of any well-born young woman with a sense of decency. Amberdrake had a reputation for things that were rather—*exotic.* Conn Levas had used the fact that he had gone to this particular kestra'chern to taunt her with her inadequacies, and the things *he* had said had gone on here were considerably more than exotic.

And worst of all, she had *no* clue what Urtho had ordered for her . . . treatment.

If anyone back in her wing found out she was here, she would never hear the end of it.

And her back *still* hurt! That was reason enough to wish herself elsewhere!

The gods only know what's going to happen to my back if—if— She found herself flushing and resenting her own embarrassment. *A lot of arching would be very bad for my spine right now. And I doubt he has any notion of that.*

Her suspicions hardened into certainty when she recognized the taste of the vero-grass tea. It was a calmative, yes, but it also had a reputation for enhacing other things than calm. But it *was* a muscle relaxant as well, and right now. . . .

Right now, my back needs it badly enough that I'll drink the damned stuff, she thought grimly. *Maybe he thinks that if he drugs me enough, I'll be too limp to stop him. Huh. Not with* this *back. One cup of tea isn't going to do worse than take the edge off the pain.*

Then he looked at her as if he was sizing her up for purchase, and said, "Disrobe and get on the table, please."

She stared at him, utterly taken aback, as much by his clinical coldness as by the words. Wasn't there supposed to be some—well—*finesse* involved here?

She looked from Amberdrake to the table, and back again. "You want me to *what?*" she asked, still stunned.

Amberdrake sighed with exasperation. What was wrong with the stupid woman? Couldn't she understand that in order to massage her he would have to have her unclothed and on the table? Surely she didn't think he could do anything with her standing in the middle of the room like a statue!

"You *are* who Urtho sent me, aren't you?" he asked, with just a touch of irony.

She swallowed, but with difficulty. "Yes—" she replied.

"And you *do* have a back injury, do you not?" he persisted. What was going on in her mind?

She answered with more reluctance than before. "Yes—"

He sighed with open exasperation, which seemed to annoy her. Well, good. Up until this moment, *he'd* been the one who was annoyed. Let *her* enjoy the sensation for a change. "Then please, lady, let me help you, as I was assigned to do. I cannot help you if you will not disrobe and get on the table."

"Help me *how?*" she replied sharply, her eyes darting this way and that. "I thought I was being sent to a Healer!"

He gritted his teeth so hard it hurt. "You *have* been sent to a Healer," he replied, allowing his tone to tell her that there was *no doubt* that he was exasperated. "Apparently, you are not aware that a human cannot be effectively massaged through her clothing. If you would rather this were done by someone other than myself, you are quite free to leave. But *you* can explain to Urtho why you walked out on this rather expensive session. *I* perform my services in a professional manner, even with reluctant clients—and the services I intended to perform on you are entirely different from the ones I think you have imagined."

Beneath his calm, cool exterior he was seething, and his back teeth jammed so tightly together that it was a wonder they didn't split. *Another gods-be-damned, pure-as-rain Healer. I should have known she'd react this way. Tamsin and Cinnabar were only too accurate in the way they described her. Bright Keros, how much more am I going to have to put up with this kind of nonsense? I'm besieged, truly I am!*

And as for Winterhart the Pure—well, from the pinched look on her face, I'd say she's certainly living down to her reputation as the Princess of Prim and Proper.

She hadn't budged a thumblength since he'd begun talking, and if his muscle readings were correct, she was so tense that he was rather mildly surprised that her eyes weren't bulging out.

And it was all too obvious that she not only didn't believe he was a Healer, she was certain it was just some kind of a ploy to take advantage of her.

As if I'd want to. I like my partners willing, thank you.

His headache worsened. Wonderful. It wasn't just *his* headache, it was coming from her as well. No wonder she had a pinched and sour look to her.

Now how do I convince her that I am a Healer? Chop off Gesten's hand and fuse it back on? I wonder if Her Majesty the Ice-Maiden here would even react to that! She and that steel-necked lover of hers deserve each other. If Urtho hadn't sent her to me, I'd invite her to take herself and her token back to her tent.

But outwardly, years of practice kept so much as a stray expression from crossing his face. "I am no threat to your— virtue—and I do assure you that you can relax. This is a massage table. I am to work on your back injury, and perhaps see if it is something that I can Heal. It is that simple." He patted the table and smiled a cool and professional smile.

She shifted her weight uneasily and moved ever so slightly away from the tent flap and toward the table.

If that's the best she can do, we're going to be here all night before she gets on *the damned table!*

"Massage," he repeated, as if to a very simple child. "I am very good at it. Lady Cinnabar will not have anyone else work on her but me."

That earned him another couple of steps toward the table; he closed his eyes for just a moment, and counted to ten. She was turning what should have been a simple session into an ordeal for both of them!

"If you are body-shy with a stranger, I will turn my back while you disrobe. You may drape yourself with the sheet that is folded beside the table," he said; he pointed out the sheet to her, and turned away.

The sound of clothing rustling told him that he had finally convinced her of his sincerity, if not his expertise.

His head was absolutely pounding with shared pain; he shielded himself against her, and it finally ebbed a bit. That was a shame. He generally didn't need to shield himself against a fellow-Healer, and allowing his Empathy to remain wide-open generally got him some useful information. Remaining that way also improved his sensitivity to what was going on with injuries and pain and helped him block it; before a client even realized that something hurt, he would be able to correct the problem and move on.

Correct the problem. Well. Unfortunately, he could very well imagine why Urtho had sent the woman *here.* The few notes he had on her indicated some trauma in her life that she simply had not faced—something that she had done or that had been done to her. Trondi'irn were generally not so busy they disregarded their own health. There was the possibility she was punishing herself by leaving her conditions unattended, or worsening them in her mind. Oh, he had no doubt that there was a real, physical injury there as well, but the way she acted told him that this was not a healthy, well-adjusted woman. Urtho must have seen that, too; here was the implied message in his sending her here.

You're supposed to Heal minds, so Heal this one.

What had Urtho said about her?

That she had abusive parents. But the signs are all wrong for them to have been physically abusive. . . .

Urtho was known for having a very enlightened idea of what constituted "abuse."

No, this woman hadn't been mistreated or neglected physically. But emotionally—ah, there was the theory that fit the pattern.

I would bet a bolt of silk on cold, demanding parents, who expected perfection—and got it. Very little real affection in her life, and most of it delivered when she managed, somehow, to achieve the impossible goals her parents set. Yes, that fits the picture.

And now, she was as demanding of everyone else as her parents had been to her. More than that, she was as demanding of herself as they used to be.

Well, that was why she would have gotten involved with an arrogant manipulator like that mage in the first place.

She doesn't see herself as "deserving" anyone who cares, so she picks someone who reminds her of what she grew up with. And then treats him the same, since she never learned to do otherwise.

He ran his fingers across his forehead as the creaking of the table behind him told him he had managed to convince her to trust him that far. *I can't undo decades of harm in a few candlemarks. Start with the easy stuff and release the pain. Then take it from there.*

Amberdrake turned back to find her on her stomach, draped from neck to knee with the sheet, as modest as a village maiden. He selected one of the oils, one with a lavender base; that would be clean and fresh enough to help convince her that he was not going to seduce her. Then, before she could react, he turned the sheet down with brisk efficiency worthy of Gesten, poured some of the oil in his hands to warm it, then rubbed his palms together. A moment later, he was kneading the muscles of her back and shoulders.

He had not been boasting; he was particularly good at massage. Lady Cinnabar *did* prefer his services to anyone else in or out of the camp. Slowly, as he worked the knots of tension out of her back and shoulders, he sensed other tension ebbing. His expertise at massage was convincing her that he was, at least in part, what he claimed to be.

Some of the barriers she was holding against him came down. But he did not take immediate advantage of the altered situation.

No, my dear Icicle; I intend to show you that I am everything I said I was and a lot more besides.

You are a challenge. And I never could resist a challenge. And Urtho, damn his hide, knows that.

When Winterhart realized that the man really did know what he was doing—at least insofar as massage was concerned—she let the fear ebb from her body. The more she relaxed, the more his hands seemed to be actually soothing away the pain in her poor back.

Odd. I always thought massage was supposed to be painful. . . .

In fact, it was so soothing that she felt herself drifting

away, not quite asleep, but certainly not quite awake. Several moments passed before she realized that the tingling sensation in her back really *was* something very familiar, after all. The difference was that she had never experienced it before as the recipient.

Her eyes opened wide although she did not move. She didn't dare. The man was Healing her, and you didn't interrupt a Healing trance!

"Well," came the conversational voice from behind her. "You certainly have broken up your back in a most spectacular fashion."

He was *talking!* How could you trance and talk at the same time?

"Your main problem is with one of the pads between the vertebrae," the voice continued. "It's squashed rather messily. I'm putting back what I can; if I can get the inflammation down, that will clear the way to stop most of the pain you've been enduring."

"Oh—" she replied, weakly. "I'd thought perhaps that I had cracked a vertebra."

"Nothing nearly so exciting," the voice replied. "But this could have been worse. It is good that Urtho sent you to me when he did. Do you feel any tension here. . . ?"

Winterhart felt a spot of cold amid the sea of warmth in her back. This man was amazing; the Healers she knew could activate the nerves in a specific point of the body, but never a specific sensation. By the time her training had been terminated, she could not activate a circle of nerves smaller than her thumb's width without causing the patient to feel heat, cold, pressure, and pain there all at once. And here this—this kestra'chern—was pinpointing the nerves in a tenth of that area, and making her feel only a chill. *Not* pain!

She could only grunt an affirmative and let her defenses slip a little more. He knew what he was doing, and he felt so competent, so *good*. . . .

Amberdrake let the fluids around the damage balance slower than absolutely necessary, partly out of caution but mostly to buy some more time.

This was not going to be as easy as he had thought.

Winterhart was like an onion; you peeled away one layer, thinking you had found the core, only to find just another layer. She had so many defenses, that he was forced to wonder just what it was she thought she was defending herself *against.*

"How did you manage to do this?" he asked quietly, letting the soothing qualities he put into his voice lull her a little more. "This kind of injury doesn't usually happen all at once; didn't you notice anything wrong earlier?"

"Well, my back had been bothering me for a while," she replied with obvious reluctance, "but I never really thought about it. My fami—I've always had a little problem with my back, you know how it is, tensions always strike at your weakest point, right?"

"True," he replied, wondering why she had changed "my family" to "I." How would revealing a family history of back trouble reveal anything about her? "And your back is your weakest point, I take it?" He thought carefully before asking his next question; he didn't want to put her more on the defensive than she already was. "I suppose you must have seen how busy all the Healers were, and you decided just to ignore the pain. Not necessarily *wise,* but certainly considerate of you."

She grunted, and the skin on the back of her neck reddened a little. "I don't like to whine about things," she said. "Especially not things I can't change. So I kept my mouth shut and drank a lot of willow. Anyway, after the defensive at Polda, one of the Sixth Wing gryphons was brought in with some extensive lacerations to its underbelly, delirious, and when I tried to restrain it, it nearly went berserk."

Interesting. Resentment there. As if she somehow thought that the gryphon in question had been acting unreasonably.

"Who was it?" Amberdrake asked.

"What are you talking about?" she replied suspiciously.

"Who was the gryphon?" Amberdrake repeated mildly. "I knew about Aubri's burns, but I didn't know anything about a Sixth Wing gryphon with lacerations. I was wondering if it was Sheran; if it was, I'm not surprised she reacted badly to being restrained. She was one of the gryphons that Third

Wing rescued just before Stelvi Pass. Ma'ar had them all in chains and was going to pinion them. We don't know what else he did to them, but we do know they had been tortured in some fairly sophisticated and sadistic ways."

There. Make her think of the gryphon in question as a personality, and not an "it." See what that unlocks.

"It could have been," Winterhart said slowly, as if the notion startled her. "There was a lot of scar tissue I couldn't account for, and it was a female. . . ."

Amberdrake probed the injury again, before he spoke. "Ma'ar saves some of his worst tortures for the gryphons. Urtho thinks it's because Ma'ar knows *he* thinks of them as his children, not as simply his 'creations.' "

"I didn't know that." Silence for a while, as the flames of the lanterns overhead burned with faint hissing and crackling sounds. "I like animals; I was always good with horses and dogs. That was why I became a Trondi'irn."

"Gryphons—" He started to say, "Gryphons aren't animals," then stopped himself just in time.

"I thought gryphons were just animals, like the Kaled'a'in warhorses. I thought they only spoke like the messenger-birds . . . just mimicking without really understanding more than simple orders." She sighed; the muscles of her back heaved and trembled a little beneath his hands, and he exerted his powers to keep them from going into a full and painful spasm. "I kept telling myself that, but it isn't true. They aren't just animals. I hate to see anything in pain, and it's worse to see something that can think in a state like that gryphon was."

"Well," Amberdrake replied, choosing his words with care, "I've always thought it was worse to see an animal in pain than a creature like the hertasi, the gryphons, the kyree, or the tervardi injured. You can't explain to an animal that you are going to hurt it a little more *now* to make it feel better later. You *can* explain those things to a thinking creature, and chances are it will believe you and cooperate. And it has always been worse, for me, to see an animal die— especially one that is attached to you. They've come to think of you as a kind of god, and expect you to make everything better—and when you can't, it's shattering, to have to betray that trust, even though you can't avoid it."

"You sound as if you've thought this sort of thing over quite a bit," she said, her voice sounding rather odd; very, very controlled. Over-controlled, in fact.

"It is my job," he reminded her with irony. "You would be amazed at the number of people who come to me after a dreadful battle with nightmares of seeing their favorite puppy dying on the battlefield. Part of what I do is to explain to them why they see the puppy, and not the friends they just lost. Only I don't explain it quite that clinically."

There wasn't much she could say to that, so after a few breaths, she returned to the safer topic. "Anyway, I was trying to treat the gryphon, and I'd gotten bent over in quite an odd position to stitch her up without tying her down, when she lashed out at me with both hindlegs. She sent me flying, and I landed badly. I got up, felt a little more pain but not much, and thought I was all right."

Good. The gryphon has gone from "it" to "she." That's progress anyway.

"But the pain kept getting worse instead of better, right?" he probed. "That's the sign you've done something to one of those spinal pads."

"I think that's one lesson I'm not likely to forget very soon," she countered, with irony as heavy as his had been. "But as you said, the Healers were all busy with injuries worse than mine, and I don't believe in whining about things as trivial as a backache."

"I would never call telling of extreme pain whining," was all he said.

She relaxed a little more; minutely, but visible to him.

"This is going to need more than one treatment," he continued. "If you can bring yourself to resort to a mere kestra'chern, that is."

The skin of her neck flushed again. "I—you are a better Healer than I am," she replied, with painful humility. She hadn't liked admitting that. "If you would be so kind—I know what your fees are for other things—but if you can spare the time—"

"To make certain the Healer of my friends is in the best of health, I would forgo the fee a king would offer for my services," Amberdrake replied with dignity. "When you are in pain, you can't do your best work; you know that as well as I do. Skan is not the only gryphon friend I have, and I want my friends to have nothing less than the finest and most competent of care."

"Ah," she said weakly. "Ah, thank you."

He examined the injury again. "I've done all I can about this spinal pad right now," he told her truthfully. "I need to finish that massage, and then you can go. I think you'll feel some difference."

"I already do," she admitted.

He rubbed some fresh scented oil into the palms of his hands to warm it, and started soothing the muscles of her back he had not reached earlier. They had gone into spasms so often they had become as tense and tight as harp-wires, and as knotted as a child's first spun thread.

She gasped as the first of them released; quivered all over in fact. Amberdrake was quite familiar with that reaction, but evidently she wasn't.

"Oh!" she exclaimed and tensed again. "I—"

"It's quite all right, don't move," he ordered. "It's the natural reaction to releasing tensed muscles. Ignore it if you can, and try to enjoy it if you can't ignore it."

She didn't reply to that; interesting. The last commoner he'd made that particular remark to had said, with dangerous irony, "What, like rape?" It was a natural thought for the ordinary soldier, who all too often found him or herself in the position of victim.

But there was no tightening of Winterhart's neck muscles, no tensing at all to indicate that thought had occurred to her.

Interesting. Very interesting. So whatever she is afraid of, it isn't that. And she is not the "ordinary soul" she says that she is.

"If I hurt you, tell me," he said. "A good massage should not hurt—and in your case, if I start to hurt you, you'll tense up again, and undo everything I've done so far other than the real Healing."

"I will," she promised. "But it doesn't hurt. It just feels very odd. My m—the massages I've had in the past were never for injuries."

What other kinds of massages are there? She can't mean sexual. So—for beauty treatments?

That would account for the superb state of her body. There were no blemishes, no signs of scarring anywhere. When the posturing and stiffness were gone from Winterhart's body, she was a magnificent sculpture of human beauty. She cared for her skin and hair scrupulously, filed her toenails, and had no calluses anywhere that he had seen, not even the calluses associated with riding or fighting.

Unusual, and definitely the marks of someone highborn, and he thought he knew all the humans of noble lineage who had ever lived near Urtho's Tower.

Perhaps she was from before I came here? But that would date back to the very beginning of the war.

"Do you get along with your commanders?" he asked, adding, "I need to know because if you don't, it is going to affect how your muscles will react and I may need to ask you to resort to herbal muscle relaxants when you are around them."

She was silent for a very long time. "They think I am the proper subordinate. I suppose I used to be; that may be why my back went badly wrong all at once. I don't ever contradict them, even now. I suppose you'll think I'm a coward, but even though I don't agree with the way they treat the gryphons, I don't want to be stripped of my rank and sent away."

"You wouldn't be, if you took your case to Urtho," he pointed out. "As Trondi'irn, it is your job to countermand even the generals if you believe your charges are being mistreated."

"I can't do that." Her skin was cold; she was afraid. Of what? Of confrontation? Of going directly to Urtho?

"Besides," she continued hurriedly. "My l . . . lover is one of Shaiknam's mages; his name is Conn Levas. If I went to Urtho, I'd still be reassigned, and I don't want to be reassigned to some other wing than his."

Untrue! Her muscles proclaimed it, and Amberdrake's intuition agreed. The way she had stumbled over the word "lover," not as if she were ashamed to say it, but because she could hardly bear to give the man that title. Amberdrake remembered Conn Levas, the mage who had come to *him* in order to shame his lover. *That lover, it seems, was Winterhart.* She and the mage might trade animal passions, but there was no love in that relationship. She didn't care that she might be reassigned someplace where he wasn't, precisely.

There is something deeper going on here. In some way, the man protects her. He must not know he is doing so, because if he did, he'd use it against her.

This was getting more and more complicated all the time.

"Well, I would say you aren't going to have to worry about that much longer," he said without thinking.

"What do you mean?" Her alarm was real and very deep; she actually started.

He put a hand in the middle of her back and soothed the jerking muscles. "Only that thanks to Zhaneel, Urtho is already aware of the situation in Sixth Wing. You won't have to confront anyone now. I suspect he'll take care of things. He always does."

"Oh." She relaxed again.

Now what on earth set her off like that? It has to be something to do with whatever it is that she is afraid of.

What that could be, he had *no* clue. Perhaps he ought to try probing farther back in her past—so far back that it would not seem like a threat.

"I learned all of my skills at Healing when I was a child," he said casually. "My parents sent me to a very odd school, one that did not admit the existence of a Healing Gift, nor of Empathy. I *did* learn quite a bit about Healing without the use of either—everything from massage to anatomy to herbal and mineral medicines. But I was also more or less trapped among very sick people with Empathy too strong to shut them out. I was miserable, and my parents didn't understand why when I wrote them letters begging to come home. They thought they were doing their best for me, and couldn't understand why I wasn't grateful."

"My parents were like that," she said, sounding sleepy.

"They *knew* their children were exceptional, and they wouldn't accept anything less than perfection. They never understood why I wasn't fawningly grateful for all the opportunities they gave me."

I thought as much! Well, this is something I can start on, right this moment.

"Like my parents, yours surely thought they had your best interests at heart," he replied quickly. "Perhaps they were too young for children. Perhaps they simply didn't understand that a child is not a small copy of one's own self. Many people think that. They feel the child *must* have the same needs and interests they do, simply because it sprang from them. They have no notion that a child can be drastically different from its parents."

"So?" she replied, probably more harshly than she intended. "Does that excuse them?"

He let her think about that for a long time before he answered. "There are no excuses," he said at last. "But there are reasons. Reasons why we are what we are. Reasons why we do not have to stay that way. Even Ma'ar has reasons for what he does."

That turned the discussion into one of philosophy, and by the time he sent her away, he had come, grudgingly, not only to feel sorry for her, but even to like her a little.

But she was going to have to change, and she would have a hard time doing so all alone. He was going to have to help her. As she was, she was a danger, not only to herself, but possibly to everyone she came in contact with. No matter how she tried to hide it, she was unbalanced and afraid.

And fear was Ma'ar's best weapon.

Vikteren

Eleven

Skandranon cautiously pushed his way into Tamsin's work tent with a careful talon, and the tail of a playful breeze followed him inside, teasing his crest feathers. As he had expected, Tamsin and Cinnabar mumbled to each other over their notes, oblivious to anything else going on. They made quite a pretty picture, with their heads so close they just touched, lamplight shining down on them, the table, and the precious stack of paper. Dark hair and bright shone beneath the lantern. They were a vision of peace. But pretty pictures were not precisely what he was after at the moment, and all peace was illusory as long as Ma'ar kept moving. And he knew that, despite his motivations, stealing this secret was a dangerous game to play.

But this secret would at least ensure the survival of his people, no matter what befell Urtho.

"Took you long enough to get here," Tamsin said without looking up, though Cinnabar gave him a wink and wry grin. He wrote another word or two, then set aside the paper he had been scrawling on and raised his eyes to meet Skan's. "What did you do, stop to seduce half a dozen gryphons on the way here?"

Skan's nares flushed, but he managed to keep his voice from betraying him. Half a dozen gryphons? Well—one female, and there certainly wasn't a seduction involved. And until he had a chance to think out a plan, he'd rather not discuss Kechara with anyone. "Not at all; I just stopped to look at something very interesting in the Tower. So what have you discovered?"

By the gleam in Tamsin's eyes, it was good news, very good news. "That your so-called 'spell' isn't precisely that," Tamsin replied. "Enabling fertility in male and female gryphons takes a combination of things, and all of them are the sort of preparation that any gryphon could do without magical help, though a little magic makes it easier. Urtho just shrouds the whole procedure in mysticism, so that you *think* it's something powerfully magical. His notes detail what to do to make the most impressive effects for the least expenditure of energy. He's been bluffing you all, Skan."

Skan's head jerked up so quickly that he hit the top of the doorframe with it and blinked. He'd hoped for simple spells; he had *not* expected anything like this. *"What?"* he exclaimed.

Tamsin chuckled, and leaned back in his chair, lacing his fingers behind his head. "When he designed you, he wanted to have some automatic controls on your fertility, so he borrowed some things from a number of different beasties. Take the Great White Owl—the females don't lay fertile eggs unless their mate has stuffed them first with tundra mice. The sudden increase in meat triggers their bodies to permit fertilization of the eggs; and the more meat, the more eggs they lay. Well, Urtho borrowed that for your females. The 'ritual' for the female gryphon is to fast for two days, then gorge on fresh meat just before the mating flight. That gorging tells her instincts that there's food enough to support a family, just like with the tundra owls, and she becomes fertile."

"But—" Skan protested weakly. "We don't lay eggs. How can that—"

Tamsin ignored him. "He borrowed from the snow tigers as well; they would have litters four times a year in a colder climate, but they only have one because the male's body temperature is so high that his seed is sterile except in the winter. So Urtho designed you males so that your body temperature is normally so high that your seed is dormant, just like theirs. So *your* half of the 'ritual' is that business of sleeping and meditating in the cave for two days while the female fasts. That drops your body temperature enough that your seed becomes active. That, or a very simple spell ensures that the male's temperature *stays* lower than normal until after the mating flight is over. And that is the only bit of magic that Urtho performs that actually accomplishes anything. It's such a minor spell that even an untrained Healer could do it—or there are drugs and infusions we could give you that have that effect, temporarily."

"Or you could sit on a chunk of ice," Cinnabar added gleefully, tossing her hair over her shoulder. Another breath of breeze entered the open tent flap, and made the flame of the lantern flicker for a moment.

"Thank you," Skan said with as much dignity as he could muster. "But I doubt I shall."

"Seriously, though, that means that in the total absence of Healers or herbs, a male gryphon could keep his seed active simply by mating in the winter like a snow tiger, or by sleeping for two days in a cave and then flying *very* high during the mating flight, where the air is cold even in the summer," Tamsin said. Then he laughed. It had been a long time since Skan had heard the Healer laughing with such ease. It was a good sound. "But as hot-blooded as the Black Gryphon is, he may need to go to the northernmost edge of the world!"

Cinnabar joined her lover in laughter, and even Skandranon wheezed a slight chuckle. It had been a long time since Tamsin had researched anything that concerned creation, rather than destruction. For this brief time, perhaps he had been able to forget the war and all it meant. "Oh, and there's the mating flight itself. The better the flight, the easier it is for—ah—everything to get together. Gets the blood and other things moving. And with a strenuous flight . . . there," he said, proferring a sheet of notes, "the better the flight, the more likely that there will be more than one gryphlet conceived. But that's basically it."

Skan sat down heavily, right in the doorway. Hard to believe, after all the mystery, all the bitterness, that it could be so simple. "But that's *all?*" he asked, too surprised to feel elation yet.

"That's it." Cinnabar shrugged and idly braided a strand of hair. "The rest is simply Urtho's own indulgence in theatrics—which is considerable. He is quite an artist. Most of his notes were involved with that and only that. I promise you, though, that unless those guidelines are *strictly* adhered to, you gryphons will be as sterile as always." She tilted her head to one side, and regarded him with dark, thoughtful eyes. "He designed you very well, and I think you ought to know that his notes said precisely *why* he made you sterile unless elaborate preparations were made."

Skan waited for her to elaborate, but she was obviously enjoying herself in a peculiar way and intended to make him *ask* why.

"Well, why did he?" The gryphon growled. Some of the anger he had felt at Urtho was back. "Not that I can't think of a number of reasons. We are supposed to be warriors, after all, and it's difficult to wreak destruction away from home while there are gryphlets in the nest to tend to."

"You have a flair for the dramatic yourself. 'Wreak destruction?' " Cinnabar teased.

Skandranon tried to ignore her. "He might not have wanted to discover himself neckdeep in fledglings. That would mean a strain on food supplies, and hungry gryphons could decimate wild game over a wide area. Also, we're his creations; he might have wanted more control over which pairings produced offspring."

That breeding program. He might have wanted nothing but pure "types." He wouldn't have wanted hybrids, I would imagine. Breeders usually don't.

"He might only have wanted the control over us that holding this 'secret' had." The bitterness he felt in discovering Kechara's plight and the records of the "breeding program" showed more than he liked. "So. Was I close?"

Cinnabar's expression was understanding, and her tone softened. She leaned forward earnestly. "Skan, it was for none of those reasons. Here it is, in his own words. Let me read it for you, and I think you might feel a little better about all of this."

She bent over the notes and read them quietly aloud. " 'Too often have I seen human parents who were too young, too unstable, or otherwise unfit or unready for children produce child after doomed, mistreated child. I will have none of this for these, my gryphons. By watching them, and then training others what to watch for, I can discover which pairings are loving and stable, which would-be parents have the patience and understanding to *be* parents. And in this way, perhaps my creations will have a happier start in life than most of the humans around them. While I may not be an expert in such things, I have at least learned how to observe the actions of others, and experience may give me an edge in judging which couples are ready for little ones. Those who desire children must not bring them into our dangerous world out of a wish for a replica of themselves, a creature to mold and control, a way to achieve what they could not, or the need for something that will offer unconditional love. For that, they must look elsewhere and most likely into themselves.' "

Cinnabar paused, giving him a moment to absorb it all, then continued. " 'The reasons for bearing young should simply be love and respect for the incipient child, and for the world they will be born into. If it took more effort to produce a child than the exercise of a moment's lust, perhaps there might be less misery in this world. Perhaps my gryphons will be happier creatures than their creator.' "

Cinnabar looked back up at him expectantly. Skan simply sat where he was, blinking, surrounded by silence. The sounds of the camp seemed very distant and somewhat removed from reality. Or, perhaps, eclipsed by a more important reality.

Skandranon's internal image of Urtho had undergone multiple drastic changes over the course of the evening. But this—

Elation—and a crazy joy began to grow in him again. Simple, uncomplicated joy; the same joy that he'd had in his friendship with Urtho and had thought he had lost. *This is more than I ever hoped to hear. A reason, a good one, a sound one. One even I can agree with. He wrote that in his own hand, to himself and no other. The whole secret makes sense. And look how even with all those precautions in place, a mistake can happen. One happened with Zhaneel; her parents died, and she was neglected by others who thought her to be misborn. I had no idea he had put such thought into this. . . .*

"Urtho is wiser than I thought," he said at last, his voice

thick with emotion that he simply could not express. "He was right to guide us so."

"Oh, I dare say you all can do well enough on your own," Tamsin told him, with a twinkle in his eye. "If nothing else, all this takes considerable effort on the gryphons' part, and a pair will probably think carefully before going to all that effort."

Skandranon squinted his eyes shut tightly and took a deep breath, then shook his body and flared his breast and back feathers. "There's no 'probably' about it," he told Tamsin, with some of his humor returning. "We can be as lazy as any other race. There *will* be more young, but not that many more, not at first. For one thing—with the war, there is rarely the leisure to make such extensive preparations."

Cinnabar smiled, and nodded her understanding. Tamsin sighed. "By the way," he said, "it's obvious from the notes that a male or female *can't* be overweight if they want to produce a youngster, and a mating flight has to be *damned* impressive in order to get everything moving well enough that fertility is assured. If you can't put everything you've got into that flight, well, you won't get anything *out* of it except a bit of exercise." He raised his eyebrow suggestively.

"Sometimes exercise can be very beneficial," Skan replied with dignity.

"Well," Lady Cinnabar replied, with a face so innocent that Skan knew she was intending to prod him. "You should know. I've heard you're probably the biggest expert in that type of gryphon exercise that has ever lived."

"I?" Skan contrived to look *just* as innocent as she. He would never miss a chance to boast a little in good company. Anyone as well-known as he had detractors to belittle any and all of his traits; so it was up to him to say otherwise, wasn't it? "I suppose, since I am an expert dancer, attractive, and skilled in aerobatics, you might be correct about that."

Tamsin's shoulders shook with silent laughter; Cinnabar simply smiled serenely and released the bit of hair she had been braiding. "I'd have been worried about you if you'd said otherwise, Skan," she said gravely a heartbeat later. "In all of this, it would be easy to lose yourself."

"I won't say that I am not feeling like a feather in a gale, my Lady. But I have to maintain who and what I am. And since I *am* irresistible, it is only responsible for me to say so to reassure you all that I have not been overwhelmed."

"I owe you most *profound* thanks, my friends," he quickly continued, changing the subject before Cinnabar could ask him who he was supposedly irresistible *to.* "I could not have done this alone. And that is perhaps the first and last time you will have heard the Black Gryphon admit he could not do something."

"Indeed!" Tamsin's brows rose. "Quite a concession, Your Highness. We were going to ask for all your possessions as payment, but that concession is rarer than—"

Cinnabar elbowed her lover sharply. "He's serious, dolt," she scolded. "About the thanks, that is."

"So much so, that I cannot think how to properly repay you," Skan told her softly. "It will not only be me that owes you a tremendous debt, but all of us."

But Cinnabar only shook her head. "Don't think of it as *owing* anyone," she replied. The expression in her face was affectionate. "Think of it simply as a gift between friends. Perhaps the greatest gift that we could ever give you—and it was a privilege to do so, not a burden."

He regarded her with surprise. He had not known that she felt that way—oh, he had known that they were his friends, but he had never realized just how much that word could mean. "Why?" he asked, making no secret of his surprise.

Cinnabar looked thoughtful for a moment. "Tamsin, Amberdrake and I are greater admirers of your folk than you know, I think. It is the same with nearly all the Trondi'irn as well. One cannot deal with gryphons without feeling that admiration, there is so much about you that is good."

Skan ground his beak, torn between pleasure and embarrassment. It was one thing for *him* to boast about gryphons in general and himself in particular—it was quite another thing to hear such effusive praise coming from the sweet lips of Lady Cinnabar, who had traveled the world, been entertained in the highest Courts, and seldom praised anything or anyone.

"Still, you are an *aggravating* lot," she continued, her expression lightening with mischief, "and an abundance of equally aggravating nestlings is exactly what you all deserve to teach you proper humility!"

Skan snorted and drew himself up to his full height, until his crest flattened against the canvas roof of the tent. "Indeed," he replied. "We shall be put in our place, if you would be so kind as to teach me that 'simple Healing spell' of yours, then tell me what herbs are needed. I will start circulating the information among the others."

"All ready, my friend." Tamsin flourished a neatly-lettered paper at him. "Memorize this, follow it through to the letter, and the joys of parenthood will be yours! And any other gryphon that you want to condemn to years of nestling-feeding, baby-chasing, and endless rounds of 'Whyyyyyyy?'—just give them this."

Skan took it from him, and quickly committed the contents to memory. As soon as he had finished reading it, he tucked the paper away in his neck-pouch for safekeeping. "Have either of you heard anything from the mages yet?" he asked.

Both shook their heads. "I know I won't be able to sleep until I do," Tamsin said in all seriousness. "What happens with the mages is very likely to affect what happens to you and the other nonhumans."

"I know." Skan tongued the point of his beak for a moment. "Well. I have a reasonable idea. Shall we lie in wait for Vikteren? He will want to know what happened to us as much as we want to know what happened to him."

Tamsin rose, and offered his hand to Cinnabar. "Let's go ambush the man."

They found Vikteren coming to look for them, on the path halfway between the Tower and Healer's Hill, weary and not terribly coherent. And in the end, it turned out that the resolution wasn't much of a resolution at all. Vikteren was exhausted by the time the meeting broke up, and all he would say to them when he met them was, "Well, we have a solution of sorts. Nobody's entirely happy, so I guess it must have been a good compromise."

That was enough for Tamsin and Cinnabar, particularly

since Cinnabar knew she would hear Urtho's version soon enough, but not soon enough for Skan.

The young mage promised Skan an explanation after he had gotten some rest, and Skan made certain to assail him again the next day. When they headed for Zhaneel's obstacle course, Vikteren was able to elaborate a little more on what had evidently turned out to be one of the most anarchic meetings ever perpetrated in Urtho's ranks. "There was a lot of complaining, a lot of yelling, a lot of talking, but I can pretty much boil it down in a couple of sentences. We bitched and moaned, named names, and pointed fingers. That took up most of the night. Urtho said the mages don't know strategy, so they're in no position to dictate it. But he agreed that we had some points, that there *were* certain leaders who acted as if troops were expendable, and that he would take care of it. And in the meantime, the mages were to retain their assignments, but now to report directly to that Kaled'a'in Adept, Snowstar, who would report directly to him. That's where we left it." Vikteren shrugged. "Snowstar wasn't really pleased about being appointed like that, but he's the most organized Adept next to Urtho that I know, so I figure he's the logical choice. He has a huge staff of attendants to keep records, and a dozen messenger-birds. Anyway, the mages bitched about so little actually being done, but the generals bitched, too, about giving up any of their power, so I guess we came out ahead."

"I would say you did." They settled down on a little rise in the shade. Skan had come here to watch Zhaneel again, but Vikteren was not participating in this run; she was supervising other gryphons on the obstacle course. Vikteren was not up to helping her *and* all these others in what was still unofficial training.

Of course, according to rumor, that would change. Trainer Shire was pushing for it, and he had the backing of some of the mages, who saw this as an excellent place to train apprentices in combative magics. But until this training became official, anything Vikteren did here was going to be with strictly limited resources.

Neither of them knew what had gone on in Zhaneel's "little talk" with Winterhart, other than the fact that Zhaneel appeared much more confident—and that she had told Aubri that the Trondi'irn Winterhart actually "had a point" worth considering. The "point," it seemed, was that gryphons who were unsuited to *her* style of attack-and-evasion tried to emulate it, and that she and the trainer needed to supervise them before they hurt themselves. So now Zhaneel actually found herself in a position of authority, which had to be a unique experience for her.

It seemed to be doing her a great deal of good, at least from what Skan could see. He observed that there were a number of positive changes in her. She walked, stood, and even flew with more confidence, more energy. She looked others straight in the eyes, even humans, to whom she had formerly deferred with abject humility. Her feathers were crisp and neatly preened, her coat shone with health.

In short, she was the most desirable creature he had ever laid eyes on in his life. However, he wasn't the only gryphon to make that particular observation.

It did *not* escape his notice that the other male gryphons exerted themselves and—posed—whenever she happened to look their way. It was also apparent that she was perfectly well aware of their interest.

It was enough to make him grind his beak in frustration.

She treated them all impartially, which was some relief, but she wasn't paying the least bit of attention to *him,* which was no relief at all. He was sitting quite prominently in the open, after all. He was always conspicuous to gryphons, especially in the daylight. Surely she saw him. Had she forgotten already how he had defended her to Winterhart?

"So, how are you coming with spreading your little secret around?" Vikteren asked, idly braiding grass stems into a string.

"It spreads itself," Skan replied, watching as Zhaneel demonstrated a tuck-and-roll maneuver, and wondering if his poor flesh and bones had healed enough to permit him to join her pupils. His dancing skills would surely help him in becoming a star pupil. What had become of that shy little gryfalcon who had so aroused his protective instincts? The instinct she aroused now was anything but protective! "I told the eight wingleaders and their mates. They in turn told four more gryphons each, and so forth. As Tamsin said, it is an absurdly simple thing, once you know how much was simple misdirection. I expect that in three days, every gryphon here will know."

And that includes Zhaneel. But the information I want to give her—I must find a way to get her alone. I need to tell her what she really is.

"Has anyone asked how you came by this?" The young mage glanced at him sideways. "Or are you playing stupid?"

Skan laughed and raised his ear-tufts. "I seldom need to *play* stupid! If anyone asks, I have half a dozen different tales to explain how I learned this information. None of them are true, and all of them are plausible. The greater truth is that this is so important to us all that no one is likely to question the origin, so long as Tamsin and Cinnabar can verify that it is accurate. And it is so important that I do not believe there is a single gryphon who will even tell his hertasi that he is privy to the secret. At least, not soon. No one wishes Urtho to learn that we have this knowledge until I am ready to tell him."

Vikteren raised both eyebrows. "So you're the victim— sorry—the volunteer who'll take him the bad news and get nailed to his workroom wall?"

Skandranon's nares flushed deep red. He could have done without hearing that. "Urtho is my friend. And right or wrong, it was my idea to steal the secret. I should be the one to face Urtho, and not a messenger. The gryphons are all agreed that I will be the one to tell him that he no longer controls us through our wish for progeny. They believe I am the one who can best express this without causing him to react badly."

"You mean, they think he's less likely to remove portions of *your* hide than that of any other gryphon," Vikteren observed. "They're probably right."

"I can only hope," Skan muttered. "I can only hope."

Will Zhaneel know where the knowledge came from when it is passed to her? He sighed. *I wish I dared tell her myself. . . .*

* * *

Amberdrake had taken to finding Zhaneel for a few moments every day just to talk, if he could; this evening was no exception, and this evening, for a change, he had quite a bit of free time. That was just as well; all the recent improvement in her spirits and morale had triggered a partial molt, and she had a number of new blood-feathers with feather-sheaths that needed to be flaked and preened away. He hadn't done *that* for any gryphon except Skan since his days as an apprentice and a feather-painter. The simple task was oddly soothing. Feeling the hardness of the feather-shaft against the softness of the insulating down, the pulse of her heartbeat just under the deep red skin, and the incredible heat a gryphon's body generated was always exhilarating.

"He was there again today," Zhaneel told Amberdrake, as he helped her groom her itching feathers. "I saw him. He looked thin."

Amberdrake did not need to ask who "he" was, and the kestra'chern smiled to think of the mighty Skandranon watching Zhaneel from afar like a lovesick brancher in a juvenile infatuation. "He is thin," Amberdrake replied. "That's partially because he's recovering from his injuries. We haven't been letting him exercise as much as he'd like; he always overstresses himself too soon after he's been hurt. But I think he might benefit from one of your classes; should I see if he's interested?"

Interested? He'll probably claw his way through anyone who stands in his way to get in!

"Oh. . . ." Zhaneel's nares paled. "I . . . he. . . ."

"Don't let him overawe you, my dear," Amberdrake said sharply. "He is *just* a gryphon, like any other. Yes, he is beautiful, but he has as many faults as he has virtues. *You* are an expert on these new tactics of yours. He is not." Amberdrake tapped her gently and playfully on the beak. "Furthermore, if you are interested in him, *don't show it.* He has females flinging themselves at him all the time. You need to establish yourself as different from them. Pretend you think of him with simple admiration for what he's done, but no more."

"I do not know. . . ." She looked at him over her shoulder, doubtfully. "I do not know that I can do that. He is *Skandra-*

non. How can I not show—" Her nares flushed with embarrassment.

"Why not?" he countered. "Zhaneel, you are every bit as good as he is. You know that; Trainer Shire and I have told you that daily. Haven't we?"

"Ye–es," she said slowly.

"So just be yourself. It isn't as hard as you might think. Haven't you always been yourself with me? Let your respect show, and let him guess at the rest." Amberdrake carefully crumbled a bit of feather-sheath from around a newly-emerging wing feather. "Try to think of him the way you think of all those admiring gryphons who are showing off for you on your obstacle course. You don't treat any of *them* specially."

She blinked at him in perplexity. Amberdrake sighed; lessons in the games-playing of love never went easily. It was a concept totally foreign to Zhaneel, but eventually she grasped it.

"The quail that escapes is always fatter than the one you catch," she observed. "I will try, if you think that will work."

"Since no one has ever succeeded in playing that particular game with Skan before, I suspect that it will," Amberdrake replied with amusement. "And what's more, I think it will serve him right. It will do him good to think that he suddenly *can't* have any lovely lady he wants. Should surprise him that there's one who is immune to all his charms."

He brushed Zhaneel's feathers down with a slightly oiled cloth, both to pick up the feather-sheath dust and to shine the feathers themselves. "There," he said, stepping back. "You look wonderful. Sleek, tough, competent, ready for anything."

Zhaneel bobbed her head with modest embarrassment. "Or anyone?"

He put his hand beneath her beak and raised it.

"I tell you again, you are a match for any gryphon that ever existed." He nodded approval as she lifted her head again. "Never forget that, and remember who told you. I am a kestra'chern. I *know.*"

"I shall try," she promised solemnly.

"Good." Amberdrake tossed the cloth into a pile of things

for Gesten to clean up and sort, pulled the tent flap aside, and gestured to her to walk beside him. "Care to take a stroll with me? I have time, if you do."

But she shook her head. "I would like this, but truly, I must go. I have a mission to fly in the morning." She glowed with pride. "A real mission, and not makework for a misborn."

His heart plummeted. It had been so easy to think of those exercises of hers as mere games, and to forget that they were intended to make her fit for combat. It had been possible to pretend that she would never go where so many others had been lost. "A long one?" he asked, trying not to show his apprehension. There was no more reason to be apprehensive about her than about any other gryphon. Less so, in fact, for the makaar could not anticipate her moves as they could those of a gryphon with conventional training. Wasn't that what made Skan so successful, that the makaar couldn't anticipate what he would do next?

Nevertheless, a chill he knew only too well settled over him. *That is what makes Skan so much of a target as well. Eliminate him, and you strike a terrible blow at the gryphons as a whole, for it makes them more predictable.*

Once again, someone he knew and cared for would be going away, making herself into a *thing* the enemy could strike at and—

And this was a war, however he might like to forget the fact. It was Zhaneel's responsibility to obey her orders, wherever they took her, a responsibility for which she had been bred and trained.

And she was so pleased, so happy about this assignment; so very proud that she had been entrusted with it. How could he spoil it with his own fears and nerves?

He couldn't, of course. So, as always, he tried to ignore the way his insides knotted up around a ball of ice in the pit of his stomach, and smiled and praised her, as he had smiled and praised every fighter he had sent out to this war. And despite the anxiety he felt, he did mean every word.

That was his duty, his responsibility. *Give them confidence; relax them. Make them forget the past if they must, and remind them of what their reasons for fighting are.*

Show them that they have a life beyond the fighting, a life worth saving.

"It is a high-flight mission," Zhaneel continued, blissfully unaware of the way his heart ached, and the pain in his soul. "The place where Skandranon found those stick-things. I am to carry the thing that Urtho made, which undoes them, and fly a pattern while I make it work; the rest of Sixth Wing East is to rain them with smoke-boxes. Then the fighters come, under cover of the smoke."

So she would be above the general level of the fighting, presumably out of reach of any ground weapons. But makaar?

They'll have to fight their way through Sixth Wing to get to her, he reminded himself. *She's carrying one of Urtho's magic boxes, which makes her nonexpendable. They'll protect her.*

If they can. If the makaar don't get through. If the magic really does work on those lightning-sticks.

If, if, if. Who commanded this mission anyway? If it was General Shaiknam—then even carrying a precious magical artifact, Zhaneel was considered expendable by virtue of the fact that she was a gryphon.

"Urtho planned this," Zhaneel continued, thereby easing some of his unspoken fears. "He commands the mission, and General Sulma Farle is the field commander. And I am to carry the magic thing because I have true hands to make it work. If it is triggered too far away, it will not work, Urtho says."

"Then fly high and well, warrior," Amberdrake told her, patting her shoulder with expertly simulated confidence. "I shall have fresh fish waiting for your return, and a victory feast."

Zhaneel's tiny ear-tufts rose at that. "Fresh fish?" she said, clicking her beak in anticipation. "Truly?" She adored fresh fish—by which she meant, still *alive*—and liked it better when they wiggled as she swallowed them. Where she had acquired this particular taste, Amberdrake could not imagine; most gryphons preferred raw, red meat, and *none* but she liked their fish still living.

Maybe there's some osprey in her somewhere. Or there

are some eagles that have a liking for fish. Or maybe it is only because it is Zhaneel. "Truly," he promised. "A victory feast between friends, though I shall have *my* fish nicely cooked."

Zhaneel made a little hiss of distaste to tease him, but readily agreed to the celebration.

What Amberdrake had not told her was that it was not going to be a victory dinner for two, but for four. Zhaneel, himself, Gesten—and Skandranon. Though he would not tell Skan either. This should be very amusing, at the very least, and with luck it would come off well.

Now let her only survive this, he thought, as he saw her off to her roost for the night. *Let her only survive this. . . .*

Zhaneel held the precious box between her foreclaws, although it was quite securely fastened to her elaborate harness by clips and straps so that it did not interfere with her flying in any way. Her orders from Urtho had been quite detailed and just as specific. She must come in very high, far above the rest of the Sixth Wing; she must then dive as steeply as she could, then level off at about treetop height, making a fast pass above the heads of Ma'ar's troopers, and press the catch that opened the bottom of the box as she did so.

A spy had confirmed that lightning-sticks had been distributed to the fighters. Urtho had told her before she left—Urtho himself!—that the thing in the box was something like a lantern, and its "light" would make the lightning-sticks useless as its rays fell on them. She would have to make several passes in order to be certain of getting most of the lightning-sticks, and each time he wanted her to come in from high above at great speed—hopefully so great that no one could train his weapons on her in time, and no makaar would be swift enough to follow. Like a peregrine falcon on a flock of ducks—or a merlin harassing pigeons.

It would take several passes to be certain of most of the lightning-sticks, for the box was useless past a certain range. And even Urtho was not sure how many passes it would take to neutralize the bulk of them. It depended on how closely the troops had been packed together, and whether Ma'ar's mages had put shielding on the sticks themselves, or those who carried them.

It would likely be on the stick. Ma'ar would not care if the man survived, so long as the stick did.

The box would work through a shield, Urtho was confident of that. He'd warned her not to use any spells if she had them, saying the box was simply a thing that *negated* the controlling force on magic. It would negate the shield as well as the stick's power pent within. The trick was, he couldn't anticipate the effect of two spells being negated at the same time. He had used the only example of the stick that they had in making *certain* the box worked at a reasonable distance. Zhaneel had seen the effect of that—not much. A little light, and that was all.

But there were easily twenty *types* of shields, Urtho had said, and the troops could possibly be protected by a barrier-shield, a force deflector, a pain-bringer, or a concussion field—the complex interaction of three spells could not be anticipated without knowing what *kind* of shield Ma'ar would use.

Whatever it is, I do not think it will affect us. Unless it unleashes winds. That could happen. I must anticipate that. Or great light that might blind us; I must think of that as well.

They neared the target; Zhaneel signaled her flight and took herself high up above the clouds, so high that the other gryphons of her wing were scarcely more than ranks of dots below her, even to her keen eyes. Wisps of clouds passed between her and them. The sun overhead scorched her outstretched wings and back, but the wind bit bitterly against her nares, her underbelly, and her foreclaws.

The precious box protected her chest from the wind, but the icy currents chilled her throat and her breath only warmed when it reached her lungs. Was she high enough? The air was very thin up here, and her lungs and wings burned with the effort of staying aloft.

Soon enough, though, she would be a spear from the heavens. They neared their objective, Laisfaar at the Pass of Stelvi. Zhaneel had never seen the town when it had been in Urtho's hands, but she had been told that the invaders had wrought terrible changes there.

They bring terrible change wherever they go; why should here be any different?

There had been gryphons here. Well, she knew well enough what Ma'ar's forces did to gryphons. They had assuredly done such terrible things to her own parents. . . .

Reason enough to hate the creatures below. Reason enough to wish that what she carried might do terrible things to *them*.

It was time; she swept her wings back slowly.

There! There was the Pass, and below it, Ma'ar's troops, a moving blotch upon the land below her fellows of the wing. Black makaar labored up from their perches on the heights, a swarm of evil. They rose like biting flies to attack the oncoming forces, to pull the gryphons to the ground where the men there could capture them in cruel wire nets, and stab them with terrible, biting spears.

The men below. Who have the lightning-sticks.

She folded her wings, and dropped like a stone from heaven, foreclaws clutched around the precious weapon the Mage of Silence had entrusted to her.

Faster, faster; the wind of her dive pressed against her as the earth rose up in her eyes, and it seemed as if the earth was trying to pull her down and swallow her. She narrowed her eyes and kept her wings pulled in tightly against her body, guiding herself with a tiny flick of a primary, a movement of the tail, even a single claw outstretched for a fraction of a heartbeat. The other gryphons could not spare an eye for her; she must watch out for *them*. She must avoid them as she lanced through the center of their formation; this would take timing of the most delicate kind, and the control of the best.

But not for nothing had she danced her dance of speed and skill against the imaginary enemies of her obstacle course. Even as the makaar closed with the leaders, she shot arrow-swift straight past makaar and gryphon alike, unstoppable.

The ground rushed at her.

Now!

Zhaneel arched her neck and fanned her wings open, feeling them vibrate as if the mountains themselves pushed her toward the ground as she strained. By treetop height she had changed her angle just enough to pull out of the dive, but she was still streaking almost as rapidly as her initial stooping dive. And her foreclaws tightened, opening the shutter on Urtho's magic box, as she skimmed over the heads of the fighters—who were nothing but so many uptilted heads, and round, open mouths to her, passing below in a blur.

Her course took her straight for the cliff, and she headed for it unswervingly. These fighters did not seem to have the magic sticks, but the ones between this lot and the cliff could—

An explosion of—not light, but actual fire!—flashed up at her from below, startling her, causing her to veer and slow a trifle. What was that? Did Ma'ar have some new weapon to use against her?

Taking no chances, she aborted the run, closing the shutter and shooting skyward again, opening her wings as she pumped furiously, laboring back up above the clouds to her position of superiority.

Only then did she look down, to focus on the place where the fire had come from.

The ground there was littered with blackened bodies, most of them still afire, and they did not move—while the troops around that area tried to flee.

Slowly, the answer came to her. *Ma'ar shielded these new weapons of his, just as we thought he might. And Urtho said he could not tell what canceling two such spells would do . . . perhaps the shield holds just enough that it contains the force of the lightning-stick and turns it into a fireball.*

Savage joy filled her heart as she realized the havoc she could wreak among her enemies, and she folded her wings again.

This time they saw her coming; pointing, running, they tried to evade her. She knew what was in their minds. They thought that it was the box she carried that was the source of the attack on them, and not the properties of one of the weapons they themselves carried. Zhaneel quickly learned the range of the "light" as she purposefully pursued the flee-ing men, rising into the sky only to descend again, leaving fire, death, and terror in her wake.

Her heart pounded with lust and excitement; the blood sang in her veins. Makaar tried to stop her, but she was too swift for them. Either they fell by the wayside, or they got too close to her, and she sent them tumbling injured out of the sky, slashed by one of her wicked hindfeet, to be finished off by one of the other gryphons. When they tried to set an ambush for her, the others broke it up. When makaar tried to get above her, the cold and thin air drove them back down, gasping for breath.

Again and again, she made her runs, as flashes of orange and blossoming flames traced her path on the ground, and her fellow gryphons pursued the makaar pursuing her. But finally, there were no more of those explosions, and the ma-kaar turned tail and ran, their numbers depleted to less than half of those that had risen to fight off the gryphons.

Zhaneel's instincts screamed at her to pursue the makaar, but she remembered her orders, and fought the impulse, tak-ing herself and her burden up into the clouds again, where the makaar could not go. Now was her moment of retreat, and the Sixth Wing's moment of glory. It was time for the other gryphons to detach the canisters on the harnesses around their shoulders and drop them, creating a pall of choking smoke to confuse the enemy. The few mages below would be trying to negate the "magical attack" of Urtho's box, not knowing it would simply negate any spell they threw at her. They would assume that the smoke was magi-cal in nature as well, and waste precious time trying to de-stroy an "illusion" or cancel out a smoke-spell. By the time they realized that it was real smoke and called up winds to disperse it, it would be too late.

She would not be there to see the result. Urtho's orders were specific. *When there are no more fighters carrying lightning-sticks, return home.*

Perhaps Skandranon might have ignored those orders to fight makaar, but as Zhaneel reached her altitude again, the elation and battle-lust drained away, leaving her only weary and ready to drop and perch at the first possible moment.

Her wings ached; holding them tight and steady against her dives, over and over again, had taken a toll of her muscles that not even preparation and strengthening on the obstacle course had prepared her for. Her neck and back felt strained, and she longed for a high peak, where she could rest for just a moment. . . .

No rest, not now. No telling who is watching, and one gryphon with a magic box is no match for Ma'ar or another Great Mage! And he will want *you, little gryphon, for spoiling his lovely lightning-sticks and hurting his fighters. Fly fast, Zhaneel! If you are lucky, he will not track you!*

Now fear, which battle-heat had kept away for so long, set hard, cold claws into her, and gave her wings new strength. How far could Ma'ar scry? Would he know to look for one particular gryphon? Would he look high, or among the others? Would he look for one lone gryphon, retreating?

No way to tell, Zhaneel. The only escape is to fly, fly, fly away, back to Urtho and his shields, his mages!

Her wings pumped, her lungs labored, and she cast a look behind her.

Smoke rose above the battlefield, thick and white, obscuring everything to the rear. Under the cover of that smoke, Urtho's ground-fighters Gated in to retake Stelvi Pass.

And behind her, below her, just above the level of the smoke, were little dots of brown and gold, blue-gray and white, moving in her direction. The gryphons of Sixth Wing, *properly* deployed, turning to follow her home, their job done as well.

Ma'ar had more things to think about than one little gray gryphon, swiftly winging her way back to his enemy's home. Urtho had sent enough troops to take Stelvi Pass *without* the devastating effect of the explosions Zhaneel had inadvertently set off. Now, the fighters of the Sixth would be encountering a demoralized and frightened enemy, as well as one confused by the smoke.

Her fear ebbed, and she slowed to let her fellows catch up with her. Yes, Ma'ar had more than enough on his hands at the moment; he would not waste scrying on her. Her task was over, but the reclaiming of Laisfaar had only begun. She and the others would learn the end of it with everyone else, and not until it was long over. But their chances were good, and the odds were with them to win this one.

And at the moment, that is enough.

Gesten

Twelve

Winterhart paused at the threshold of Amberdrake's tent, squinting out into the sunlight. Amberdrake dropped his hand down onto her shoulder, in a gesture meant to convey comfort and support.

"Remember," he said. "Right now nothing that you or I will do can change the outcome of what's happening with the Sixth. If you did everything in your power to get each and every gryphon ready for this, then you have contributed enough. And if you have prepared for the worst case you can imagine, then you are ready for their return. No one could expect any more than that; only the gods have the ability to do more."

"I know, I mean, my *head* knows, but—" Winterhart began.

"Then listen to your head, and stop thinking you have to be superhuman." He patted her shoulder once, and then gave her a little nudge in the direction of the path to the gryphons' landing field. "They'll be coming back soon, I think."

"Right. And—thank you, Amberdrake. For the advice as well as the massage." Winterhart smiled wanly, but it was a real smile, and one of the few he had seen on her face. It was a start, at any rate.

She took herself off, and Amberdrake dropped the tent flap as soon as Winterhart was out of sight, sighed, and retreated to the comforting surroundings of his private quarters. Once there, he flung himself down on his bed, and performed the little mental exercises that allowed him to relax each and every muscle in his back and neck without benefit of a massage.

Not that I wouldn't love one, but I don't have time to call in any favors right now. Not and still get my little "victory feast" together.

He still had his share to do, though the bulk of that preparation had fallen, as always, on the capable shoulders of Gesten. They had raided Amberdrake's hoard of tokens to prepare for this, but it had been Gesten who had done the truly impossible when it came to the feast itself. He had found a party of convalescing fighters willing and able to go hunting and fishing in exchange for those tokens, and now there was a prime raebuck waiting for Skan, a tub full of moon-trout for Zhaneel, and, most precious of all, a covey of fat young quail as appetizers before the main course. Amberdrake could not recall the last time he had seen a quail in the camp, and he had purloined one of them for his meal without a blush. And for Gesten, the hunters had picked a basket full of the succulent sponge-mushrooms that the hertasi prized so much. It would, indeed, be a feast, and a welcome change for all of them from camp-rations. Skan had assured him any number of times that different creatures tasted differently, even to a carnivore that did not cook or season its meals, and that he and every other gryphon grew as tired of the taste of herd beasts as any soldier grew of field rations.

But before he could do anything, Winterhart had had a therapy session scheduled, the last one of the day before the feast. She was making progress, both physically and mentally, but with all of the Sixth Wing gone, Winterhart had nothing to do. And that meant that she started thinking. . . .

She needs to think less, and act more. That was just one of her many, many problems. She thought too much, and there were times when she became paralyzed with indecision as one possibility after another occurred to her. Those were the times when she was most vulnerable to anyone who would come along and give her orders—for if she followed someone *else's* orders, she could not be blamed if something went wrong. Or so her insidious little circle of reasoning went.

So seldom did Winterhart do anything on impulse that she

literally could not recall the last time she had followed such a course.

Or so she says. Then again, given what I surmise of her upbringing, it probably is true.

Part of that was due in no small part to that lover of hers—better say, "bedmate," since love had very little to do with *that* relationship—the Sixth Wing mage, Conn Levas.

Amberdrake still had no more idea of how she had come to be involved with that selfish bastard than he did of how she had come by a Kaled'a'in name when she was no more Kaled'a'in than Lady Cinnabar was. Information about her past came in tiny bits, pieces that she let loose with extreme reluctance.

He had guesses, that was all. Everything about Winterhart that showed on the surface was an illusion, a mask intended to keep the observer from asking questions.

She was not Kaled'a'in, but she knew enough about them to choose an appropriate Kaled'a'in name—since most of the Trondi'irn *were* Kaled'a'in, having such a name would tend to keep a casual acquaintance (which was all she allowed) from asking why she had chosen such a service. That made him think she must have had exposure to the Kaled'a'in in the past.

She had parents who had expected the infinite of her, and would reward nothing less. Hence the self-expectation that she must be superhuman.

She had impeccable manners.

That, in and of itself, was interesting, for she tried to pretend that she was nothing more than an ordinary Trondi'irn. Whatever their virtues, the Kaled'a'in did not cultivate the kind of manners that the elite of Urtho's land learned as a matter of course. She tried to act as much like Conn Levas and his ilk as she could. But it was an act, and it slipped when she was under stress. She had to *think* in order to act "thoughtlessly." Insults did not fall easily from her lips, and she could not bring herself to curse under any circumstance whatsoever.

In short, whenever she did not think she was observed, or when she was under stress, she acted like a lady.

In a camp where it was often difficult to find the time to

bathe thoroughly and regularly, she was immaculate at all times.

In an army where no one cared if your uniform was a little shabby, hers looked as if it had been newly issued, neatly pressed, pristine.

And far more to the point, she had "the manner born." She carried herself as if she never doubted her own authority, nor that she had the *right* to that authority.

To Amberdrake's mind, that spelled out only one thing.

Far from being the commoner she pretended to be, she was of noble birth, perhaps as high as Cinnabar's. That might be why she avoided Cinnabar's presence as much as possible. If the Lady ever got a good look at her, long enough for unconscious mannerisms to show through the Trondi'irn's carefully cultivated facade, Winterhart's ruse might well be over. One could change one's face, gain weight or lose it, alter clothing and hair with the exchange of a little coin, but habits and mannerisms often proved impossible to break.

Then again, Cinnabar is the soul of discretion. She might already have recognized Winterhart, and she's keeping quiet about it. If there were no compelling reasons to unmask Winterhart, Cinnabar would probably let things stand.

Now that he came to think about it, ever since he had begun Winterhart's treatments, Lady Cinnabar had been very silent on the subject of that particular Trondi'irn. This despite Cinnabar's intervention at the time of the "hertasi incident." The Healer had been as angry as anyone else over Winterhart's parroted orders, but since then she had not said a word about Winterhart even when others discussed something she had said or done. Perhaps Cinnabar recognized her, or perhaps not; in any event, the Lady was a powerful enough Empath as well as a Healer to realize, once she had been around the Trondi'irn for any length of time, how much of Winterhart's coldness was due to emotional damage and fear.

Little by little, she reveals herself to me, as she begins to trust me. But I think this may be the most difficult case I have ever dealt with. Zhaneel was simple in comparison;

she only needed to learn how outstanding she was, and to be given a way to succeed on her own terms. Once she had those, she blossomed. Winterhart has so pent herself up that I do not even know who she truly is, only what the facade and the cracks in it tell me. Winterhart is afraid, every moment of her life, and she has yet to show me what she is afraid of.

Maybe that was why she had taken Conn Levas into her bed. The man was appallingly simple to understand.

Simply give him everything he wants, and he is happy to let you have an identity as "his woman." He is protection, of a sort, because he is so possessive about everything he thinks is his. He doesn't even know she isn't a Kaled'a'in. He thinks she is, just because of the name, that's how unobservant he is.

Then again, that was simply a reflection of what Amberdrake already knew. A mercenary mage, in this war only for the pay, would have to be unobservant. Anyone who could even *consider* being in the pay of Ma'ar would have to be completely amoral.

But Conn Levas was incidental to the puzzle. Amberdrake laid his forearm across his eyes for a moment, and tried to put the pieces he had so far into some kind of an arrangement. *When she joined the army, it had to be for a reason. I don't know what that reason is yet. But she joined it under a cloud of fear, terrified that her identity would be revealed, even though, since she is very intelligent, she must have chosen the profession of Trondi'irn because it was utterly unlike anything else she had been known for in her previous identity. She may also have taken that position because of another fear; the Trondi'irn do not normally go anywhere near the front lines. I know that fighting terrifies her. I know that she is horribly afraid of what Ma'ar and his mages can do.*

He had seen her in the grip of that fear himself, more than once, when the two of them had been together at a moment when news came in from the front lines. She controlled herself well, but there was always an instant when absolute terror painted her features with a different kind of mask than the facade of coldness she habitually wore.

So, when Conn Levas propositioned her, it must have seemed sent from the gods. Perhaps he even wooed, charmed her. I am certain that he has the ability to do just that, when he chooses. He had a position with Sixth Wing; so would she. He had an identity that no one questioned; so would she, as "his woman." No one would ask her anything personal. And she could do her job among the gryphons impersonally—after all, they were "obviously" nothing more than sophisticated animals. She could deal with them on terms that cost her nothing, other than a bit of energy.

That was where Zhaneel had inadvertently shaken up her world as much as Amberdrake had. The gryfalcon had forced Winterhart to accept the fact that the gryphons in her charge were *not* "sophisticated animals" with limited ability to ape human speech—for she had tried to convince herself that they were only something a little larger than a messenger-bird, but along the same lines.

But Zhaneel changed all that. Zhaneel showed her in no uncertain terms that these charges of hers were people. And she had an obligation to them, to see that they received treatment as such, with consideration, politeness, and decency. She had an obligation to act as their advocate to the commander of Sixth Wing.

She was in every way as responsible for them as their commander was.

She had not wanted to know that; it was putting stresses on her that showed up when she came to get her treatments for her back from Amberdrake. So long as the gryphons had not been "people" to her, she had been able to cope. Now they were real to her, as they had not been before. Now she had to look at them and know there were personalities there behind the beaks and alien eyes, personalities like those of every human in the ranks. She was sending *people* off into the war to be swallowed up, and she could no longer ignore that fact.

She had begun to feel again, and ironically, it was that very fact that was sending tremors through her relationship with her lover. As long as she had not been able to feel, she did not care what he did to her, said to her, or how he treated her. Now she did care, and she was no longer giving him the absolute deference he required. That much came through in the edited things that she told Amberdrake.

Circumstances have been keeping them separated quite a bit, but once this operation is over, he'll be back, wanting "his rights." She's not going put up with his arrogance and indifference to her feelings anymore; she is bound to break off with him. I don't think she's been sleeping with him much even when he's in camp; maybe she's been finding reasons to avoid their tent. I wonder if I should see if he's been going to any of the perchi*! Or should I stay out of it!*

It was hard to tell; this was not the usual client-kestra'-chern relationship, and had not been since the beginning. And of the two people in the relationship, only one was currently his client. How much interference was too much? When did "need to know" end and "snooping" begin?

And she was so profoundly damaged, so terribly brittle. A confrontation with Conn Levas would shatter her, for he would not hesitate to use the most hurtful things he could think of against her. Yet, under her fragility, there was a core of strength that *he* would like to have the privilege of calling on, from time to time. He needed a confidant as much as she did, and he had the feeling that once she sorted herself out, she would be able to fill that need better than anyone he knew. He sensed that he could trust her, and there were not many people that a kestra'chern *could* trust. All too often, the profession became a bone of contention, or a cause for derision. But somehow he knew that Winterhart would never do that to him; no matter what, she would keep the things she knew would hurt the most under the tightest control.

He *knew* that. Even though he couldn't have told why he was so certain about it.

This end of camp was very quiet, unusually so for the middle of the day. Off in the distance, he heard a sergeant bellowing orders, but here there was scarcely more than the chattering of messenger-birds and the occasional rattle of equipment. He guessed that most of the other kestra'chern had opted for a nap, in anticipation of being needed when the Sixth returned. *Well, all this thinking is not getting the dinner taken care of. And I do have my share of it to do!*

He was as relaxed as he was going to get, and the tension-headache that had threatened to bloom while he was counseling Winterhart had gone away.

He took his arm away from his eyes and rolled off the bed. Time to get to work. First thing; find out what was happening with the Sixth and the attempt to retake Stelvi Pass. If all went well, the first gryphons from Sixth Wing, Zhaneel leading, should be coming back about now. But there would be more than enough folk crowding the landing field at the moment, and this was not supposed to be a mission whose purpose was widely known. No point in making a spectacle when someone might make some inferences.

So—find a messenger-bird, or appropriate one.

The birds were easy enough to come by most times; they swarmed the camp, and all you had to do to attract one was to scatter some of their favorite seed on the ground and wait. Amberdrake didn't need the services of a bird often, but he did have a small store of the succulent sunseeds handy, since people liked the savory seeds as well as the little birds did. And Amberdrake was no exception to that liking.

He had a bag in his quarters, next to the bed; he dug out a handful, and took the fat, striped seeds to the cleared area in front of the tent, where he scattered them in a patch of sunlight. A few moments later, he had his choice of a dozen birds, all patterned in every color imaginable. They pounced on the seeds with chortles and chirps, making a racket all out of proportion to their small size.

He watched them for a moment, trying to pick out a smart one, then chose a clever little fellow whose colors of red and black with vivid blue streaks in his hackles made him easy to see at a distance. He whistled to it and leaned down to extend his hand, sending it a little tendril of comforting thought to attract it. The bird hopped onto his outstretched hand with no sign of fear and waited for his orders, cocking its head sideways to look at him.

While these were *not* the altered birds of prey favored by the Kaled'a'in, they were able to respond fairly well to limited mental commands. Amberdrake held the bird so that he could look directly into one bright bronze eye, and made his orders as simple as he could.

:Go to gryphon-field. Wait for gryphons. Look for this one—: He mentally sent an image of Zhaneel. *:Listen, return, and repeat what you heard.:*

That last was a fairly common order, when someone wanted to know what was going on in another part of the camp. The birds could recall and repeat several sentences, and the odds were good that at least one of those sentences would give some idea of what was happening at a distant location. And if it didn't—well you could send the bird back to eavesdrop some more.

The bird flew off, lumbering away rather like a beetle. They weren't strong flyers, and they were fairly noisy about it; their wings *whirred* with the effort of keeping their plump little bodies aloft, and they usually chirped or screeched as they flew. So if you didn't want anyone to know what you were about, you had plenty of warning before you actually saw a messenger-bird arrive to snoop. But many people made pets of specific birds, as much for their engaging personalities and clownish antics as for their usefulness, so you had to really go to an extraordinary amount of effort to avoid them.

There would, without a doubt, be hundreds of birds waiting at the gryphons' landing field. Although it was supposed to be something of a secret that the Sixth Wing was going to try to retake Stelvi Pass, enough people knew that the area would look as if the birds had learned of a major sunseed spill there. That was the discreet way of learning about something the outcome of which was supposed to be a secret; send a bird to watch, rather than looking around yourself.

And I am nothing if not discreet.

Well, now that he had a winged informant aloft, it was time to get on with the dinner itself. The preparations on his part were fairly simple, since a dinner with gryphons was by necessity informal. He cleared the front of the tent of everything except the piles of pillows. He saved one each for himself and Gesten, and arranged the rest in two gryphon-sized "couches." On the rugs in front of these he placed waterproof tarpaulins; gryphons were not neat eaters.

The buck, the quail, and the tub of trout were behind the tent, and Gesten was seeing to the cooking of his mushrooms and Amberdrake's quail. He had hinted that he would see to a few more small culinary surprises. So that much was taken care of.

Amberdrake changed into his Kaled'a'in festival clothing; the real thing this time, and not the fancy kestra'chern fakery. A silk shirt, leather tunic and tight breeches, both beaded and fringed, and knee-high fringed boots. It was amazing how comfortable the leathers and silks felt, and how simply shedding his "identity" of Amberdrake the Kestra'chern made him relax a little further.

I wonder if Winterhart has ever actually seen Kaled'a'in festival clothing—or if she is only familiar with what we would wear to blend in with folk from outClan?

He was tying up his hair when the chattering of the messenger-bird brought him to the front of his tent.

He held up his hand, his eyes straining to spot the red dot of the bird against the bright sky. The little red-and-black creature whirred in, and backwinged to a landing on his finger, still chattering at a high rate of speed. He placed one hand on its back to calm it, and it fell silent for a moment.

As he took his hand away, it muttered to itself a little, then began repeating what it had heard. Although its voice was very much that of a bird, the cadences and accents were readily identifiable as individual people. Sometimes the clever little things could imitate a favorite person so well that you would swear the person it was imitating was there before you.

But the first thing that the bird produced was a series of crowd noises, among which a few phrases were discernible. "She's exhausted." "Get water!" "It isss all rrright—" this last obviously being Zhaneel.

Then the voice of Trainer Shire. "Zhaneel, I have a link to Urtho here, can you give him a quick report?"

The bird spoke again in Zhaneel's voice, her sibilants hissed and r's rolled, much as Skan spoke when he was agitated or weary. "The box hasss worrrrked. It made explosss-sionssss, and killed many, ssso the ssstickssss mussst have been sssshielded. Therrrre arrre injurrrred gryphonssss, but no dead. The ssssmoke wasss sssprrreading when we rrrre-turrrned, and the fighterrrsss moving in. The rrressst follow me."

The bird imitated the sound of a cheering crowd with uncanny accuracy, Zhaneel saying that she was fine and would take care of herself, and the voice of Winterhart countermanding that, and ordering hertasi to be in readiness for injured gryphons coming in.

Amberdrake very nearly cheered himself; he gave the little bird his reward of fruit and sent him off to rejoin his flock with such elation that he came close to giving the bird more fruit than it could carry away. He *did* kiss it, an endearment which the little clown accepted with a chortle, returning the caress with its mobile tongue.

Zhaneel would be along after she made her longer report to Urtho in person, rested, and cleaned herself up a bit. Skan was due before she arrived; Amberdrake had decided to get the Black Gryphon settled first. Skan did *not* know that Zhaneel was the guest of honor at this feast; he thought it was simply a whim of Amberdrake's.

In a short time the camp was alive with rumors, a steady hum of conversation coming from everywhere. Amberdrake knew that Skan, if he had not been at the landing field, would surely be in the thick of things and have all the news by the time he arrived.

Gesten arrived even before Skan, pulling a laden cart. Amberdrake raised an eyebrow at that; he was not particularly concerned with the cost in tokens, but *where* in a war camp had the hertasi found so much in the way of treats?

Never mind. Better not to ask. There were always those who had hoards of rarities, and were willing to part with them for a price. And tokens for the kestra'chern were prized possessions. Eventually, in an irony that Amberdrake certainly appreciated, there was no doubt that a fair number of those tokens would find their way back to *his* coffers, anyway.

"Skan's on the way," Gesten said, as Amberdrake hurried to give him a hand. "I've got some real goodies in here. Hope he appreciates 'em."

"Save the best for Zhaneel, she deserves it," Amberdrake told him with amusement.

"Huh. Got a couple things for you, too, Drake. And don't tell me *you* don't need a treat, you've been wearing yourself out between that Winterhart, Zhaneel, and the Black Boy." Gesten pushed the cart to the back wall of the "public" room, and opened it up. "Look here—fresh nut-bread, *good* cheese, an' not that tasteless army stuff, a nice mess of vegetables, pastry, eels for Zhaneel, an' heart for Skan. Couldn't ask for better."

"I have to agree to that," Amberdrake replied, a little dazed. "I don't think I want to know where you got most of that."

"Legally," the hertasi said, turning up his snout saucily. "So none of your lip."

"What about lip?" Skan said, pushing aside the tent flap. "Is Drake trying to give you excuses about why he can't have a proper meal for a change?"

"Oh, you know Drake," the hertasi replied before Amberdrake could even say a word in his own defense. "If no one else has something, he doesn't think he should have it either. Martyr, martyr, martyr."

"That is *not* true," Amberdrake replied, going straight over to the cart and popping a bit of pastry into his mouth to prove Gesten wrong. "It is only that I do not think that I should take advantage of my position to indulge myself alone."

"Oh?" Skan chuckled. "And what do you call this?"

"Indulging a client," Amberdrake told him promptly. "You *are* one of my clients, aren't you?"

"Well, yes—"

"And you *have* been undergoing a prolonged and painful convalescence, haven't you?"

"Well, yes—"

"And you *do* deserve a bit of indulgence, don't you?"

Skan coughed. "Well, I happen to—"

"There, you see?" Amberdrake turned to Gesten in triumph. "Moral indulgence!"

"My eye," the hertasi replied, chuckling, and began taking things out of the cart. Skan eyed the heart appreciatively and moved a little nearer.

"Away from that, you!" Gesten slapped his beak. "That's your dessert. And stop drooling."

"I wasn't drooling!" Skan replied with indignation. "I never drool!"

It was on the tip of Amberdrake's tongue to say, "not even over Zhaneel?" but that would spoil the surprise. So he winked at Gesten, and gave the hertasi a hand in unloading the gloriously laden cart, while Skan stood by and made helpful comments.

"I hope you weren't planning on eating right away," Amberdrake said, as Skan settled down on his pile of pillows. "This is a little early for me, and I'd rather appreciate good food with a good appetite."

"Oh, I can wait," the Black Gryphon replied lazily. "Besides, by now everyone knows about the operation at Stelvi and I expect you want to hear how the Sixth did."

"I'm sure you'd tell us even if we didn't care," Gesten sniped. "But since we do care, you might as well give us the benefit of your superior oration."

Skandranon pretended to be offended for just a moment, then tossed a pillow at him, which Gesten ducked expertly. "You cannot spoil my mood, I am feeling far too pleased. The Sixth has retaken the Pass. The messages are in from the mages, and the town is back in our hands." He continued at length, with as much detail as Amberdrake could have wished for, then concluded, "But I have saved the best for last." His eyes gleamed with malicious enjoyment. "General Shaiknam and Commander Garber have been placed on 'detached duty for medical reasons,' and General Farle has been given the Sixth Wing as a reward for successfully commanding them in this operation—and for, I quote, 'appropriate and strategic use of the air forces' end quote."

"Meaning the gryphons," Amberdrake said with pleasure. "Including Zhaneel."

It was not his imagination; Skan's nostrils flared at the sound of her name, and his nares flushed a deep scarlet.

He was going to probe a little further, but a shadow fell upon the closed flap of the tent. "Ah, here is our fourth guest," he said instead, and rose and went to the door of the tent himself. "Lovely lady," he said, bowing and gesturing for Zhaneel to come in, "you brighten our company with your presence."

Zhaneel *was* looking very lovely, if rather tired; Winterhart must have helped her with her grooming. But then, since Zhaneel had been ordered to report directly to Urtho before she came here, the Trondi'irn would have taken pains to make her look especially good, at least to human eyes.

From the stunned expression on Skan's face, she looked especially good to gryphon eyes as well.

She stepped inside, and only then did she see who was waiting there. She froze in place, and Amberdrake put one hand on her shoulder to keep her from fleeing.

"You know Gesten, of course," he said quickly, "and this, as you know, is Skandranon—I do not believe you have actually been introduced, but as I recall, he gave you some good advice on the disposition of a valor-token."

Amberdrake had no difficulty in reading Skan's eyes. *I'll get you for this one, Drake.* Well, this was fair return for the false impression that Skan had given poor little Zhaneel—however well the whole affair had turned out, *he* owed *Skan* for that one.

"I took the liberty of adding him to your victory dinner, Zhaneel," he added. "I didn't think you would mind."

"No," she replied faintly. "Of course not."

But to her credit, she did *not* bolt, she did not become tongue-tied—in fact, she recovered her poise in a much shorter time than he would have thought. She blinked once or twice, then moved forward into the room, and took her place on the pile of pillows that Amberdrake pointed out to her.

Skan recovered some, but by no means all, of his aplomb. As the dinner progressed, he was much quieter than usual, leaving most of the conversation to Amberdrake and Gesten.

Zhaneel managed to seem friendly toward Skan, and full of admiration, but not particularly overwhelmed by him, an attitude that clearly took him rather aback.

As darkness fell, and Gesten got up to light the lamps, she seemed to relax quite a bit. Of course, these were familiar surroundings to her by now, and perhaps that helped put her at ease. Before the dinner was over, Skan *did* manage to ask if she would accept him into one of her training classes, subject, of course, to Amberdrake's approval—

"He's my Healer, you know," Skan added hastily. "Best gryphon-Healer there is."

He fell silent then, as Amberdrake grinned. "Why, thank you, Skan," the kestra'chern replied. "I personally think you're more than overdue for some retraining, if Zhaneel is willing to accept someone who's as likely to give her arguments as not."

"I should be pleased," she said with dignity, as her eyes caught the light of the lamps. "Skandranon is wise enough to know that one does not argue with the trainer on the field, I think."

Her nares were flushed, but in the dim light of the tent, only Amberdrake was near enough to notice. "Did you know that General Farle is being given command of the Sixth?" he asked, changing the subject. "Skan brought us the news."

"No!" she exclaimed, with delight and pleasure. "But that is excellent! Most excellent indeed! He is a *good* commander; most went according to plan, there were no missed commands, and when things happened outside of the plan, General Farle had an answer for them."

"That leaves Shaiknam and Garber at loose ends, though," Gesten put in, his voice full of concern. "I don't know, I just don't like thinking of those two with nothing to do but think about how they've been wronged."

"But they haven't been," Skandranon protested. "They retain their rank, they retain all their privileges; they simply do not have a command anymore."

"Which means they have no power," Gesten countered. "They have no prestige. They messed up, and everyone knows it. They've been shamed, they've lost face. That's a dangerous mood for a man like Shaiknam to be in."

Amberdrake only shrugged. "Dangerous if he still had any power, or any kind of following—but he doesn't, and thinking of him is spoiling my appetite. General Shaiknam will descend to his deserved obscurity with or without us, so let's forget him."

"I second that motion," Skan rumbled, and applied himself to his coveted heart, as Zhaneel ate her eels.

And yet, somehow, despite his own words, Amberdrake could not forget the General—

—or his well-deserved reputation for vindictiveness.

Skandranon ached in every muscle, and he needed more than a bath, he needed a soak to get the mud and muck out of his feathers. But that was not why he came looking for Amberdrake, hoping that his friend was between appointments. Drake wasn't in the "public" portion of his tent, but the disheveled state of the place told Skan that the kestra'-chern *had* been there so short a time ago that Gesten hadn't had time to tidy up.

As it happened, luck was with him; Drake was lying on a heap of pillows in his own quarters, looking about the same way that Skan felt, when the gryphon poked his nose through the slit in the partition.

"Thunderheads!" Skan exclaimed. "Who've *you* been wrestling with? Or should I ask 'what' rather than 'who'? You look like you've been fighting the war by yourself!"

"Don't ask," Amberdrake sighed, levering himself up off the bed. "It isn't what you think. You don't look much better." The kestra'chern pulled sweaty hair out of his eyes, and regarded Skan with a certain weary amusement. "Zhaneel, I trust?"

Skan flung himself down on the rug right where he stood. "Yes," he replied, "But it isn't what you think. Unfortunately. It was a lesson." He groaned, as his weary muscles complained about just how weary they were. "I thought I might impress her. It was a bad idea. She decided that if I was that much better than the rest of the class, I could run *her* course along with *her*."

Amberdrake passed a hand over his mouth.

Skan glowered. "You'd better not be laughing," he said accusingly.

Amberdrake gave him a look full of limpid innocence. "Now *why* would I be laughing?" he asked guilessly. "You look all in; you've obviously been pushing yourself just as hard as you could. Why would I laugh at that?"

Skan only glowered more. He couldn't put it into words, but he had the distinct feeling that Drake was behind all of this, somehow. Zhaneel, the lessons, the private lesson—all of it. "I have been pushing, and pushed, and I am *exhausted*. I need to borrow Gesten, Drake, or I'm never going to get the mud out of my coat and feathers. And I wish you'd let me steal your magic fingers for a bit. And—" he sighed, finally admitting his downfall, "—and I need to talk to you."

Amberdrake nodded, as if he had expected as much. *Which, if he really is behind all this, shouldn't surprise me.*

"In private, I take it?" the kestra'chern asked. As if he didn't know.

"Very private," Skan confirmed, and flattened his ear-tufts to his skull in real misery. "Drake, it's Zhaneel. She's the one—*the* one. And I'm nothing more to her than one of her students."

"And just how do you figure that?" Amberdrake asked casually.

"Because she—I just don't impress her, no matter what I do!" Skan exclaimed in desperation. "It's driving me insane! I don't know what to do!"

"Let me see if I understand what you're saying correctly," Amberdrake replied, leaning back on one elbow. "You have decided that Zhaneel is your ideal mate, and you are upset because she isn't following you and draping herself all over you like every other gryphon you've wanted. Then, when you strut and puff and act in general like a peacock, she *still* isn't impressed. Is that it?"

Skan felt his nares flushing hotly. "I wouldn't put it *that* way!" he protested.

"I would," Gesten said, from behind him. The hertasi

pushed his way in through the curtains past Skan. "Feh," he added, "You look like a used mop. If I were a female, I wouldn't have you either."

"Drake!" Skan cried.

"Gesten, that's enough," Amberdrake admonished. "Skan, has it ever once occurred to you to go and *talk* with the lady? Just talk? Not to try to impress her, but to find out what she's like, what she thinks is important, what kind of a person she is? Find out about *her* instead of talking about yourself?"

"Ah—" the gryphon stammered.

"Try it some time," Amberdrake said, leaning back into his pillows. "You might be surprised by the results. Gesten, this used mop would like to know if you're willing to help him look more like a gryphon. I can go get a bath in the shower tent for once; I look worse than I feel."

"If you want," Gesten said dubiously. "I think you sprained something."

"Then I can get Cinnabar to unsprain it for me," Amberdrake said to the roof of the tent. "Go on, Skan needs your help more than I do at the moment, and we *are* supposed to be sharing your very excellent services."

"All right," the hertasi said with resignation. "Come on, Black Boy. But you'll have to put up with my massaging; Drake is definitely not going to be up to it."

Skan climbed to his feet with more groans. "Right now, I'd accept a massage from a makaar," he replied. "And I'd court the damned thing, if it would get the muck off me."

Gesten looked back over his shoulder and batted his eyes at Skan in a clever imitation of a flirtatious human. "Why, Skan, I never guessed! Harboring an unfulfilled passion for little me?"

Skan only snorted and followed the hertasi into the sunlight behind the tent. Gesten opened up a box built into the side of the wagon that carried Amberdrake and all his gear when the entire army was on the move, and got out the brushes and special combs needed for grooming gryphons. "You really ought to go find a vacant tub and have a bath," the hertasi said, looking him over. "You're mage enough to heat the water so your muscles don't stiffen up in the cold."

"Once you brush me out, please," Skan pleaded. "If I go in like this, it'll be a mud bath."

"You have a point." The hertasi picked up one of the brushes and set to work with a will. Bits of dried, caked mud flew everywhere with the force of Gesten's vigorous strokes. "So besides you being infatuated with Zhaneel, and her having the good sense to see through you, what else is new out there?"

Skan ignored the first part of the question to answer the second. "What's new is that we may have the Pass, but Ma'ar isn't budging another toe-length." He shook his head, and leaned into Gesten's brush. "I don't know, Gesten. I can't tell if things look good for us, or bad."

"Neither can anyone else." Gesten put the brush down and picked up one with finer bristles. "Urtho doesn't know what to do, I hear. Ma'ar won't leave us be, and Urtho won't spend troops like Ma'ar does to get rid of him. That's the problem with an ethical commander; the leader who doesn't care how many of his men he kills has an edge."

Skan shook his head. "Too much for me, at least right now."

The hertasi snickered. "Yah. I know what's on your mind—what there is of it. Don't know how Drake thinks you're going to impress Zhaneel with it, since I haven't seen much evidence of a mind in you since I met you."

Skan did not rise to his teasing this time. "Gesten," he said hesitantly, "do you really think she'd ever pay any attention to me if I did what Drake said? Nothing I've done has worked."

"So try it. Who knows?" Gesten slapped him on the shoulder, raising a cloud of dust. "The man's job is the heart, you know. I figure he probably knows what he's talking about."

Skan considered that. Gesten was right. *And besides, I have to tell her what she is, what I learned in the Tower. Might as well kill two birds with the same stone, as they say.*

"But first, Skan," Gesten cautioned, "there's something that's *really* important you need to do."

Skan craned his neck around to look at him, the hertasi sounded so serious. "What is it?" he asked anxiously.

Gesten fixed him with a sobering gaze for a long moment, then said with deadpan seriousness, "Skan—get a bath."

The hertasi made it all the way to the tent flap before the flung brush caught up with him.

Conn Levas

Thirteen

Zhaneel preened a talon thoughtfully, then looked down at her hand. *Hand*, and not a misshapen collection of foreclaws. She was not some kind of an accident. As Amberdrake had surmised, she was the living result of something that had been planned.

"So." She looked from the talon to Skandranon, and even though she managed to keep her expression calm and serene, her heart raced to have *him* here beside her, on her favorite rock overlooking the obstacle course. "I am the first of a breed, you say? And you saw evidence of that in Urtho's Tower?"

Skan nodded; his great golden eyes fixed upon her as steadily as if he were the needle of a compass, and she were the Northern Cross. The sun shone down on his black feathers, bringing up the patterns in them that were normally concealed by the dye he used. "There seem to be about fifty different types altogether. Mostly broadwings, eagle-types. You are based on the only kind that looks really falcon-based. I don't know what Urtho had in mind to call your type, but I'd call you a gryfalcon."

"Gryfalcon." She rolled the word around on her tongue. It sounded even better when Skan had said it than when Amberdrake had come up with it. "And none of *this*," she spread her foreclaws wide," is accidental. I am simply the only one of my kind."

"Not that I saw. But, Zhaneel—" He hesitated a long moment, and she looked at him curiously. From the tension in his body, he was trying to make up his mind about saying something more. "—Zhaneel, you aren't precisely the only one of your type. Only the first *successful* gryfalcon." He ground his beak for a moment, then clearly made up his mind to continue. "There's—well, what we'd call a *real* misborn in the Tower, too. It looks as if she started out to be a gryfalcon, but something went wrong. She's distorted, like a child in her head, I think she's a neuter, and there are probably other things wrong with her as well."

Zhaneel's tiny ear-tufts rose. "In the Tower? But why— why would Urtho keep her there? I—" But then all of the slights and insults, the teasing and the bullying of her own childhood returned to her, and she *knew* why. "—no. I see." Gryphons did not cry, but sadness made their throats tighten, and triggered a need to utter a keening sound. She bowed her head and stifled the urge to keen. *The poor, poor thing. Perhaps it is as well that it is like a child, for it cannot understand how cruel the world can be, and it will not mourn what it has never seen.* "Does it have a name, this poor little one?"

Skan nodded. "Urtho calls her 'Kechara,' and she says that he visits and plays with her often. I don't think she is in any kind of pain or want."

"Kechara—beloved—" She took a deep breath, and her throat opened again. "Yes, that would be like Urtho, to care for the poor thing that was not quite what he wanted, to make it as happy as he could." She had come to understand their leader very well during the past several weeks. She wondered if Skandranon knew how often Urtho had taken the time to talk to her; Amberdrake knew, and several times, things that Amberdrake had told her made her think that Urtho had been talking with him about her. "But what does this mean for us? I think that if we can, we should find a way to free Kechara. With two of us to protect her, she will not suffer taunts as I did, do you not think? With two of us, acting as her family—? We should not have younglings just yet, I think, but Kechara will serve as practice of a kind. Now that you have made it possible for us to do so, whether or not Urtho approves."

Shyly, she cocked her head to one side. Skan gaped at her,

looking extremely silly, as the sense of what she had just suggested penetrated to him.

He looked even sillier a moment later, but it was because he was giddy with elation. But then, so was she.

She knew how exhausted he must be after the workout of this afternoon, yet from somewhere he found the strength to follow as she leapt into the air, giving him a playful, come-hither look over her shoulder. And as the moon rose, she led him on a true courtship chase, a chase that ended when they caught each other, landing in the warm grass of a hillside far above Urtho's Tower.

As was the only way to end a courtship chase, after all.

This was the face of defeat. Chaos on the landing field; shouting and the screaming of gryphons hurt too badly to keep still. Healers and Trondi'irn from the Hill and every wing swarmed the site, somehow never getting in each others' way. Winterhart ignored it all as she held the bleeding gryphon in life by the barest of margins, holding the mangled body together with Gift and hands both, until a more Gifted Healer could reach her. She swore at and coaxed the poor creature by turns, stopping only to breathe and to scrub tears from her eyes by rubbing her cheek against her blood-stained shoulder.

"Don't you die on me, Feliss!" she scolded. "Not after all the work Zhaneel's put in on you! If you die, I swear, I'm going to have Urtho catch your spirit and put it in the body of a celibate Priestess of Kylan the Chaste! That'd teach you!"

Tears rose up again to blind and choke her; she wiped them away again, and ignored the way her own energy was running out of her the way Feliss' blood ran between her fingers. Gods, gods, it had been easier a few short weeks ago—before she had been forced to see these gryphons the way Amberdrake saw them. Before she had found herself caring for them, and about what happened to them. Before she learned to think of them as something more than a simple responsibility. . . .

Before Amberdrake made her *like* them, and Zhaneel made her respect them.

Tears rose again, but there was no time now to wipe them away; she held on, grief-blinded, unable to see—

Until a Gift so much greater than hers that it dazzled her touched her, and used her as the conduit to bring the Healing to Feliss that she had not been able to give. Emerald-green Healing energy poured through her, and beneath her hands the gaping wounds closed, the flesh knit up, the bleeding stopped.

Winterhart closed her eyes and concentrated only on *being* that conduit, on keeping Feliss' heartbeat strong, until the energy faded, blood no longer flowed through her fingers, and the heartbeat strengthened of itself. Only then did she open her eyes again.

Lady Cinnabar removed her long, aristocratic hands from where they rested atop Winterhart's and looked deeply into the Trondi'irn's eyes. Winterhart was paralyzed, frozen in place like a terrified rabbit. She had been trying for weeks to avoid the Lady's presence, ever since the moment she'd thought she'd seen a flicker of recognition in Cinnabar's face.

Who would ever have thought that a song would give me away? She'd been humming, on her way back from a session with Amberdrake; her back felt normal for the first time in ages, Conn was still in the field and *not* in her bed, and she'd actually been cheerful enough to hum under her breath.

But she hadn't thought about what she was humming, until she passed Lady Cinnabar (hurriedly, and with her face a little averted), and the Lady turned to give her a penetrating stare.

Only then did she realize that she had been humming a song that had been all the rage at High King Leodhan's Court—for the single week just before Ma'ar had challenged the King to defend his land. Like the nobles who had fled the challenge in terror, or simply melted away in abject fear, the song had vanished into obscurity. Only someone like Lady Cinnabar, who had been at the High King's Court at that time, would recognize it.

Only someone else who had been part of the Court for that brief period of time would have known it well enough to hum it.

Winterhart had seen Cinnabar's eyes narrow in specula-
tion, just before she hurried away, hoping against hope that
Cinnabar would decide that she was mistaken in what she
thought she had heard.

But the Lady was more persistent than that. More than
once, Winterhart had caught Cinnabar studying her at a distance. And she knew, because this was the one thing she
had dreaded, that Cinnabar was the kind of person who knew
enough about the woman she had once been, that the Lady
would uncover her secret simply by catching her in habitual
things no amount of control could change or eliminate.

And now—here the Lady was, staring into Winterhart's
eyes, with the look on her face of one who has finally solved
a perplexing little puzzle.

"You are a good channel, and you worked today to better
effect than I have ever seen you work before," Cinnabar said
mildly. "And your ability and encouragement kept this
feathered one clinging to life. You are a better Trondi'irn
and Healer than you were a few weeks ago."

"Thank you," Winterhart said faintly, trying to look away
from Cinnabar's strange reddish-brown eyes, and failing.

"Altogether you are much improved; get rid of that Conn
Levas creature, and stand upon your own worth, and you
will be outstanding." Cinnabar's crisp words came to Winterhart as from a great distance. "He is not worthy of you,
and you do not need him, Reanna."

And with that, she turned and moved on to the next patient, leaving Winterhart standing there, stunned.

Not just by the blunt advice, but by Cinnabar's last word.
Reanna.

Winterhart went on to her next patient in a daze; fortunately her hands knew what to do without needing any direction from her mind. Her mind ran in circles, like a mouse
in a barrel.

Lady Cinnabar *knew.* Winterhart had been unmasked.

How long before the Lady told her kinsman Urtho that
Reanna Laury—missing and presumed fled—was working in
the ranks as a simple Trondi'irn? How long before everyone
knew? How long before her shame was revealed to the entire
army?

But before Winterhart could free herself from her paralysis, Cinnabar was back. "You and the rest can handle everything else from here on," the Healer said quietly. "I'm needed back up on the Hill. The gryphons are not the only injured. And Reanna—"

Winterhart started at the sound of her old name.

Cinnabar laid one cool hand on Winterhart's arm. "No one will know what I have just spoken, if you do not tell," the Healer said quietly. "If you choose to be only Winterhart, then Winterhart is all anyone will know. But I believe you should tell Amberdrake. He has some information that you should hear."

The Lady smiled her famous, dazzling smile.

"Sometimes being in the middle of a situation gives one a very skewed notion of what is actually going on. If I were a minnow in the middle of a school, I would not know *why* the school moved this way and that. I would only see that the rest of the school was in flight, and not what they fled. I would never know when they ran from a pike, or a shadow."

And with that rather obscure bit of observation, the Lady turned and was gone.

Winterhart sat in her own austere tent, braiding and re-braiding a bit of leather; her nerves had completely eroded. In another few moments, she was scheduled for a treatment for her back—treatments she had come to look forward to. The kestra'chern Amberdrake was the easiest person to talk to that she had ever known, although the changes he had caused in her were not so easy to deal with.

But now—Cinnabar knew. And although she had said that she would not reveal Winterhart's secret, she had also said something else.

"I believe you should tell Amberdrake." Cinnabar's words haunted her. Who and what was this man, that she should tell *him* what she had not told anyone, the secret of her past that she would rather remained buried?

Why would Cinnabar say anything so outrageous?

And most of all, *why* did she want to follow the Lady's advice?

Oh, gods—what am I going to do? What am I going to say?

She could say nothing, of course, but Amberdrake was skilled at reading all the nuances of the body, and he would know she was upset about something. He had a way of getting whatever he wanted to know out of a person, as easily as she could extract a thorn from the claw of one of her charges.

I could stop going to him. I could find someone else to handle the rest of the treatments.

But she was not just seeing him for her back, and she knew it. Not anymore. Amberdrake was the closest thing she had to a real friend in this place, and what was more, he was the only person she would ever consider telling her secrets to.

So why not do it?

Because she didn't want to lose that friendship. If he heard what she was, how could he have any respect for her, ever again?

Then there was the rest of what Lady Cinnabar had said. *"Get rid of that Conn Levas creature and stand on your own."* Oh, Cinnabar was right about that; she and Conn were no more suited for each other than a bird and a fish. And dealing with Conn took more out of her than anyone ever guessed.

She had always known, whether or not Conn was aware of it, that her liaison with the mage was temporary. She had thought when she first accepted his invitation to "be his woman" that it would only last until Ma'ar overran them all, and killed them. A matter of weeks, months at the most. But Urtho was a better leader than anyone had thought, and she found herself living long past the time when she had thought she would be dead.

Then she had decided that sooner or later Conn would grow tired of her, and get rid of her. But it seemed that either most women around the Sixth knew the mage for the kind of man he was—an overgrown child in many ways, with a child's tantrums and possessiveness—or else he perversely prized her. He made no move to be rid of her, for all his complaints of her coldness.

Then again, he was a master of manipulation, and one of the people he manipulated as easily as breathing was her. She didn't like unpleasantness; she hated a scene. She was easily embarrassed. He knew how to threaten, what to threaten her with, and when to turn from threats to charming cajolery.

On her part the relationship originally had been as cool and prearranged as any marriage of state. He supplied her with an identity, and she gave him what he wanted. They maintained their own separate gear and sleeping quarters; they shared nothing except company.

But you don't allow someone into your bed without getting some emotional baggage out of it. She was wise enough to admit that. And even though she would have been glad enough to be rid of him, as long as he claimed he had some feelings for her, and he needed her, she knew she would stay. Not until *he* walked away would she feel free of him.

Amberdrake had skillfully pried that out of her already— and in so doing, had made her face squarely what she had not been willing to admit until that moment. She didn't want Conn anymore, she heartily wished him out of her life, and the most he would ever be able to evoke in her was a mild pity. There was no passion there anymore, not even physical passion. Amberdrake gave her more pleasure than he did, without ever once venturing into the amorous or erotic. And now Cinnabar, saying she should be rid of him—

Cinnabar must think he's a drain on me, on my resources. I suppose he is. Every time he comes back from the front lines, there's a scene. I spend half the night trying to make him feel better, and I end up feeling worse. I find myself wishing that he would die out there, and then I'm torn up with guilt for ill-wishing him. . . .

Oh, it was all too tangled. Amberdrake could help her sort it all out—but if she kept her appointment, Amberdrake would learn her secrets.

Her stomach hurt. Her stomach always hurt when she was like this. Amberdrake knew everything that there was to know about herbal remedies, maybe he would have something for her stomach as well as her back, and if she just kept the subject on *that* she could avoid telling him anything important.

She put the bit of leather aside, and got up off her bedroll, pushing aside the tent flaps to emerge into the blue-gray of twilight.

Time to go. There was no place to run from it now. And no point in running.

Amberdrake knew the moment that Winterhart slipped through the tent door that there was something wrong. Even if he hadn't been an Empath, even if he were still an apprentice in the various arts of the kestra'chern, he'd have known it. She moved stiffly, her muscles taut with tension, and the little frown-line between her brows was much deeper than usual. Her eyes looked red and irritated, and she held her shoulders as if she expected a blow to come down out of the sky at any moment.

"Is Conn Levas back yet?" he asked casually, assuming that the mage was the reason for her tension.

But the startled look of surprise, as if that was the very last thing she had expected him to say, told him that the shot had gone far wide of the mark. Whatever was troubling her, it was not her erstwhile lover.

"No," she replied, and turned her back to him, modest as always, to disrobe so that he could work on her back. "No, the foot-troops are still out. They aren't doing well, though. I suppose you know that Ma'ar is pushing them out of the Pass again. The Sixth got hit badly, and the Fourth and Third sent in gryphons with carry-nets to evacuate the wounded. It was bad on the landing field."

"So I'd heard." Skan was out there now; as the only gryphon who could keep up with Zhaneel, Urtho had assigned him to fly protective cover on her. No standard scouting raids for *them*; they only flew at Urtho's express orders, usually bearing one or more of his magic weapons or protections. The Black Gryphon had already given Amberdrake a terse account of the damage, before going out on a second sortie. "After a day like today, I'm not surprised that you're tense."

"And my stomach's in a knot," she said, wrapping herself

in a loose robe, before she turned back to face him. Her expression mingled wry hope with resignation, as if she hated to admit that her body had failed her. "I don't suppose you have anything for that, do you?"

"Assuming you trust my intentions," he countered, trying to make a joke of it. "I'd prescribe an infusion of vero-grass, alem-lily root, and mallow. All of which I *do* have on hand. You aren't the only person who's come to me today with your muscles and stomach all in knots."

Her eyes widened a little, for all three herbs were very powerful, and had a deserved reputation for loosening the tongue and giving it free rein—and for loosening inhibitions as well. "I don't know," she replied hesitantly. "Then again, between the state of my back and my stomach, maybe I'd better."

He had made the same concoction often enough for himself that he could nod sympathetically as he went to his chest of herbs. He put measured amounts of each into a cup, poured in hot water, and left the medicine to steep. "Believe me, I know how you feel. As I said, I've had to resort to my own herbs more than once since this war started. I've been with Urtho's forces since—let me think— right after the High King collapsed, and Urtho more-or-less took over as leader."

She accepted the cup of bitter tea carefully, made a face as she tasted it, and drank it down all at once. "That's longer than I have," she remarked. "If you've been with Urtho that long, I suppose you must have seen quite a bit of the Court, then."

"Me? Hardly." He laughed and could have *sworn* that she relaxed a little. "No, I was just one kestra'chern with the Kaled'a'in; all the Clans came as fast as they could when Urtho called us in, and he didn't sort us out for several months after that. He just gave the Clan Chiefs his orders and let them decide how to carry them out, while he tried to organize what was left of the defenses. At that point, no one knew what ranking I was qualified for. Kestra'chern aren't given a rank among the Clans the way they are in the outside world. My rank and all that came later, as things got organized."

She arranged herself on the massage table, facedown. "The way that the Clans stood by him, though—you must have been disgusted by the way the nobles just panicked and deserted him."

He paused, a bottle of warm oil in his hand, at the odd tone in her voice. She surely knew that *he* knew she was no Kaled'a'in, but there was something about the way she had phrased that last that was sending little half-understood signals to him. And the direction the conversation had been going in—

Go slowly, go carefully with this, he thought. *There is more going on here than there appears to be. I think, if I am very careful, all my questions about her are about to be answered.*

"We stood by him because we were protected and never felt the fear," he replied, pouring a little oil in the palm of his hand and spreading it on her back. "We have our own mages, you know. Granted, we don't go about making much of the fact, and they only serve Kaled'a'in, but between the mages and the shaman, Ma'ar couldn't touch us—and there was no way that he could insinuate agents into our midst to bring us down. Not the way he did the High King and his Court."

The muscles under his hand jumped. "What do you mean by that?" she demanded, her voice sharp and anxious.

He soothed her back with his hands, and deliberately injected a soothing tone into his voice. "Well, Ma'ar has *always* been a master of opportunity, and he's never used a direct attack when an indirect one would work as well. Treachery, betrayal, manipulation—those are his favorite weapons. That was how he got control in his own land in the first place, and that is how he prefers to weaken other lands before he moves in to take them with his troops. He may be ruthless and heartless, but he never spends more than he has to in order to get what he wants."

"But what does that have to do with us?" she demanded, harshly. "What does that have to do with the way those cowards simply *deserted* the High King, fled and left the Court and their own holdings in complete chaos?"

"Why, everything," he told her in mild surprise. "Ma'ar

had a dozen agents in the Court, didn't you know that? Their job was to spread rumors, create dissension, make things as difficult as possible for the High King to get anything accomplished. *I* don't know their names, but Cinnabar does; she was instrumental in winkling them out and dealing with them after the King collapsed. But the major thing was that once Ma'ar believed that his agents had done everything they could to get the Court just below the boiling point, he sent one of them into the Palace with a little 'present' for the King and his supporters." His mouth twisted in distaste. "Treachery of the worst sort. Have you ever heard of something called a *dyrstaf*?"

"No," she said, blankly.

"Skan could tell you more about it. He was there at the time, in Urtho's Tower, and he found out about everything pretty much as it happened. For that matter, so was Lady Cinnabar, but she's not a mage, and Skan is." He tried to recall everything that Cinnabar and Skan had told him. "It's a rather nasty little thing. It's an object, usually a rod or a staff of some kind, that holds a *very* insidious version of a fear-spell. It looks perfectly ordinary until it's been triggered, and even then it doesn't show to anything but Magesight. It starts out just creating low-level anxiety, and works up to a full panic over the course of a day and a night. And since it isn't *precisely* attacking anyone or anything, most protective spells won't shield from it. And of course, since it wasn't active when the agent brought it into the Palace, no one knew it was there, and it didn't trip any of the protections laid around the King."

"A fear spell?" she asked softly. "But why didn't the Palace shields—oh. Never mind, it was *inside* the shields when it started to work. So of course the shields wouldn't keep anything out."

"And by the time anyone realized what was going on, it was too late to do anything about it," Amberdrake replied. "In fact, it did most of its worst work after dark, at a time when people are most subject to their fears anyway. The *mages* always slept under all kinds of personal shielding, so of course they weren't affected. Anyone with Healer training would also sleep under shields; remember, most Healers have some degree of Empathy, and this was an *emotion*. They would also have been protected against it."

"But anyone else—" She shuddered.

"And what most people did was simply to run away." Amberdrake sighed. "By morning, the Palace was deserted, and it wasn't only the nobles who ran, no matter what you might have heard to the contrary. It was *everyone*. Cinnabar said that the only ones left were the mages and Healers; there wasn't a horse, donkey, or mule fit to ride left in the stables, the servants and the Palace guards had deserted their posts, and the King was in a virtual state of collapse. She and the others called Urtho from his Tower. By the time that Urtho found the *dyrstaf*, it was too late; the worst damage had been done."

"But they didn't come back." No mistake about it; Winterhart's tone was incredibly bitter and full of self-accusation. "They could have returned, but they didn't. They were cowards, all of them."

"No." He made his voice firm, his answer unequivocal. "No, they didn't come back, not because they were cowards, but because they were *hurt*. The *dyrstaf* inflicts a wound on the heart and soul as deep as any weapon of steel can inflict on the body; an invisible wound of terror that is all the worse because it can't be seen and doesn't bleed. They weren't cowards, they were so badly wounded that most of them had gone beyond thinking of anything but their fear and their shame. Some of them, like the King, died of that wound."

"He—died?" she faltered. "I didn't know that."

Amberdrake sighed. "His heart was never that strong, and he was an old man; being found by Urtho hiding in his own wardrobe shamed him past telling. It broke his spirit, and he simply faded away over the course of the next month. Since he was childless, and everyone else in direct line had fled past recalling, Urtho thought it better just to let people think he'd gone into exile."

"What about Cinnabar?" she demanded sharply. "Why didn't *she* run? Doesn't that just prove that everyone who did really *is* a coward?"

"Cinnabar was already a trained Healer, dearheart," he

said. *Not like you, little one. You might have had the Gift, but your family didn't indulge you enough to let you get it trained.* "You've worked with her, you know how powerful she is, and her Empathy is only a little weaker than her Healing powers. *She* was shielded against outside emotions and didn't even know what was going on. Then in the morning, she was able to tell that the fear was coming from *outside,* and she was one of the ones who got Urtho and helped him in a search for the *dyrstaf.* They all came in by way of Urtho's private Gate into the throne room—all but Skan, he was too big to fit. Unfortunately, by the time Urtho and the mages found it, it was too late to do any good."

"They always said her family was eccentric," Winterhart said, as if to herself. "Letting the children get training, as if they were ever going to have to actually *be* Healers and mages and all. I envied her—" A gasp told him she had realized too late that she had let that clue to her past slip.

"If your parents had allowed you to have Healer training, instead of forcing you to learn what you could on your own, you probably wouldn't be here right now," he told her quietly. "Don't you realize that if you'd been properly trained, you'd have been standing beside Cinnabar, helping her, on that day? There is nothing more vulnerable than an untrained Empath. You were perhaps the single *most* vulnerable person in the entire Palace when the *dyrstaf* started working. Didn't you ever realize that? If Ma'ar's spell of fear *wounded* others, I am truly surprised that it didn't strike you dead."

Her shoulders shook with sobs. "I wish it had!" she wept into the pillow. "Oh, *gods!* I wish it *had!*"

Carefully, very carefully, he sat down on the edge of the massage table, and took her shoulders in his strong hands, helping her to sit up and turn, so that she was weeping into his shoulder instead of into a comfortless pillow. For some time, he simply held her, letting her long-pent grief wear itself out, rocking her a little, and stroking her hair and the back of her neck.

She shivered, and her skin chilled. Gesten slipped in, silent as a shadow, and laid a thick, warmed robe beside him. He thanked the hertasi with his eyes, and picked it up, wrapping it around her shoulders. She relaxed as the heat seeped into her, and gradually her sobs lost their strength.

"So that was why you chose the name 'Winterhart,' " he said into the silence. "I'd wondered. It wasn't because it was Kaled'a'in at all—it was because a hart is a hunted creature, and because you hoped that the cold of winter would close around you and keep you from ever feeling anything again."

"I never even saw a Kaled'a'in until I came here," came the whisper from his shoulder.

"Ah." He massaged the back of her neck with one hand, while the other remained holding her to his chest. "So. You know, you don't have to answer me, but who are you? If you have any relatives still alive, they would probably like to know that you are living, too."

"How would you know?" The reply sounded harsh, but he did not react to it, he simply answered it.

"I know—partly because one of my tasks as a kestra'chern is to pass that information on to Urtho in case any of your relations *have* been looking for others of their blood. And I know because I lost my family when they fled without me, and I have never found them again. And there is a void there, an emptiness, and a pain that comes with *not* knowing, not being able to at least write 'finished' to the question."

"Oh. I'm—sorry," she said awkwardly.

"Thank you," he replied, accepting the spirit of the apology.

He sensed that she was not finished, and waited.

Finally, she spoke again.

"Once, my name was Lady Reanna Laury. . . ."

Winterhart spoke, and Amberdrake listened, long into the night. She was his last client; he had instinctively scheduled her as the last client of any night she had an appointment, knowing that if her barriers ever broke, he would need many candlemarks to deal with the consequences. So she had all the time she needed.

He talked to her, soothed her—and did not lay a finger on her that was not strictly platonic. He knew that she half expected him to seduce her. He also knew that given any encouragement whatsoever, *she* would seduce *him*. But the situation was too complicated to allow for one more complication, and he would have been not only unprofessional but less than a friend if he permitted that complication to take place.

Much as he wanted to.

She was very sweet, very pliant, in his arms. He sensed a passionate nature in her that he doubted Conn Levas even guessed at. She was quite ready to show that nature to him.

But the essence of a kestra'chern's talent was a finely-honed sense of timing, and he knew that this was *not* the time.

So he sent her back to her tent exhausted, but only emotionally and mentally—comforted, but not physically. And he flung himself into his bed in a fever, to stare at the tent roof and fantasize all the things that he wished he *had* done.

He had never really expected that he would find anyone he wanted to share his life with. He had always thought that he would be lucky to find a casual lover or two, outside of his profession.

He had certainly never expected to find anyone so well suited to him—little though she knew the extent of it. Right now, she only knew that he could comfort her, that he had answers for the things that had eaten away at her heart until it bled. He did *not* want her until she had recovered from all this—until she knew what and who she was, and wanted him as an equal, and not as a comforter and protector.

She got enough of that with Conn.

For Winterhart, whatever she *had* been, was now a strong, vital, and competent woman. She had a deep capacity for compassion that she had been denying, fearing to be hurt if she gave way to it. She had overcome her fears to find some kind of training that would make her useful to Urtho's forces, and then had *returned* to take her place there, when hundreds of others who had not been affected as profoundly as she had remained deserters. Granted, she had not come back as herself, but at this point, any attempt to reveal her name and nature would only disrupt some of what Urtho had accomplished. The House and forces of Laury answered now to Urtho and not to those who had once commanded them and their loyalty by right of birth. Why disturb an established arrangement?

He thought he had persuaded her of that—and what was more, he thought *she* had figured that out for herself, but had been afraid that saying anything of the sort would only be taken for further cowardice. It wasn't, of course. It was only good sense, which in itself was in all-too-short supply.

"It would be different," he'd told her, "if we had a situation like Lord Cory's. He was back on his estate, in retirement, and was left the only member of his line to command his levy. So he did, even though he is far too old for the task. He's a fine commander, though, so Urtho isn't going to ask him to step down—but if one of his sons or daughters ever showed up, willing to take the old man's orders, there'd be a new field commander before you could blink."

"But the Laury people are commanded by General Micherone," Winterhart had observed, and sighed. "Bet Micherone is a better commander than I could ever be, and Urtho has the utmost confidence in her. I don't see any reason to come back to life."

"Nor do I," Amberdrake had told her. "You might ask Lady Cinnabar, since she knows the political situation better than I, but if she says not to bother, then there is no reason why you can't remain 'Winterhart' for the rest of your life." He chuckled a little, then, and added, "And if anyone asks why you have a Kaled'a'in name, tell them it's because you have been adopted into my sept and Clan. I'll even arrange it, if you like."

She'd looked up at him thoughtfully. "I would like that, please," she had replied. "Very much."

He wondered if she knew or guessed the significance of that. Kaled'a'in did not take in those from outside the Clans lightly or often—and it was usually someone who was about to marry into the Clans, someone who had sworn blood-brotherhood with a Kaled'a'in, or someone who had done the Clan a great service.

Still, he did not regret making the offer, and he would gladly see that the matter was taken care of. Because if things fell out the way he hoped—

Not now, he told himself. *Take one day at a time. First*

she will have to deal with Conn Levas. Only then should you make overtures. Otherwise she will be certain that she betrayed him, somehow, and she has had more than enough of thinking she was a traitor.

All it would take was patience. Every Kaled'a'in was familiar with patience. It took patience to train a hawk or a horse—patience to perform the delicate manipulations that would bring the lines of bondbirds and warsteeds to their fulfillment. It took patience to learn everything needed to become a shaman, or a Healer, or a kestra'chern.

But, oh, I have had enough of patience to last me the rest of my life! I should like some immediate return for my efforts for a change!

He would like it, but he knew better than to expect or even hope for it. It was enough that in the midst of all this pain and death, there was a little life and warmth, and that he was sharing in it.

And it was with that thought uppermost in his mind that he finally fell asleep.

Skandranon In Flight

Fourteen

A bird-scream woke Amberdrake out of a sound and dreamless sleep. He knew those screams; high-pitched, and sounding exactly as if a child were shrieking. He sat straight up in bed, blinking fog out of his eyes.

What—a messenger, at this hour! It was morning! What could—

But if someone had sent a messenger-bird to screech at the entrance to his tent, there was grave trouble. Anything less and there would have been time to send a hertasi rather than a bird. Before Gesten could get to the door flap, he had rolled out of bed and flung open the flap to let the bird in. It *whirred* up from the ground and hit his shoulder, muttered in agitation for a moment, then spoke in Tamsin's voice.

"Drake, we need you on the Hill—now."

That was all there was to the message, and normally the last person that Tamsin would ask for help on the Hill was Amberdrake, despite his early training. Amberdrake knew that Tamsin was only too well aware of his limitations— how his Empathic Gift tended to get right out of control even now. He was much better suited to the profession he had chosen, and they both knew it. But if Tamsin had sent a bird for him, then the situation up on the Hill was out of hand, and the Healers were dragging in every horse doctor and herb collector within running distance—and every other kestra'chern who knew anything of Healing or could hold a wound for stitching or soothe pain.

He flung on some clothing and headed for the Healers' tents at a dead run. There were plenty of other people boiling out of their tents wearing hastily-donned clothing; as he had surmised, he was not the only kestra'chern on the way up there. Whatever had happened, it was bad, as bad as could possibly be.

He found out just how bad it was when he arrived at the Healers' tents and stopped dead in his tracks, panting with effort, struck dumb by the sheer numbers of near-dead.

The victims overflowed the tents and had been laid out in rows wherever there was space. There was blood everywhere; soaking into the ground, making spreading scarlet stains on clothing and hastily-wrapped bandages. The *pain* hammered at him, making him reel back for a moment with the force of it pounding against his disciplined shields.

"Amberdrake!"

He turned at the sound of his name; Vikteren grabbed his arm and steered him into a tent. "Tamsin said to watch for you, they need you here, with the nonhumans," he said, speaking so quickly that he ran everything together. "I know some farrier-work, I'm supposed to assist you if you want me."

"Yes, I want you," Amberdrake answered quickly, squinting into the semidarkness of the tent. After the bright sunlight outside, it took a moment for his eyes to adjust.

When they did, he could have wished they hadn't. There were half a dozen kyree lying nearest the entrance, and they seemed to be the worst off; next to them, lying on pallets, were some tervardi and hertasi—he couldn't tell how many—and at the back of the tent, three dyheli. There was only one division of the forces that had that many nonhumans in combat positions, and his heart sank. "Oh, gods— the Second—?"

"All but gone," Vikteren confirmed. "Ma'ar came in behind them, and no one knows how."

But there was no time for discussion. He and his self-appointed assistant took over their first patient, a kyree that had been slashed from throat to tail, and then there was no time for *anything* but the work at hand.

Amberdrake worked with hands and Gift, stitching wounds and Healing them, blocking pain, setting bones, knitting up flesh. He worked until the world narrowed to his hands and the flesh beneath them. He worked until he lost all track of time or even who he was working *on*, trusting to training and instinct to see him through. And at last, he worked until he couldn't even see his hands, until he was so exhausted and battered by the pain and fear of others that the world went gray, and then black, then went away altogether.

And he found himself being supported by Vikteren, his head under the spout of a pump, the young mage frantically pumping water over him.

He spluttered and waved at Vikteren to stop, pushed himself up to a kneeling position, and shook the cold water out of his eyes. He was barely able to do that; he had never in all of his life felt so weak.

"You passed out," the mage said simply. "I figured that what worked for drunks would probably work for you."

"Probably the best thing you could have done," Amberdrake admitted and coughed. How many more wounded were there? His job wasn't done yet. "I'd better get back—"

He started to get up, but Vikteren restrained him with a hand on his shoulder. He didn't do much but let it rest there, yet that was enough to keep Amberdrake from moving.

"There's nothing left to go back to. You didn't pass out till you got the last tervardi and a couple of the humans that the others hadn't gotten to yet. The rest no one could have helped," Vikteren told him. Amberdrake blinked at that, and then blinked again. The mage was a mess—his clothing stiff with blood, his hands bloodstained. He had blood in his hair, his eyes were reddened and swollen, and his skin was pale.

"We're done?" he asked, trying not to sound too hopeful.

Vikteren nodded. "Near as I can tell. They brought the last of the wounded in through the Jerlag Gate, evacuated the rearguard, and shut it down about a candlemark ago."

Evacuated? Shut the Gate down? Amberdrake blinked, and realized then that the light shining down on both of them was entirely artificial, one of the very brilliant mage-lights used by the Healers. Beyond the light, the sky was completely black, with a sprinkling of stars.

We've been working all day?

"Sunset was about the same time they shut the Gate

down," Vikteren told him, answering his unspoken question. "Urtho's up at the terminus now, and—"

A ripple in the mage-energies, and an unsettled and unsettling sensation, as if the world had just dropped suddenly out from underneath them, made them both look instinctively to the north. The Jerlag Gate was in the north, beyond those mountains in the far distance.

Far, far off on the horizon, behind the mountains, there was a brilliant flash of light. It covered the entire northern horizon, so bright that Vikteren cursed and Amberdrake blinked away tears of pain and had false-lights dancing before his eyes for several moments.

It took much longer than that before either of them could speak.

Vikteren said carefully, "So much for the Jerlag Gate."

"Did he—" Amberdrake could hardly believe it, but Vikteren was a mage, and *he* would recognize what Urtho had done better than any kestra'chern.

Vikteren nodded. "Fed it back on itself. Ma'ar may have taken Jerlag, but it's cost him a hell of a lot more than he thought it would. That's the first time Urtho's ever imploded one of his permanent Gates."

The thought hung between them, ominous and unspoken. *And it probably won't be the last.*

Amberdrake swallowed; he could not begin to imagine the forces let loose in the implosion of a fixed Gate. Vikteren could, though, and the young mage squinted off at the horizon.

"Probably a hole about as big as this camp, and as deep as the Tower there now," he said absently.

And then it was Amberdrake's turn to grab for *his* arm and steady him, as he trembled, lost his balance, and started to fall. He was heavier than Amberdrake could support in his own weakened condition; he lowered the mage down to the muddy ground in a kind of controlled fall, and leaned against him. Vikteren blinked at him with glazed eyes.

"You collapsed," Amberdrake told him gently. "You aren't in much better shape than I am."

"You can say that again, Drake." Gesten padded up into the circle of light cast by the mage-light overhead, with

Aubri and two of Lady Cinnabar's hertasi with him. "The Lady told me where you were. She and Tamsin and Skan are worried sick. I'm supposed to have Dierne and Lysle help Vikteren back to his tent and get some food in *him*, while Aubri helps me get you back to yours." The hertasi patted the young mage on the shoulder. "Good work, boy. Tamsin says you two basically took care of every badly injured non-human that came in. *Real* good work. If I had a steak, I'd cook it up for you myself."

"Right now a couple of boiled eggs and some cheese sounds fine," Vikteren croaked, his face gone ashen. "I'd rather not look at meat just now—could look like someone I knew. . . ."

Gesten gestured to the other two hertasi who levered Vikteren back up to a standing position and supported him on his feet. "Get some food, get some rest. And *drink* what these two give you. It'll keep you from having dreams."

"Nightmares, you mean," Amberdrake murmured, as the hertasi helped the mage down the hill, step by wavering step. "I remember *my* first war-wounded."

"As do we all," Aubri rumbled. "Gesten, if you can get him standing—Amberdrake, you lean on my back—"

As he got to his feet, he began to black out again, and Gesten *tsked* at him as he sat abruptly back down. "I thought as much," the hertasi said. "You've drained yourself. You're going to be a right mess in the morning."

"I'm a right mess now." Amberdrake put his head down between his knees until the world stopped spinning around him. "I hope you have a solution for this. I'd hate to spend the rest of the night sleeping in the mud."

"That's why I brought Aubri. Just give us a moment." The hertasi hustled into one of the supply tents, and came back out again with a number of restraining straps and a two-man litter. While Aubri muttered instructions, Gesten rigged a harness over Aubri's hindquarters, and stuck one set of the litter handles through loops in the harness. "Get yourself on that, Drake," the hertasi ordered. "I've got this inclined so Aubri takes most of your weight."

Amberdrake did manage to crawl onto the litter, but he was so dizzy that it took much longer than he thought it

would, and his head pounded in time with his pulse until
he wanted nothing more than to have someone knock him
out. He knew what it was; he'd overextended himself,
drained himself down to nothing. He was paying the price
of overextending, and he wouldn't be the only Healer who'd
done that today.

He closed his eyes for the journey back to his tent; when
he opened his eyes again, he was being lifted into his bed.
But the moment he tried to move, his head exploded with
pain, so he closed his eyes again and passively let them do
whatever Gesten told them to. He wound up in a half-sitting
position, propped in place by pillows.

When he opened his eyes again, the tent was silent, lit
only by a single, heavily-shaded lantern, and Gesten was still
there, although Aubri and the rest of the hertasi's recruits
were long gone. Gesten turned with a cup in his foreclaw,
and pushed it at him.

"Here," he said brusquely. "Drink this, you know what it
is."

Indeed he did; a compound of herbs for his head and to
make him sleep, so thick with honey he was surprised the
spoon didn't stand in it. At this point, he was too spent to
protest, and too dizzy to care. Obediently, he let the too-
sweet, sticky liquid ooze down his throat.

Then he closed his eyes, waiting for the moment when
the herbs would take effect. And when they did, he slid into
the dark waters of sleep without a single ripple—for a while.

Winterhart had never wanted quite so much to crawl away
into a hole and sleep for a hundred years. Instead, she
dragged herself back to her tent and collapsed on her bedroll.
She curled into a fetal position, and waited for her muscles
to stop twitching with fatigue, too tired even to undress.

Urtho was losing. That was the general consensus. The
only question was if their side would continue to lose
ground, or if Urtho would come up with something that
would hold Ma'ar off for a little longer.

*We're being eroded by bits and pieces, instead of being
overrun the way I thought we'd go.* Even that stark certainty

failed to bring her a shiver of fear. She was just too tired.

It wasn't just tending her own charges now, it was being called up the Hill at a moment's notice whenever too many wounded came in. And it wasn't just her—it was everyone, anyone who even knew how to wrap a bandage. She'd seen Amberdrake working so long and so hard today that he'd become a casualty himself, and he wasn't the only one, either. The rest of the kestra'chern worked just as hard, and even the *perchi* came in to mix herbal potions and change bandages. For now, all the little feuds and personality conflicts were set aside.

Unfortunately, Shaiknam and Garber have their commands again. Although General Shaiknam no longer had nonhumans or mages under his command, he was still managing to account for far too many casualties. When he succeeded, he did so in grand style, but it was always at a high cost in terms of fighters.

I wish that Urtho would just put him in charge of siege engines and catapults. They don't die.

Well, she no longer had to parrot Garber's stupid orders, or try to make excuses for him. And the Sixth was holding its own at the moment. Perhaps they would continue to hold, and Ma'ar would give up for a while, let things stand at stalemate, and give them all time to breathe.

Footsteps outside the tent warned her in time to roll over to face the back of the tent and feign sleep. It was Conn, of course, and wanting the usual; she could not imagine where he got any energy to spare when everyone else was exhausted.

He shoved the tent flap open roughly, and stood beside her bedroll, waiting for her to wake up. Except that she wasn't going to "wake up."

I'm tired of you, Conn. I'm tired of your so-called "temperament." I'm tired of acting like your mother as well as your lover. I'm very tired of being your lover; you have no couth and no consideration.

It occurred to her then that he had so little consideration for her that he might well try to shake her awake. Then she would have no choice but to give up the ruse.

But I'm damned if I'll perform for you, Conn. You'll get me the way I feel—too tired to move a muscle, with nothing left over for anything or anyone, not even myself.

He stood there a moment longer, and experimentally prodded her with his toe once or twice.

Very romantic, Conn.

But she had seen people fallen so deeply asleep that nothing short of an earthquake would wake them. She knew how to simulate the same thing. She remained absolutely limp, neither resisting the push from his toe, nor reacting to it. Finally he muttered something uncomplimentary and left the tent.

She stayed in the same position in a kind of wary stupor; there was no telling how Conn would react to having his wishes flaunted. He might just linger outside the tent, waiting to see if she moved or even came out. He might even come back with a bucket of cold water—

No, he won't do that. He wouldn't want to use the bedroll if it had been soaked.

But he might find some other way of waking her up and return with it.

It's a good thing he won't be able to find a messenger-bird now that it's past sunset. He'd probably bring one back here and have it shriek in my ear. The little beggars love dramatics; he wouldn't have any trouble getting one to cooperate.

But nothing happened, and when her arm fell asleep, she finally turned over, keeping her eyes cracked to mere slits.

There was a light right outside her tent, and if there had been anyone lurking out there he'd have shown up as a silhouette against the canvas. There wasn't a sign of Conn, and as her arm came back to life and she sat up, swearing softly, he didn't come bursting into the tent.

She sighed and massaged her left hand with her right, cursing as it tingled and burned. Her eyes felt dry, and gritty, as if she'd been caught in a sandstorm. She left off massaging her hand and rubbed them; it didn't stop the itching, but at least they didn't feel quite so dry anymore.

This end of camp was silent—frighteningly silent. Anyone not on duty was sleeping, wasting not a single moment in any other pursuits. As she listened, she heard the deliberate pacing of a sentry up and down the rows of tents, and the rustle of flags in the breeze, the creaking of guy ropes and the flapping of loose canvas.

And something muttered just overhead.

She peered up, where the tent supports met in a cross. There was a tiny creature up there, perched on the poles.

She got to her feet, somehow, and reached up to it without thinking. Only as her hand touched it and she felt feathers did it occur to her that it could have been *anything*—a rat, a bat, some nasty little mage-accident.

But it wasn't; it was only a messenger-bird. She slipped her fingers under its breast-feathers as it woke and muttered sleepily, and it transferred its hold on the pole to a perch on her hand.

She brought it down carefully. While they were very tame, they were also known to nip when they were startled. She scratched it with one finger around its neck-ruff while it slowly woke, grumbled to itself, and then, finally, pulled away and fluffed itself up.

It tilted its head and looked up at her; obligingly, she got into the light from outside so that it could see her face and identify her. It snapped its beak meditatively once or twice, then roused all its feathers again and spoke.

Canceling your appointment tonight, it said in Amberdrake's voice, and it was uncanny the way the tiny bird was able to imitate sheer exhaustion overlaying the words and making him slur his sentences. *Too tired. Tomorrow, if we can. 'M sorry.*

She sat back down again, obscurely disappointed. Not that she was up to so much as a walk to the mess tent, much less halfway across camp! And *he* certainly wasn't up to giving her any kind of a massage, not after the way she'd seen him slaving today.

But we could have talked, she thought wistfully. *We could have cried on each other's shoulders . . . comforted each other.*

Suddenly she realized that she no longer thought of him as "the kestra'chern Amberdrake"—not even as her Healer. She *wanted* to tell him every grisly detail—the men that had died under her hands, the fighters who were never going to see, or walk, or use a weapon again. She wanted to weep on his shoulder, and then offer him that same comfort back again. She needed it, and she guessed that he did, too. His friends were as mind-sick and exhausted as he was, and would be in no position to console him.

Or else they have others they would rather turn to.

If only he hadn't canceled the appointment! If only she could go to him—

Well, why not? came the unbidden thought. *Friends don't need appointments to see each other.*

That was true enough, but—

Dear gods, it was a long walk! She held the little bird in her cupped hand, petting its back and head absently as it chuckled in content. Just the bare thought of that walk was enough to make her weep. *He* might have exhausted his Healing powers, but *she* had been lifting and reaching, pulling and hauling, all day. Small wonder her muscles burned with fatigue, and felt about as strong as a glass of water.

Footsteps crunched on the gravel of the path between the rows of tents, drawing nearer, but they were too light to be Conn's, so she dismissed them as she tried to muster the strength just to stand. *If I can get to my feet, maybe I can get as far as the mess tent. If I can get as far as the mess tent, maybe I can get to the bath house. If I can get that far—*

The footsteps paused just outside her door flap, and the silhouette against the canvas was not at all familiar. Until the man turned sideways, as if to go back the way he came.

"Amberdrake?" she said aloud, incredulously. The man outside paused in mid-step, and turned back to the doorflap. "Winterhart?" Amberdrake said cautiously. "I thought you were probably asleep."

"I—I'm too tired to sleep, if that makes any sense," she replied, so grateful that he was here that she couldn't think of anything else. "Oh, please, come in! I was just trying to get up the energy to come visit you!"

He pushed open the tent flap and looked down at her, sitting on her bedroll, little messenger-bird in her hands. "You got my message—" he said hesitantly.

"Since when do friends need an appointment to talk?" she retorted, and was rewarded with his slow, grateful smile. "I had the feeling we both needed someone to talk to tonight."

"You'll never know how much," he sighed, collapsing on the bedroll beside her.

As she looked at him, sitting there in the shadows of the tent, and wanting nothing more than to *talk*, a warmth started somewhere inside her and began to spread, as if a cold place within had thawed at long last, and the warmth was reaching every part of her.

"Would you like to start first, or may I?" he asked, courteous as always.

He needed her! *He* needed *her*, and not the other way around! She sensed the pain inside him, an ache that was so seldom eased that he no longer expected to find relief for it. How long had he been carrying this burden of grief? Certainly longer than just today.

"You first," she said, acting on generous impulse. "I think you must need to talk more than I do. After all, you were the one who made the long walk here."

It was too dark to see his face, but she sensed that he was startled. "Perhaps I do. . . ." he said, slowly.

She put the bird on the dressing stand, and reached out and took one of his hands. It was cold; she cupped it in both of hers to warm it.

Sharing the warmth; sometimes that's all that's needed, I think. . . .

Skan wheeled sideways and left an opening for Zhaneel to stoop on the pursuing makaar. The one behind him, intent upon making the Black Gryphon into shredded flesh, was a nasty, mottled deep blue, with freshly-broken horns still bleeding from colliding with another of his misshapen brethren. Skandranon acted as the lure for Zhaneel's stoops, flying against the thin clouds to show up better from the ground. The gryfalcon, high above, saw through the wispy clouds easily, and it was simplicity to time when she would fall upon the pursuing makaar.

On time, a cracking sound followed by a descending scream marked Zhaneel's arrival behind him, and she shot past and under him at well over three times his speed. Skandranon's eyes blazed with approval, as they did every time Zhaneel fought beside him. He went into his follow-up while she arced upward to retake her position of superior altitude, higher than any makaar could fly.

Beautiful! And it's working. She's unstoppable when she is in her element, and the new makaar are more fragile than the last breed. Two breeds since Kili . . . wonder if he's still alive? Tchah, next group—

While the battle raged behind and below them, they managed to keep most of the makaar occupied so they wouldn't harry the retreat. *Retreat! Another one! And I warned Urtho to fortify and trap the valley to at least slow Ma'ar's advance, but we ran too thin on time and resources. Now our troops are beating their way back from the latest rout, and the best the gryphons can do is keep the makaar busy dying. Granted, it's fun, but all in all I'd rather be fat and happy in a warm tent, feeding Zhaneel tidbits of rabbit.*

In broad daylight, the Black Gryphon wasn't the most effective at stealthiness, so he and Zhaneel had worked out this particular style of combat on the way. It had turned into a predictable pattern by now, and the new makaar had apparently figured out that it took Zhaneel a certain amount of time to regain her aerial advantage. It was no longer quite so easy to kill makaar, but at least the makaar at this battle were down to manageable numbers. There couldn't be more than thirty.

Another flight of makaar—four, this time, in a height-staggered diamond—closed on Skandranon sooner than the previous flights had. They were going to clash with him behind Zhaneel's upward flight path, too soon for her to strike at them, but too close for Skan to make an effective stoop of his own. The result—they could chase Skan and exhaust him at their leisure, unless he slowed and fell to strike at them.

Either result reduces my chances of survival significantly, and I am not interested in that at all. Isn't there something better you could be doing, stupid gryphon? Maybe eating. Or dancing. Dancing—

Ah! Now that is something the makaar wouldn't expect.

They're counting on me speeding past them, or slowing—but if I pull up and stop, that might just break up their formation. Makaar without a formation are also known as scattered bodies. This may be fun again after all!

So, that hertasi backspin-pointe that Poidon had shown him before the Harvest festival could finally come to some use, if his back could stand up to the deceleration. Amberdrake's Healing, coupled with Tamsin and Cinnabar's periodic care, should have his tendons and muscles in good enough shape to handle it. Since he was a broadwing, cupping enough air to stop should not be a problem, but the speed was going to be a critical factor.

Zhaneel was about to clear the cloud layer on her upswing, but couldn't know what was going on behind her. She'd be expecting Skandranon to be in the next quarterspan, and he wouldn't be there on time; she'd stay on station until she located him. If he slowed his flight too much right now, the makaar could guess his intention and swarm him. And even if. . . .

You'll talk yourself out of doing anything at all, while those four uglies are debating what sauce to put on your bones! Honestly, gryphon, you should know better. Urtho's given you more than wings, you know. You have a brain to think with. That brain's learned spells, you silly side of beef, and the makaar won't be expecting that. Makaar only act on what they expect, remember? They're expecting you to be dead, dead, dead, not the proud father of little gryphlets.

Basic dazzling should do the job, but that took a moment of time and repose—*repose? Who told you that? It takes a moment of concentration, nothing more, you worrying lump. You can't do it while you're flying, but you can do it while you're falling. Falling should be in your immediate future, if you can do the backspin-pointe. You only need one calm moment.*

The makaar gained and shrieked at him, Skan recognized Kili in the lead, and that immediate future became *now.* Skandranon pointed his beak toward the clouds, and arched his body backward. The air rushing against his throat was nearly enough to stop the blood flow to his head, despite the cushioning effects of his feathers. Slowly and deliberately, in what seemed like years of constant effort, he changed the angle of attack of his broad wings until he kited upward. His forward speed was decreasing rapidly, and in this deadly game, speed and endurance were all that kept a flier alive.

To the makaar, it must have appeared at first that he was surrendering. The old maxim of trading speed for altitude held true as long as Skandranon kept his wings at a good angle of attack. He would be higher, but eventually he'd come to a stall and stop completely. Then, as his old enemy Kili surely knew, he would fall, and four makaar were sure to slice him open as he hurtled toward the unforgiving ground.

Zhaneel, if this doesn't work, don't tell anyone I did something this stupid, please?

The makaar screamed their glee as he slowed in midair, his arms and wings spread. Kili started to shriek a victory cry. He straightened his body in midair with one leg pulled close, the other at pointe. The Black Gryphon hung at the apogee of his climb for a moment.

A calm moment.

Just one calm moment. . . .

Zhaneel pumped her wings furiously, still game for the hunt but growing physically weary. The air was thin above the filmy layer of clouds that she and the Black Gryphon were using for cover, and her lungs had trouble supplying her body for long up here. Her claws hurt from hammering makaar, too.

But she was making a *difference.* Fighting beside the Black Gryphon was everything she had dreamed it could be, and more. They worked so well together, it seemed like nothing could go wrong—but she knew better than to believe such things. Ma'ar and his commanders were cunning, and each strike the gryphon pair made could be their last. That made the elation at every success all the sweeter.

They'd been devastating on the makaar so far today, but the knowledge that it was to cover a withdrawal weighed on her mind. It was one thing to be greeted as heroes for making a glorious advance; it was quite another to dodge the enemy as you ran for home. Things looked bad enough already by the time the army came boiling out of Ma'ar's ground-Gate, rank after rank of identically uniformed humans with pole arms and bows. Urtho's mage apparently hadn't arrived in time to stop Ma'ar's mage from opening the Gate, so the two gryphons took it upon themselves to disable Ma'ar's man. Skandranon was unable to hit him until after the majority of Ma'ar's ground troops had come through, and then the makaar had clouded like gnats.

That had resulted in one of Zhaneel's proudest moments; the mighty Black Gryphon had gotten his foot caught in the camouflage net the mage had been hiding behind. He was tangled and could not free himself, anchored to the ground by the body of the mage which was also trapped in the downed net, and the mage's men were advancing on Skandranon from the escarpment below. Zhaneel streaked in and cut the net away with her shears, then pushed the broken body of the mage, net and all, down the rocky slope to slow down the troops while Skan beat his way skyward. Just the kind of rescue she'd dreamed of!

And now, her beloved Black Gryphon was down below the clouds, waiting for her to strike again at the makaar that would inevitably be pursuing him. She lined up on where he should be, readied for her stoop, and peered through the thin clouds—and Skandranon wasn't there!

Her voice caught and she felt her throat going tight. This high up, her instinct to keen could strangle her, she realized with growing horror. The air was thinner, she couldn't let herself keen—but where *was* he? She couldn't *help* but cry out in worry!

But sure enough, there was no broadwinged black shape moving relentlessly under the haze of cloud that she could see. He *should* be right *there*! That's where his momentum would have him, and he wasn't *there*! She folded her wings and looped in a frantic search for him—

—and then there was a flash of light below her. Her eyes darted to the location of the dazzling burst, and at the center of a diamond of four stunned makaar was a falling black mass.

Skandranon!

Zhaneel fell upon the helpless makaar, as unstoppable as

lightning. *No* damned makaar were going to harm *her* beloved!

Skandranon opened his eyes to find a planet spiraling closer and closer to him at high speed. Given the other things he could have been seeing at the moment—his internal organs dotting the sky, for instance, or makaar claws in his face—seeing that he was only falling was quite a welcome sight.

There were no makaar below him or to the sides, so he followed another bit of personal philosophy—*never look behind you, there may be an arrow gaining*—and forced himself to stay stone-still so that gravity could work its magic on him. Another few seconds, and he should be moving quickly enough that his wings would do him some good. *Then* he would see what shape the makaar behind him were in, and he'd try to find Zhaneel somewhere.

She must be on station by now and looking for him, and he wouldn't be where he was supposed to be. *You've lasted this long, skydancer, but will you survive what she'll do to you after the worry you'll cause her?*

Before he could formulate a rebuttal to his own question, the air around him shook from a massive displacement—and a makaar wing entered his vision only a handsbreadth from his face!

Kili's wing!

Skan desperately twisted sideways to bring his claws to bear on the enemy that was only a heartbeat away from disemboweling him. He lashed out with both foreclaws to latch onto the wing, intent upon taking the monster down with him—

—and found Zhaneel screaming past him in triumph, her shears clutched tightly in her hands. She was followed a second later by a mist of dark, cold blood, another wing, and the dying body of the now-wingless makaar flight leader. Zhaneel arced back up to come beside Skandranon and laugh along with him as he dropped the lifeless makaar wing and resumed controlled flight.

Oh, gods above, I am in love.

The other three makaar, still bedazzled by Skandranon's

spell, scattered and took their remaining brethren along with them. No more makaar harried the retreat, and Ma'ar's troops had already halted to assess their own losses.

Safe again, and there she was, flying beside him, every bit as confident and beautiful as Skandranon's wildest dreams.

Yes, Zhaneel, I am definitely in love. You are worth living for, no matter what comes. You are worth anything. . . .

Makaar

Fifteen

Peace, at last.

Amberdrake dropped the tent flap behind his last client for the evening; he turned with a whisper of silk to look back into the brightly-lit public chamber, and sighed with relief. Gesten raised his blunt snout from the towel chest, where he had been working, and looked straight at him and then away, as if the hertasi were going to say something, then thought better of it.

Not a comment or a complaint, or he wouldn't have hesitated, so it must be a request.

"Spit it out, Gesten," Amberdrake said patiently. "You want something. Whatever it is, you've more than earned it a dozen times over. What is it?"

"I'm tired, and I'd like to quit early and get some sleep," Gesten admitted, "But I don't want to leave you with all this mess to take care of alone, if you're tired, too. I thought you felt pretty good until I heard you sigh just now."

Amberdrake shook his head, and pulled his hair back behind his neck. "That *sigh* was because it is damned nice to be doing the job I'm trained for, and not playing second-rate Healer," he told the hertasi. "It was a sigh of contentment."

Amberdrake turned aside and went over to the portable folding table beside the couch, a table that currently held a selection of lotions and unguents, scented and not. He picked up the first, a half-empty bottle of camil-lotion, and put them in their proper order. He made very sure that the lid of each was properly tightened down before he put it away. Right now, there was no way of telling when he'd ever find replacements, and each drop was too precious to waste in evaporation or spillage. Cosmetics and lotions no longer appeared on the list of any herbalist's priorities. He knew how to make his own, of course, but when would he ever have the time or the materials?

Of course he might not ever need to find replacements. Ma'ar might very well make the question of where or how he would find them moot at any point.

Better not to think of that. Better just to enjoy the respite and try not to think of how brief it might be.

"No, Gesten, I'm not tired. Oddly enough, I think that exhausting myself on a regular basis up on the Hill only made me learn how to make better use of my resources," he continued. "Either that, or I'm fitter now than I was before. It's just such a pleasure to get back to being nothing more than a simple kestra'chern. . . ." A pregnant silence alerted him, and he turned to see that Gesten was grinning a toothy hertasi grin. He made a face. "And you can wipe that smug smile off your snout, my little friend. No puns, and no clever sallies. Just go get some rest. I had to clean up after myself long before *you* came along, and I think I can remember how."

If anything, Gesten's smile widened a bit more, but there was no doubt that the hertasi was as tired as he claimed. Probably more so; the past few days had not been easy ones for him, either. If anything, he had gotten less rest than Amberdrake. His scales had dulled, and he carried his tail as if the weight of it was a burden to him. That didn't stop him from exercising his tongue, however.

He bowed, spreading his foreclaws wide. "Yes, O greatest of the kestra'chern, O master of massage, O summit of the sensuous, O acme of the erogenous, O prelate of—"

"That'll do," Amberdrake interrupted. "One of these days, Gesten, you're going to get me annoyed."

"And when that happens, the moon will turn purple and there'll be fish flying and birds under the sea," Gesten jeered. "You almost *never* get angry, Drake, not even with people who deserve it. Demonsblood! The last time I saw you get angry was with that uppity Healer, the one that came all the way down from the Hill to tell you off, and *then* you cooled off by the time you got back to the tent! You ought to get angry a lot more often; you're too polite. You've got too much control for your own good. Dams break, you know."

But Amberdrake shook his head, and continued to put the jars and bottles back into their special places, each one in order. The sendel-wood lined case had cushioned slots for each, so that no matter how roughly the case was handled, the contents would never break or spill. And, after all the times of trouble in the recent past, doing a simple task was relaxing. So was simply talking to his dear hertasi rather than trading snap opinions of how to deflect this emergency or that crisis. "It's not that I'm polite, it's that I know too much about human nature—and I know how it can be twisted and deformed until people turn into monsters. That makes it difficult to stay angry with anyone for very long, since I generally know what their feelings and motivations are. Now that I've talked with Urtho about our enemy, I even know why Ma'ar is the way he is. I *can* manage to stay angry with Ma'ar; I just wish that knowing the reasons for his behavior would make some difference in stopping him."

"But you never stay angry with anyone else," Gesten argued. "And people think you're weak because of that. They think that they can walk all over you. And they think that because you don't fight back, you must really think that *they* are in the right."

He had to raise a surprised eyebrow at that. "Do they really?" he replied. "Interesting. Well, Gesten, that's all to the good, don't you think? If they believe that I'm a weakling, they'll underestimate me. If they think I'm harboring some kind of secret guilt or shame, they'll believe that I'm handicapped in dealing with them. I'll be able to defeat their purposes or get around them with a minimum of effort, and they'll have spent their strategy-time gloating that they've already won."

Gesten snorted scornfully. "Maybe you think so—but what about all the folk like that damned Healer? The ones who look down their noses at you, think they're better'n you, and say rotten things behind your back? How're you going to stop a whispering campaign against you? How're you going to deal with people who slander you?"

Amberdrake shrugged. "I'll do what I always do. Find out who they are and what they're saying. Once I know who the dagger is likely to come from, I have options. I can duck, I can find something to use as a shield, or I can tell the right people to deal with my detractors from a position of authority without my getting personally involved."

Gesten growled, and it was clear that he was annoyed at Amberdrake's calm reasoning. "Mostly, you duck. And they go on thinking you're weak. Worse, they figure you've just *proved* that they're right, because you won't come after them!"

He thought about that carefully for a moment, then lifted the now-filled chest and returned it to its proper place against the tent wall. "That's true," he said at last. "But as long as what they say and do does me no real harm, *why should I care?* As long as I know who they are, so that I can guard against real harm in the future, there's no point in dealing with them on any level. And it makes them happy."

Gesten's mouth dropped open and his eyes widened. "I don't believe I just heard that," he said, aghast. "That poison they spread—it's like stinky, sticky mud, it sticks to everything it touches and makes it filthy, contaminates everyone who hears it! Worse, it makes other people want to spread the same poison! Why would you want to make *them* happy?"

Amberdrake turned back to his little friend, and sat with a sad smile on his face. "Because they are bitter, unhappy people, and very little else makes them happy. They say what they do out of envy, for any number of reasons. It may be because I lead a more luxurious life than they, or at least they believe I do. It may be because there are many people who *do* call me friend, and those are all folk of great personal worth; a few of them are people that occupy high position and deservedly so. Perhaps it is because they cannot do what I can, and for some reason, this galls them. But they have so little else that gives them pleasure, I see no reason to deprive them of the few drops of enjoyment they can extract from heaping scorn and derision on me."

Gesten shook his head. "Drake, you're crazy. But I already knew that. I'm getting some sleep; this is all too much for me. Good night."

"Good night, Gesten," Amberdrake said softly, rising again and beginning to pick up scattered pieces of clothing.

I wonder if I should have told him the whole truth? he thought, as he stacked pillows neatly in the corner. *Maybe he was right, maybe I should get angry, but I don't have the energy to waste on anger anymore. There are more important things to use that energy for than to squander it on petty fools.*

If there hadn't been a war, would he still feel the same way? *No way of knowing. Maybe.* He thought for a moment about the "enemies" he had among Urtho's ranks—most of them on the Hill, Healers who felt that he was debasing *their* noble calling; some few among the officers, people he had refused to "serve" for any amount of money.

The motives of the latter were easy to guess; those that Amberdrake sent away were not likely to advertise the fact, but the rejection infuriated them. For most of them, it was one of the few times anyone had ever dared to tell them "no." But the motives of the Healers were nearly as transparent. The fact that he used much the same training and *identical* Gifts to bring something as trivial as "mere" pleasure to others sent them into a rage. The fact that he was well paid for doing so made them even angrier.

He could see their point; they had spent many years honing their craft, and they felt that it should never be used for trivial purposes. But how was giving pleasure trivial? Why must everything in life be deadly and deathly serious? Yes, they were in the middle of a war camp, but he had discovered this gave most folk an even greater need for a moment of pleasure, a moment of forgetfulness. Look at Skan; even in the midst of war and death, he found reasons for laughter and love.

Maybe that was why those enemies often included the Black Gryphon on the list of those to be scorned.

Oh, these are people who would never coat a bitter pill, for fear that the patient would not know that it was good for him. Never mind that honey-coating something makes it easier—and more likely—to be swallowed. And if this had been a time of peace, they would probably be agitating at Urtho's gates to have Amberdrake thrown out of the city without a rag to his name.

And they would be angry and unhappy because if this were a time of peace—I would be a very rich kestra'chern. That is not boasting, I do not think.

And in that time of peace, Urtho would listen to their poison, and nod, and send for Amberdrake. And Amberdrake would come, and the two would have a pleasant meal, and all would remain precisely as it had been before—except that Amberdrake would then know exactly who was saying what.

Which is exactly what happens now. Except that it's Tamsin and Skan, Gesten and Cinnabar, who tell me these things rather than Urtho. We kestra'chern are officially serving, even as they, and it is obvious that we have a place here as far as Urtho is concerned. Besides, if they tried to rid the camp of us and of the perchi, *there would be a riot among the line fighters.*

But would he hate his enemies, if he had the time and the energy to do so?

I don't think so, he decided. *But I would be very hurt by what they said. I am now, though I try not to dwell on it. I may not hate people, but I do hate the things that they do. Whispering campaigns, hiding behind anonymity—those I hate. As Gesten said, they are poison, a poison that works by touch. It makes everyone it touches sick, and it takes effort and energy to become well again.*

For all of his brave words to Gesten, he felt that way now, hurt and unhappy, and it took effort to shrug off the feelings.

He immersed himself in the simpler tasks of his work, things he had not done since Gesten had come to serve him, to help push the hurt into the background. Putting towels away, draining and emptying the steam-cabinet, rearranging the furniture . . . these things all became a meditative exercise, expending the energy of anger and hurt into something useful. As he brought order into his tent, he could bring order into his mind.

Although Skan claims that a neat and orderly living space is the sign of a dangerously sick mind, he thought with amusement, as he folded coverings and stacked them on one end of the couch. *It's a good thing that gryphons don't have much in the way of personal possessions, because I've seen his lair.*

"Amberdrake?" It was a thin whisper behind him, female, and it was followed by what sounded like a strangled sob.

He dropped the last blanket and turned quickly, wondering if his mind was playing tricks on him. But—no, he had *not* imagined it; Winterhart stood in the doorway, tent flap drawn aside in one hand, clearly in tears.

He quickly reached out, grasped her hand in both of his, and drew her inside. The tent flap fell from her nerveless fingers and he took a moment to tie it shut, ensuring their privacy. "What happened?" he asked, as she took a few stumbling steps, then crumpled onto the couch, clutching a pillow to her chest with fresh tears pouring down her face. "What's the matter? Don't worry about being interrupted, my last client just left, and I have all night for you if you need it."

"I may," she said, rubbing the back of her hand fiercely across her eyes. "I'm sorry, I didn't mean to fall apart on you like this—it's just—I saw you standing there and you looked so confident, so strong—and I feel so—so—*horrible.*"

He sat down beside her, and took her into his arms, handing her a clean towel to dry her tears and blow her nose with. It might not be a handkerchief, but it was at hand.

"Tell me from the beginning," he said, as she took several deep breaths, each of which ended in a strangled sob. "What happened?"

"It—it's Conn," she said, muffled in the towel. "You knew we haven't been—for a couple of weeks now. Mostly it was because I was exhausted, but sometimes—Amberdrake, I just didn't *want* to. There's nothing there for him anymore, even if there ever was. I just wished he'd go away. So tonight, when his group came back in and he started on me—well, that's when I told him that I wanted him to leave—and not just for right then, but permanently."

"And?" Amberdrake prompted gently.

"He said—" she burst into tears again. "He started yelling at me, telling me how worthless I am. He said I was a cold, heartless bitch, that I didn't have the capacity to love anyone but myself. He said I was selfish and spoiled, and all I cared about was myself. He said I was the worst lover he'd ever had, that it was like making love to a board, and that I'd never find another man as tolerant as he was. He said I was probably a Trondi'irn because no human would have me as a Healer, and if it weren't for the fact that there's no one checking on the Trondi'irn's competence, I wouldn't even have that job. He said I was clumsy, incompetent, and if there weren't a war on, I'd be a total failure—" She was weeping uncontrollably now, and if Amberdrake hadn't been listening carefully, he wouldn't have been able to understand more than half of what she said.

"And you're afraid that it's all true, right?" he said gently, as soon as she gave him the chance.

She nodded, quite unable to speak, her eyes swollen and bloodshot, her nose a brilliant pink. She looked horrible. He wanted to hold her in his arms and protect her from the rest of the world.

And then he wanted to take the nearest crossbow and go hunting for Conn Levas.

And I told Gesten I couldn't be angry with anyone anymore. . . .

But none of that would solve anything. She did not need to be coddled or protected; she needed to regain confidence in herself, so that she could stand on her own feet without having to hide behind anyone else.

"You think that what he said is true, only because you are very self-critical, and there *is* just enough truth in what he said to make you believe all of it," he said firmly. "We both know what kind of a manipulator he is. He plays people the way a musician plays his instruments—and he can do that because he simply doesn't care what happens to them so long as he gets the tune he wants." He pulled away a little, and looked her straight in the eyes. "Think about him for a moment. Right now, the one thing he is afraid of is that someone will think *you* left *him* because he isn't 'man enough to keep you.' He said what he did to make you feel too afraid to leave him. Let's take the things he said one at a time. What is the first thing that you can think of?"

"Th–that I'm a c–cold bitch?" she said, in a small voice.

"By which he means that you are both uncaring and an unsatisfactory lover?" he replied. "Well, so far as *he* is concerned, that's correct. You told me yourself that you didn't care in the least for him, emotionally, when you made your arrangement with him. You used him to protect your real identity. Reanna would never have had anything to do with someone like him, which made him perfect as part of your disguise. Right?"

"Reanna would never have taken *any* lover, much less a lowborn one," she replied, her cheeks flaming. "I—I—"

He shook his head gently. "You made an unemotional bargain, and you expected it to remain that way. It didn't. In part, because he was good enough at winkling out your real feelings and using them against you. Which by definition means that you are *not* without emotion. Yes?"

She nodded, still blushing, her eyes averted.

"He also claimed that you are incompetent and clumsy, and you are professional enough to fear that he is correct in that assessment as well." He thought for a moment. "The worst that I ever heard about you—and trust me, kechara, a kestra'chern hears a great deal—was that you parroted rotten orders without questioning them, and treated your charges as if they were so many animals. No one ever questioned your competence, only your—ah—manner. And now that you treat your gryphons as the people they *are*, you have the highest marks from everyone. Cinnabar included."

"I do?" She looked at him again, shocked.

"I don't know Conn Levas very well on a personal level, nor do I wish to," Amberdrake continued. "I had him as a client once, and I managed to avoid a second session; I have seen far too many people with his attitudes, and I don't feel I need to see any more. Furthermore, every other kestra'-chern that he has gone to feels the same about him as I do. The center of Conn's world is Conn; he is interested only in someone else insofar as they can do something for him. In his world, there are users and the used; once you took yourself out of the ranks of the latter, you must have become one of the former, and thus, you went from being his *possession* to his *rival*. So that is why he flung the other insults at you, about being selfish and spoiled. To his eyes, the universe is a mirror—he sees himself reflected everywhere, both his good and bad traits. People who are good to him must be like him—and people who are bad to him must *also* be like him."

She nodded, and rubbed her eyes with the corner of the towel.

"As for the rest of his accusations . . ." he paused a moment, and assessed his own feelings. *Should I? What happens if I do? And what would happen if I don't?* ". . . would you care to have a professional assessment?"

She pulled away, eyes wide with surprise. But not with fear or revulsion, the two things he had been worried that he would see in her expression.

"You can't—I mean, do you mean—" she stammered.

He smiled, and nodded. "The assessment would be professional," he told her, very quietly. "But the motives are purely selfish. I find you exceedingly attractive, Winterhart. I do not want to complicate our friendship, nor do I want to jeopardize it, but I wish that we were more than just friends."

She blinked for several moments, as her cheeks flushed and paled and flushed again. For a moment, he thought that she was going to refuse, and he wished that he had never said a word. Then, to his own delight and surprise, she suddenly flung herself at him. But not like a drowning woman grasping after safety, but like an eagle coming home to her aerie after a long and weary flight, and there was no doubt left at all, of her feelings—or of his.

The afternoon respite was rare enough for Skan—and that Amberdrake had time to spare was a gift from the hand of the gods. Time for the two of them to sit in the warm sun together—and as an excuse to keep others away, Amberdrake tasked himself with repairing feathers Skan had broken in the last engagement with the enemy.

"The word on the lines is—stalemate," said Skan, as Amberdrake imped in one of his old feathers on the shaft of a broken primary. "Again. Not a quiet stalemate though, at least not for us."

The warm sun felt so good on his back and neck . . . he stretched his head out and half-closed his eyes, flattening his ear-tufts and crest-feathers with pleasure.

"That seems to be the case up and down the lines," Amberdrake replied, his brows furrowed with concentration, as he carefully inserted the pin that would hold the new shaft to the old.

Skan turned his head a little, and watched him with interest, and not a little envy. He would have loved to have the hands to do things like this for himself. Even Zhaneel couldn't imp in her own feathers, for all that she had those wonderful, clever "hands." She could do plenty of other things he relied on a human for, though.

She no longer had the disadvantage of shortened foreclaws that had handicapped her in aerial combat. A human in the Sixth who had once been a trainer of fighting cocks had made her a set of removable, razor-sharp fighting "claws," that fit over the backs of her hands. She could still manipulate objects while wearing them, for they worked best when she held her own foreclaws fisted. Now she was as formidable as the strongest of the broadwings and wouldn't need to rely on her shears to take down makaar! These new claws were made of steel, sharp as file and stone could make them, and much longer than natural claws.

She had been so effective in claw-to-claw combat with the makaar while wearing these contraptions that the man had been pulled out of the ranks and set to making modified "claws" and "spurs" that other gryphons could wear. The makaar dropped with gratifying frequency, and gryphons wearing the new contraptions found themselves able to take out two and even three makaar more per sortie.

The trouble was, of course, that as soon as someone in the enemy ranks figured out what the gryphons' new advantage was, it would be copied for the makaar. It was only a matter of time.

As long as every makaar that gets close enough to see the new claws winds up dead, we can keep our secret weapon secret a little longer, Skan told himself. *And every makaar dead is one more that won't rise to fight us and will have to be replaced.*

"I understand that the word in the camp is much more interesting than that," Skan continued casually, looking back at his friend through slitted eyes.

Amberdrake fitted the trimmed feather onto the spike of the pin, and slowly eased it into place. Skan had expected him to hem and haw, but the kestra'chern surprised him by glancing up and smiling. "If you mean what's going on between Winterhart and me, you're right," he said, with a nod. "The situation between us is not a stalemate anymore." He looked back down and finished the work of gluing the feather to the steel pin and the place where both shafts met. "Hold still. Don't move. If you can sit there patiently until this sets, it's going to be perfect."

"Not a stalemate?" Skan asked, suppressing the urge to flip his wings, which would ruin Amberdrake's careful work. "Is that all you can say?"

Amberdrake peeled the last of the glue from his fingers, and tossed aside the rag he had used to clean up before he answered. "What else do you want me to say?" he asked. "She's the Sixth Wing East Trondi'irn, I'm theoretically the chief kestra'chern. She can't and won't abandon her duties, and neither will I. Mine take up a great deal of the evening and night, and hers take up a great deal of the daytime. Aside from that—we are managing. Conn Levas is back out in the field. He has made no moves to cause her trouble other than gossip and backbiting which we can both ignore. He chooses to believe that she is proving what a fool she truly is by taking up with a manipulating kestra'chern, and if that makes him happy and causes him to leave her alone, then he can spread all the gossip he wants so far as we are concerned. We have an ear among the mages in the person of Vikteren, so we know everything he says."

"Huh." Skan cast Amberdrake a look of dissatisfaction, but the kestra'chern ignored it. "Tamsin and Cinnabar had a lot more to say about it than that."

"Tamsin is a romantic, and Cinnabar was raised on ballads," Amberdrake retorted, his neck and ears flushing a little. "Winterhart and I are satisfied with the arrangement we have. We are fulfilling our duties exactly as we did before. That is all anyone needs to know."

Skan raised his head carefully and flattened his ear-tufts. "Heyla, excuse me!" he said in surprise at Amberdrake's controlled vehemence. "Didn't mean to pry. When you're in love, you know, you like to hear that the whole world's in love, too!"

Amberdrake finally looked into his eyes, and patted his shoulder. "Sorry, old bird," he said apologetically. "There've been too many people who want to make up some kind of romantic nonsense about the two of us being lifebonded, and just as many who want to turn me into the evil *perchi* who seduced the virtuous Winterhart away from the equally virtuous Conn Levas. I'm a little tired of both stories."

Skan nodded, but for all of Amberdrake's denials, there was very little doubt in his mind that Amberdrake and Winterhart *were* a lifebonded pair. Tamsin and Cinnabar said so, and they also said that those who were lifebonded tended to be able to recognize the state in others.

"It won't be easy for either of them," Tamsin had added pensively. "Lifebonding is hardly as romantic as the ballads make it out to be. Both of you have got to be strong in order to keep one from devouring the other alive. And you'd better hope that both of you are ready for the kind of *closeness* that lifebonding brings, especially between two people who are Empaths. You *can't* fight or argue—you feel your partner's pain as much as your own. You become, not two people precisely, but a kind of two-headed, two-personalitied entity, Tamsin-and-Cinnabar, and you'd better hope that one of you doesn't suddenly come to like something that the other detests because you wind up sharing just about everything!"

"But when it finally works," Cinnabar had added, with an affectionate caress for Tamsin, "it is a good thing, a partnership where strengths are shared and weaknesses minimized. *I* think that the good points all outweigh the bad, but I have reason to."

Neither of them had bothered to point out the obvious— that Tamsin was as low-born as Cinnabar was high, and if there had *not* been a war on, there would have been considerable opposition to their pairing even from Cinnabar's conspicuously liberal and broad-minded family. In fact, there had been terrible tragedies over such pairings in the past, which was why there were as many tragic ballads about life-bondings as there were romantic ones. Even Skan knew that much.

Well, if Amberdrake chose not to admit to such a tie with Winterhart, that was his business and not Skan's. And if he preferred to make the relationship seem as casual as possible, well, that was only good sense.

"Can't help what people say, and you know that Conn is the origin of most of the spiteful talk," Skan observed. "And as for the people who are spreading it, well, you know who *they* are, too. If it wasn't Winterhart, they'd make something up about you, and that's a fact. I just want to know one thing. Are you *happy*? Both of you?"

Amberdrake nodded, soberly. "I think that we are as happy as any two people can be, in this whole situation. We aren't *unhappy*, if that makes any difference." He sighed and smoothed down the vanes of the feather, blending the old one into the new. "This is a war; she deals with the physical hurts, I try to deal with the emotional ones. Every day brings more grief; I help her through hers, and she helps me through mine. Maybe—"

He didn't finish the sentence, but Skan knew the rest of it. It was the litany of everyone in Urtho's forces, from the lowest to the highest. "Maybe someday, when the war is over—"

The war had gone on so long that there was an entire generation of gryphons now fighting who had never known anything *but* the war. That probably went for humans, too. The war had turned the society that older folks sometimes talked about completely upside down, and even Skan could not remember most of what his elders talked about with such longing. The repercussions of that were *still* going on.

"Is it set?" Skan asked finally, when the silence between them had lingered for some time. Amberdrake seemed to jar himself awake from some pensive dream, and checked the joint with a careful finger.

"I think so," he replied. "Give yourself a good shake. If it holds through that, it's set."

Skan did so, gratefully. There was *nothing* like being told to hold still that made a gryphon *wild* for a good shake!

Amberdrake laughed and backed out of the way as the gryphon roused all of his feathers and then shook himself so vigorously that bits of down and dust went everywhere.

The newly-imped feather held, feeling and acting entirely as strong as any of the undamaged ones. He grinned in satisfaction and saluted Amberdrake with a jaunty wave.

"Excellent as always, my friend," he said cheerfully. "You should give up your wicked ways and become a full-time feather-artist."

"Very few gryphons are as *enthusiastic* in the performance of their duties as you are," Amberdrake countered. "I don't think I've had to imp in more than a dozen feathers in the last two years, and most of those were yours. I'd starve for lack of work."

"You could always tend hawks as well as gryphons," Skan suggested.

"*You* could always pull a travel-wagon," Amberdrake replied. "Thank you, no. I enjoy my duties. I would *not* enjoy tending psychotic goshawks, neurotic peregrines, murderous hawkeagles, and demented gyrefalcons. Have you ever heard the story about how you tell what a falconer flies?"

"No," Skan replied, with ear-tufts up. Hawks and falcons fascinated him, because they were so outwardly like and inwardly unlike a gryphon. "How do you?"

"The man who flies a falcon has puncture wounds all over his fist from nervous talons. The man who flies a goshawk has an arm that is white to the elbow, because he never dares go without his gauntlet. And the man who flies a hawkeagle is the one with the eye patch." Amberdrake's mouth quirked slightly, and Skan chuckled.

"I presume that must be a very old Kaled'a'in proverb," Skan told him, with the sigh that was supposed to tell Amberdrake he had quoted far too many Kaled'a'in proverbs. "But—nervous talons? What does that mean?"

"Tense birds have tense toes, and peregrines are notoriously nervous," Amberdrake said, his mouth quirking a little more, this time with a distinctly wicked glint in his eye. "Remember that the next time your little gryfalcon is startled when she's got some portion of you in her 'hands.' "

Skan laid her ear-tufts back with dismay. "You aren't serious, surely."

Amberdrake laughed and slapped the gryphon's shoulder. "You wouldn't do anything to make Zhaneel nervous, would you?"

"Of course not," he said firmly and wondered in the next moment if there was any chance. . . .

Amberdrake only chuckled. "I've spent enough time with you, featherhead. There are some things I need to take care of, and I'm certain that you have plenty to do yourself. So if you don't mind, I'll get on with my cleaning, and you get back to your mate."

Skan's crest rose with pleasure at that last word. *Mate.* He had a *mate.* And that mate was Zhaneel; swift, strong, and altogether lovely. . . .

He tugged affectionately on a mouthful of Amberdrake's hair, and then shoved the kestra'chern back in the direction of his own tent. "Back to your housekeeping, then. If you prefer it to my company. You really ought to know that a clean and neat dwelling place—"

"—is the sign of a disturbed mind, yes, I know." Amberdrake combed the hair Skan had mouthed back with his fingers, grinned, and took himself back into his tent before Skan could retort with anything else.

Such respites were doomed to be short in wartime.

The flight back to the gryphons' lairs was a short one, and normally completely uneventful. But as Skan took to the air and got above the tops of the tents, he saw evidence of a great deal of disturbance in that direction. Gryphons flew in to the lairs from all over the camp, their irregular wingbeats betraying agitation. Even at a distance he saw ruffled feathers and flattened ear-tufts, crests raised in alarm and clenched foreclaws. Yet there was no other sign of agitation in the camp, so either the gryphons were privy to something the rest of Urtho's forces hadn't found out yet or the information was pertinent only to gryphons.

It wouldn't be the first time we found out about something no one else knew, he thought with a sinking heart.

Immediately, he lengthened and strengthened his

wingstrokes, to gain more speed. Whatever had occurred, it was imperative that he learn what was going on!

The lairs had been built into an artificial hill, terraced in three rings, so that each lair had clear space in front of it. There was a small field full of sunning rocks between the lairs and the rest of the camp. That was where everyone had gathered. He landed next to a cluster of half a dozen gryphons from the Sixth that included Aubri. All of them listened intently to what the broadwing had to say, necks stretched out, and heads cocked a little to one side. Their sides heaved as they panted heavily, one of them hissed to himself; their neck-feathers stood straight out from their necks like a fighting-cock's ruff, and two of them rocked back and forth as their feet flexed. All of this was quite unconscious, and a sign of great agitation.

Aubri stopped in mid-sentence as Skan backwinged down on the top of a rock beside them, and waved Skan over with an outstretched foreclaw. "I've got bad news, Skan," he called out, as Skan leapt down off the rock and hurried over to join the group. "It's not all over camp yet, but it will be soon. General Farle's dead."

"What?" Skan could not have been more surprised if Aubri had told him that the Tower had just burned down. Farle? *Dead?* How did you kill a General without wiping out the entire Command? Chief officers were *never* anywhere near the front lines!

Granted, Farle had a reputation for wanting to be near the action, but the General wasn't stupid, and he was certainly the best-protected man in the Sixth! How had anyone gotten to him? Was it accident? Could it have been treachery?

"I was telling the others—we think that some kind of suicide group got through and took him out, him and most of the other chief officers of the Sixth," Aubri said. "We don't even know how or who did it. There was just an explosion in the command tent, and when the smoke and dust cleared, there wasn't much there but a smoking hole. The mages are trying to figure out just what happened, but the main thing for us is that we've lost him."

Skan swore. There was only one man of Farle's rank that was not already in a command position: Shaiknam, the General that Farle had replaced. The official story was that Shaiknam was on leave while Farle got more command experience, although the real reason Shaiknam had been taken out of the post was his incompetence.

But Urtho could not help being his optimistic self, nor could he stop giving unworthy people so many second chances that they might as well not even have gotten reprimanded. Urtho would remember all the great things that Shaiknam's father had done, probably assume that Shaiknam had learned his lesson and would give him back the command he had taken away, rather than promoting someone else.

After all, it would look very bad for General Shaiknam if Urtho *did* promote someone of a lower rank to command the Sixth, when Shaiknam was sitting there on his thumbs, doing nothing. Until now, Urtho had been able to maintain that polite fiction that he was "seasoning" Farle, and that General Shaiknam was taking a well-earned leave of absence to rest.

He would not be able to maintain it for more than a moment after the rest of the forces learned of Farle's death. It was either shame Shaiknam, with all the attendant problems that would cause, or give the Sixth back to the man who'd never completed a task in his life.

There was no doubt in Skan's mind which it would be. Shaiknam was too well-born, too well-connected. The Sixth would go back to him.

That seemed to be the conclusion everyone else had come to as well. With Shaiknam in charge, the gryphons of the Sixth just became deployable decoys again. Right now, the big question seemed to be what, if anything, they could *do* about it.

Skan moved from group to group, just listening, saying nothing. He heard much the same from each group; *this is dreadful, and we're all going to get killed by this madman, but we can't do anything about it.* There was a great deal of anxiety—panic, in fact—but no one was emerging with any ideas, or even as a leader willing and able to represent them all.

Which leaves—me. Well, this was the moment, if ever, to

act on the theories of leadership he had been researching all this time. *Can you be a leader, featherhead?* He looked around once more at the gathering of his kind; gryphons had started to pick at their feathers like hysterical messenger-birds, they were so upset.

I guess there isn't a choice. It's me, or no one.

He jumped up onto the highest sunbathing rock, and let loose with a battle-screech that stunned everyone else to silence.

"Excuse me," he said into the quiet, as startled eyes met his, and upturned beaks gaped at him. "But this seems to be a problem that we already have the solution to. Urtho doesn't control us anymore, remember? We are just as autonomous as the mages, if we want to be. We can all fly off into the wilderness and leave the whole war behind any time we want."

A moment more of silence, and then the assembled gryphons met his words with a roar of objections. He nodded and listened without trying to stem the noise or counter their initial words; most of the objections boiled down to the simple fact of the gryphons' loyalty to their creator. No one *wanted* to abandon Urtho or his cause. They just wanted to be rid of Shaiknam.

When the last objection had been cried out onto the air, and the assemblage quieted down again, he spoke.

"I agree with you," he said, marveling that not a single gryphon in the lot had made any objection to his assumption of leadership. "We owe loyalty—everything—to Urtho. We shouldn't even *consider* abandoning him. But we do not have to tell him that. The mages all felt exactly the same way, but they were perfectly willing to use the fact that they *could* all pack up and leave as a bargaining-chit. We should do the same thing. If the situation was less dangerous for us than it is, I would never suggest this course of action, but I think we all know what life for the Sixth was like under Shaiknam, and we can't allow a fool to throw our lives away."

Heads nodded vigorously all around him as crest-feathers slowly smoothed down, ear-tufts rising with interest. "You've got to be the one, Black Boy," Aubri called out from somewhere in the rear. "You've got to be the one to speak for us. You're the best choice for the job."

Another chorus, this time of assent, greeted Aubri's statement. Skan's nares flushed with mingled embarrassment and pride.

"I'll tell you what, then," he told them all, wondering if what he was doing was suicidally stupid, or would be their salvation. "I was trying to come up with a plan to get the confrontation over with quickly, before Shaiknam has a chance to entrench himself. Now, we all know that where Shaiknam goes, Garber follows, and I'm pretty certain he is going to be the one to try to bring us to heel initially. This is the tactic that just might work best. . . ."

Two messages came by bird from Garber, both of which he ignored. One of the gryphons who had a particularly good relationship with the birds smugly took the second one off for a moment when it arrived. When the gryphon was finished, the bird flew off. Shortly thereafter, messenger-birds rose in a cloud from the area around Shaiknam's tent, and scattered to the far corners of the camp.

That left Shaiknam and Garber with no choice but to use a human messenger. The gryphons of the Sixth took to their lairs to hide while the rest made themselves scarce, and Skan was the only gryphon in sight. He reclined at his ease up on the sunbathing rock, as an aide-de-camp in the colors of the Sixth came trudging up the path to the lairs, looking for the gryphons Garber had summoned so imperiously.

The gryphons in question hid in the shadows just out of sight, although they had a clear view of Skan and the aide. They were not going to show so much as a feather until Skan gave them the word.

The young man glanced curiously around the area—which looked, for all intents and purposes, to be completely deserted. Skan wondered what was going on in his mind. The gryphons were *not* with their Trondi'irn, who obviously had not been told of this impromptu conspiracy. They were not on the practice grounds, nor on Zhaneel's now-sanctioned obstacle course. They were not with the Command. They could only be at their lairs, unless they had all taken leave out of the area, and leave had not been approved.

Yet the lawn in front of the lairs was completely deserted. No sign of gryphons, nor where they had gone to. There was no one in the dustbathing pits, nor at the water-baths. No one lounged in the shady "porch" of his or her lair. No one reclined on a sunbathing rock.

Except Skan.

The Black Gryphon watched the man's expression as he tried to reconcile his orders with what he'd found. Skan was not precisely assigned to the Sixth, but he had been flying cover for Zhaneel. Skan would have to do.

The aide-de-camp took another look around, then squared his shoulder, and marched straight up to the Black Gryphon. Skan raised his head to watch him approach, but said and did nothing else.

"General Shaiknam has sent two messenger-birds here to rally the gryphons of the Sixth," the young man said crisply. "Why was there no answer?"

Skan simply looked at him—exactly the same way that he would have regarded a nice plump deer.

But the youngster was made of sterner stuff than most, and obviously was not going to be rattled simply by the stare of an unfriendly carnivore with a beak large and sharp enough to make short work of his torso. He continued bravely. "General Shaiknam orders that the gryphons of the Sixth report immediately to the landing field for deployment."

"Why?" Skan rumbled.

The young man blinked, as if he had not expected Skan to say anything, much less demand information. He was so startled that he actually *gave* it.

"You'll be making runs against the troops below Panjir," he said. "Flying in at treetop level. Dropping rocks and—"

"And making ourselves targets for the *seven batteries* of ballistas and other sky-pointing missile-throwers," Skan replied caustically. "Scarcely-moving targets, at that. There isn't room between those cliff-walls for more than one gryphon to fly at a time, much less a decent formation. We'll look like beads on a string. If the missiles don't get us, the makaar will, coming down on us from the heights. You can tell the General that we'll be declining his little invitation. Tell him the message is from the Black Gryphon."

And with that, Skan put his head back down on his foreclaws, closed his eyes to mere slits, and pretended to go to sleep.

The aide's mouth dropped completely open for a moment, then closed quickly. But to his credit, he did not try to bluster or argue; he simply turned on his heel and left, trudging back down the hill, leaving behind a trail of little puffs of dust. Skan watched him until he was well out of sight, then jumped to his feet.

"Now what?" one of the others called from the shelter of his lair.

"Now I go to Urtho before Shaiknam does," Skan replied, and leapt skyward, wings laboring to gain altitude, heading straight for the Tower.

Where would Urtho be at this hour? Probably the Strategy Room. That wasn't exactly convenient; he couldn't go to something deep inside the Tower without passing a door and at least one guard. Skan was going to have to go through channels, rather than landing directly on Urtho's balcony the way he would have preferred.

He backwinged down onto the pavement in front of the Tower, paced regally up to the guard just outside the door, and bowed his head in salute.

"Skandranon to see Urtho on a matter of extreme urgency," he said politely and with strictest formality. "I would appreciate it if you would send him a message to that effect."

He was rather proud of the fact that, despite his own agitation, his sibilants had no hissing, and he pronounced his r's without a trill. The guard nodded, tapped on the door and whispered to someone just inside for a moment, and turned back to Skan.

"Taken care of, Skandranon," he said. "If you'd care to wait, I don't think it'll take long."

Skan nodded. "Thank you," he replied. He longed to pace; his feet itched with the need to tear something up out of sheer nerves. But he kept as still and as serene as a statue of black granite—except for his tail, which twitched and lashed, no matter how hard he concentrated on keeping it quiet.

With every moment that passed, he expected to hear a messenger from Shaiknam running up behind him— messenger-birds still probably avoided the General and his underlings, so Shaiknam would have to use a much slower method of requesting his own audience with the Mage of Silence.

As time continued to crawl past, Skan wanted to grind his beak. He felt like a very large target in the middle of all the pale stone.

Finally, after far too long a wait, a faint tap on the door behind him caused the guard to open it and listen for a moment. He flung it wide, and gestured for Skan to enter. "Urtho will see you," he said. "The Mage is in the Strategy Room."

No point in the guard telling him the way, as they both knew. Skan was perfectly at home in the Tower. He simply nodded and walked in the open door. A second guard stationed inside gave him a brief nod of recognition as Skan passed. Urtho had planned most of his Tower with creatures like his gryphons in mind; the floors were of natural, rough-textured stone, so that claws and talons did not slip on them, the doors and hallways were all made tall and wide enough for things larger than a human to pass. There wasn't a great deal to see, otherwise—just the hallway itself, plain and un-adorned, with closed doors on either side of it. The room that Skan wanted was behind the third door on the right, and he hurried right to it.

The door opened for him, but by human agency, and not magical. Urtho stood behind the table-sized contour map used for all major planning sessions. Areas held by Ma'ar had been magically tinted red; everything else was blue.

There was an alarming amount of red on that map.

"Urtho," Skan began, as soon as he was in the door. "I—"

"You and the Sixth Wing gryphons are staging a revolt," Urtho replied, with dangerous gentleness.

Skan's ear-tufts flattened. "How did you know?" he blurted, backing up a pace or two. Behind him, a hertasi shut the door and took himself out of the room by a side passage, leaving the two of them alone.

"I am a mage," Urtho reminded him. "While I don't squander my energies, I *do* use them on occasion to keep an eye on something. I knew you lot wouldn't care for having Shaiknam set over you, but I didn't think you'd start a revolution." He crossed his arms over his chest and gazed levelly at Skan. "That's not a particularly clever thing to do. You can't survive without me, you know."

Ah, hells. Well, might as well drop it all at once.

"Yes, we can," Skan replied, raising his head so that he looked down on Urtho, rather than dropping his eyes below the level of Urtho's as all his training screamed at him to do. "I'm sorry, Urtho, but we don't need you anymore. We know how to make ourselves fertile now. Zhaneel is the proof of that, if you doubt my unadorned word on it."

He had never in all of his life seen Urtho taken aback before. Surprised, yes. Shocked, certainly. But completely dumbfounded—never.

The expression of complete blankness on Urtho's face was so funny that Skan couldn't help himself. He started laughing.

Urtho's face flushed, and the blank expression he wore turned to one of annoyance and a little anger. "What are you laughing at, you overgrown chicken?" the mage spluttered. "What is so damned funny?"

Skan could only shake his head, still laughing. "Your face—" was all he was able to manage, before he ran out of breath.

Urtho reddened a little more, but then, grudgingly, he smiled. "So, you think you have the upper hand, do you?" he said, challenge in his tone.

Skan got himself back under control, and quickly, even though laughter threatened to bubble up through his chest at any moment. "Yes and no," he replied. "We can leave now. You no longer control us by means of our future, Urtho. That doesn't mean we *will* leave, though, it just means that we won't have to put up with idiots like Shaiknam and Garber who think we're to be thrown away by the handful. Wait!" He held up a foreclaw as Urtho started to say something. "Listen to me first. *This* is what Shaiknam planned to do with the gryphons as soon as he got the Sixth out into the field again!"

He told Urtho what the aide had told *him*, then traced out the planned maneuvers on the map. "You see?" he said, as Urtho's brow furrowed. "You see what that would do? Maybe we would provide a distraction for Ma'ar's troops, but there are better ways of supplying distraction than sacrificing half the Wings!"

"I do see," Urtho replied, nodding thoughtfully. "I do see."

"We don't want to make trouble, Urtho," Skan continued earnestly, taking a cautious step nearer, "but we don't want to be blackmailed into suicidal missions. Maybe that's not how it seemed to you, but that was how it felt to us." He raised his head a little higher. "You built our urges to reproduce as strongly as our will to eat and breathe, and used that to control us. We'd rather serve you out of loyalty than coercion."

"I would rather have you out of loyalty," Urtho murmured, blinking rapidly once or twice. He coughed, hiding his face for just a moment, then looked up again. "And just how did you obtain this knowledge?" he asked. "I'm sure it was you—I can't think of another gryphon who would have tried, let alone succeeded."

Skan gaped his beak wide in an insolent grin, hoping to charm Urtho into good humor. "That, Urtho, would be telling."

Ma'ar

Sixteen

For one brief moment when Skandranon defied him, Urtho had been in a white-hot rage. How *dared* this creature, a thing that *he* had created, presume to dictate the terms of this war? How *dared* this same creature usurp the knowledge it had no right to, and was not intelligent enough to use properly?

But that rage burned itself out as quickly as it came, for Urtho had lived too long to let his rage control his intellect. Intellect came to his rescue, with all of the answers to the questions of "how dared. . . ." Skan dared because he was not a "creature"; he was a living, thinking, rightfully independent being, as were all the rest of the gryphons. They were precisely what he had hoped and planned for and had never thought they would become in his lifetime. They had the right to control their own destinies. Perhaps he was responsible for their form, but their spirits were their own. He was now the one who "had no right" to dictate anything to them—and in a blinding instant of insight he realized that he was incredibly lucky that they didn't harbor resentment against him for what he'd withheld from them. Instead, they were still loyal to him.

They would have been perfectly within their rights to fly off as they threatened, he thought, as Skan laughed at the expression on his face. *It's nothing short of a miracle that they didn't. Dear gods, we have been lucky. . . .*

He didn't realize how lucky, until Skan told him just what Shaiknam had been planning. A quick survey of the topography of the area told him what it did not tell Skan; that

Shaiknam had intended to launch an all-or-nothing glory-strike against the heavily-fortified valley. Such things succeeded brilliantly when they succeeded at all, but this particular battle-plan didn't have the chances of a snowflake in a frying pan of working. It was just another one of Shaiknam's insane attempts to pull off some maneuver that would have him hailed as a military genius and a hero.

The only trouble was that military geniuses and heroes had sound reasoning behind their plans. Shaiknam, unfortunately, had only wild ideas.

Urtho cursed the man silently as Skan pointed out all the ways that the gryphons would be cut down without being able to defend themselves. Shaiknam's father was such a brilliant strategist and commander. *How* had the man avoided learning even the simplest of strategies from him?

Well, there was no hope for it; the only way to get rid of the man now would be to strip the Sixth of all nonhuman troops and mages on the excuse that all the other Commands were undermanned, and reassign the personnel elsewhere. Shaiknam could still *be* Commander of the Sixth, but he would only command foot-troops, all of them human. With no aerial support, and no mages, he would be forced into caution.

That should keep him out of trouble, and his inept assistant, Garber, too.

He growled a little when Skan refused to tell him *who* his co-conspirators had been, but it was a good bet that Lady Cinnabar was involved in this, right up to her aristocratic chin. And where you found Cinnabar, you found Tamsin, and probably Amberdrake. *No doubt they got in when Cinnabar asked to "look at my records on the gryphons." I thought she was looking for a cure for belly ache!* The kestra'chern must have gotten a client to make him a set of "keys" for mage-locks; that would account for how they'd gotten into the book.

The wonder of it was that they had managed to penetrate past all the fireworks and folderol in order to find the *real* triggers for fertility.

"How many of you know the spell?" he asked, as reluctant admiration set in.

"All," Skan said, without so much as blinking an eye. "And it's not exactly a flashy spell, Urtho. It was simply good design. There was no point in holding the information back. Every gryphon outside this Tower knows the secret."

He couldn't help it; he had to shake his head with pure admiration. "And you've kept this whole thing from me all this time! Unbelievable."

"We had reason to keep it among ourselves," Skan replied. "Good reason. We didn't know how you would feel or act, and we didn't want you finding out before the time was right for me to tell you."

"So you were the sacrificial goat, hmm?" Urtho eyed Skan dubiously. "I don't know; a sacrifice is supposed to be savory, not scrawny."

Skan drew himself up in an exaggerated pose. "A sacrifice is suppose to be the best of the best. I believe I fill that description."

His eyes twinkled as he watched Urtho from beneath his heavy lids, and his beak gaped in a broad grin when Urtho laughed aloud.

"I submit to the inevitable, my friend," Urtho said, still laughing, as he slapped Skan on the shoulder. "I suppose I must consider this as your test of adulthood, as the Kaled'-a'in give their youngsters. You gryphons are certainly not my children any longer—not anyone's children."

Then he sobered. "I am glad that this has happened now, Skan. And I am glad that you are here. I need to pass along some grave news of my own, and this will probably be the best opportunity to do so."

He called in the hertasi, who waited discreetly just on the other side of the door, and gave him swift instructions. "I wish you to summon General Shaiknam and take him to the Marble Office; once you have left him there, summon the commanders of the other forces to the Strategy Room."

He turned back to Skan. "I am splitting the nonhuman manpower of the Sixth among all the other commanders—I have reason enough since all of them have been complaining that they are shorthanded. That will leave Shaiknam in command of nothing but humans. Is there any commander that you think the gryphons of the Sixth would prefer to serve?"

For once, he had caught the Black Gryphon by surprise; Skan's grin-gape turned into a jaw-dropped gape of surprise, and his eyes went blank for a moment. "Ah—ah—Judeth of the Fifth, I think."

Urtho nodded, pleased with his choice. "Excellent. And she has had no real gryphon wings assigned to her forces until now, only those on loan from the Sixth or the Fourth. Consider it done." Urtho regarded Skan measuringly. "Still, the gryphons should have their own collective voice, even as the mages do. There are things that you know about yourselves that no human could. There should be one gryphon assigned to speak for all gryphons, so that things will not come to the pass they have with Shaiknam before I come to hear about it." He stabbed out a finger. "You. You, Skan. I hereby assign you to be the overall commander of all the gryphon wings and to speak for them directly to me."

Skan's surprise turned to stupefaction. His head came up as if someone had poked him in the rear. *"Me?"* he squeaked—yes, squeaked, he sounded like a mouse. He cleared his throat and tried again. "Me? Why me? I am honored, Urtho, but—"

Urtho waved his objections aside. "You've obviously thought about becoming the leader of the gryphons, or why else would you have read all my history books about the great leaders of the past? The others clearly think that you should have that position, or why else would they have sent you here to confront me over Shaiknam?"

Is it unusually warm in here? Skan felt his nares flushing, and he hung his head. "They didn't exactly *pick* me," he admitted. "They couldn't seem to do much besides panic and complain, so I . . . I took over. Nobody seemed to mind."

"All the more reason to place you in charge, if you were the only one to *take* charge," Urtho said implacably. "How do you think *I* wound up in charge of this so-called army?"

Skan ducked his head between his shoulder blades, his nares positively burning. "I'm not sure that's a fit comparison—"

"Now, I have a few things to tell you," Urtho continued. "I don't know if you've been aware of it, but I've been sending groups of families and noncombatants into the west ever since we first thought we'd have to abandon the Tower." He turned back to the map and stood over it, brooding. "I didn't like having such a great concentration of folk here in the first place, and when I realized what chaos an evacuation would be, I liked it even less."

Skan nodded with admiration. He *hadn't* realized that Urtho was moving people out in a systematic way. That in itself spoke for how cleverly the mage had arranged it all.

"I've been posting the groups at the farthest edges of the territory we still hold, near enough to the permanent Gates there that they can still keep in touch with everyone here as if nothing had changed, but far enough so that if anything happens—" Urtho did not complete the sentence.

"If anything happens, we have advance groups already in place," Skan said quickly. "An evacuation will be much easier that way. Faster, too. And if the fighters know their families are already safe, their minds will be on defense and retreat, rather than on worrying."

"I don't want another Laisfaar," Urtho said, his head bent over the table, so that his face was hidden. "I don't want another Stelvi Pass."

Skan had his own reasons to second that. The lost gryphons there sometimes visited him in dreams, haunting him. . . .

. . . *fly again, as Urtho wills.* . . .

"Who will you pick for your second, Skan?" Urtho asked after a long silence, briskly changing the subject. "I assume it's going to be one of the experienced fighters. And—" he cast a quick glance out of the corner of his eye at Skan, who caught a sly twinkle there. "—I count Zhaneel as an experienced fighter."

Skan coughed. "Well, it will be Zhaneel, of course, but because she has the respect of the others. Even gryphons who haven't trained on her course know how hard it is, and they admire her for all she's accomplished. But there's something else I'd like to ask you for as well."

Urtho turned away from the table. "Oh?" he said, imbuing the single syllable with a multitude of flavorings.

Once again, Skan's stomach and crop churned with anxiety, and his nares flushed. "I—ah—did a little exploring on that level of your Tower."

"And?" Urtho's face and voice were carefully neutral.

"I found the—the models."

"How did you—" Urtho exclaimed, flushing for a moment with anger, but he quickly calmed. "Never mind. What—"

Skan interrupted. "I met Kechara."

Urtho stared at him blankly for a moment, then grew just a little pale. "I believe," he said carefully, "that I had better sit down. You must hate me."

Skan shook his head as Urtho lowered himself into a chair, and if he was any judge of human reactions, the Mage had been profoundly shaken. "How could I hate you? The more time I spent with her, the more I realized that you had done the best you could for her. And once I had a few days to think about it, I believe I managed to puzzle out why you had her up *there,* instead of down with the rest of the gryphons. It wasn't just to protect her from being teased and getting her feelings hurt." He took a deep breath, and ventured everything on his guess. "It was because she's a very powerful Mindspeaker. Probably the most powerful you've ever seen."

Urtho's eyes widened, and he caught his breath. "Did she Mindspeak at you?" he asked.

Skan nodded, pleased that he had been clever enough to figure out the puzzle. "I realized that I had been getting a great deal more information from her than she had the words to tell me. That was when I remembered that she had hit me with a mind-blast just before she attacked me, and I figured out that she wasn't just *telling* me things with her voice, but with her mind as well."

He told Urtho the tale from beginning to end, saving only that he had gotten into the chamber in the first place with Vikteren's mage-keys. "That's why she's in the Tower, in a room with such heavy shields, and why she creates the *presence* of a dozen gryphons when there's only her. And that's why Zhaneel and I would like to have her. *We'll* protect her from teasing and ridicule, and she can act as—oh—a kind of relay for groups of gryphons that may need to speak with each other. We have Mindspeakers, of course, but none as powerful as she is."

"I see that you put a great deal of thought into this." Urtho mopped his forehead with a sleeve, as small beads of perspiration sprang up. "I must confess—that use for her had occurred to me. I was too softhearted to . . . well . . . misborn usually die young anyway, and I assumed that her nature would take care of the problems she represented for me. When she didn't die, though, I had to do something about her. She's as old as you are, Skan. She only seems younger because she's so childlike, and because her memory for things longer ago than a year is very poor. I knew that if anyone ever discovered her and her power, she'd be a target for our enemies. In the wrong hands, she could be a terrible weapon. I was afraid that I would have to go to war just to protect her, and I couldn't reconcile the safety and freedom of one misborn with compromising the safety of all those who depend on me. You see? That was why I hid her in the Tower and kept her existence secret. I simply could not protect her otherwise, and I would not risk a war over her."

"Urtho, I hate to point this out, but we *are* in a war, and it isn't over Kechara," Skan retorted, with a little more sarcasm than he intended. "No one is going to get into this camp to steal her, and there isn't much point in keeping her mewed up anymore."

Skandranon sat down across from Urtho. He was rather surprised to learn that Kechara was as old as he was; as Urtho said, the misborn generally did not live past their teens, much less grow to be as old as he. It was something of a tribute to Urtho's care that she had lived as long as she had.

Urtho sighed. "You're right," he admitted reluctantly. "She deserves a little freedom anyway. But keep her here—if not in the Tower, then near it."

"Of course." Skan nodded. "I should like to start moving the gryphon families out to where the other noncombatants are going, if you don't mind. All pairs with nestlings and fledglings, and all fledged still in training. I don't see any reason why they can't complete their training elsewhere." He thought for a moment. "I'll tell them that you are concerned that with all of us consolidated here, we make a very tempting target for some terrible weapon. You want to get us spread out, so we aren't quite so easy to get all at once."

Urtho considered that as he studied the map. "What about here and here." He pointed to two valleys, easily defended, at the farthest range for a permanent Gate. "I can set two of the Gates for those places, and move not only gryphons, but Kaled'a'in and all the nonhumans who are not combatants there. Anyone who wants to visit them, can."

"I have an even better idea," Skan suggested. "Set up a secondary Gate and put the gryphons out farther. Use the excuse that we are big eaters and need the territory. Send the Kaled'a'in to this valley in the south, and convalescents and volunteers there to the north. That gets them out from underfoot, and they can train your human youngsters while they're recovering."

Urtho snapped his fingers. "Of course—and what's more, I'll have the ambulatory and the youngsters run foraging parties! Make them as self-sufficient as possible!"

"Have them send the surplus here," Skan added, with growing enthusiasm. "It won't be much, but it will make them feel as if we need to have them out there. And a little fresh game now and then—"

His mouth tingled at the very thought. *Herd beasts have no real flavor. A good raebuck, though. . . .*

"With hertasi in charge, Skan, I am not certain I would be too ready to say that they 'won't send back much.' Hertasi are remarkable scavengers." Urtho's eyebrows quirked a little. "That's largely why I have them in charge of supply here. They find ways to make ten loaves feed a hundred fighters."

But Skan noticed that Urtho was much more subdued than usual. *Perhaps there is something he hasn't told me? Are things even worse than I thought?*

A light tap at the door prevented him from asking any further questions. Cautiously, Urtho's chief hertasi stuck his snout inside.

"The commanders are here, Urtho," the lizard said quietly. Urtho glanced over at Skan and shrugged.

"Let them in, Seri," he said. "They might as well hear it all at once."

The commanders filed in, General Judeth last of all, impeccable and austere in her chosen colors of black and silver. They gathered around the table, and Skan saw one or two turn a little pale when they looked over the latest conquests of Ma'ar's forces.

Didn't they know? Or does this mean something I can't guess at?

"Gentlemen, ladies." Urtho nodded to the group. "I brought you here for several reasons. The first—General Farle is dead. Assassinated, as far as we can tell."

A sharp intake of breath around the table told Skan that none of the commanders had heard the bad news yet.

"I am afraid that under the circumstances, I must dismantle the Sixth as it has been known, and spread its nonhuman and magical resources among all of you. General Judeth." As Urtho spoke her name, the lady sat up straighter, and lost her look of shocked dismay. "At the specific request of the new commander of all the gryphon wings, I am assigning the wings that formerly belonged to the Sixth to you. I know that you will command them well."

The General did not salute or snap to attention, but she gave the impression that she had. "I will do my best, sir," she replied simply.

"The rest of you may decide among yourselves how to apportion up the rest of the Sixth's available manpower. General Shaiknam will command the human foot-soldiers, but all else will be available to you." Urtho nodded, and Skan saw with satisfaction that the commanders were already getting over their shock and thinking about the situation. "I am certain that you will not allow any kind of rivalry to interfere with the best possible deployment of that manpower. Now—I am certain you all know Skandranon, the Black Gryphon, either on sight or by reputation."

Nods and some slight smiles met that, as Skan bowed his head in a brief salute to all of them, but especially to General Judeth.

"I have appointed him to be the overall commander of the

gryphon wings, in the same arrangement that I made with the mages." Urtho paused and waited for their reaction.

Skan saw only slight frowns, and one or two nods. General Judeth was the first to speak.

She cleared her throat delicately, then spoke to both Urtho and to Skan. "The arrangement is working better with the mages than we had thought it would," she admitted. "We thought it might make for problems, if not outright mutiny among the mages, but it didn't work out that way." Her mouth twitched a little, although she did not actually smile. "There are even some mages who have shown a remarkable *increase* in their abilities. Apparently, having someone to evaluate their performance who *knows* what they can do has made them a little more—eager—to do their best. I trust, both because Urtho has chosen you, Skandranon, and from *some* of your reputation, that you will act in a similar manner."

Skan's nares flushed, for there was no doubt just what the General meant by "some of your reputation," but he answered her steadily enough.

"I can promise you that no gryphon will balk at anything he is asked to do without a reason for objecting," Skan replied gravely. "We all understand that this is a war, and in war there is the risk of death. We only ask that we not be sent into a *certainty* of death. I can also promise you that if there are objections to what we are asked to do, it will be because the loss will outweigh the gain for all concerned. The gryphons will defend all the races."

The General nodded at that, and turned her attention back to the table.

"I see that you are all concerned by the amount of territory that Ma'ar has taken," Urtho continued. "You should be; I have only just updated the map, and a great deal of that gain has been within the last month. You all knew you'd lost ground, but none of you has seen the real scope of the loss until now. We are in trouble, and I will not hide that fact from you. In fact, we have lost so much, that Ma'ar himself has moved into the Palace and made it his headquarters."

They took all that without flinching, although Skan was incensed at the idea that Ma'ar would have taken the Palace for his own. The idea of that—that beast, that tyrant, soiling the halls that great leaders had called home, soiling them with his bloody boots—

"It would be rather difficult to hide that we are in trouble, with *this* spread out before us," General Movat said dryly. "The question is, what are your plans to deal with it?"

Urtho considered the map, as heavy silence reigned. "The first thing I intend to do is to begin a quiet evacuation of the noncombatants from around the Tower," he replied. "Some preliminary work has been done in that direction, but now I want it to become a priority. I want to move them into the West. I'm going to take six of the permanent Gates here on the Tower grounds and activate them, targeting them to six points on the western border. That's mostly wilderness area, mountains and forested valleys, too steep to farm and not really suited for grazing. My very first Tower was there," he added wistfully, "and I rather liked keeping it wilderness."

"Yes, well, now it's a good thing it *is* wilderness," General Korad said briskly. "Ma'ar won't consider that you might have sent people into it."

"My idea precisely." Urtho tapped the map, pointing to the six places where the Gates would have their other ends. "If we have to abandon the Tower, we'll have most of the people who would be trouble already out of the way. They, in turn, will have advance camps ready for us. If we inform our people that we are doing this only to spread out our resources and make one spot less of a target, I believe we can keep them from panicking."

The Generals contemplated the plan quietly for some time, each one studying the map and making mental calculations. Urtho watched their faces; Skan watched Urtho.

He looks satisfied; well, if they have simply accepted the plan, that must mean it's strategically sound. So that's how he does it! He puts out a plan, waits to see what they think of it, and changes it with their suggestions and objections! I wondered how a mage had become such a good strategist!

General Judeth broke the silence first. "I'd like to have one strong mage with each group," she said. "Adept-class. Perhaps this would be a good place to send those who are frail, or those who have moral objections to combative magics, and those who simply do not have skill at combative magics. This way, if further Gates need to be built, there will be someone at hand, rested, and prepared to build those Gates."

Urtho nodded. "My Kaled'a'in will be *here*—" he pointed. "They will have mages enough in their ranks to cover that point. If any of you can think of particular mages who would be suitable, please let me know, especially if they are familiar with this kind of terrain."

If they can deal with primitive conditions, he means. Some of his older mages—well, they ought to go with the Kaled'a'in. The Clans can make a home anywhere, if they have to, and the horse-nomads are already set up for wandering.

There was more discussion, and they put together a tacit agreement. Skan was impressed. He hadn't known that there were humans anywhere who could agree to so much with so few wasted words.

"But this is secondary," General Korad said at last. "The real question is—how in the name of all the gods are we going to defend the Tower?"

Urtho hesitated, then asked humbly, "Are you certain that we should?"

A chorus of objections met that statement, but it seemed to Skan that most of them boiled down to—"of course we should, it's *your* Tower."

Urtho waved them to silence. "There is a great deal in the Tower that can't be moved and shouldn't be allowed to fall into Ma'ar's hands. But things can be destroyed. The knowledge that made those things possible is as portable as the minds and the books that hold it. This place may be my home, and it is true that I have invested a great deal of my life in it, but that is no reason to remain here when the situation becomes untenable. Others have lost their homes; it would be arrogant of me to think mine was any more sacred than theirs. I would be as foolish as my critics have claimed if I clung to this Tower when every wise person would have fled."

He pondered the map. "If Ma'ar breaches our defenses *here*

and *here,* he can spread out his troops along this line. He has manpower far exceeding ours. If he does that, he can force us to try to counter him until we are spread so thin we can't defend ourselves. From here, on the Plain, he has a clear run to the Tower itself. We cannot hold a line against him, unless we can suddenly multiply our own troops by a factor of ten."

The Generals studied the map with varying expressions of gloom.

"You're right," Korad said, with no emphasis. "Damn, but I hate to admit it. If he can get that far, he's got us."

"*If* we remain at the Tower," Urtho reminded them all. "If we retreat, we can pick our place to make a stand, or make no stand at all, simply keep retreating, making *him* string out his supply lines and his forces. Eventually, even Ma'ar must become sated with conquest! We can go west, then retreat to the farthest south, in the lands that the Haighlei Emperors hold."

"The Black Kings?" said Judeth. Skan knew that referred not to their predilections, but their skin, which was supposedly as dark as a moonless, starless sky. "Would they help us?"

Urtho shrugged. "I don't know. I *do* know they would shelter us against a conqueror and despot like Ma'ar, and their magic is so different from ours that I think even Ma'ar would hesitate before he attacked them. It's not wise to attack an unknown."

Judeth bit her lip, then nodded, slowly and grudgingly. "It's our best hope, *if* Ma'ar gets that far. I am going to see that he doesn't, if it takes every drop of blood in my body to stop him." She sounded and looked grim, and Skan shivered in a sudden chill, as ice threaded down his spine as if a cold wind had just ruffled his feathers.

"How are you going to explain—everything—to Shaiknam?" Korad wanted to know, after an uncomfortable silence.

Urtho shrugged. "I'll tell him that I've seen he is best with ground maneuvers, and I'm giving him the chance to concentrate on them without the distractions and annoyances of a mixed force. Then I'll show him what I've shown you, and we'll all meet tonight to plan the overall strategy to hold Ma'ar. Right now, I want you all to go to your people and get those who are not essential ready to evacuate. I'd like to start moving people out steadily starting tomorrow."

That sounded like a dismissal to Skan, and so the other commanders took it. They saluted and filed out, with only General Judeth pausing long enough to have a brief word with the Black Gryphon.

"As soon as you've seen to your new command, come see me with the old Sixth Wingleaders," she said. "And best of luck, Skandranon. I think Urtho's chosen wisely."

She turned smartly and left, leaving Skan to gape at her back as the door closed behind her. He turned to look at Urtho.

The mage smiled wearily. "I think I've chosen wisely, too, Skan," he said. "Now—go deal with your people, while I see to mine. We both have a great deal to do, and only the Kaled'a'in Lady knows if we will be given the time to get it all done."

Skan bowed, deeply and profoundly, but he hesitated at the door. Urtho had turned back to the map, staring at it blankly.

"Urtho—" Skan said. The mage started, turned to face him, and stared at him as if he had not expected his new commander to still be in the room.

"I want you to know something. We never really considered flying off and abandoning you. We are not only loyal to you—we love you. That is *why* we are loyal to you. Love is harder to earn than loyalty, and you are more than my friend. You are my beloved Father."

He turned quickly and left, and the door swung shut behind him—but for one moment, just before it closed completely, he thought he saw Urtho's eyes glittering, as if with tears.

Packing too many people in this mess tent made it stiflingly hot. Amberdrake stood on a table and ran one hand through his damp hair, in a nervous gesture that had become habit over the past few days. Every kestra'chern in the camp had squeezed into the mess tent, and they all stared at him with varying levels of anxiety. Wild tales had spread all through the camp since word came from the Sixth that General Farle had been killed, and Shaiknam assigned to his old command again. Most of those tales were variations on older rumors, but some were entirely new. All the stories that Amberdrake had heard had been told with varying degrees of hysteria.

He held up a hand and got instant silence. Lamplight glittered in dozens of eyes, all fixed on him, all wide with fear or hope. "You've heard the rumors for weeks, now the rumors are coming true," he said abruptly. "We are evacuating all noncombatants from around the Tower." A murmur started, but he shook his head and the murmurings died away. "Urtho gave me complete control of what to tell you. I am going to tell you the whole truth because Urtho and I are counting on you to help keep people calm. Ma'ar is in a dangerous position for us. Urtho is *telling* people that he wants the noncombatants spread out so that we don't make such a tempting target with everything clustered here. The real reason is that if he has to evacuate, he doesn't want to have civilians at the Tower to get in the way, or have the ones left worry about them."

He let them absorb that for a moment. "We will be one of the last groups out because we are also useful as Healers. I'm going to interview each of you tonight and tomorrow, and you will decide which of the six evacuation sites you wish to go to. I will give you an assignment-chit, and when the last of the civilians are gone, you will pack up your tents and go to your chosen sites. You will *still* be able to service your clients there; the Gates will be open for two-way traffic, and Urtho expects a certain amount of coming and going."

Someone down in front waved his hand. "What if Urtho decides to evacuate completely? What about people who are visiting over here?"

"Good question. Anyone who goes from his evacuation site to the Tower must be aware that at any moment Urtho could call for a retreat. At that point, a noncombatant will have to fend for himself, and count himself lucky if he gets to *any* Gate, much less the one to his own site." Amberdrake shrugged helplessly. "You would be much better off for your clients to come to you, rather than vice versa. We are going to try to discourage traffic *from* the sites *to* the Tower. For instance, there is going to be a curfew in force once the civilians are theoretically gone, and meals on the Tower side will be strictly rationed to those supposed to be there—no visitors allowed."

He let them absorb that for a moment. Another hand appeared. "Is it really looking that bad?" asked a young woman with frightened eyes.

He hesitated a moment. "I can't tell you everything," he said finally. "But Urtho is seriously worried, and he has already undertaken the enormous task of stripping the Tower of as much as possible and sending it to safer places."

Another murmur arose, but it died on its own. Finally Lily rose to her feet and lifted her head defiantly. "There *has* to be something else we can do!" she said. "You know very well that most of our clients are going to postpone visits until the civilian evacuation is over—so there must be something practical we can do to help!"

Amberdrake relaxed marginally as a chorus of agreement met her brave words. "Thank you, Lily," he said softly. "I was hoping someone would bring that up. Yes. There is a *great* deal that we can do to help, both on this side of the Gates and the other." He sat down slowly on the table top. "The very first job is to help with the children. . . ."

Gesten looked out beyond the campfire, counted noses, and came up with a satisfactory total. Every hertasi tribe had sent at least one representative, and most had sent several. Why *he* should have been chosen to be the leader of the whole lot, he had no notion, but Urtho said he was, and that was the end of it.

"Right," he said, and dozens of eyes blinked at him. "You know the story. Nonfighters are pulling out, and we're nonfighters. The only hertasi who are supposed to stay here after the civilians leave are the ones serving the Healers and the gryphons. Everyone else goes. Once you've gotten your own kit out, come back and start helping the families. The kestra'chern are minding the children, so you'll be doing what we do best—you'll be helping to pack up the households and get 'em moving. Once *that's* done, you go report to the Tower. If they need you, they'll tell you. If they don't, you get back over to your assigned place and *stay* there. Got it?"

"What if you're doing split duty—with a Healer and a civilian, say?" someone called from the back.

Gesten's briefing hadn't covered that, but Urtho had told him that he could and should use his own judgment when it came to things that hadn't been covered. "Depends on how close to the fighting you think you can stand to be," he said, finally. "If you're feeling brave, stay here, go full-time with the Healer. If you're not, stay on the evacuation site and help with whatever needs doing. There's going to be a *lot* that needs doing." He tilted his head to one side and narrowed his eyes as he recited the list Urtho had given him. "We'll need winter-proof housing built for everyone, and that includes the fighters, in case they have to come over. We'll need food supplies located. We'll need wells dug, sanitary and washing facilities set up. A lot of the families are going to consist of mothers with children; they'll all need that extra hand to help. We'll need facilities for the sick and injured, and overland vehicles in case we have to retreat from there."

"Will there be mages to help us with all this?" asked an anxious voice. "And Healers? There are pregnant females with those civilians, and I don't know a *thing* about birthing babies, especially not human babies!"

"We'll have a lot of mages, all of the Apprentices, most of the Journeymen, and at least one Adept at each site," Gesten promised. "The Healers are sending some of their Apprentices, a couple of Masters, and as soon as all the civilians are over, the kestra'chern will be joining them. There're plenty of Healers with them, and they all have some Healer training."

Gesten sensed an easing of tension at that. Hertasi considered the kestra'chern the most level-headed of the humans, and the ones most likely to react properly in a crisis. "Right," he said again. "We can do this."

"We can do this," they echoed.

It was, after all, the hertasi motto.

*　　*　　*

Amberdrake rubbed his blurring, burning eyes until they cleared, then turned his attention back to the list he was compiling. *Protea to tend a creche of tervardi little ones; that will work. Loren with the Healers, putting together packs of supplies for the evacuees. Renton, Lily, Marlina, Rilei—*

"Amberdrake? Have I come at a bad time?"

He looked up, squinting across the barrier formed by the light from his lantern, and made out the face of Lionwind, the Clan Chief of his own Kaled'a'in clan of k'Leshya. "What are you doing still awake?" he asked, out of sheer surprise to see the perpetual Dawn greeter up and active long past the hour of midnight.

Lionwind stepped farther into the tent, his heavy braids swinging with each soft, silent step. "We had a clan meeting," he said. "And we'd rather not go off with the rest of the Kaled'a'in, if it's all right with Urtho."

But Amberdrake shook his head. "You can't stay," he said flatly. "Urtho can't make any exceptions."

Lionwind half-smiled, and folded himself gracefully onto a stool on the other side of the desk. "We didn't want to stay, we just want to be where the gryphons are," he told Amberdrake. "We've supplied most of the Kaled'a'in Trondi'-irn for the gryphons, we've worked with Urtho on his breeding program—and we *like* them. They'll need someone besides hertasi with them, after all. Hertasi are all very well, but they don't like to hunt, they can't lift what a human can, and they're a little short of imagination."

Amberdrake listened to this calm assessment with growing relief. He'd wondered how the gryphons were going to manage, for Urtho's plan called for a second Gate to be built from the Kaled'a'in evacuation site, and the gryphon families to be sent farther out from there. The gryphons were huge eaters, and it was doubtful that they would be able to stay anywhere that there was a large concentration of any other species. All of the Kaled'a'in Clans, for instance. But if k'Leshya was basically volunteering to be sent off beyond the rest, that would solve the problem neatly.

"Are you certain you want to do this?" he asked.

Lionwind shrugged. "I'm not certain we *want* to do anything at the moment," he replied. "We don't want to run, but we don't want to stay here to be slaughtered either. We'd like it best if Urtho could suddenly produce a magic weapon that would eliminate Ma'ar and all his troops without harming anyone or anything else, but short of the Goddess working a miracle, that isn't going to happen. So this is our best choice, and if Urtho will allow it, we'll take it."

"I'm certain he'll allow it," Amberdrake said, and rubbed his eyes again as Lionwind's face blurred and went out of focus. "I'll take care of it."

Lionwind rose and leaned over the table. Amberdrake rubbed his eyes again, but they wouldn't stop blurring.

"Is there anything else I can do?" he asked, blinking rapidly. That didn't help, either.

"Only—get some rest," Lionwind answered, leaning closer. "That's your Clan Chief's order."

"I can't, there's too much to do," he objected—as Lionwind reached across and touched his forehead. And only then did he remember, belatedly, that Lionwind was also a Mindhealer, fully capable of imposing his will on the most recalcitrant.

" 'The best attack is the one no one sees coming,' kestra'chern," Lionwind quoted, and chuckled, as sleep snatched him up in surprisingly gentle talons and carried him away. . . .

The six permanent Gates were enormous, quite large enough to accommodate the biggest of the floating land barges. Urtho had constructed them using fused-stone arches, and tied each of them into its own node to power it. Only Urtho had ever accomplished the construction of a Gate that did not require the internal knowledge and resources of a single mage to target and power the Gate. Only Urtho had uncovered the secret of keeping such a Gate stable. Of all of his secrets, that was probably the one that Ma'ar wanted the most.

He had, for the first time in many years, left the Tower briefly to journey through one of his own creations and set up a second permanent Gate at that evacuation point. This one he targeted deep in the western wilderness, to a lovely valley he himself had once called home. The gryphon families, all those gryphons that were not fighters, and those who were injured, had all been sent there. Now the Kaled'a'in clan k'Leshya, of all the Clans, the only one not named for a totemic animal, but called simply "the Spirit Clan," slowly filed through the first Gate to follow them.

He could not have said truthfully that he had a "favorite" Clan, but of all of them, k'Leshya held the greatest number of his favorite Kaled'a'in. Lionwind, the Clan Chief, was one of the wisest men he knew, with a wisdom that did not fit with the smooth, youthful face and the night-black hair that hung in two thick braids on either side of his face. Lionwind's father and mother had both been shaman; perhaps that explained it. Or perhaps, as Lionwind himself had once claimed, only half in jest, he was an "old soul." The Clan Chief—not then the Chief, but nearly as wise—had been of great comfort to Amberdrake when the young kestra'chern first joined his ancestral Clan. He continued to be of comfort, on the rare occasions that Amberdrake would permit anyone to help him.

Lionwind had been first through the Gate, riding his tall, rangy warmare. He had not looked in any direction but forward, although he surely knew he would never see the Tower again, and likely would not see many of those he left behind. He had made his farewells, as had all the Kaled'a'in, and it was not the Kaled'a'in way to linger over such things.

"Long farewells give time for the enemy to aim." That was what Lionwind said to Urtho as he clasped his hand, and the words were sure to become a Kaled'a'in proverb. Although there was no enemy here, k'Leshya followed that precept now.

Urtho watched them go, hiding his pain beneath a calm smile. He did not know if he would ever see any of them again. All he could be certain of was that he had sent them into a safer place than this one. And now that the gryphons were in full control of their own destinies, he could at least be certain that no matter what Ma'ar undid of his, there would always be gryphons in the world. If Ma'ar conquered the Tower, they would scatter, using their mobility to take them beyond his reach.

So something of mine will survive, in spite of everything that Ma'ar can do.

Odd that it should be the gryphons, creatures that his contemporaries had considered eccentric toys. He had always had faith in them, though. Of everything he had created, they were his favorites. He had given them the ability to do great good; it only remained to see if they would fulfill that promise as well as they had fulfilled all the rest.

The last k'Leshya herdsman, driving the last of the Clan herds under a great cloud of dust, passed through the Gate. The Gate "sensed" that there was no one else waiting to cross it, and the view of the crowd of Kaled'a'in at the terminus faded, as the Gate shut itself down to conserve power. The space inside the arch went to black—then showed only what was on the other side of the physical arch.

Only then did Urtho realize that he was not alone.

Amberdrake stood behind and to one side of him, staring at the now-blank Gate. The kestra'chern was not wearing any of his elaborate robes or costumes, only a pair of breeches and a sleeved tunic in a soft, faded blue. His hair had been tied up into a tail at the nape of his neck, and he wore a headband of blue that matched his tunic.

Urtho regarded him with a touch of surprise. He had *thought* that it was understood that Amberdrake would go with his own Clan. The rest of the kestra'chern all had their assignments in the evacuation, and as soon as they had completed those tasks, they would head for their own evacuation sites. He was not needed as their leader anymore, and it was unlikely that anyone would have leisure in the coming days and weeks for the ministrations of a kestra'chern, however expert.

Amberdrake seemed to divine Urtho's thoughts from his expression. He raised one elegant eyebrow in a gesture so graceful it could only have been unconscious. "You're wondering why I'm still here," he said.

Urtho nodded.

"Winterhart is still here. She's the Trondi'irn of the fighting gryphon wings of the Fifth, and I am not going to leave her alone in a camp that still holds her former lover." There was a note of steel in his voice that was new to Urtho—or perhaps it had been there all along, and Amberdrake had simply hidden it better. "Skan is still here, and Zhaneel, and Gesten to serve the two of them. They are all the family I have."

Urtho allowed a bit of steel to creep into his own voice. "I said, 'no exceptions,' and you are not excused from that. You heard it clearly enough, Kestra'chern Amberdrake. You do not belong here."

"I am a Healer, Urtho. You can verify that with Lady Cinnabar if you wish; I volunteered for her group." Pain and fear shadowed Amberdrake's eyes for a moment, and Urtho knew why and marveled at his bravery. He knew all about Amberdrake's past; he knew how much it would cost Amberdrake to work with the Healers, every waking hour—how vulnerable he was to losing control of his Empathic abilities—how he feared that pain, physical and mental, more than anything else.

Yet here he was, facing his worst fear, in order to remain with his odd and tenuous "family." Urtho bowed his head a little in acknowledgment of courage.

"I stand corrected, Healer Amberdrake. You have every right to be here." The lines at the corners of Amberdrake's eyes softened a bit, and Urtho decided that he would ease another of Amberdrake's worries. "There is a single mage still working with Shaiknam and the Sixth, at his own request. I approved his petition for field duty myself. I am told his name is Conn Levas." He let his own eyebrow rise, just a little. "I believe the Sixth is currently away on assignment."

Urtho turned then, not waiting for thanks. Already he had turned his mind to the next task.

And so, probably, had Amberdrake.

Long farewells give the enemy time to aim. And they did not dare give the enemy time for anything.

Amberdrake Alone

Seventeen

Aubri's wings ached from shoulder to tip; they burned with exhaustion on the downstroke of each wingbeat. The heavy, damp air in this particular valley always meant difficult flying, but that was not why he was tired. He had been flying scout for the Fifth since dawn, and it only lacked a few hours until sunset. He had flown a double shift already, and by the time he finished, long after dark, it would be a triple.

At least all the innocents were far beyond the reach of any disaster now. The last of the noncombatants, including the kestra'chern, had passed through the Gates to their new locations several days ago. And as Urtho had expected, there was steady traffic between the Tower and the evacuation points, but not in the opposite direction. The word that any noncombatant caught on the Tower side in an emergency would have to fend for himself kept the evacuees in their new homes. Aubri missed seeing the youngsters, missed the sound of fledglings playing—but he would rather miss these things than have them at the Tower lairs, and at risk. One slaughtered youngster was one too many—and he had seen the pathetic corpses of considerably more than one in the time he had been fighting for Urtho.

His chest muscles complained, growing tight and stiff from built-up fatigue poisons, and he knew that by the time he landed, he'd be one sore gryphon. At least on this second shift, he *wasn't* fighting makaar. This was all simple coordination scouting, making sure that the Sixth and the First were where they were supposed to be, so that the mages with the Fifth didn't hit their own troops with friendly fire.

Huh. "Friendly fire, isn't." That's what the Kaled'a'in say anyway. Ma'ar's generals hadn't pressed an attack on this point all day, holding a purely defensive line, and Shaiknam hadn't made any offensive moves, a reflection of the inertia here for the past two or three days. Both forces glared at each other from the opposite sides of a wide, shallow ravine, but the only attacking going on was from little presents the mages dropped which were easily deflected by their opposite numbers.

The situation was a stalemate, at least here.

No—wait. He caught a hint of movement through the heavy haze. *Something's going on down there!*

Aubri circled higher, to get a better perspective on the situation. So far as *he* had been told, Shaiknam wasn't supposed to order any kind of attack unless an opportunity too ripe to ignore arose, and Aubri hadn't seen any evidence of that. Was this just false movement? A little shuffling in place to make the enemy think that Shaiknam was about to press an attack?

He pumped harder, gaining more height, and looked down half a minute later.

At first he couldn't make out anything at all. Then the haze parted a little, giving him a clearer view of Shaiknam's troops. His wingstrokes faltered with shock, and he sideslipped a little before catching and steadying himself in the air. *Demonsblood! What does he— Why— He* can't *be that stupid! Can he?*

Shaiknam's troops had parted right down the middle, and were pulling back, leaving the easiest place to cross the ravine wide open.

This would have been a classic move, giving the enemy a place to penetrate and then closing companies in on either side of him while the troops to the rear cut his forces off from the rest. The only problem was that there *were* no other companies in place, and no time to get any in place. Shaiknam had not been positioned directly protecting one of the two vital passes, but from here Ma'ar's forces could easily *get* to one of those vital passes.

He's bluffing. Ma'ar's commanders won't believe this and

he knows it. He's just giving them something to occupy them. . . .

He couldn't hover; the best he could do was to glide in a tight circle, panting with weariness and disbelief. Even as Aubri watched, the two groups that had pulled back moved on in a clear retreat, and Ma'ar's army marched across the ravine and into Urtho's territory with all the calm precision of a close-order drill.

What in hell is going on here?

Now he wished he was one of those gryphons with any kind of Mindspeech; if *only* he could tell someone what was happening! By the time he lumbered through the sky to a message-relay, it would be too late to stop the advance.

Damn, it's already too late. . . . If I can't stop it, maybe I'd better find out who ordered this. That's what Skan would do. Has Shaiknam lost what little mind he used to have? Or have his troops somehow been sent false orders?

Aubri dropped through the haze, well behind the line of advancement, and landed just outside of Shaiknam's all-but-deserted command post. He got out of sight, just in case someone from the other side was watching, under cover of a grove of trees right behind the command tent. *Predictable,* he thought savagely. *Trust Shaiknam; ignore the fact that someone can sneak up to your tent in favor of the fact that you get to sit in the shade all day. I hope there're red ants in those trees biting on his fat behind.* He'd wondered why there seemed to be so little activity going on around the command tent, but he'd figured it was simply because there was *no* activity along this section of the front lines. *Now I know, maybe. Either Shaiknam's been assassinated or replaced or—*

—or something worse has been going on.

He tried to emulate Skan, blessing Zhaneel for all those hours on the obstacle course, as he slithered on his belly through the underbrush. The lessons were second nature now; shove the branches aside with your beak, close your eyes, and let them slide over your neck and your tight-folded wings. Creep forward with forefeet until you were as stretched-out you could get, then inch the hindfeet up until your back hunched, and start over again. Vary the intervals and your steps. Make no patterns.

And why the hell aren't there guards around the tent, after what happened to Farle? Because Shaiknam isn't there? Or because he knows he doesn't need guards? Or because he has no guards left?

He had concentrated so hard on his stealthy approach that he didn't keep track of how far he'd come. The buff canvas of the tent suddenly loomed up in a wall from out of the underbrush a few talon-lengths in front of his beak, just as he heard voices coming from inside.

Well, there's someone in there, anyway.

He closed his eyes and listened. Whoever was in there murmured, rather than speaking in normal conversational tones, as if they wanted to be certain they weren't overheard from outside.

". . . going very well, my lord," whispered an unctuous voice. "And Ma'ar is keeping his side of the bargain. By the time Judeth of the Fifth realizes what has happened, Ma'ar's troops will have the Pass."

"Well, good." That was Shaiknam, all right; Aubri had heard his whining tones often enough to be certain of that. "Once he has the Pass, we can close behind him, and no one will know we let him through. His mages can set up Gates to pour troops down onto the plains, and I can 'surrender' with no one the wiser. My command and holdings will remain intact. And without you, Levas, I would not have been able to contact Ma'ar's commander and bring all this to pass."

Levas? Conn Levas? Wasn't that the mage Winterhart used to—

"Thank you, my lord." The unctuous voice was back. "I always make certain to be on the winning side, and I was pleased to find you are a commander as pragmatic as I."

Shaiknam laughed. "I have another task for you, if you think you're up to it. Urtho may yet be able to pull off a miracle; he has a disconcerting habit of doing so. But without Urtho . . ."

There was a certain archness to the mage's reply that held Aubri frozen. "I am a mercenary, my lord; you knew that when we made our bargain. There will be an additional price for additional services."

Shaiknam laughed very softly. "Name it," he said, as arrogantly as if he had all the resources of all the world to call upon. "Whatever coin you choose."

"Twenty-four thousand silver, and the coin of bodies, my lord." The mage's voice, already cold, grew icy. "Two bodies, to be precise, and both still alive and in a condition to be amusing to me. The Trondi'irn, Winterhart, and the kestra'chern, Amberdrake."

"Done and done," Shaiknam replied instantly. "Neither are combatants; they should be easy to subdue. Cheap at the price. You could have sold your services more dearly, mercenary."

"Their value is peculiar to me—"

Aubri could bear it no longer.

I have to stop them! Now!

He lunged at the tent wall, slashing it open with his sharp talons, back agape to bite the spines of one or both of them in half—

And tumbled ignominiously to the ground, unable to move even his eyes. He landed with bone-bruising impact right at the feet of General Shaiknam, skidding a little on the canvas of the tent floor.

If he could have struggled, he would have, but there wasn't a muscle of his body that would obey him. His heart continued to beat, and his lungs to breathe, but that was all the movement he was allowed.

He'd been the recipient of a spell of paralysis, of course. *Idiot! Conn Levas is a* mage, *idiot! How could you have been so incredibly stupid?*

General Shaiknam looked down at him with mild interest in his catlike eyes, then searched his pockets for a moment. Then he turned to Conn Levas, and flipped him a coin. The mage caught it deftly, and pocketed it. Shaiknam's serene, round face produced a smile that went no further than his lips. "Payment for additional services," he said, his voice ripe with satisfaction.

"Indeed, my lord," Conn Levas replied. "As I expect payment on completion of your other task."

Shaiknam shrugged, and his eyes reflected his boredom. "They have no interest for me. I will see that they are captured unharmed. It should not be terribly difficult."

"What of—*this*—my lord?" A new voice, but another one that Aubri recognized. *Garber.*

Shaiknam's second-in-command spoke from out of Aubri's line-of-sight, but there was no doubt of where he was. A toe prodded him in the ribs, waking pain in his chest muscles.

"I can dispose of him if you like," Conn Levas began, but Shaiknam held up a hand to forestall him.

"No," he said. "There is a use for him. Ma'ar is rather fond of gryphons. I believe we should send him this one, as a gift, in earnest of many more to come." He waved at the unseen Garber. "Package this up for me, would you, and deliver it to General Polden with my compliments to the Emperor."

"So the Emperor enjoys the antics of these creatures?" Conn said with interest.

"He does," Shaiknam replied. He smiled down at Aubri; the gryphon gasped, as the ice of horror and the chill of pure fear swept over him. "I hope you can learn some new tricks, beast," he said sweetly. "Other than 'playing dead.' 'Dance,' for instance, or better yet, 'beg.' Make certain to learn 'beg.' The longer you entertain the Emperor, the longer you will live. Or so I'm told."

Urtho flung a plate across the room; it shattered against the wall but did nothing to help relieve his feelings. *"Gods!"* he cried. The cadre of hertasi and human messengers ignored him. There were no messenger-birds in camp anymore; Urtho had not wanted to leave these smallest and most helpless of his creatures behind even by accident. They had been the first through the Gate, to go with k'Leshya and the gryphons.

Urtho paced the side of the map table, issuing orders as fast as hertasi and humans could take them, doing his best *not* to seize handfuls of hair and start yanking them out by the roots. What in the name of all the gods had happened? *How* had Ma'ar's men gotten past the defensive line? Why hadn't anyone noticed until they'd already taken the Pass of Korbast and had set up a Gate to bring more troops in?

Never mind, it's happened, now deal with it! This was his worst nightmare come true; the Tower still full of things he hadn't gotten out yet, the traps not yet set, and the enemy pouring down into the plain, behind his own lines. Already the Sixth and the Third had been cut off from the rest and from retreat; they would have to fend for themselves. Judeth was bringing the Fifth in, but no one knew for certain about the rest. *They have mages, they can Gate here. They can even Gate straight to their evacuation sites. They'll be all right. I have to believe that.*

He sent the last of his messengers off on their errands with orders to send the Healers and other support personnel to their Gates, and forced himself to stop pacing. He clutched the edge of the table and stared down at it, as if staring at it fiercely enough would make the situation reverse itself.

"Sir!" A hertasi scrambled in the door, all out of breath. "The mage Conn Levas is here from the Sixth!"

He started and turned toward the door, just as Conn Levas pushed his way past the lizard. He looked as if he had personally fought his way through all of Ma'ar's troopers to reach the Tower; his robes were filthy, torn, and bloodstained, his hair matted down to his head with sweat.

"Go." Urtho told the breathless hertasi. "Find me Skan and bring him here. I'll need him in a moment."

The hertasi let the door swing shut behind Conn Levas as Urtho took three steps toward the mercenary mage. "What *happened?*" he cried, eager only to hear what had gone wrong.

Too late, he saw Conn's hand move, saw an empty bag in it, and felt the stinging of a hundred thousand tiny needles in his face and hands, in every bit of flesh left exposed by his clothing. He brushed at his face frantically, while Conn Levas laughed.

"That won't help," the mercenary said very softly as Urtho tried to cry out for help and realized that he couldn't do more than whisper. "*Miranda* thorns, Urtho. Very potent. *Quite* impossible to magic away. A little invention of my new employer; I believe you might have seen their effects, once or twice. Mages never do consider that someone might attack them physically."

Urtho's knees crumpled beneath him; he managed to stagger back enough that he landed in the chair behind him before his legs gave out altogether. His entire body tingled, burned, twitched uncontrollably. His lips moved, but nothing emerged. Strange swirls of light and color invaded his vision; the furniture stretched and warped. Conn's head floated about a foot above his body as the mercenary mage approached, and the head looked down at him malevolently.

"It's a poison, of course," the head said, each word emerging from his mouth in flowing script, and encapsulated inside a brightly-colored bubble. "You should enjoy the effects. I knew that all the defenses of the Tower are keyed to you, of course, as well as the node beneath it, and I knew that if I slew you outright, I would die before I had a chance to escape. I expect Shaiknam knew that, too, and was counting on not needing to fulfill his part of the bargain. But you'll live long enough for me to get clear, and he'll just have to keep his word, hmm?"

Urtho's chest nearly burst with the need to howl in anguish, but all that he could manage was a pathetic whimper. Conn Levas' head floated around the room for a moment, then suddenly produced a new body as the old one faded away. A large, furry body, of an eye-searing pink. Urtho shuddered as the fur turned into spines, like those of a hedgehog. Then Conn shook his body, and all those spines shot forward, piercing Urtho's limbs with excruciating pain. The furniture grew tentacles, and the walls opened up into pulsing starscapes.

"I see you can't answer," the mercenary said silkily. "No matter."

He turned to go—that is, his head turned. His body remained the way it had been, and began walking backward toward the door. With every step he took, bleeding wounds appeared in the floor, and it felt to Urtho as if the wounds were to *his* flesh. He whimpered again, and Conn's head turned back.

"Oh, one more thing," the mage said casually. "In case

you might have worried about that little misborn gryphon you named so charmingly. Kechara. I offered her a nice bit of rabbit and she followed me out to the Emperor's new lines. I decided to make certain that Shaiknam would keep his word, by ensuring that the Emperor knows my name, and what he owes to me. She's my gift to Ma'ar to pave the way for my new rank and position. I expect to be a Duke at the very least."

Kechara! Oh, GODS! His anguish translated into more whimpers, and streams of blood began to flow from his open hands. Conn laughed and turned to open the door, which warped and deformed as he touched it, becoming a blood clot lodged in an open wound. The walls throbbed in time with Conn's laughter.

But the door opened before Conn, and there was someone out there—

Skan hurried after the frantic hertasi, talons clicking on the stone of the floor. "Aubri missing, the Sixth gone silent, why did you *leave* that lying bastard alone with Urtho?" Vikteren scolded the little lizard, as they ran toward the Strategy Room.

"He told me to get you!" the hertasi wailed, caught in a dilemma between what he had been ordered to do and what Vikteren thought he should have done. "I couldn't get you and stay there at the same time!"

"Leave it, Vikteren," Skan snapped. "It's done—let's just hope that—"

The young mage sprinted for the door and shoved it open in the surprised face of Conn Levas. The mercenary mage recovered quickly from his surprise, and backed up a pace when Skan loomed up behind Vikteren.

From his greater height, Skan could see right past Conn, and spotted Urtho, clearly in terrible pain, collapsed into a chair in the corner. Conn followed his glance, paled, and began babbling.

"Urtho—" he said. "He said he wasn't feeling well. The strain—"

But Skan's hearing was better than a human's, and the

word Urtho was forcing through spittle-frothed lips was "*—poison—*"

Skan's vision clouded with the red of rage; he saw Conn's hands move, and he didn't hesitate. The Black Gryphon lashed out with an open talon, and caught the mage across the throat, tearing it out in a spray of blood. His second blow, the backhanded return of the talon-strike, flung the mercenary's body across the room to slam against the table with the wet crack of a snapping spine.

There the body of Conn Levas lay atop the tiny space of land that was still theirs, blood pumping down onto the map, flooding the representation of the Tower and the plain around it with sticky scarlet.

Vikteren had headed straight for Urtho, as Skan stalked in through the doorway with every feather and hair erect in battle-anger. "Poison," the young mage said shortly, his face flushed and his voice tight with grief. "*Miranda*-thorns, very rare, no antidote. The bastard probably had enough in his pockets to hit us both, too; that's what he was reaching for when you got him."

The hertasi gasped and scrambled off, presumably to fetch help.

Skan only heard and heeded one thing. *"No antidote?"* he roared, so that Urtho whimpered and Vikteren winced. "What do you mean, *no antidote?*"

"Skan, I *can't change the facts,*" Vikteren shouted back. "There's no antidote! It's something Ma'ar created as an assassination-tool, and we haven't seen more than three victims since the war started! All we can do is buy him some time and counteract some of the effects."

"Do it," Skan snapped, spreading out his bloodstained claws over the body of his creator and friend, invoking every tiny bit of magery he had. He opened himself to Urtho, found the places in his mind that the *miranda* had muddled, bringing hallucinations and pain, and joined with Vikteren to help Urtho straighten the mental paths and banish those symptoms.

He fought with every bit of his grief and rage, every atom of energy. And still, it was not enough. He saw for himself that Vikteren was right. The poison replicated itself within

Urtho's body, spreading like some evil, sentient disease, and with every passing moment it destroyed a little more of Urtho's life-force, corroding it away inexorably.

At last, his mage-energies exhausted, he dropped his outstretched claw and opened the eyes he did not realize he had closed.

Vikteren supported Urtho in his chair, and the face that looked up at Skan was sane again. "The evacuation—" Urtho whispered harshly. "Get me—Healers. I have to hold on—"

Vikteren looked up into Skan's puzzled face. "I think he's keyed some kind of destructive spells into himself—if he leaves the Tower, the place is going to go unstable. And if you thought what happened with that Gate at Jerlag Pass was impressive—"

The young mage left the rest unsaid. *Leaves the Tower, or dies, he means. And there must be two dozen permanent Gates here, not to mention the Tower itself and everything still in it.* The destructive potential staggered him. Anyone still here would be obliterated by the result, pulverized to dust. . . .

The noise of running feet from the hallway made him turn sharply, ready to attack again, but these were friends. The hertasi had returned with Tamsin and three more senior Healers, who squeezed through the door as one. *Not Cinnabar. He must have sent her through the Gate while he could.*

"We know," Tamsin said shortly, taking Vikteren's place at Urtho's side. "We'll buy him all the time we can."

Skan did not move out of the way. The Healers shoved past him, ignoring him as if he had been an inconveniently placed piece of furniture.

He started to say something, but Vikteren motioned to him to remain silent. Tears trickled down the mage's face, and his shoulders shook, but he didn't produce so much as a stifled sob to distract the Healers from their work.

Skan himself shook from beak to talons with the effort of repressing a keen of grief. He closed his eyes and clamped his beak shut, flexing his talons into the wood of the floor, feeling it splinter beneath them, and wishing he could kill Conn Levas a hundred more times.

Someone tapped him on the shoulder, startling him, making him jump. His eyes snapped open and focused on Tamsin's face, not more than a finger away from his beak.

"We've done all anyone can," the Healer said, in a voice gone flat and dull with sorrow and exhaustion. "He needs to tell you something."

The four Healers staggered out the door, holding each other in pairs and not once looking back. Vikteren still stood beside Urtho's chair, tears falling steadily down his cheeks and dropping onto the breast of his tunic.

"Get all the gryphons you can find," one of the Healers told the hertasi who waited, trembling, beside the door. "He's going to try to get everything open that he can before the end, and he wants them to take all they can carry."

The hertasi looked up at the Healer for a moment, too grief-stricken to reply. The man spoke again. "Knowledge will always be the best weapon against tyrants," he choked out. "*Urtho* said that." And at that the hertasi ran to carry out the orders.

"Skan—there's a weapon." Urtho's voice was the merest whisper, but his words were clear enough. "Never meant to use it, but—now, Ma'ar is coming. Help me—weapons room."

Vikteren helped him to his feet and got under one shoulder, while Skan supported him on the other side. They both knew where the weapons room was, and that it was locked, to be unsealed by Urtho's presence alone. They carried him across the Strategy Room and to the door across the hallway; Urtho had no more strength than a newborn kitten. He fell against the door to the weapons room to open it, and directed them both to a box on a stand in the far corner of the room.

"It's—like the box I gave Zhaneel. But bigger. Got one on the Tower roof. Dissolves the bonds—of spells. Take it to Ma'ar when you can, trigger it. Same thing that happened at Jerlag." Urtho did not look at Skan; the gryphon had the feeling that perhaps he couldn't bear to. "Made it for gryphons. Stick your talons—in the holes. All at once."

Skan saw then that what he had taken for decorative perforations in the side were actually holes made to fit a gryphon's talons, in a pattern of two on each side to fit the two-forward, two back-curved talons of the foreclaws.

"You have—a count of a hundred—to get away," Urtho finished. "Better have—a Gate handy. And closed fast."

The Mage of Silence tried to smile, and coughed instead. *"Go!"* he whispered fiercely, when the coughing fit was over. "Go. Get Ma'ar later. Survive now."

Skan lifted the box from its stand, and saw that it had a carry-strap meant to go around the neck. He pulled the strap over his head, awkwardly, and turned back to the Mage.

Urtho's eyes were clouded with pain, and his lips formed the word, "Go."

Beak clamped down on the death-keen, Skan backed out of the room. But before he left, he saw Vikteren helping Urtho to the next door to be unlocked.

And the first of the combat-gryphons arrived, to carry away what he could.

Knowledge will always be the best weapon against tyrants. Unable to hold it back any longer, Skan fled down the hallway and into the sunset, his death-keen echoing through the Tower as he ran.

Winterhart flung books and packages through the Gate whenever there wasn't someone actually traversing it, from the pile that formed as the gryphons brought them to her, her arms and back one long pulled muscle. There would be some time after Urtho succumbed before everything went dangerously unstable. They *should* all have time to get out.

All but Urtho. . . .

Her eyes stung with tears, but she would mourn him later, when they were all, temporarily at least, safe.

Somewhere on the other side of this Gate was another Trondi'irn, pitching packages through the Gate to k'Leshya. The farther away this dangerous knowledge went, the better off they would all be. She did not bother to think about how they would continue this war, or even if they would be able to regroup. The important thing now was simply to escape, to live, and to worry about the rest later.

Other gryphons, too exhausted to be of any use, staggered up to and through the Gate while she paused in her labor.

Humans and hertasi, tervardi and kyree and dyheli also presented themselves for passage, burdened with everything they could carry. There were fewer of them now than there had been; as combatants staggered in from the field, they grabbed what they could and headed for their evacuation-Gates, and by now virtually everyone who *could* make it back, had.

That left only the few faithful, like her and Amberdrake, who would stay until the bitter end to help save as much as they could from the wreckage.

She *still* did not know why Urtho was reportedly dying, although she trusted the news. It could not have been something simple like heart failure, or the Healers would be able to save him. Had Ma'ar somehow penetrated their defenses with a mage-attack?

Another pair of exhausted gryphons and a pack of mud-stained kyree staggered up to the Gate, and she stopped long enough to let them pass. But before she could pick up another package from the pile, someone else appeared, a human this time. But he headed for her, and not the Gate, and it took her a moment to recognize Amberdrake.

His face was absolutely blank with shock, and he was as pale as snow. She leapt for him as he stumbled and started to fall, catching him and holding him upright.

"What—" she began.

"I just saw Skan," he replied dully. "I just said good-bye to him."

Something in the way he phrased that made her freeze. Good-bye? As in—permanently?

"We have to get Zhaneel out of here, now, to k'Leshya," he continued numbly. "We can't let her find out Skan is gone, or she'll try to follow him. Urtho gave him a weapon, and told him to use it to stop Ma'ar. Skan is determined that Urtho meant him to do it *now*."

Winterhart realized that she was clutching her hand in her hair at the side of her head only when it began to hurt. She let go slowly. "Couldn't you stop him?" she cried involuntarily.

"I tried. He wouldn't listen." Amberdrake stared at her,

eyes blank and blind. "He told me that Shaiknam, Garber, and Conn Levas went over to the enemy."

A cold ring of terror constricted her throat, cutting off her gasp. "But—"

"He said he caught Conn Levas right after he'd poisoned Urtho with *miranda* thorns, and he tore the traitor's throat out. By then it was too late; there was nothing they could do for Urtho but buy him time." She sensed his pain as if it were her own—if *she* wanted to mourn for Urtho, *he* would have ten times the grief to deal with—and ten times that for Skan.

"I'll—wait, there she is." Zhaneel came hurrying up with a bundle of books in her beak and another clutched to her chest, running on three legs with her wings spread to help her balance.

Winterhart grabbed the edge of her wing before she could put her burden down. "Zhaneel!" she cried, "I need someone on the k'Leshya side to make certain all this is carried as far away from the Gate as possible. We don't know how unstable these things are—"

Zhaneel nodded and darted through the Gate without waiting for further explanation. "You go after her," Winterhart ordered. "I'll follow you as soon as I get the last of this stuff across."

At least she had something to do. Something to keep her from thinking.

"Are you all right?" Amberdrake asked suddenly, a little life coming into his eyes. She knew what he meant.

Conn is dead. Conn is a traitor, and he's dead. She paused and collected herself, examined her heart.

"It's best that Skan took care of the problem," she said firmly, looking deeply into Amberdrake's eyes, so that he would know she meant what she said. "If he hadn't—I'd have done so, but with less elegance. Myself."

Beneath all the pain, all the grief, she saw a moment of relief. It was enough for now. She shoved him gently toward the Gate.

"I'll see you on the other side," she said. "Take care of her." He took a last, long look at the Tower, then turned and stumbled blindly across the threshold.

She picked up another package as soon as he was clear, and pitched it across.

Skan knew exactly who he was looking for—the Kaled'a'in Adept, Snowstar, the person Urtho himself had appointed as the chief of all the mages. He knew Snowstar, knew that the man was truly second only to Urtho in knowledge and ability, and knew one other, crucial fact.

Snowstar had been working with Urtho long before the King collapsed. Snowstar was one of the mages that Urtho had with him when Cinnabar called them all to the Palace that terrible morning.

Snowstar *knew* the Palace as well as Skan did. Which meant that Snowstar, unlike many of the other mages, could build a Gate there.

And Ma'ar was at the Palace.

After three false tries, he located Snowstar at the Tower stables, turning away from the last empty stall. An odd place for a mage perhaps, unless the mage was Kaled'a'in, and the horses here were the precious warsteeds. Skan grinned savagely to himself; Snowstar had not expected an ambush—and doubtless intended to head straight for the Kaled'a'in Gate from here, hot on the heels of his beloved equines.

There would be a brief delay.

As he turned, Skan stood in the aisle between the stalls and spread his wings to block his way. The mage looked up at him blankly. "Skandranon? What—"

"I need a favor," Skan said quietly, but with an edge to his voice. "And you don't have a choice. I need a Gate to the old Palace, and I need it now."

Snowstar's eyes went wide and he shook his head with disbelief. "Are you out of your mind?" he cried, putting out his hands to shove Skan out of the way. "There's no time for this kind of nonsense! We have to get out of here!"

"There *is* time and you *will* do this," Skan hissed. "I have a prrresssent to deliver to Ma'ar. From Urtho."

Snowstar blanched, and his eyes dropped to the box around Skan's neck as if he had only just this moment noticed that it was there. Skan was gambling on a number of things. The Black Gryphon was known as Urtho's confidant; Snowstar should assume that Urtho's request was an *order*, and that it was not meant to be implemented at some far future date, but *now*. Snowstar knew very well what kind of shape Urtho was in; he would not risk a single precious moment by going to Urtho or sending a messenger to confirm what Skan had just told him. He might even assume that Urtho had ordered Skan to *find* Snowstar, knowing that the Adept would be one of the few at full strength and capable of building a Gate that far away.

Snowstar's pupils widened and contracted, as all those thoughts—and likely, a few more—raced through his mind.

"Right," he said then, still pale, but grimly determined. "I won't Gate you into the Palace itself, if that is agreeable to you. I have no idea who or what Ma'ar has stationed where. I could Gate you into the servants' quarters only to find out that he's got it full of soldiers or traps. But there's one place I know *very* well where you won't find much opposition, and the little you find, I suspect you can silence."

"The stables," Skan breathed, amazed at Snowstar's quick thinking.

"Exactly." Snowstar shoved at Skan again, but this time to make some room to work, and Skan gladly moved over. "I'll position the Gate to come out of the last stall in the back; it's a big loose-box, partitioned off from the rest with floor-to-ceiling walls, and with no outside windows. We never put a horse in it unless it was one that was so sick it needed dark and quiet. No grooms are likely to change that."

It sounded perfect, and Skan nodded. "Put it up, and bring it down once I'm through," he said decisively. "Then get yourself out of here."

"What about—" Snowstar began, then saw the look in Skan's eyes. The rage Skan held bottled up inside must have been blazing. Snowstar grew just a bit paler, then turned away, raised his hands, and began.

The Adept had had decades of practice to refine and hone his craft; the Gate went up with scarcely a ripple in mage-energies. Skan did not even wait to thank him; clutching his precious burden with one foreclaw, he dove through to the other side.

This is poorly planned, stupid gryphon, but there isn't

time. Urtho can't die without knowing Ma'ar's dead and gone. You don't do helplessness well at all. And if you can't save Urtho, you can still do something.

He landed, feet skidding a little in the straw, in the dark and empty loose-box. As Snowstar had guessed, it had not been used in so long that the straw covering the stone floor smelled musty and was full of dust. He suppressed a sneeze and moved cautiously to the door.

He listened carefully, all senses straining against the darkness.

Odd. Lots of voices, and the sound of something struggling. *What did they have penned up in here, some kind of feral stallion?*

"Are you sure that's going to hold the beast?" The voice was doubtful, and very frightened. "I tell you, orders or no orders, if that thing breaks free, don't think I'm going to stand here and try to stop it!"

The *crack* of hand on flesh, and an exclamation of pain.

"You'll do as you're told, and like it, coward!" a second voice growled. "If I tell you to stand there and let the thing take your arm off, you'll damned well *do* it!"

Not a stallion, then. A bull? Some new monster Ma'ar just dreamed up?

A muttered, sullen curse; the sound of spitting. Heavy boots, walking away. More struggles; chains rattling, muffled *thuds*, more mutters, a stream of ill-wishes directed against the second voice, his family, and all his progeny to come.

The thin, high wail of a young gryphon.

"Faaaather!"

A voice he knew! *Kechara!*

He pushed against the stall-door, and it swung wide while he stepped out and mantled. His eyes locked with those of one poor, spotty-faced groom clutching a pitchfork in one hand, a bloody rag held to his mouth with the other. The boy couldn't have been more than sixteen. He took one look at Skan, went pale as milk, and fainted dead away.

Skan stepped over him, and looked into the stall he'd been guarding.

There were two canvas-covered bundles there; one thrashing, one whimpering. The whimpering bundle was the smaller, and the whimpers were definitely in Kechara's voice!

How did she—never mind. Conn Levas or Shaiknam, or both. Quickly, he squeezed into the stall, but he did not free the little one. Not yet. The larger bundle of the two also smelled of blood and of *gryphon*, and it was a scent that he thought he recognized.

"Hold still," he whispered. "It's Skan."

The bundle stilled immediately. He took a moment to examine the situation.

Chains wrapped around the bundle, but they were not fastened to the stall itself. If he could get the gryphon inside to bend a little, he might be able to slip one loop off, and that would give him enough slack to undo the whole thing without having to unlock it.

"Can you bend this way?" he whispered harshly, pushing down on what he thought was the back of the gryphon's head. It must have been; the place bent over in response to his pressure, and he was able to work the loop of chain off as he had hoped. Once he had the slack he needed, two more loops followed, and he worked the entire chain down, with the squirming assistance of the gryphon inside.

Now he could slit the canvas bag and see if the contents were who he *thought* it was. He ripped open the canvas with a slash of a talon, and a head popped out—a head covered in an enormous version of a falcon's hood, with the beak tied firmly shut.

He pulled off the bindings, and the beak opened.

"Damn it, Skan," Aubri croaked, in a whisper no louder than his had been. "You took your own sweet time getting here!"

It took both of them to convince Kechara that she *had* to be quiet, but for once Ma'ar's men had done them all a favor. They had cut off all the primaries on both her wings and Aubri's, and in Kechara's case, that meant she wasn't tripping over her own awkward wings.

Kechara wasn't at all clear on how she had gotten there, but the picture in her mind, projected strongly, was of a blurred Conn Levas offering something that smelled lovely.

Skan assured her that he had "gone away" and that Skan had made certain he wouldn't come back.

Not in this lifetime, anyway.

Aubri was a lot clearer on what had happened to him, and kept his explanation down to a terse couple of sentences. He only wanted to know one thing.

"Urtho?" he asked, with a sideways glance to see if Kechara was listening.

Skan closed his eyes, letting his grief show for just the briefest of moments, and shook his head.

Aubri's beak clamped shut, and when Skan opened his own eyes, the broadwing's eyes were blazing as red with madness as any goshawk's.

"I got Conn Levas," Skan said, around the lump of rage and grief in his own throat. "*This* will take care of Ma'ar. If we can get it to him." He tilted his head to one side. "I have to admit—I was told that I'd have a count of a hundred to get away, and then this thing will make Jerlag look like a campfire." He shook his head. "If you can think of any way you can get yourself and Kechara out of range. . . ."

Aubri's pupils dilated, and he produced a harsh bark of a laugh. "On clipped wings? I don't think so. Besides, all I ever asked was to go down fighting. I'm sorry about the little one, but this is going to be clean, right?"

He nodded. "As clean as fire. And I can still send you both into the Light if all seems hopeless."

As you've done too many times before—Urtho, why must we feel these burdens? Why?

"Well," Aubri rumbled. "You need me. Bet we can even find a way Kechara'll be useful. And if it gets Ma'ar—" Aubri's savage grin and the scrape of his talons on the stone told the rest. "And—ah, demonsblood, Skan, you always *were* the luckiest son of a vulture I ever saw. *Your* luck, you'll find a way out for us. I'll take my chances with you."

Skan let out the breath he had been holding in. "Well," he said lightly. "That was the hard part. Now the easy part."

"Which is?" Aubri asked as Kechara gave a breathy squeal of glee and pounced on something. She stuffed it in her mouth and looked up innocently, the tail of a rat hanging out of one corner of her beak for a heartbeat, before she swallowed and it vanished.

Skan looked cautiously around the corner; the doors to the stable stood open wide, and the apparently-deserted stable-yard stretched between them and the Palace kitchens. "Oh, it's nothing much," he replied, offhandedly. "Just getting into the Palace and the throne room."

The last Tower door had been opened; there were still books and devices here Urtho wished he could save, but the vital things had been carried off. He had persuaded Vikteren and the rest to leave. Now there was only the small matter of hanging on, living every possible second, for every second meant more time to ensure that all of his people who *could,* would reach safety.

The Tower echoed with the whisper of air through doors long locked, and the occasional *thud* of something falling, echoing through stone corridors suddenly more empty than imagination could bear. In all of his life, Urtho had never felt so alone.

He had never expected to die alone, much less like this. At least the mages and Healers had taken all the pain, blocked the hallucinations and the convulsions, and left him only with growing weakness.

He was so tired, so very, very tired. . . .

No! He had to fight it, to stay conscious, awake! Every heartbeat was vital!

All we have done, and all I have learned, and I cannot slow the progress of my own death by even a candlemark.

He had never thought much about revenge, but now he burned with longing for it. *Revenge—no, I want to protect my people, my children! And when the Tower goes, I want it to be something more than the end, I want it to mean something, to* accomplish *some purpose!* He had always hoped, if it came to that, he would be able to lure Ma'ar, or at least some chief mages of Ma'ar's, into the Tower-turned-trap. He'd planned for that, all along; a desperate gambit that, if nothing else, would keep Ma'ar so busy cleaning up the damage that his children and his people would be able to get far beyond Ma'ar's reach or ability to find.

Now, when he died, the Tower would die in an expanding ring of sound and light, and it would be no more than the most impressive funeral pyre the world had ever seen—

—*wait a moment.*

Something stirred under the morass the poison had made of his mind. An idea, and a hope. *Ma'ar cannot know that Conn Levas succeeded. What would happen if I challenged him?*

There was a permanent Gate, a small one, big enough only for one human at a time, not more than a room away. It would take no effort at all to open it. A moment of clear thought, and it could be set for the Palace, the Throne Room. Urtho had used it to step directly from his own audience chamber into the King's—an impressive bit of nonsense that never failed to leave foreigners gaping and a little frightened. That was how he had gotten to the Palace the night that Cinnabar had summoned him; he had opened a larger Gate elsewhere for Skan. He hadn't been certain what the effect of trying to squeeze through a too-small Gate might be, and that had not been the moment to find out.

The odds are good that he'll be in the Throne Room, waiting to hear from his army. What if I opened that Gate and challenged him to come over? A fierce and feral joy flooded him, and for the first time he understood how his gryphons felt at the kill. *I open the Gate; he can't fight me through the Gate, he has to come over. I close it. He can't reopen it while I keep him busy, and by the time he gets his own Gate up, I'm dead. And so is he. If I were alive, I would never consider it—but I am dead already.*

That terrible joy gave him the strength to rise to his feet, stagger into the next room, and take his place on his own, modest version of a throne. Hardly a throne at all, really, just a large, comfortable chair, raised off the floor on a platform about half a stair-step high. He had never seen any reason to build a dazzling audience chamber; everything in the small room was made of old, time-mellowed wood. On the few occasions that he had needed to impress someone, he'd transformed the whole place with illusions. Much cheaper, and *much* easier to clean.

He gasped with effort as he stumbled up onto the platform

and lowered himself down into his throne. The exertion left him dizzy and disoriented for a moment; he closed his eyes, and when he opened them again, there was a faint haze of rainbow around everything.

The hallucinations, or what's left of them. I don't have much time. If this doesn't work—at least I tried. And Skan can make his own try, someday. That in itself comforted him, a little. Skan would get to safety, plot and plan with the sharpest minds of the Kaled'a'in, and make his own attempt. Ma'ar had not, and would not, win. Not while there was a single gryphon or Kaled'a'in left to oppose him.

He stared fixedly at the ornamental arch across the room from him, an arch built right into the wall, that seemed only to frame a shallow, purposeless nook. He wrapped his mind and his fading powers around the mage-energies woven into wood and stone beneath, and *twisted.*

Within the frame of the arch, the blank wall writhed, then turned into a swirling haze of colors, like oil on water, for just the barest instant.

Then the colors darkened, steadied—and Urtho looked across the leagues into the Throne Room of the Palace of High King Leodhan, a massive room constructed of six different kinds and colors of the rarest marbles, a place that seemed vast even when it was packed full of courtiers. Now it held only one man, but that man had presence enough to fill it.

Ma'ar stared fixedly at the Gate that had suddenly opened up in his Throne Room, a Gate he clearly had no notion ever existed. He had not been born a handsome man, but over the years he had sculpted his body into the image of a young god. His square-jawed face, with precisely chiseled cheekbones and sensuous mouth, framed with a mane of hair of dark copper, topped a body that would be the envy of any warrior in his ranks. All that remained of the old Ma'ar were the eyes; small, shrewd, and of an odd yellow-green.

"Kiyamvir Ma'ar," Urtho said genially. "It has been a very long time."

Ma'ar recovered his poise much more quickly than Urtho would have credited him for. "Urtho." He leaned back in his throne, a *real* throne, much more impressive than the alabaster bench the King had used. This one might not be solid gold, but it certainly looked as though it was, and the single red-black ruby over Ma'ar's head, carved in the shape of the head of a snarling cat, was twice the size of the largest such stone Urtho had ever seen. "Have you called on me to offer your surrender?"

Urtho smiled, gently. "Not at all," he countered. "I recall that you used to enjoy a gamble. I am offering you just that."

Ma'ar barked his laughter. "You? And what have you to offer me that I cannot take?"

Urtho waved, a gesture that made him dizzy again. "Why, this. I'm sure you realize that I've had as much carried away as I could—but I am sure you also realize that there is *far* more than could ever be carried away. I'm sure you also realize that what I did at Jerlag, I can do here."

Ma'ar's face darkened, and his lips formed a soundless snarl.

"However—" Urtho held up a finger to forestall any reply. "I'm proposing a challenge. The prize—the Tower and everything that's left. If you kill me, I obviously cannot trigger the destructive spells." *And let's hope he hasn't figured out, as Conn Levas did, that it isn't a spell that does the destruction, it's the lack of one.* "You have the Tower and everything you want. If, on the other hand, I kill you—well, I suspect that your underlings will immediately begin fighting among themselves, and leave me and mine alone. The bickering is inevitable, and I will have protected my own."

Ma'ar frowned, but he was obviously intrigued. "You underestimate what I have done here, Urtho. I took a weak land, torn apart by internal quarreling and wrecked by the greed of shortsighted idiots who thought no further than their own fat profits. I forged it into an Empire that will live long beyond me, and I intend to live a *very* long time! What makes you think I would risk all that for your stupid wager?"

Urtho leaned forward in his chair, ignoring another wave of dizziness, and spoke two words. "Knowledge. Power."

Then he settled back, and closed his eyes. "Think about it, Kiyamvir Ma'ar. You win, or I do. All the knowledge, and all the power. I can afford to wait, but feel as though I should retire. Your army is on the way, and I prefer to reset this Gate to—somewhere else, somewhere *very warm*, and leave your army with an unpleasant surprise."

He slitted open his lids just a little, and saw to his satisfaction that Ma'ar was staring at the Gate, chewing his lip in vexation.

He's going to do it!

"I always said you were the luckiest—" Aubri muttered, before Skan hushed him.

"It's not luck," he muttered back. "It's memory. Cinnabar used to play with the Princes, and she showed me all the secret passages. I took a chance that Ma'ar wouldn't have found them all, and that I could take care of the traps he put in the ones he *did* find."

He didn't like to think of how Cinnabar had shown him all the secret passages; she'd impressed them directly into his mind, and it hadn't been a pleasant experience. Nor had the circumstances been pleasant. She'd put him in charge of searching the passages for that damned *dyrstaf*, because he was the only mage there she *could* do that to.

She took the human-sized passages, and I took the ones big enough for a gryphon. . . .

He shook off the memory; it didn't matter, anyway. What mattered was how many guards Kiyamvir Ma'ar had with him in that Throne Room.

Please, please, please, O Lady of the Kaled'a'in, make him so arrogant that he does without guards entirely! Please. . . .
The gryphons didn't have a deity as such, and this was the first time he'd ever felt the urgent need to call on one. The gryphons had only had Urtho and themselves.

And when this is over—take Kechara somewhere safe and warm, and bring Urtho to her—and keep Amberdrake and Zhaneel happy.

There were no peepholes in this passage, and no human would have been able to hear what was going on in the Throne Room. Anyone using the entrance here would have to do so blindly, trusting that there was no one there.

Unless that someone was a gryphon.

He closed his eyes, and concentrated, becoming nothing in his mind but a pair of broad, tufted ears, *listening. . . .*

He's talking to someone! Demonsblood! It's now or never!

"Go!" he hissed at Aubri. The broadwing hit the release on the doorway, and rammed it with his shoulder, tumbling through as the panel gave way. Skan leapt his prone body and skidded to a halt on the slick marble, Kechara romping puppylike behind him.

Ma'ar swung around to stare at the open panel, and now faced away from—

Urtho! Oh, Star-Eyed Lady, is that a Gate!

What else could it be, when Urtho lay back in a chair framed by an archway, with a faint shimmering of energy across the portal?

Skan did not even stop to think about his incredible, unbelievable good fortune; did not stop to think about the pole-axed expression on Urtho's weary face. "Aubri!" he screeched, "Get Kechara across *now.*"

But Aubri didn't have to do anything. Kechara spotted Urtho on her own, screamed, *"Father!"* in a joyful, shrill voice, and shot across the intervening space like an arrow, squeezing through the Gate as if she'd been greased.

Aubri followed—and stuck.

Skan reached for the box, while Ma'ar stared at all of them as if he thought they were some kind of hallucination. Finally he spoke.

"All of this was to save two gryphons?"

The Black Gryphon held the weapon before him and slid his foreclaws home, and triggered the box.

"No. To save all of us."

He ducked out of the carry-strap, and slung the whole thing across the floor at Ma'ar, who dodged in purest reflex. But dodging didn't help; the box's strap caught his feet and tripped him. The fall knocked the breath out of him, and delayed any reaction he might have for a crucial moment.

Ma'ar clutched at the box, which glowed and sparked when his hands touched it. His expression changed from one of indignation to one of surprise and then—fear. Then insane anger. He stood, trembling with rage, and kicked the box aside. It clattered on the marble floor to rest by the throne.

"You think this is it?" he screamed. "This toy of Urtho's is supposed to kill me, gryphon? *Watch.*"

The Emperor drew a glittering silver knife—and with both hands, drove it into his own chest.

His face wrenched into a maniacal grin and he locked his eyes on Skandranon's. As blood streamed down his sumptuous clothing, the grin grew wider.

"You see, I know some things you don't. I have won! I will live *forever!* And I will hate you *forever*—all of Urtho's people, all your children, and their children, and I will hunt you *all* down. Do you hear?"

Skandranon Rashkae! Will you wake up! Ma'ar is playing for time! He'll keep you occupied with his little spectacle until the box goes and takes you with it!

The gryphon snapped himself awake from Ma'ar's mesmerizing speech. Ma'ar withdrew the dagger from his chest; blood blossomed anew and dripped to the floor. Without saying anything else, the Emperor's face went ashen, and he fixed his gaze of madness on Skandranon. With both hands, he held the dagger's point to his throat, behind the chin— and in one swift movement, thrust the long dagger upward.

Skandranon was running toward the Gate before Ma'ar fell. Behind him, over the clatter of his own talons, he could hear the dagger's pommel strike chips from the stone floor, muffled only by the sound of the body. The Black Gryphon hurtled to the Gate at full speed; Aubri was still wedged there, and if this didn't work, they were both doomed.

He hit Aubri from behind with all of his weight.

With a scream of pain from two throats, they ripped through, leaving behind feathers and a little skin, and the Gate came down so quickly that it took off the end of Skan's tail.

Kechara was already cuddling in Urtho's lap, unable to understand why her Father looked so sick. Skan picked himself up off the floor and limped over to the mage, who looked up with his eyes full of tears.

"I never thought I'd see you again," he whispered hoarsely. "What did you think you were doing? I meant you to *save* that weapon—"

But before Skan could reply, he shook his head, carefully,

as if any movement pained him. "Never mind. You are the salvation of everyone, you brave, vain gryphon. Everyone we saved will be safe for the rest of their lives. I have never been so proud of any creature in my life, and never felt so unworthy of you."

Skan opened his beak, trying to say something wonderful, but all he could manage was a broken, "Father—I love you."

Urtho raised one trembling hand, and Skan moved his head so that the mage could place it there.

"Son," he said, very softly. "Son of all of the best things in me. I love you."

Skan's throat closed, as Urtho took his hand away, and he was unable to say anything more.

Kechara looked at them both with bewildered eyes. "Father?" she said timidly to Urtho.

"Father has to go away, Kechara," Urtho said, gently. "Skan will be your Father for a while, do you understand? It may be for a long time, but Skan will be your Father, and when the bad men who hurt you are all gone, you can come join me."

She nodded, clearly unhappy, but her one taste of the "bad men" had been enough. She gazed up at Urtho in supreme confidence that he could and would deal with the "bad men," and nibbled his fingers in a caress.

Aubri limped over to both of them. " 'Scuze me, Urtho?" he asked humbly. "Can that Gate go somewhere else?"

Urtho closed his eyes, then opened them with visible effort.

"I can try," he said.

Amberdrake thought that he was prepared for the inevitable, but when the great flash of light in the East turned night into full day for one long, horrible moment, he realized that he was not ready. He had accepted the loss of Skan, of Urtho, of everything he had known with his mind, but not his heart. The entire world turned inside out for a fraction of a heartbeat; as if he had crossed a Gate, the universe shook and trembled, his vision blurred—but there was no Gate, it was all in himself.

Then everything was normal again. The night sky returned, spangled with stars, but wreathed in the East with ever-expanding multi colored rings of light, and a cool breeze brought the scents of crushed grass and dust.

Normal—except all was gone.

"No!" he cried out, one voice of fruitless denial among a multitude. *"Nooooooo—"*

He started to fall to his knees—a terrible moaning burst from his chest, and tears etched their way down his face in long trails of pain. *Urtho—Skan—*

Hands caught him and supported him; Winterhart. But another set of hands took his shoulders and shook them.

"Dammit, man, *no one* can fall apart yet!" Vikteren snarled at him, tears of his own leaving trails down his dusty face. "We aren't safe! Didn't you feel what happened, back there? When the Tower went up, something more happened than even Urtho thought! Gods only know what's going to happen now, we need to get under shields."

"But—" he protested. "But—"

"Just *don't fall apart on me.* People are watching you! You can collapse after I get the shields organized." Vikteren punctuated every word with another shake of his shoulders, and Amberdrake finally nodded weakly. Vikteren let him go, and he got a wavering grip on his emotions, turning his face into the serene mask of the kestra'chern, although deep within, pain was eating him alive.

Vikteren turned away from him, and waved his arms frantically over his head. "Listen!" he shouted, over the keens, the weeping. "Everybody! This—the trap didn't do what we thought, all right? We don't know how much is left of Ma'ar's forces, we don't know how far away is *safe,* we don't know who or how many of the rest survived. All we *do* know is that what happened was worse than we thought, and we have a couple of hours to get ready for it! It's going to be a—we'll have to call it a mage-storm, I guess. I can't tell you how bad. Just listen, I need all the mages over here with me, no matter how drained you are, and the rest of you, start getting things tied down, like for a really bad storm, the worst you've ever seen!"

Somehow the desperation in his words penetrated; hertasi carried the bad news to the rest of the camp, to those who had been too far away to hear him. Mages pushed their way through the crowd to reach his side; the others stopped milling and started acting in a purposeful manner, glancing at the slowly-expanding rings of light with a new respect and no little fear.

Winterhart went looking for her gryphons; her first duty was to them. Amberdrake let her go, then stumbled through the darkness to the small floating barge that held his own belongings.

But once there—it all left him. There was nothing left in him but the dull ache of grief. He couldn't even bring himself to care what might happen next.

He sat down on the side of the barge, and his hand fell on the feather he still had tied to his belt. Zhaneel's feather.

How would he tell her? She still didn't know. . . .

There's nothing left, nothing left for any of us.

He didn't even hear them come up beside him, he was so lost in despair, so dark that not even tears served to relieve it. One moment he was alone; the next, Zhaneel sat beside him, and Winterhart took a place next to him on the edge of the barge.

"When he did not follow, I guessed," Zhaneel said, her voice no more than a whisper, and although he had not thought that his grief could grow any greater, it threatened to swallow him now.

The tears choked his breath and stole his sight, and left him nothing.

:Nothing?: said a voice in his mind, as a hand closed over his.

"Nothing?" said Zhaneel aloud. "Are we nothing?"

And Amberdrake sensed the two of them joining, reaching into *his* heart to Heal it, reaching to bring him out of the darkness. The gryfalcon touched one talon to the feather he still held.

"Will you not redeem this now, my friend, my brother?" she asked softly. "We need each other so much."

"And the rest of them need you," Winterhart added. "I've heard you used to ask, 'who Heals the Healer'—and we have at least one answer for you."

"Those he Healed," Zhaneel said. "Giving back what he gave."

Blindly, he reached for them; they reached back as he held tightly to feathered shoulder and human and shook with sobs that finally brought some release.

The first flood of tears was over, for the moment at least, when he heard someone shouting his name.

"Amberdrake!" It sounded like Vikteren. "Amberdrake! *The Gate! It's opening again!*"

The what! He stumbled to his feet, and ran back to the site of the old Gate-terminus, a roughly-made arch of stone. Sure enough, there was a shimmer of energy there, energy that fluxed and crackled and made him a little sick to look at.

"What is it?" he asked, as Vikteren ran across the clearing to him.

"I don't know—can't be Ma'ar—" The energy inside the Gate surged again. "Whatever it is, whoever, it's been affected by the mage-blast." He turned hopeful eyes on Amberdrake. "You don't suppose it's Skan, do you?"

Amberdrake only shook his head numbly, heart in mouth. The energies built a third time; the mouth of the Gate turned a blinding white—

And Kechara tumbled through, squalling with fear. Winterhart and Zhaneel both cried out and ran to her to comfort her, but before they could reach her side, the Gate flared whitely a second time, and Aubri leapt across the threshold, smelling of burned fur and feathers, to land in an exhausted heap.

"Skan!" the broadwing screeched, turning his head blindly back toward the Gate. "Skan! He's still in there!"

The Gate fluxed—and collapsed in on itself, slowly, taking the stones of the arch with it. The entire structure began to fall as if in a dream.

"No!" Vikteren screamed.

Amberdrake was not certain what the young mage *thought* he was doing; he was only *supposed* to be of Master rank, and Amberdrake had always been told that only Adepts could build Gates. But Vikteren reached out his hands, in a clutching, clawlike motion, and Amberdrake *felt* the ener-

gies pouring from him into the collapsing Gate, seizing it—
and somehow, holding it steady!

Amberdrake sensed Vikteren faltering, and added his own
heart's strength to the young mage's—

—and felt Winterhart join him, and Zhaneel—

The Gate flared a third and final time, but this time it
was so bright that Amberdrake cried out in pain, blinded.

Vikteren cried out, too, but in triumph.

Amberdrake's vision cleared after much blinking and eye-
rubbing, and lying before them was Skandranon—shocked
senseless, and no longer as he—*was*. The elegant black form
they had known was thinner and bleached to snow-white,
but it was unmistakably Skandranon.

The Gate and Vikteren collapsed together.

Then there was no time to think of anything, as the East-
ern horizon erupted with fire—again. And for some reason
Amberdrake could not understand, he could feel the death,
far away, of the Mage of Silence, content that his people,
including those he loved most, were safe at last.

They had just enough time—barely—to establish their
shields before the double mage-storm hit. The worst effects
lasted from before dawn to sunset. But their preparations
held, and they all emerged from shelter to find a blood-red
sun sinking over a deceptively normal landscape.

Normal—until you noticed the places where trees had
been flattened; where strange little energy-fields danced over
warped and twisted cairns of half-melted rocks. Normal—
until night fell, and did not bring darkness, but an odd half-
light, full of wisps of glowing fog and dancing balls of
luminescence.

"We can't stay here," Winterhart said wearily as she returned to Amberdrake's hastily-pitched tent. It was the only
one big enough to hold four gryphons—Skan and Aubri, and
Zhaneel and Kechara, the former two because of their injuries, and the latter because *they* would not leave Skan's
moon-white form.

"I'd assumed that. We'll have to pack up and move West,
I suppose." He looked up at her and smiled, then turned his

watchful gaze back down to the slumbering Skandranon. "I don't mind, if you don't."

"Well, I wish we knew how many of the others survived," she sighed, "But the mages can't get anything through this— whatever it is. Magical noise and smoke. No scrying, no mage-messages, and we don't want to risk the poor little messenger-birds. The tervardi don't want to scout, the kyree are as scared as we are, the hertasi are traumatized, and the gryphons don't trust the winds. We'll have to go West and assume any others are doing whatever they have to."

"So we're back to ordinary, human senses." He reached out for her, caught her hand, and drew her down beside him. "Not so bad, when you come to think about it."

"I have no complaints." She leaned her head on his shoulder, and stroked one ice-white wing-feather of the still-shocky Skandranon. "Except one."

"Oh?" he replied. *She probably wishes we could stay here long enough to rest—but at least we know there won't be anyone following us—*

"This—" she pointed to Skandranon, curled around Zhaneel like a carving of the purest alabaster, "—is going to make him *twice* as vain as he was!"

"Of course it will," came a sleepy rumble. A pale, sky-blue eye opened and winked slyly. "And deservedly so."

Amberdrake smiled and held his beloved. No matter what tears were shed or what trials were faced, some things would stay the same. There would always be day and night, stars and sky, hope and rest. There would always be love, always compassion, and there would always be Skandranon. And forever, in the hearts of all the Clans, there would be Urtho—and for his memory, a moment of silence.